Holly H..ng as she
can rem...day she
decided to be brave and dipped a toe into the bubble bath
of romantic fiction with her first novella, *Cupidity*, and she's
nev...................................... funny, except for
when faced with traffic wardens and border control staff. Her
favourite things are making people smile and Aidan Turner.

She's tried many jobs over the years, from barmaid to
market researcher and she even had a brief flirtation with
modelling. These days she is mostly found writing.

She lives near London with her grey tabby cat, Portia.
They both have an unhealthy obsession with Marmite.

Follow Holly on Twitter @HollyH_Author.

Praise for Holly Hepburn:

'A fresh new voice, brings wit and warmth to this
charming tale of two sisters' Rowan Coleman

'You'll fall in love with this fantastic new series from a new
star of women's fiction, Holly Hepburn. Filled to the brim
with captivating characters and fantastic storylines in a
gorgeous setting, *Snowdrops at the Star and Sixpence* is simply
wonderful. I want to hear more!' Miranda Dickinson

'The Star and Sixpence sparkles with fun, romance,
mystery and a hunky blacksmith. It's a real delight'
Julie Cohen

holly hepburn

A Year at Castle Court

**SIMON &
SCHUSTER**

London · New York · Sydney · Toronto · New Delhi

A CBS COMPANY

First published individually as *Snowy Nights at Castle Court, Frosty Mornings at Castle Court, Stormy Weather at Castle Court* and *Starry Skies at Castle Court* in Great Britain by Simon & Schuster UK Ltd, 2017, 2018
A CBS COMPANY

3 5 7 9 10 8 6 4 2

Simon & Schuster UK Ltd
1st Floor
222 Gray's Inn Road
London WC1X 8HB

Simon & Schuster Australia, Sydney
Simon & Schuster India, New Delhi

www.simonandschuster.co.uk
www.simonandschuster.com.au
www.simonandschuster.co.in

A CIP catalogue record for this book is available from the British Library

Paperback ISBN: 978-1-4711-7029-4
eBook ISBN: 978-1-4711-7030-0
Audio ISBN: 978-1-4711-8323-2

Typeset in the UK by M Rules
Printed and bound by CPI Group (UK) Ltd, Croydon, CR0 4YY

Simon & Schuster UK Ltd are committed to sourcing paper that is made from wood grown in sustainable forests and support the Forest Stewardship Council, the leading international forest certification organisation. Our books displaying the FSC logo are printed on FSC certified paper.

To Jo Williamson,
who has been my guiding star for ten years.
I'm afraid you're stuck with me now.

Snowy Nights at Castle Court

Chapter One

Cat Garcia held up a small bunch of silver keys and jangled them in front of her best friend's nose. 'Do you want to do it or shall I?'

Sadie Smart felt a shiver run down her spine that had nothing to do with the chilly November air. They'd been building up to this for the last six weeks – the moment she and Cat stepped inside the newly refurbished Smart Cookies Biscuit Emporium together for the very first time. It had been a dream they'd cherished since school; their very own business, one that combined Cat's love of cookery and Sadie's artistic flair. And what better place to open a food shop than quirky Castle Court, in the heart of their home town, a secret oasis tucked away behind the time-worn streets of the Rows.

Glancing up at the swirling blue and gold sign she'd painted above the door, Sadie allowed herself a half-smile. Art college seemed like something she'd done in another lifetime; marriage and the arrival of her daughter, Lissy, had given her student days a dreamlike, distant quality. It had felt good to dust off both her brushes and her creativity, especially for something so important, although she'd felt horribly rusty. She hoped it didn't show in her work.

'Why don't you do the honours?' she asked Cat. 'You've done most of the hard graft so far, being here every day to oversee the building work.'

'You were working too,' Cat pointed out. 'Just not here. And you have a five-year-old to look after.'

Sadie thought back to the previous afternoon, when she'd said goodbye for the last time at the doctor's surgery where she'd been working part-time. She'd been nervous about leaving – worried about being further away from Lissy's school too – but there was no way Cat could continue to do everything to get Smart Cookies off the ground. Besides, she wanted to be involved – they were building their dream together.

'But I'm here now and ready to get stuck in,' she said firmly. 'Although I'm relieved I won't have to deal with any of the workmen. I don't know how you didn't kill the guy fitting the oven.'

Cat gave her a dead-eyed stare. 'Who says I didn't? Maybe he's the reason the new cement floor in the basement isn't quite level.' Her expression dissolved into a grin as she slid the key into the lock. 'We're a team, so we'll do it together. On three . . .'

Sadie clasped her gloved hand over Cat's. 'One, two, three!'

They twisted the key to one side and the door nudged open. Both women let go and allowed it to swing back. The not-unpleasant scent of fresh putty and new paint wafted over them in a cloud of warm air as they gazed inside. The walls were lined with clean white shelves. The wood floor had been sanded and re-varnished; it was now dotted with multi-tiered circular tables that rose like wedding cakes, waiting to be decorated with Sadie and Cat's creations. A glass counter ran along the back wall, next to an alcove where the computerised till system would sit. Gleaming white banisters invited customers to take the curving stair-case downstairs to the basement, where a small but perfectly equipped kitchen was tucked away off a galley room filled with benches and long tables; Sadie planned to use them to offer icing classes and birthday parties. But that was for the future, she reminded herself with a small inner shake. There was a lot to be done before Smart Cookies was ready to open its doors to the public.

'What first?' she asked, glancing at Cat with a quizzically raised eyebrow.

Cat stepped forwards, wiping her boots on the doormat. 'First we put the kettle on. And then we make a plan.'

Sadie didn't try to hide her amusement. That was Cat all over: organised, methodical and a firm believer in the power of tea and a To-Do List. It was probably inevitable, given her friend's glittering career as a chef – what was a recipe, if not a very specific to-do list, after all? 'Okay,' she said, following her into the pristine shop and closing the door behind her, noting the pleasing tinkle of the little brass bell over their heads. 'I hope you've brought some biscuits.'

'Believe me, I have eaten, slept and breathed the bloody things for the last month.' Cat patted her large tote bag, which bulged with boxes, her expression rueful. 'I've given away so many free samples that I'm pretty sure my new neighbours think I'm some kind of cookie pusher.'

Sadie noted the dark circles under Cat's eyes, and the sallow tinge to her Mediterranean skin; she didn't doubt that her friend had been burning the midnight oil in pursuit of perfection. 'And?'

'And I *think* we're there. Baking a biscuit that will stay

crisp and crunchy under all the icing you're going to pour on top hasn't been easy.' Cat gave a melodramatic sigh and tucked her long dark curls behind her ears. 'You don't want to know how many disappointingly soggy bottoms I've bitten into recently.'

'Mary Berry would be proud,' Sadie said, fighting to keep her face straight. 'But I want you to know that I appreciate both the pun and the sacrifice.'

Cat shrugged off her coat. 'There's plenty more of both in our future. But the first order of business is tea. I think better with a cuppa in my hand.'

She led the way down the stairs, past the galley and into the kitchen. Two floor-to-ceiling fridges lined one wall; another was filled with gleaming silver ovens. A third wall had white cupboards, beneath which lay glittering marble worktops studded with industrial-sized stand mixers, and a high-level table lay flush against the final wall. Sadie couldn't help glancing at the tiled floor as Cat walked across it to reach for the kettle. It was perfectly even; clearly the woeful oven-fitter had redeemed himself eventually. Cat was used to working to the highest standards in the Michelin-starred restaurants of Paris and anything less than perfection would not be tolerated. Sadie had heard stories of sous-chefs reduced to tears by Cat's blistering tongue, although she'd never experienced the fury herself. But she'd also never worked with her; being business partners increased the likelihood that sparks would fly, Sadie thought, squashing a faint bubble of unease. She'd have to make sure she brought her A-game to everything she did, especially where the biscuits were concerned. And that might be easier said than done now that she was a single parent. Lissy had coped well with the turmoil caused by her parents' separation just over six months earlier, but Sadie still struggled to juggle the demands of having to do it all herself. She couldn't even rely on her own parents to help out; they'd retired to the idyllic town of Bowness, overlooking Lake Windermere in the Lake District. In spite of the difficulties of coping alone, Sadie was determined to give Smart Cookies everything she had. She owed it to both herself and Cat.

The tea was strong, brewed with the Yorkshire tea bags that Cat loved so much that she'd taken boxes with her as she travelled the world, studying different cuisines. Now she'd settled back in Chester, in a glossy two-bedroomed rooftop apartment nestled inside the city walls, with views across the River Dee. It wasn't quite the Parisian skyline, she'd admitted to Sadie on the day she'd moved in, but it was home.

'So,' Cat said, as they settled on leather-topped stools around the high table. 'Here's where we are.'

She tapped at her tablet and pulled up the detailed spreadsheet that made up the blueprint for the whole business.

'We're on schedule for our opening day at the start of December,' Cat said, scanning the rows of highlighted numbers. 'But we really need to start advertising, to build up a buzz. And we need the website to be finished – it can't go live until we have photographs of our products.'

Sadie glanced at the date on her watch: it was 9 November,

just three and a half weeks until the shop was due to open. They were cutting it fine if they wanted to get the word out to build up the all-important Christmas trade.

'And we need the biscuits to be iced before we can have photos,' she said, thinking of the designs laid out across the dining-room table in the tiny two-bedroomed cottage she shared with Lissy. She'd planned to start small but Cat had wanted more and more. A Welcome Baby range in pink, blue and yellow, presented in little keepsake boxes. Butterflies, birds and bees that just begged to be bitten. Birthday balloon biscuits that could be personalised. Individually iced letters arranged to spell out Thank You. And of course there was a Christmas range: edible bauble biscuits, gleaming red and white candy canes, snowflakes and colourful box-shaped presents. And that was just the basic stock. Cat also wanted plenty of display biscuits dotted around the shop, plus an irresistible window display that would tempt customers inside. It all made sense to Sadie but there was no denying it would be a Herculean task to get it all done in time.

'Do you think you can ice these overnight?' Cat asked, reaching into her bag, and pulled out a large Tupperware box. 'I thought I might nip them over to the photographer in the morning.'

Sadie eyed the box with some trepidation. 'What shapes are in there?'

'Two of everything,' Cat said, placing another large box on the table. 'One for you to practise on and another that needs to be picture-perfect. That's okay, isn't it?'

Sadie's heart sank. The whole range numbered more than seventy individual biscuits. Each one needed at least two different types and shades of icing, matched perfectly against a custom-made colour chart, to decorate them. Getting them all ready by the next day was going to be a huge task – preparing the icing alone would take well over an hour.

Cat studied her apologetically. 'I'm sorry to dump this on you, especially since it took me forever to perfect the bake. Say if I'm being unreasonable – I know you've got Lissy to think about too.'

The trouble was that they needed the website to be up as soon as possible, Sadie thought, trying not to feel daunted. But she didn't want to let Cat down, not when time was so pressing and it really should be fine – she'd practised the designs on greaseproof paper, after all. 'No problem,' she said, squaring her shoulders. 'I'll make a start before the school run later.'

'Amazing,' Cat said, flashing her a grateful look. 'Thank you.'

The conversation moved on to the presentation of the shop itself. They went back upstairs, discussing how the stock should be arranged across the shelves. Sadie felt herself relax as she slipped into her comfort zone; design and aesthetics were where she had always excelled.

'I've probably gone overboard with the bunting and fairy lights order,' Cat said, pursing her lips. 'But actually we should go straight into festive mode – a tree, tinsel, the works. The window should be Christmas-themed too.'

Sadie's creative instincts sat up. 'We could do a miniature

snowy village in biscuits, with Father Christmas and his reindeer flying overhead and star-shaped cookies sparkling in the sky.'

'That would look amazing,' Cat said, her eyes gleaming. 'I could make the houses out of gingerbread. It would be a great showcase for our talents and I'm sure it would pull in the festive crowds.'

'And in the meantime, I could paint some pictures on the glass,' Sadie suggested, glancing at the barren window. 'To give people an idea of what's coming.'

She pulled her notepad towards her and started to doodle some designs on the smooth white paper, while Cat absorbed herself in the spreadsheet. Sadie was so engrossed in her drawing that she barely noticed when the bell above the door tinkled. It was only when she heard a male voice that she looked up.

'Hello, neighbours.'

The speaker was holding the door half open, leaning through as though he couldn't decide whether to come in or not. Sadie took in his tousled dark hair, dancing brown eyes and wide smile, before moving on to the black biker jacket and white T-shirt beneath. His black jeans were narrow and led downwards into heavy Doc Marten boots. Wow, Sadie thought, dragging her gaze back to his face. He's the kind of neighbour I could get used to.

Cat evidently agreed because she didn't seem to be able to take her eyes off him. Amused, Sadie summoned up a businesslike smile. 'Hi there. How can we help?'

Their neighbour's smile widened. 'I've been watching the workmen come and go for weeks,' he said, nodding at Cat. 'And now that it seems you are almost finished, I thought I should come and say hello.'

His voice had a trace of an accent, one that lifted each word out of the ordinary and made them instantly more interesting. French? Sadie wondered, hoping that wasn't the case. Although Cat had loved living in Paris, she'd left the city under a cloud; the last thing she needed was an ever-present reminder of what she saw as her failure.

Cat still hadn't spoken so Sadie put down her pen and extended a hand to the stranger. 'I'm Sadie, the arty half of Smart Cookies.'

The man shook her hand. 'Great name for a biscuit business,' he said approvingly. 'I'm Jaren Smit. I run the Dutch pancake house opposite.'

That certainly explained the accent, Sadie decided, glancing beyond the ancient oak tree in the heart of the courtyard towards the orange and green Let's Go Dutch sign that hung above a double-bayed shop front. She turned her head to give Cat a meaningful look. 'And this is the brains of the operation – Cat Garcia.'

Hearing her name seemed to wake Cat from her daydream. Her cheeks reddened slightly as she stepped forwards to take Jaren's outstretched hand. 'It's nice to meet you.'

'Likewise,' he said, smiling. 'Although I should probably warn you that I am the first of many nosy shopkeepers who will be banging on your door. Your shop has been the subject of much speculation around Castle Court for some time now and everyone is keen to meet you.'

Cat and Sadie exchanged looks. 'We're looking forward to getting to know everyone too,' Sadie said cautiously. 'This is a brand new venture for us so it's good to know our fellow shopkeepers are friendly.'

Jaren nodded. 'Castle Court is a special place – we all look out for each other here. Which isn't to say we all get along, of course, but we're a bit like a family – we try to help if and when it's needed. All you have to do is ask.'

He smiled again and Sadie wondered if it was having the same effect on Cat as it was on her; it certainly looked as though her friend was having some distinctly non-familial thoughts about their new neighbour. 'That's great,' she said. 'Isn't it, Cat?'

'Absolutely,' Cat replied. 'Really great. We look forward to becoming part of the Castle Court family.'

Jaren gazed back and forth between them and Sadie thought his eyes lingered a fraction of a second longer on Cat before he spoke again. 'Well, don't let me get in your way. I'm sure you have plenty to do.' He raised a hand and waved. 'See you around.'

Both Sadie and Cat waved their goodbyes and watched Jaren make his way back across Castle Court. A busy silence filled the shop.

'Well,' Cat said, after a moment had passed. 'If all our neighbours look like him then it's going to make coming to work a whole lot more enjoyable.'

Sadie laughed. 'He's certainly very easy on the eye. More your type than mine.'

'Maybe. But probably not single,' Cat said with a sigh. 'The good-looking ones never are.'

'You never know,' Sadie replied. 'It shouldn't be too hard to find out, anyway.'

Cat's expression brightened. 'That's true.' She glanced sideways at Sadie. 'And if he is single, he might have a friend for you.'

Sadie shook her head hard. 'Oh no, you're not dragging me into this. The last time we double-dated was our Sixth Form prom and I ended up headfirst in the college fountain.'

'It's not my fault your date was a moron,' Cat countered. She sent Sadie a wide-eyed look. 'Come on, you and Daniel have been separated for more than six months now. It's time you had some fun.'

'I do have fun,' Sadie said, folding her arms. 'I take Lissy to the park, play football with her, build Lego castles. Those things are lots of fun.'

Cat's face became obstinate. 'You know what I mean. The thrill of attraction, the frisson of kissing someone you've never kissed before. Adult fun.'

Sadie shifted from one foot to the other, uncomfortably hoping her cheeks weren't as flame-red as they felt. 'Cat—'

Her friend held up her hands in mock-surrender. 'I know, I know – you're not ready. But you'll forgive me for pointing out that Daniel didn't waste any time moving on. I don't see why you should.'

Cat meant well, Sadie knew, but that didn't stop her words from hurting. Daniel hadn't wasted any time in starting a new relationship once their marriage had broken down. In fact, it turned out there'd been some overlap, which had been the final nail in the coffin for Sadie – she'd moved out and taken Lissy with her. As far as she knew, Daniel was still dating his other woman, although now he was perfectly free to do so, of course.

'It's not that simple,' she said quietly. 'Besides, between motherhood and this place, I have my hands pretty full right now, don't you think?'

'Okay, I'll give you that,' Cat conceded. 'But don't think you can hide forever, Sadie Smart. One of these days someone will catch your eye and I'll be there to make sure you don't let him slip away.'

She glanced over at the pancake house opposite as she spoke and Sadie had to hide a grin. Settling in to Castle Court had just become a whole lot more interesting.

Chapter Two

Lissy's eyes were wide as she followed Sadie into the kitchen after school.

'Mummy,' she said, her upturned face accusing. 'You've made a big mess.'

Sadie couldn't argue with her daughter; she *had* made a mess. Piping bags filled with icing bloomed from bowls like rainbow-coloured petals and every available surface was covered in sticky baking parchment; even the range had been turned into a makeshift worktop. The cream wall cupboards had Sadie's icing designs stuck to them and the dining-room table now had biscuit-laden cooling racks running from end to end. Lissy couldn't have seen those yet, Sadie decided; she'd have declared an immediate and insatiable hunger if she had.

'This is Mummy's work,' Sadie told her. 'You remember – Auntie Cat and I are opening a shop together and my job is to make the biscuits look nice and tasty. That's what all the icing is for.'

Lissy's face brightened. Her auburn curls, so like Sadie's own, bounced as an idea struck her. 'Can I help you? I coloured in a triceratops today and my teacher said it was really good.'

'I'm sure it was beautiful,' Sadie said, casting around for something Lissy could decorate without depleting the stock Cat had provided. Her gaze came to rest on a half-opened packet of Digestives. 'Want to ice some of these?'

Lissy nodded enthusiastically. Sadie fastened an apron around her daughter and then took down her own from behind the kitchen door. 'First things first, you need to decide what you're going to draw,' she said, placing a biscuit on the work surface and moving the plastic step Lissy used to stand on to wash her hands nearer to the worktop. 'Start with something simple – like a flower. And then you need to pick a colour to draw your shape with.'

Lissy narrowed her eyes thoughtfully. 'A daisy. Except I want it to be yellow, like a buttercup.'

Sadie reached for a sunflower-yellow piping bag. This was line icing, used for creating the outlines of shapes. Once it had set a little, they would be able to flood the shape with a slightly runnier icing mixture and perhaps even add some extra design details.

'Okay, first of all you need to picture a daisy in your head,' Sadie said. 'Can you remember what they look like?'

Lissy pointed to the picture of some flowers she'd drawn back in nursery. It peeped out from its lofty position high up on the fridge. 'Like that.'

'That's right. Now I need to teach you how to hold the bag so that the icing doesn't splurge out when you get going.' Sadie stood behind her daughter and twisted the top of the icing bag around to seal it. 'The trick is to keep a gentle but steady pressure on the bag — like this.'

She spread Lissy's small fingers around the squishy mass below the twist. 'Dip the tip of the bag down until it touches your biscuits then lift it up and let the icing string fall into the shape you want.'

Sadie steadied Lissy's hand as a thin ribbon of yellow curled onto the biscuit and into the rough shape of a flower. She dabbed at the centre of the final petal and the icing line broke. 'There — all done.'

Lissy gave the biscuit a disappointed look. 'But it's all wobbly.'

'Don't worry,' Sadie said with an encouraging smile. 'Once the outline has dried a little bit, we're going to fill the middle with icing too, and then we can add some detail to make it look more like a yellow daisy. Why don't you try another while we wait?'

Lissy took another biscuit and tried again, her tongue poking out between her rosebud lips as she concentrated. By her third attempt, the line of icing was much less wobbly and she was starting to smile.

'Excellent work,' Sadie said, giving Lissy's shoulder a tiny squeeze. 'Ready to fill your first one in?'

'Yes.'

Sadie reached for a second piping bag, stashed in another

bowl. This was flood icing, with a consistency that was almost like custard that spread more easily across the biscuit surface. The trick here was not to overfill the shape and break the line icing.

'Well done,' Sadie said, as Lissy filled the last petal. 'Now you need to pop all the little bubbles in the icing – here, use this cocktail stick to dab them.'

Once all Lissy's yellow daisies were ready, Sadie put them into the warm oven to dry and turned to her daughter. 'Do you think you'd like to try a few on your own, while I get on with my designs?'

The little girl nodded and reached for another Digestive biscuit. 'I'm going to try a butterfly,' she announced, her voice ringing with confidence.

They worked side by side for half an hour before Lissy remembered that biscuits were also for eating. Sadie took the baking tray with the iced daisy biscuits out of the oven and slid them onto a cooling rack. 'These will be ready to eat in a few minutes. Do you want to ice any more?'

Lissy shook her head. 'No, thank you. I want to play dinosaurs.'

Sadie glanced at the boxes of biscuits still to be iced; she wasn't even halfway through the collection yet. 'Why don't you bring your toys in here? That way I can keep an eye on you as you play.'

But it wasn't long before Sadie was sitting on the floor, in charge of the vegetarian dinosaurs as they faced an invasion by the carnivores. Lissy had always had an active imagination and Sadie frequently had to hide a smile as her daughter adopted a different growl for each dinosaur. Eventually, Lissy lowered her T-Rex and rubbed her stomach. 'I'm hungry.'

Sadie glanced up at the untidy kitchen; she'd have to clear up before she could make Lissy's supper and then it would be time for her bath and bed. Only then would Sadie be able to get back to work; it looked as though it was going to be her turn to burn the midnight oil for Smart Cookies.

Swallowing a sigh, she turned her gaze back to Lissy. 'Okay, what can I make you to eat?' Before the little girl could speak, Sadie held up a warning hand. 'And don't say biscuits.'

It was almost seven-thirty that evening when Cat stretched her aching back and decided to call it a night. She hadn't meant to stay so late but the temptation to test the new ovens had been hard to resist. The bulk of the biscuit baking so far had been done at her apartment, where Cat had already got approval from the local council's environmental health department, but she planned to do most of the baking on the Smart Cookies premises eventually. The shop wasn't due for its visit from environmental health for another week, so technically Cat couldn't sell any of the biscuits she made there to the public, but since they weren't actually open yet, that wasn't likely to happen. These were samples so that she could gauge where the oven's hotspots were and get used to its idiosyncrasies. Every oven had a personality, she'd decided right at the start of her career, and the best chefs got to know them.

Rolling her shoulders, Cat winced as her neck muscles twinged. Another fourteen-hour day and most of it spent on her feet – wasn't that what she'd left Paris to escape? That and the immense pressure of producing more than a hundred Michelin star-worthy meals every night? Of course, the only person checking the quality of Cat's work now was herself, and perhaps Sadie if the biscuits didn't hold the icing as well as they needed to, but nobody was going to bawl her out in front of the rest of the staff if the tiniest aspect of the product wasn't up to scratch. No one was going to reduce her almost to tears, night after night. That was what had driven her out of Paris and a career she'd once loved; that, and a man who had thought he could get away with anything.

The air outside bit with cold. The three timber-framed storeys of Castle Court glowed against the November night sky as Cat locked the door of Smart Cookies, but her eye was drawn to the ancient oak tree in the centre. It must be a few centuries old, at least, and perhaps even pre-dated the Tudor-style buildings themselves. The trunk and branches had been strewn with tiny lights that sparkled and made her half-wonder if there was an enchantress hiding inside.

In the summer, Cat knew the courtyard would be full of tables and chairs that were packed with al fresco diners but tonight was too frosty for that. A few tables were dotted here and there, warmed by the glow of outdoor heaters, but they were mostly empty, aside from the occasional smoker.

The businesses around the Court were most definitely not empty, however; even Let's Go Dutch seemed to be doing a brisk trade when Cat would have assumed most locals would consider pancakes to be more of a breakfast treat. Then again, she knew the Dutch ate savoury pancakes that could be every bit as substantial as a heavier meal; maybe the diners of Chester had discovered that too. She'd have to check out the menu, see what Jaren was offering that meant his restaurant was almost full on a wintry Wednesday evening. But the pancake house wasn't the busiest of Castle Court's businesses. The French bistro at the far end of the Court seemed to be doing well and the cocktail bar on the top floor appeared to be packed too. Neither could compete with the kitsch charm of The Bus Stop diner, which boasted a wide yellow US school bus as its frontispiece. Through its oblong windows, she caught sight of a waitress wearing a stripy red and white shirt and a dainty hat on her head as she moved between the tables with a tray full of tall milkshake glasses. A queue snaked out of the door and wound its way past a patisserie and a chocolaterie, both of which had been closed for hours. Not all of the neighbouring shops sold food, Cat noted; there was an upmarket stationery store in one corner and she'd yet to explore the rest of the second and third floors. But there did seem to be a definite leaning towards culinary delights in Castle Court. It was what had drawn Cat there in the first place.

A voice cut across her thoughts, making her jump. 'A euro for your thoughts.'

She turned to see Jaren beside her. 'Oh! Hi.'

He gave her an apologetic smile. 'I made you jump – I'm sorry. It's just that you looked so deeply engrossed in your thoughts and I wanted to know what was making you frown.' He waved a hand at the courtyard around them. 'Don't you like what you see?'

Cat shook her head. 'It's nothing like that. I was just taking everything in – it's a long time since I've been here in the evening and the crowds caught me a little by surprise, I suppose.'

'Ah, the crowds,' Jaren said, his expression growing serious. 'Yes, I can see why they might have surprised you. Rumour has it that Chester was once twinned with New York, as the city that never sleeps. In fact, I wouldn't be surprised if New York's nickname was borrowed from Castle Court itself – the party often goes on into the early hours.'

His eyes crinkled as he spoke and Cat couldn't help smiling back. 'Something tells me I'm going to like it here.'

Jaren tipped his head. 'I hope so. Speaking of late nights, I came out here to tell you that a group of us are having some after-hours drinks in Seb's bar on the third floor this Saturday, if you and Sadie would like to come? Most of the Castle Court shopkeepers will be there – the food lovers, anyway. It might be a good way for you to meet everyone.'

He held out a card with the same logo Cat could see picked out in neon lights up above them. 'Thanks,' she said as she took it. 'I'll have to check with Sadie to see what her plans are but I'll definitely be there.'

'I hope so,' Jaren replied, meeting her gaze. 'I am looking forward to getting to know you.'

Cat looked into his dark brown eyes, made almost black by the night around them. Was he flirting with her or simply being friendly? It was hard to tell. 'Thanks for passing on the invitation,' she said, filling her voice with warmth. 'It's kind of you to make us feel so welcome.'

Jaren smiled. 'Believe me, the pleasure is all mine.'

It felt as though someone had sprinkled grit in Sadie's eyes the following morning as she negotiated the short drive from her cottage to Lissy's school in nearby Christleton. Dubbed one of Cheshire's prettiest villages, it had been Sadie's home for seven years and she hadn't wanted to disrupt her daughter's life any more than necessary when she'd left Daniel, so Lissy still attended the small village primary school there. Unfortunately for Sadie that meant driving past the house on Windmill Lane she'd shared with Daniel, a daily reminder of what they'd had together, but she supposed it was a small price to pay for Lissy's happiness. And it wasn't as though she ever saw him as they passed; his job as an investment banker meant early starts and long days, which had been ultimately part of the problem in their marriage.

By the time Sadie had parked in the underground car park beneath Cat's apartment and made her way along a frost-touched Eastgate Street to the Old Boot Inn, she was in desperate need of caffeine. An arched tunnel beneath the first-floor pub led to the hidden delights of Castle Court;

Sadie hurried through, her head nestled down into her scarf against the cold. She didn't see the man barrelling towards her until it was too late – they collided mid-tunnel. Sadie let out a yelp of surprise and clutched at the wildly swinging bag containing her precious cargo of iced biscuits; Cat would kill her if they were anything other than pristine. The person she'd bumped into wasn't so lucky; his armful of boxes thudded to the ground.

'Sorry!' Sadie gasped, as he reached out a gloved hand to steady her. 'I didn't see you.'

The man gazed at her from beneath his beanie hat, his hazel eyes wide with concern as he pulled down his scarf to reveal a beard. 'Are you okay?'

'I'm fine,' Sadie said, glancing in distress at the ground, which was now strewn with Brussels sprouts. 'But your boxes . . .'

His mouth twisted into a smile. 'Sprouts are hardy vegetables – a quick wash and they'll be fine.'

He knelt down and started to gather the loose vegetables back into their boxes. Sadie started to help. 'I really am sorry. I was off in my own little world.'

'Me too,' the man said. 'But no harm done, as long as you're all right?'

He glanced across at her then and Sadie felt a shiver of something quite unexpected as she met his gaze. She looked away fast, grateful that her suddenly rosy cheeks could be blamed on the sub-zero temperature. 'Honestly, I'm fine. Don't give it another thought.'

He dropped the last of the sprouts into the box and closed the lid. 'Okay. Well, sorry again,' he said, straightening up with an embarrassed-looking smile. 'Nice bumping into you, ha ha.'

Now it was his turn to blush but Sadie couldn't stop a small smile from creeping across her own face as she stood up. 'No problem. I hope your day gets better.'

He opened his mouth as though about to say something, then closed it fast. They stood still for a moment, smiling at each other. Then the man seemed to wake up and stepped to one side. 'Well. Bye then.'

'Bye,' she echoed as he walked away. 'Enjoy your sprouts.'

She forced her legs to move. By the time she'd reached Castle Court and stopped to look back, he was gone. Sadie let out a groan – had she really just told a total stranger to enjoy his sprouts? It was quite possibly the lamest parting shot ever spoken. She shook her head and hurried for the safety of Smart Cookies. And this time she watched where she was going.

'You look how I feel,' Cat observed, looking up from the dough she was rolling out as Sadie stashed her coat in one of the basement cupboards. 'Late night?'

Sadie placed her bag full of biscuits onto the work surface, deciding not to mention her encounter with the runaway greens. 'Early morning,' she said, pulling a face. 'I thought I'd get everything done in time for a nice early night after Lissy went to bed but the icing separated while I was giving her a bath and I had to remake it.'

Cat's eyes widened in sympathy. 'All of it?'

'All of it,' Sadie confirmed. 'And then it was one o'clock in the morning before I got everything finished.'

Cat winced. 'Sorry. What time did Lissy get up?'

'Five-thirty,' Sadie said with a weary sigh. 'So I really hope we've got some Nespresso pods here or I might fall asleep on the job.'

'Coming right up,' Cat said, dusting off her hands. 'And then I'll take a look at your handiwork. I can't wait to see the finished biscuits.'

Coffee in hand, Sadie held her breath as Cat opened up the boxes. She'd been so worried about them rubbing together in transit and damaging the delicate icing that she'd used a blob of icing to stick each one to its layer of greaseproof paper. But would that be enough to have saved them from the jolt of her collision with Sprout Man?

Cat said nothing as she inspected each biscuit. Sadie's palms began to itch with sweat – were they about to have their first professional bust-up? But Cat was smiling when her eyes finally met Sadie's. 'Has anyone ever told you you're amazing?'

Sadie let out her breath in a whoosh. Her cheeks grew warm with pleasure at the praise. 'Not today.'

'Well, you are,' Cat said. 'This is exactly how I imagined them – high quality, unusual and really desirable. I love them and so will everyone else – well done.'

'It's a team effort,' Sadie said. 'If you hadn't made such a great base, I'd never have been able to make them look like that.'

27

'I can't wait to see how they photograph,' Cat said, lifting up a pink and silver butterfly laced onto a dark chocolate base. She tilted it so that the delicate wings caught in the light. 'The website is going to look awesome.'

Sadie took a long sip of the espresso Cat had given her and almost sighed at the rich bitterness that flowed down her throat. 'Is that what you're going to do today – photograph the biscuits?'

'That's my plan,' Cat replied, nodding. 'I've got a photographer friend who says I can use his studio, as long as I'm quick. I'm hoping he might even give me some tips, since what I know about food photography can be written on the back of a Post-it note.'

'I could come along, if you like?' Sadie offered. 'I know a little bit about photographic composition.'

'Great,' Cat said. Then her eyes clouded over with doubt. 'Weren't you going to paint the window, though? It would be a great way of sparking curiosity in passers-by.'

'You're right. Once that's done, I might take a walk around, check out some of the other shops before I go and collect Lissy.'

And maybe see if I can bump into any more good-looking strangers, Sadie thought dreamily, before giving herself a mental shake. Hadn't she told Cat the day before that she didn't have time to spend day-dreaming about men?

Her best friend reached into a pocket and pulled out a business card. 'That reminds me – what are you doing on Saturday night?'

'Uh – nothing,' Sadie replied, forcing the memory of the blue-eyed man out of her head. 'Why, have you got another urgent load of biscuits for me to ice?'

'No,' Cat said, sliding the card towards her. 'The other shopkeepers are having after-hours drinks and we're invited. Want to go?'

Sadie thought fast. It was Daniel's weekend to have Lissy but there had been times when he'd been less than reliable over the course of the past year and she'd grown wary of making plans. 'In theory, yes. Do you?'

She needn't have asked; of course her best friend would want to go – she loved socialising. 'I think it would be a good idea to show our faces, get to know people,' Cat said slowly. 'Jaren thought it might be a nice way to break the ice too.'

'So that's where the invitation came from,' Sadie said, raising her eyebrows. 'I wondered how you'd found out about it.'

'I saw him last night, as I was heading home,' Cat replied, her tone casual. 'He mentioned it then.'

Sadie resisted the temptation to wink. 'Then it feels like it would be rude not to go, especially since we've been personally invited.'

'That's what I thought,' Cat said quickly. 'And it will be good to meet the rest of the Castle Court crew.'

'Check out the competition, you mean?' Sadie observed.

Cat offered her a disarming smile. 'Of course. But mostly, I'd love to know whether the cocktail list at Seb's tastes as good as it looks. Besides, we haven't had a night out in forever – it will do us good.'

'Mmmm,' Sadie said, making a mental note to stick to water all night. The last thing they needed was to over-indulge and be the subject of Castle Court gossip in their very first week. She decided to change the subject before Cat tested her resolve with the names of the cocktails on offer. 'So, what shall I paint on our windows?'

Chapter Three

Once Cat had left for the photographer's studio, Sadie paid a quick visit to the Court stationery shop, praying they'd have glass paint. It was clear from the moment she stepped inside that they had everything she needed and plenty more besides. She lingered by the beautiful embroidered notebooks and ran her fingers over the rainbow colours of the pen section before dragging herself to the art supplies at the back of the shop, promising herself a return visit very soon.

Back inside Smart Cookies, Sadie got to work on the window display. She and Cat had agreed that it needed to showcase the biscuits they were planning to sell without giving too much detail about the designs of the product. In the end, they settled on a gingerbread theme: children chasing butterflies, families enjoying a picnic, complete with a baby in a pram, while dogs sniffed the grass nearby and birds soared through the sky. Sadie suggested a hint of Christmas with some snow-covered rooftops and candy cane trees dotted here and there.

Several hours later, she was satisfied. Leaving her handi-work to dry, she took a stroll around Castle Court. The weather forecast predicted snow, much to Lissy's excitement, although it had yet to materialise. Sadie wouldn't be surprised to see a flurry or two; there was a definite icy stillness to the air and the temperature hadn't risen much above freezing all morning. Her breath billowed out in steaming clouds as she walked along the top floor, peering into shop windows and admiring the festive displays already on view. She was in foodie heaven, she decided as she passed a trendy whole-food store and the kind of old-fashioned sweet shop Lissy would adore; Sadie made a mental note to pop in there for some stocking fillers nearer to Christmas. Not every business sold foodstuffs; there was a lingerie shop tucked away in a corner that Sadie couldn't imagine ever needing to visit and a designer handbag store that she was certain would empty her purse with its unnecessary but oh-so-desirable stock. And of course there was Seb's, dominating the furthest end of the level and affording a bird's eye view of the whole of Castle Court. Sadie lingered at the window, checking out the cocktail list Cat had so admired. She had to admit it sounded good; even the virgin cocktails were a fusion of mouth-watering flavours that begged passers-by to try them. The window seats would be a great place for people-watching, Sadie thought, as she resisted the temptation to go inside. Another time, she decided; there'd be plenty of time to linger in the months ahead.

The second level boasted a jeweller's, a bespoke men's

tailors that Daniel would love, a delicatessen and a fromagerie that smelled like cheesy heaven. And then she was back on the ground floor, admiring the glistening, fragrant delights of Elin's, the chocolaterie, and Patisserie Cherie. Each business had an elegant, understated class, Sadie thought as she waited in line to buy raspberry and white chocolate eclairs, and now more than ever, she understood why Cat had been adamant that Castle Court was the right place for Smart Cookies to open its doors, in spite of the eye-watering rent; iced biscuits were a luxury item and they would fit right in here. But at the same time, Sadie was determined that they wouldn't just sell biscuits to people with more money than sense. She glanced across at the cheap and cheerful frontage of Let's Go Dutch and decided to talk to Cat about designing a pocket money range of affordable treats. Not everyone could spare thirty pounds for a tin of animal-shaped biscuits, after all. And they would have samples by the till, to give to any children who came in. Maybe they could even do a tie-in with Chester Zoo and create some individual animal biscuits to sell in their gift shop. There was plenty of scope to spread the joy of a perfectly iced treat all over the city, Sadie thought, and she hurried back to the shop to write down her ideas.

Cat was waiting for her when she returned, leaning over her laptop on the counter at the back of the empty shop, frowning thoughtfully at the screen.

'Problem?' Sadie asked.

'Just admiring the website,' Cat replied, turning the computer around for Sadie to see. 'Looks good, doesn't it?'

The site used the blue and gold branding Sadie herself had designed and she felt a buzz of pleasure when she saw the photographs of all the biscuits she'd made on display. She hadn't realised how much she'd missed her creative side until she'd begun working up ideas for Smart Cookies. 'That was fast.'

Cat shrugged. 'The photographer sent the pictures over to the web designer, who downloaded them and slotted them into place on the site. It isn't live yet so if there's anything you don't like then it can easily be changed.'

Sadie reached for the mouse and started to navigate her way around the web pages. It was a well-designed site – nothing was more than a couple of clicks away from the main page and the layout managed to be both intuitive and logical. And it looked tempting; hopefully it would lead to lots of online orders.

'Looks good to me,' she said, relinquishing control of the laptop.

'Great,' Cat said. 'All our web designer needs to do now is add a shopping cart and payment options and we're good to go.' She glanced up at Sadie. 'What have you been up to? The window looks great.'

'I'm rusty,' Sadie said, feeling a hot rush of embarrassment. 'It's the best I can do for now.'

Cat gave her a fierce look. 'If that's your "rusty" then I can't wait to see you at the top of your game.' She shook her head. 'You've got to start trusting yourself.'

Sadie stared at her feet, hoping her friend wouldn't notice the tears brimming behind her eyes. It was all very well for

Cat to tell her to trust her abilities; she'd never had a crisis of confidence in her life. In fact, she seemed to have lived a charmed life since graduating catering college at the top of her class and landing a job as a commis chef in one of London's most up-and-coming restaurants. And it might have all unravelled in the last year but confidence still wasn't something Cat was short of, Sadie decided. She wouldn't understand how inferior Daniel's affair had made Sadie feel; the fear that she'd become too dull and boring for even her husband to give her a second glance. But the truth was that her self-confidence had begun to seep away long before she'd discovered his affair; being with Daniel had made her smaller, somehow, less sure of herself and a shadow of the girl Cat had known so well. It was only after Sadie had left her marriage that she'd realised how much she'd changed and the journey back to who she had been before Daniel was slower than expected. Even so, she knew Cat was right; her artistic instincts were good and the window looked gloriously appealing. She really did need to give herself more credit.

'Okay,' she said, glancing up with a small smile. 'I'll try.'

'Good,' Cat said, with a nod of satisfaction. She reached under the counter and pulled out a pale pink box tied with ribbon. 'I stopped by the patisserie on my way back. How can we check out the competition if we don't know what they sell?'

Sadie grinned as she held up her own matching box filled with eclairs. 'Great minds think alike. I'll put the kettle on.'

*

Daniel was due to collect Lissy at ten o'clock on Saturday morning and the little girl was bouncing with excitement as she waited for him to arrive. Normally, Sadie made a point of dropping her off at their old home, preferring to keep her ex as separate as she could from the new life she'd made, but she'd stayed up late again decorating stock for the shop and it made sense to give in to his offer to come round. Just this once, she told herself, as she feverishly cleaned the kitchen surfaces of their visible drifts of icing sugar.

'Trying out some new make-up?' Daniel asked when she opened the front door to let him into the cramped hallway of the cottage.

She stared at him in confusion. It was very unlike him to notice her appearance these days, much less comment on it. 'No – why?'

He reached out a finger and brushed the end of her nose. 'You've got powder all over your face.'

Heat flooded Sadie's cheeks and she glanced in the hallway mirror. Sure enough, her nose and forehead were dusted with icing sugar. She'd even managed to get some in her coppery curls. Mortified, she rubbed her sleeve over her face. 'Sorry. I've been working this morning.'

Daniel gave her a sideways look, causing Sadie to review what she'd said. 'Just while Lissy was watching television. I was keeping an eye on her, obviously.'

'Relax, Sadie, it's fine,' Daniel said. 'I know Cat must be cracking the whip. I'm amazed she's not round here supervising, in fact.'

There was no malice behind the words but Sadie wasn't fooled. Daniel and Cat had never got on; they hadn't even pretended to like each other. Cat had resented Daniel for tying Sadie down to a life of drudgery and motherhood and he hadn't appreciated Cat's efforts to lure his wife away from their comfortable and happy home. To Cat's credit, she'd never once said 'I told you so' once news of his affair had broken, although Sadie knew she must have thought it.

'Cat's in charge of biscuit production, not decoration,' Sadie said coolly. 'And, for the record, she's very happy with my work so far.'

Daniel held his hands up. 'I'm sure she is. But I know you've got a lot to do – I'm more than happy to have Lissy a bit more, to give you extra time to work. All you have to do is ask.'

Sadie couldn't help it; she bristled. It wouldn't be the first time he'd hinted that she wasn't coping with life as a single parent. 'That won't be necessary. I'm quite capable—'

'Daddy!'

Lissy came barrelling into the hallway and wrapped her arms around Daniel's knees. 'Hello, princess,' he said, sweeping her up into his arms.

Her nose wrinkled in disgust. 'I'm not a princess, I'm a dinosaur trainer in charge of saving the world from the evil carnivores.'

Her father laughed. 'Sorry, my mistake. Are you ready to bring your fearsome warriors over to my house? There's a ravenous raptor causing trouble in the rose bushes.'

Lissy's delighted laughter echoed through the hall as she wriggled to get down. 'What are we waiting for? Let's go!'

She vanished into the living room and a series of thuds and clatters filled the air.

'I hope you know what you've done,' Sadie said, her tone wry. 'She'll be packing every dinosaur she has.'

'As long as she's happy,' Daniel said, staring after Lissy.

Sadie gazed at his profile; he was still as good-looking as ever. His dark hair was short and neat, his skin lightly tanned from weekends spent playing golf in sunnier climates. He had the beginnings of laughter lines around his blue eyes – had they always been there? Laughter wasn't something she associated with Daniel; he'd always been so serious and work-obsessed. An arrow of sadness cut through her; maybe she'd been the reason he hadn't laughed. He was obviously much happier now.

He glanced across at her, catching her out. She cleared her throat, embarrassed. 'I'll get her overnight bag.'

It took three attempts to get Lissy out of the front door – she kept remembering one more vital piece of dinosaur battle equipment. But at last she seemed to concede that she had everything she needed and allowed Sadie to bundle her into her coat. As she skipped down the gravel path towards Daniel's sleek Mercedes, he turned back to Sadie.

'Look, I know you think I'm poking my nose in but I meant what I said before – I'm happy to help out more with Lissy if you need me to. Getting a new business off the ground is tough and I'd hate for you to run yourself into the ground trying to do it all when you don't need to.'

Sadie shook her head. 'Daniel—'

'I don't have an agenda, I'm not trying to score points or anything like that.' He softened his voice. 'Just think about it, okay?'

He sounded so reasonable that there was nothing she could do except nod. But that was Daniel all over: reasonable and measured and charm personified while he manoeuvred you into a corner. 'Okay,' she said reluctantly. 'I'll think about it.'

Daniel reached out to squeeze her hand. 'Good. I'll see you tomorrow evening – don't work too hard.'

Sadie pushed away a stab of guilt as she thought about the party that night. It was business, not pleasure; a way of getting to know their neighbours in Castle Court, of building relationships that would stand Smart Cookies in good stead for the future. And besides, Daniel had no idea she wouldn't be slaving over row after row of perfectly cooled cookies all night. 'I'll try not to,' she called as she gave Lissy one final wave.

Now, she thought as she closed the door and wandered into the toy-strewn living room. *What the hell am I going to wear?*

Chapter Four

The problem with working practically every hour of the day, and wearing chef whites to do it, was that Cat had very little to show in terms of clothing, despite having spent three years working in the fashion capital of the world. She stood in her bedroom for a few minutes, gazing thoughtfully into her wardrobe, before grabbing her bag and deciding to hit the shops.

She'd say this for Chester: when it came to retail therapy, there was no shortage of choice. The Rows were packed with shops of all shapes and sizes, from chain stores to quirky little boutiques. The trouble was that Cat couldn't quite get a handle on what she should wear to the welcome party at Seb's; should she go dressy or casual? The shops were all gearing up for Christmas; their rails were filled with sequins and sparkle, reds and greens and golds – Christmas party clothes that Cat was sure would be too much for informal drinks at Castle Court.

After more than an hour spent battling the early festive

shopping crowds, she gave up and rang Sadie. 'I need advice. What are you wearing tonight?'

'Dressy jeans and a rose-gold top,' Sadie replied promptly, giving Cat the impression that she'd had her outfit planned from the moment she'd heard about the party. 'Where are you?'

'In a coffee shop on Northgate Street,' Cat admitted. 'I'm hiding from my woeful fashion ignorance.'

Sadie laughed. 'Cat Garcia, you know you look good no matter what you wear. Do you have any idea what you're looking for?'

'None,' Cat admitted with a sigh. 'It doesn't help that it's wall-to-wall Christmas out here.'

'Why don't you head to some of the quieter streets? There are some lovely little shops around Godstall Lane, opposite the cathedral. Maybe something will leap out at you.'

Cat took a sip of her espresso and sighed. 'Maybe. Haven't you got anything I can borrow?'

'Probably,' Sadie said, sounding even more amused. 'Shall I bring a couple of tops, just in case? I assume you can manage jeans.'

'Yes,' Cat replied dryly. 'I can manage jeans. What time are you heading into the city? Fancy grabbing dinner before we head to Seb's?'

'Sure,' Sadie replied. 'I'll aim for eight-thirty, okay?'

'Perfect,' Cat said. 'You can sleep over if you want to, in my spare room.'

There was a slight pause. 'I'd better not. I still have a lot of biscuits to ice, remember? They need a steady hand so it's probably safest if I drive and get an early start on the icing before Lissy comes home.' Sadie hesitated again, as though she knew it wasn't what Cat wanted to hear. 'I'll sleep over next time, I promise.'

Cat couldn't help laughing. 'We're not nine years old, Sadie. Of course it's okay – it sounds very sensible to me.'

'It sounds boring,' Sadie grumbled. 'But I really do need a clear head and a steady hand. Sorry.'

She sounded it too: contrite and apologetic and keen to make up for it. That was what eight years of Daniel had done, Cat thought, her mood darkening. But she kept her thoughts to herself. 'Honestly, it was just an idea. Forget it.'

Once the call had ended, Cat sipped slowly at her coffee. She'd never liked Daniel, hadn't liked who Sadie became when she was with him, and over the years they'd instinctively given each other a wide berth. When Sadie had revealed the extent of his betrayal last year, during a heartbroken late-night telephone call with Cat, her opinion of him had hit rock bottom. As far as she was concerned, the sooner Sadie moved on from her ex, the better. With a bit of luck Castle Court might provide her with a new romantic opportunity as well as a new career, Cat thought, finishing her coffee and getting to her feet. And with a bit more luck it might do the same for her.

Seb's was still full when Cat and Sadie arrived just after ten-thirty that evening. The windows were thick with condensation and the sound of laughter mingled with a grimy bass beat that made the floor vibrate as they got nearer.

'Are you sure it's tonight?' Sadie murmured as Cat pushed back the door and they were enveloped by a cloud of moist, cinnamon-scented air.

Cat paused, scanning the crowd for a familiar face. She was sure she had the right date – Jaren had definitely said this Saturday. 'Maybe we're early,' she whispered back to Sadie. She cleared her throat and raised her voice. 'Come on, let's get a drink.'

They hadn't got more than halfway to the distressed stainless steel bar when a shout rang out. Cat and Sadie turned to see Jaren waving at the back of the room, standing at the far side of a rectangular table that had a large 'Reserved' sign in the middle. 'Cat, Sadie! Over here.'

There were several others at the table already, Cat noticed as they picked their way over to Jaren; were they shopkeepers waiting for the crowd to get the message and go home? Or were they paying punters, which was equally possible? Cat did her best to study each face in turn, committing them to memory so that she wouldn't embarrass herself when she ran into them out and about in Castle Court over the coming months.

Jaren beckoned them over again and beamed at them as they approached. 'Welcome to Seb's!' he cried as soon as they slipped into empty seats around the table. He waved expansively at the strangers. 'Meet Cat and Sadie, everyone. Say hello!'

A chorus of greetings rang out. Once she was seated, Cat took the opportunity to discreetly scrutinise the others. A tiny blonde with a slight hint of a Scandinavian accent introduced herself as Elin the chocolatier and seemed friendly, although she sat so close to Jaren that Cat decided she might as well have been sitting in his lap. Were they an item? Cat wondered, remembering her suspicion that Jaren had been flirting with her a few days earlier. Perhaps she'd misunderstood, she thought with a flicker of acute disappointment.

An older but no less glamorous dark-haired woman at the table seemed considerably less eager to meet Cat and Sadie; her name was Cherie and her lips were pursed as Jaren introduced them.

'Oh, I visited your shop today,' Sadie burst out, just as Cat began to say something similar. 'What marvellous cakes you sell.'

The woman did not smile. 'I suppose you were checking out my stock, working out which ideas you could steal for your own shop,' she sniffed.

Cat blinked and she saw Sadie's eyes widen. Jaren's smile drooped a bit. 'Come on, Cherie, we talked about this. Sadie and Cat aren't running a patisserie or even anything remotely like that. They're selling biscuits, remember?'

Cherie looked as though she didn't believe a word of it. Her lips pressed into an even tighter line and her eyes flashed with barely contained annoyance.

'It's nice to meet you,' Sadie said politely, and Cat didn't dare make eye contact with her friend for fear she might giggle. 'Your cakes were delicious – thank you. I think we ate them far too fast to think about stealing your secrets, though.'

Jaren coughed and glanced hurriedly at the two clean-cut, twenty-something men seated at the end of the table. 'Speaking of stealing, make sure you don't leave anything valuable lying around when these guys are nearby. They're total magpies, as the front of their shop suggests.'

'Guilty as charged,' one of the men said amiably, with an unmistakable American twang. 'I'm Andrew and this is Earl – we run The Bus Stop diner downstairs.'

Earl nodded and pushed his glasses up his nose. 'You might have noticed it – the big yellow bus part is kinda hard to miss.'

Cat grinned; she liked them already. Sadie leaned forwards. 'I hope you don't mind my asking, but is it a genuine school bus or a replica?'

Andrew adopted an expression of wounded pride. 'A replica? Don't insult us, ma'am.'

'It's one hundred per cent genuine,' Earl added. 'Stolen from outside a school and shipped all the way over from the States.'

'Those kids can't get to school now but the good people of Chester have benefited, so it's – what's the phrase you use? –' Andrew wrinkled his nose in thought, 'swings and carousels?'

Sadie laughed. 'But how did you get it inside the Court?' she pressed. 'It's far too big to have been driven in.'

Andrew and Earl exchanged glances, then Earl leaned

towards Cat and Sadie. 'Promise me you won't breathe a word of this to anyone else, not least the authorities.'

Intrigued, Cat nodded. 'Our lips are sealed.'

Beside her, Sadie did the same. 'We promise.'

'We beamed it over using the USS Enterprise,' Earl said solemnly.

Andrew shook his head. 'Ignore this moron. Actually, our house elf did all the hard work.'

Cat grinned. 'Impressive. Mine can't even make a decent cup of tea.'

'But if we didn't have a house elf and had to do it the old-fashioned way,' Andrew went on, tapping the side of his nose, 'we might take it apart in our back yard and transport it here in pieces.'

Earl took a swig of his drink. 'Then we might rebuild it, bit by bit, to create an impossible-to-ignore centrepiece that customers would love.'

Cat gazed down at the brightly lit bus that dominated the front of The Bus Stop. It showed no signs of having been broken apart and reassembled; she was half-tempted to believe it had been done by magic. 'Wow. That's pretty dedicated.'

'What can I say?' Earl said, spreading his hands in a modest shrug. 'We're marketing geniuses. Or our house elf is.'

Everyone laughed but Cat made a mental note to talk to the two Americans more. Maybe they'd have some advice for her and Sadie about promoting Smart Cookies. She'd make a point of avoiding Cherie, though; the woman hadn't stopped glowering since they'd arrived.

'Let's see, who else is there you need to meet?' Jaren mused, glancing around. 'Oh, the guy behind the bar, spinning the bottles like he's a New York mixologist, is Seb. He'll come and say hi as soon as he's finished trying to impress you.'

Cat followed his gaze and saw a rugged, blond-haired man in his mid-thirties juggling bottles as he mixed cocktails in front of an adoring female audience. He wasn't breathtakingly good-looking, Cat thought – nowhere near as classically handsome as Jaren – but he exuded confidence and a charm that suggested he was used to getting plenty of attention. And if Jaren was off the menu then Seb might turn out to be exactly the kind of distraction she wanted, she decided.

'And that's all we have for now.'

Jaren's voice cut into Cat's thoughts, just as Seb caught her studying him. She dragged her attention away fast and focused on the Dutchman as he continued to talk. 'Greg will be over as soon as the bistro closes and by that time, the last stragglers from here should be on their way and we can start enjoying ourselves.'

'But you don't have to wait until then to order a drink,' Elin said, pushing a cocktail menu across the table. 'Go for something exotic – Seb loves an opportunity to show off.'

'I bet he does,' Cat murmured, so quietly that only Sadie could hear. She studied the menu and waited until the other shopkeepers had begun to chat amongst themselves to risk another glance across at the bar. She was both amused and unsurprised to find the bar owner's eyes were still fixed on her. They shared a long, appraising look.

The exchange didn't escape Sadie's notice. 'Down, girl,' she said in an undertone, as she peered at the menu over Cat's shoulder. 'Tonight is meant to be business, not pleasure, remember?'

Cat watched Seb pour liquid into a cocktail shaker and add a handful of ice. 'I don't see why we can't mix the two – we're all grown-ups,' she said. 'See anyone here who ticks your boxes?'

'No,' Sadie replied and Cat detected a faint hint of irritation. 'And even if I did, I wouldn't act on it. Isn't mixing business and pleasure one of the reasons you left Paris?'

Cat took a deep, calming breath; she loved her best friend very much but sometimes – *sometimes* – she wished she would let her hair down and relax. And she had no idea of the real reason Cat had fled from Paris – none at all. 'No, I left because I very nearly had a nervous breakdown brought on by stress and being overworked. Pleasure had nothing to do with it.'

Sadie flushed. 'I know. Sorry, I'm just – I don't want anything to spoil things for us here, that's all.'

'Nor do I,' Cat replied. She dredged up a crooked smile. 'But a bit of window shopping isn't going to bring about the end of the universe, is it?'

'No,' Sadie admitted, glancing across at Seb. 'And I must admit I do see the appeal. He's certainly good with his hands.'

'An excellent observation,' Cat said, grinning. She glanced across at Jaren, who was deep in conversation with Elin. 'It looks as though Castle Court has a couple of fringe benefits.

Shame Earl and Andrew are spoken for, though. I like a man who can make me laugh.'

Sadie frowned. 'You mean—'

'Definitely a couple,' Cat said firmly. 'Didn't you catch the chemistry?'

'Oh,' Sadie said, looking back and forth between the two Americans. 'No, I missed that completely.'

'Trust me,' Cat said, 'they only have eyes for each other. Now, shall we mingle a bit?'

Sadie nodded. 'That's what we're here for. I'll take the Harry Potter fans and you sweet-talk Elin.'

Cat did her best to ignore a burst of laughter from the bar; Seb was apparently funny as well as talented, and waited for a lull in Elin and Jaren's conversation. 'Are you from Switzerland, Elin?'

The blonde woman nodded, her neat bob glistening beneath the lights. 'Yes, from Geneva originally, although I have lived here for almost seven years now.' She studied Cat's dark curls and olive skin. 'And you?'

'Spanish dad and English mum,' Cat said. 'No one ever believes I'm Chester born and bred, especially since my parents now live in Castile.'

Elin glanced sideways at Jaren. 'You'll fit right in at Castle Court – it's a real melting pot of different nationalities. Greg is from Marseille and Seb is South African.'

'Really?' Cat said, mentally ticking the box marked *Interesting background* on Seb's information sheet in her brain. 'Well, maybe that isn't so surprising – food is one of the oldest ways to bring people together, after all, and Castle Court is very much foodie heaven.'

'That's true,' Jaren said, smiling. 'So what brings you here, Cat? Apart from a love of food.'

Cat hesitated. She didn't really want to go into the reasons she'd abandoned her career but, on the other hand, she wanted the other business owners to take her seriously, to recognise a fellow food professional in their midst. So she summoned up a casual smile. 'I was head chef at La Perle de Paris for three years. But I wanted a change of pace, and Sadie and I had always dreamed of running our own business, so this seemed like the perfect opportunity for both of us.'

Elin stared at her and Jaren whistled. 'You were in charge of the kitchen at La Perle? But that's a Michelin-starred restaurant – one of the most famous in the world.'

'We had two Michelin stars, actually, and were on course for a third,' Cat replied with a modest shrug. 'But all good things come to an end. It was time to move on.'

Jaren fixed her with an admiring look. 'La Perle's loss is our gain, for sure.'

Was it Cat's imagination or did Elin's eyes narrow a fraction? She couldn't tell. 'Biscuits are a lot easier than *cordon bleu*,' Cat said. 'And the hardest part is the decoration, which is Sadie's department. She's the talent, not me.'

Her self-deprecation seemed to work; Elin smiled. 'It sounds to me like you're a dream team. I look forward to tasting some of your work.'

'Just don't tell Cherie where you used to work,' Jaren advised, lowering his voice. 'She had her eye on your shop, before you swept in and snapped it up, and she's paranoid you're going to take some of her trade away. The truth is that Castle Court has room for both businesses – they're really quite different.'

Cat glanced across at the dark-haired woman, who was stabbing at her phone screen with a ferocity that suggested a lot of bottled-up anger. 'I'm sorry that she was disappointed over the shop but she's got nothing to worry about product-wise. The cakes Sadie and I bought today were top class – Smart Cookies isn't in competition with Patisserie Cherie.'

Elin let out a sigh. 'She was the same when I opened my shop – accused me of muscling in on her customers. But she'll warm to you eventually.' Her lip twisted in wry amusement. 'It's only taken five years for her to change from outright hostility to a nod of greeting each morning.'

A shadow fell across the table. Cat looked up to see Seb gazing down at her. 'Hi, I'm Seb de Jager. Nice to meet you.'

'Cat Garcia,' she replied. 'Good to meet you too – I've heard a lot about you.'

Seb raised a quizzical eyebrow and glanced at Jaren. 'From this guy? Don't listen to a word he says. He's just jealous because the beautiful women all prefer to hang out with me.'

He winked at Elin, who blushed and looked away, making Cat wonder whether they had some kind of history together. It wouldn't surprise her; food and romance were inextricably linked and it was an industry where passions often ran high, especially in a microcosm like Castle Court.

Jaren shook his head in pity. 'When will you learn that they only talk to you because they feel sorry for you, Seb?'

The other man grinned and turned his attention back to Cat. 'Seen anything you like?'

He meant the cocktail list, Cat realised, but she had no doubt there was a double-edged meaning to his words. 'Maybe,' she said lightly. 'I haven't had time to have a good look yet.'

His green eyes fixed on her. 'Take your time. I'm in no hurry.'

Cat had no idea how long they would have stared at each other if the door hadn't opened. Seb frowned and looked up. 'We're closed.'

A bearded man in a beanie hat and a duffle coat stuck his head into the room. 'Even to me?'

Seb grinned. 'Adam! I'm always open for you.'

He went over to pull the newcomer into a bear hug.

'Adam Tucker,' Elin explained, noticing Cat's curious expression. 'He supplies half the businesses in Castle Court with honey.'

'Oh,' Cat said, watching the man take his coat off and hang it on the stand behind the door. 'Does he work for a wholesaler?'

Jaren shook his head. 'He's a beekeeper. Although the bees are dormant at this time of year so he sidelines as a gardener.'

Cat frowned. 'Isn't that seasonal too?'

'Don't ask me,' Jaren said, shrugging. 'All I know is that if I need asparagus in December, Adam is the person I go to.'

Cat studied him with renewed interest. It wasn't likely she would need asparagus for Smart Cookies but honey was a different matter; she added it to her biscuit dough and much preferred to use locally sourced produce where she could. 'He sounds like a good man to know.'

Almost as though he'd heard her, Seb made his way back towards Cat, with Adam in tow. 'Sorry, that was unforgivably rude of me,' he said. 'Let me fix you a drink on the house to make up for it.'

Cat shook her head. 'There's no need.' She picked up the cocktail menu and studied the drinks listed there. 'I think I'm in the mood for something unfussy – can you manage a simple Bombay Sapphire and tonic or is that too pedestrian for you?'

Seb's expression didn't even twitch at the barb. 'Single?'

Cat tutted in mock-derision. 'Double.'

He raised an eyebrow. 'That wasn't what I was asking.'

Smooth, Cat thought with a secret grin of delight. His gaze lingered on her for a long second, then he half-turned to beckon the beekeeper forwards. 'Can I introduce you to Adam Tucker? Adam, this is Cat Garcia – she's opening the new shop on the ground floor.'

'Hi,' Cat said, as Adam smiled in greeting. 'You need to meet my business partner, Sadie.'

As Seb went to whisk up the drinks, Cat tapped Sadie on the shoulder. 'There's someone I want to introduce you to.'

Excusing herself to Andrew and Earl, Sadie swivelled around and gazed up enquiringly. Her eyes widened as they met Adam's. 'Oh! It's you.'

'Hello again,' he said, smiling.

Cat glanced back and forth between the two of them, puzzled. 'You know each other already?'

Sadie nodded. 'We – uh – bumped into each other a few days ago.'

'Literally,' Adam confirmed. 'I dropped my sprouts.'

'And I helped him pick them up,' Sadie added. 'How did they taste?'

'Fine,' Adam said. 'Like I said, they're sturdy. I fried them up with some butter and pancetta.'

Cat followed the exchange with interest, noting the sparkle in Sadie's eyes when she looked at Adam and the answering gleam in his. She sat back, a plan beginning to form in her mind. 'Adam is a beekeeper and supplies a lot of the Castle Court businesses with honey,' she told Sadie, her tone as guileless as she could make it. 'Which is lucky, because we need a good supply of honey for our biscuits. So as long as Adam doesn't mind another customer, it looks as though we might be seeing quite a bit more of him in the immediate future.'

To Cat's immense satisfaction, Adam didn't take his eyes off Sadie when he replied. 'No, I don't mind that at all.'

Chapter Five

'Ow!'

Cat opened one eye and instantly closed it again as a burst of pain shot through her skull. 'Ow, ow, ow.'

'I told you not to have that last tequila shot,' a voice said from the side of the bed.

Cat squinted up, ignoring the pain, and saw Sadie standing there with a cup of tea. 'What time is it?' she croaked, shading her eyes.

'Nine-thirty,' Sadie replied. 'I'm heading home soon to get on with the next batch of biscuits. Is there anything you need before I go?'

'Apart from a new head?' Cat groaned. 'What time did we leave Seb's last night?'

Sadie shook her head. 'Three-thirty. And I'm not surprised you don't remember – I don't think I've ever seen you drink so much.'

For a moment, Cat thought her friend was cross but her

lips were twisted into a reluctant smile. 'It's Seb's fault,' she said in a plaintive tone. 'He kept making all these amazing-looking cocktails – it would have been rude not to drink them.'

'And yet somehow I managed to resist without mortally offending him,' Sadie said. 'Although I will say that the ice is well and truly broken with our Castle Court neighbours. It's hard to stand on ceremony once you've snogged half of them.'

Cat sat up in bed. 'I did not.'

Sadie grinned. 'No, you didn't. But for what it's worth, I don't think Seb would have minded a bit of snogging action. The two of you seemed to be getting on awfully well.'

Gingerly, Cat lowered herself back onto her pillow. She remembered talking to Seb on several occasions, and laughing a lot. They'd definitely flirted. But she hadn't overstepped the mark ... had she? 'What about you and Adam?' she countered. 'You couldn't take your eyes off each other.'

Sadie's cheeks turned pink. 'I like him, he's nice. But we were both just being friendly, nothing more. Don't try to change the subject.'

'I'm too hungover for this,' Cat grumbled, closing her eyes. 'Can't you make yourself useful and cook me some breakfast?'

'Don't you remember?' Sadie said, in a voice that contained far too much gleeful satisfaction for Cat's liking.

'You've got a brunch date with Seb. That's why I woke you up – I'm sure you don't want to be late.'

Cat's eyes flew open as a hazy memory of arranging to meet Seb surfaced. 'Shit, you're right. We're going to check out that new chicken and waffles place on Watergate Street.' She rubbed a hand across her face. 'Why didn't you wake me earlier?'

'There's Berocca and ibuprofen on your bedside table and you need to be outside Water Wings in just less than an hour,' Sadie said as she headed to the bedroom door. 'I expect a full report later – don't do anything I wouldn't do!'

Seb was waiting outside the restaurant as Cat puffed up five minutes late, her breath making steamy clouds in the chilly morning air.

'I thought you were going to stand me up,' Seb said, smiling at her from behind a pair of sunglasses.

'Sorry,' she said, squinting up at him in the wintry sunlight. 'It took longer than I thought to feel human again. I am never letting you make me cocktails again.'

He grinned. 'You're not the first person to have said that, actually. Come on, what you need is medicinal protein and carbohydrates.'

It was busy for a Sunday morning, although Cat noticed a higher than usual proportion of sunglasses were on display, suggesting she wasn't the only person nursing a hangover. Seb looked as fresh as a daisy, which irritated Cat even more; he clearly hadn't been drinking his own creations.

'So,' he said, once they were seated at a table in one corner. 'What do you think of the Castle Court crew?'

Cat revisited her patchy memories of the night before. Andrew and Earl had turned out to be every bit as hilarious as she'd anticipated. Elin had relaxed once she'd observed Cat and Seb flirting, which suggested Cat's suspicions about her interest in Jaren were right. Whether Jaren himself had noticed was another thing entirely ... She hadn't spoken to Greg, the bistro owner, much, especially after he had tried to pump her for information about her time at La Perle, but he'd spent most of his time whispering with Cherie; Cat caught them firing unfriendly glances her way from time to time. And Seb – well, he'd turned out to be an extremely attentive host. Cat had enjoyed flirting with him, which was probably why she found herself sitting opposite him now. Overall, she'd found her neighbours at Castle Court to be a fun, friendly bunch. With one or two notable exceptions.

'Honestly?' she said. 'I really like them. Jaren said the Court is a bit like a family and I can really see that. So I suppose it's inevitable that there's one person I didn't really get along with.'

'Cherie,' Seb guessed.

'Cherie,' Cat repeated. 'Elin said she took a while to warm to her too so I'm trying not to take it personally but there were times last night when I could feel her eyes boring into me. I understand that she's protective of her business but really, Smart Cookies is no threat.'

Seb tilted his head. 'Give her time. Some people cope better with change than others and I don't think her relationship with Greg is necessarily what she needs. They wind each other up.'

'That makes sense,' Cat said, thinking back to the way Greg and Cherie had huddled together. 'Even so—'

'Even so, Cherie isn't a bad person,' Seb said. 'Greg is probably worse, to be honest.'

Cat rubbed her forehead as she considered his words. 'Are you sure? Because I'm starting to wonder whether these pains in my head are because Cherie made a voodoo doll of me and is sitting at home sticking pins into the skull.'

He laughed. 'I'm afraid the only spirits to blame for your hangover are vodka and gin.' Passing her a menu, he gave her a sympathetic smile. 'But luckily, I know the perfect cure.'

Their food arrived faster than Cat expected, given the bustling tables. Seb had been right, the twin hit of fried chicken and sweet syrupy waffles helped her almost immediately. She allowed him to do most of the talking, listening as he described growing up in Port Elizabeth and explained how he'd ended up living in one of the garret apartments that lined the top floor of Castle Court. 'Whirlwind romance with a model from Chester,' he confided with a grimace. 'I gave up everything to relocate. Then she met a Premier League footballer and I was unceremoniously dumped. But the city had me under its spell by then so I stayed.'

By the time he'd finished talking, she knew he was thirty-seven, had three sisters and one ex-wife, had spent several years working the bar scene in New York, learning from master mixologists there, and that he hated celery to the point that he'd reinvented the Bloody Mary to avoid 'any taint of the evil stuff'. On the surface, he was witty and charismatic but Cat was certain there was a lot more to him than he was letting her see – she sensed he used his good looks and charm as a shield to prevent anyone from getting too close.

'Now it's your turn,' he said, once Cat had mopped up the last remnants of maple syrup from her plate. 'Tell me all about you.'

'There's not much to tell,' Cat said, shrugging. 'Went to catering college, took a variety of jobs in London to get onto the career ladder, travelled a bit to expand my knowledge of food and ended up at La Perle. Now I'm here.'

Seb stared at her. 'That's it? No disastrous career moves, no sweeping romances that broke your heart but taught you more than you dreamed possible in the process? No moments of insane happiness followed by the depths of despair?'

Cat took a long sip of water and avoided his incredulous gaze. 'I didn't say that,' she said quietly.

He grew still. 'You don't want to talk about it.'

'Not really,' she said and looked up. 'For a long time, I was married to my work. Does that make me boring?'

He gave her a rueful smile. 'No. It's probably easier than being married to a person. Cheaper when you need to get divorced, too.'

He was being flippant on purpose, she realised, trying to make her laugh. 'Thank you.'

He shrugged and picked up the menu. 'Don't mention it. Now, do you think your hangover can cope with sharing a dessert or shall we save that for next time?'

'Next time?' Cat repeated, smiling at his cockiness. 'There's going to be a next time?'

Seb's gaze was warm when it met hers. 'Oh, I think there are going to be lots of next times. Don't you?'

Cat felt the flicker of attraction she'd noticed the night before turn into a surge. 'I hope so.'

Monday morning dawned grey and foggy. Sadie dropped Lissy off to school and drove into Chester, painfully aware of the slower than usual traffic. Cat had been at the shop for hours, baking fresh batches of biscuits so that they would be cool enough for Sadie to ice when she arrived. She knew it wouldn't really matter to Cat that the traffic was crawling along today, but it would be a different story once the shop was open; Cat couldn't be downstairs baking and upstairs serving customers at the same time. Sadie needed to find a way of making sure she reached the shop by nine-thirty each day. The trouble was that Lissy's school day didn't start until eight-fifty and it only took one accident on Sadie's route into the city to cause major problems. She was starting to wonder whether they were going to need some help to run the shop, especially in the run-up to Christmas.

She arrived at the shop just after ten o'clock, red-faced

and flustered from hurrying through the slippery streets. It didn't matter how many times Cat reassured her that there was no harm done, Sadie felt uncomfortable and out of sorts for the rest of the morning. She couldn't settle to pipe icing onto the biscuits, something that she'd come to find soothing now that she was more practised at it, and began to arrange the shelves instead.

Cat appeared at her elbow just after midday. 'Come on,' she said, handing Sadie her coat and bag. 'I'm taking you out for pancakes.'

Let's Go Dutch was starting to fill up with lunchtime trade. Jaren greeted them both warmly and found them a table in the window so they could observe the behaviour of customers around the Court.

'He's so thoughtful,' Sadie said, watching Jaren stop by another table and check everything was to the diners' satisfaction. 'Don't you think?'

Cat's eyes were fixed on Seb's, three floors up. 'Hmmm?'

'Jaren is so thoughtful,' Sadie repeated, narrowing her eyes at her friend. 'He and Andrew are planning to elope together on the big yellow school bus.'

'Good,' Cat replied absently. 'That sounds like a great idea.'

Sadie folded her arms. 'Is the only reason you brought me here so that you could spy on Seb?'

'What?' Cat stared at her in guilty surprise. 'No, of course not. I just thought you could do with a change of scene, that's all. And I'm quite curious about Jaren's menu so coming here seemed like a good idea, but we can go somewhere else if you'd rather.'

'Of course we can't,' Sadie said. 'What would Jaren think?'

'What would I think of what?' Jaren said, appearing at their table with a small notepad in his hand.

'Nutella-flavoured pancakes,' Cat said without missing a beat. 'They're very popular in France but I'm not sure so I wondered how you felt about them.'

Sadie wanted the ground to swallow them up. He must know Cat was lying, surely? But he shook his head, as though giving the question serious thought. 'If you asked me outside of these walls,' he said in a hushed tone of voice, 'I would tell you that Nutella and pancakes have no business even being in the same sentence. But since they are one of our most popular menu items, my official response is that they are a match made in heaven.'

Sadie laughed. 'What do you recommend for someone who only eats pancakes once a year, with lemon and syrup?'

He studied her thoughtfully. 'For you, I recommend the creamed spinach and ricotta pancake, with a side order of *bitterballen*. They're a kind of meatball, with a mustardy sauce.' He turned his gaze to Cat. 'And for you, perhaps the smoked salmon pancake with sliced green beans and a lemon and dill dressing, with cheesy *kaasballen* as a side?'

Sadie gave Cat an enquiring look. 'Sounds delicious,' Cat said, nodding.

Jaren made a note of their order and hurried away to the

kitchen. 'He's probably going to warn him that he's got a Michelin-starred chef to impress,' Sadie joked, but she knew it was probably closer to the truth than either of them wanted to admit. All of Castle Court's food business owners had seemed a little in awe of Cat once they'd discovered where she'd worked before coming back to Chester; all except Cherie and Greg, who continued to remain aloof. And Cat would probably maintain that a bit of awe and respect was no bad thing in the food industry but Sadie wasn't so sure.

'Cat, do you think we've bitten off more than we can chew by diving straight into opening a shop?' she said suddenly. 'Do you think perhaps we should have done a business course first, learned how to do things properly?'

Cat frowned. 'What do you mean, properly? What have we done so far that isn't proper?'

'It just feels a bit sudden, that's all,' Sadie said, beginning to wish she'd kept quiet. 'A bit rushed.'

'It's taken a while to get to this stage, Sadie,' Cat replied, still frowning. 'And things are starting to come together – I'm not sure what you think we ought to be doing differently.'

Sadie hesitated. Cat wasn't wrong; the various strands of Smart Cookies did seem to be dovetailing. But worry still nagged at her. 'Maybe we should have gone with an online business first,' she said, gnawing at her lip. 'Started small and worked up.'

'What is this really about?' Cat demanded, staring at Sadie. 'Come on, out with it.'

Heart thudding, Sadie explained her concerns about

getting into the shop each morning. 'What if Lissy is ill and I can't come in at all?' she said. 'How will you cope on your own?'

'We'll hire some staff,' Cat said, gazing at Sadie as though she'd grown two heads. 'I was going to wait until the shop was open but we can start the process now if it makes you feel any better. Because if there's one thing I've learned over the past few years, it's that you can't do it all yourself.'

Sadie sagged in relief; she'd expected Cat to hate the idea but it turned out they were thinking the same thing all along. 'Great,' she said weakly, just as Jaren appeared with their food.

'Here you are the finest Dutch pancakes this side of the North Sea,' he said, laying plates of delicious-smelling food before them.

Cat smiled at him. 'Do you serve all your customers personally?'

Jaren grinned back at her. 'No. Only the VIPs.' He waved a hand at the steaming plates. 'Enjoy.'

Sadie sighed as he walked off. 'I've always admired a man who can cook.'

Cat picked up her knife and fork. 'Believe me, the appeal wears off after a while. But Elin clearly agrees with you. I think she's got a bit of a thing for Jaren.'

Sadie took a mouthful of food, savouring the delicate flavours for a moment. 'You're right,' she said, once she'd swallowed. 'But I'm not sure he has a thing for her. He told me on Saturday night that he was definitely single.'

She paused. 'I also got the impression Seb and Elin had got together at some point in the past.'

'Me too,' Cat said. 'But Seb practically admitted he's been a bit of a ladies' man since his divorce came through.'

'Just be careful,' Sadie advised. 'The last thing you want is to end up just another one of his conquests.'

Cat gave her a look that suggested she wouldn't mind that at all but she said nothing. They ate in silence for a few minutes. Sadie couldn't believe how good her pancake tasted; maybe she'd try and introduce Lissy to the idea of savoury fillings too. She glanced around; everywhere she looked, people were enjoying their food. Jaren had a very successful business on his hands.

She spotted him in the corner, watching their table like a nervous parent on the first day of school. 'Don't look up, but Jaren is staring at you.'

Cat sighed. 'I knew I shouldn't have told him about working at La Perle. Now he thinks I'm judging him when all I want is a decent lunch.'

Sadie glanced over again and shook her head. There was a look on Jaren's face that she thought she recognised. She opened her mouth to explain but just at that moment, Cat glanced out of the window at Seb's. Sadie closed her mouth. Whatever Jaren did or didn't feel for Cat, now wasn't the time to mention it. Not when Cat was so clearly interested in someone else, Sadie decided.

She concentrated on finishing her pancake, swapping a few of her meatballs for some of the cheesy mozzarella balls, and pushed her reservations about Cat and Seb to the back of her mind. Because the truth was, when it came down to it, her best friend's love life was really none of her business.

Chapter Six

In what felt to Cat like the blink of an eye, it was the weekend again. With only two weeks left until Smart Cookies opened, her days seemed to be filled with an endless blur of baking, biscuits and paperwork. The stock was building up, thanks to Sadie's dedication, and the shop was actually starting to look the way it should, but Cat still found herself waking up in a cold sweat during the early hours of the morning, worrying about all the things she had forgotten.

Sadie was busy looking after Lissy and had no plans to come into the city. Cat was meant to have the weekend off too but she'd been restless at home on Saturday, unable to concentrate. She'd stopped by Castle Court just before lunchtime, intending to spend an hour or so finalising their order for packaging to keep the biscuits safe when they were sent out in the mail. Six hours later, she was still there. On the plus side, she now had an extra four batches of treacle-spiced biscuits ready for Sadie to ice on Monday morning and an advert for temporary staff to stick up in the window.

Scrunching her stiff shoulders, she climbed the stairs and gazed around the shop. Everywhere she looked, she saw signs of Sadie's artistic talent; the shelves were packed with samples of the biscuit collections they'd designed together and that Sadie's skill with icing had brought to life. A Nativity scene lay inside a Perspex box, ready to be assembled, complete with donkeys, shepherds and a tiny crib. And the Christmas tree stood by the door, waiting to be hung with shimmering edible baubles. It was going to be amazing once it was all in place, Cat thought, as she put the advert in the window and stared out at the shoppers and diners wandering through the freezing winter gloom. Everything was under control. So why couldn't she relax?

It was a throwback to her final few months in Paris, when she told herself over and over again that everything was fine when it wasn't. Not by a long way. And now she couldn't trust herself. Cat almost laughed; it would have been funny if it wasn't so tragic. She thought about going home but the idea of a long evening in front of the television made her feel even worse. It was too early to go for something to eat. But it wasn't too early for a drink.

She found herself in Seb's almost without being aware of deciding to go there. He blinked when she walked in, wincing at the noise from the early evening crowd, and then smiled. 'Hey. You're a sight for sore eyes.'

She slipped into an empty seat in front of the bar. 'What do you recommend, Mr Mixologist?'

Seb raised an eyebrow. 'For a pre-dinner drink?'

Cat shook her head. 'For when you want to stop thinking.'

'Right,' Seb said and reached for a bottle. 'How do you feel about Jack Daniel's?'

'I think he sounds like someone I could make friends with really fast,' Cat said honestly.

Nodding, Seb set to work. 'Bad day?' he asked, pouring a generous measure of whiskey into the cocktail shaker.

Cat pulled a face. 'Do you ever think about how many plates you keep spinning and wonder what would happen if you suddenly just stopped?'

'Sometimes,' Seb said. He picked up a bottle of sugar syrup and added a measure, then reached for the Angostura bitters and dropped three drops into the shaker, followed by some ice. 'Do you want to stop spinning?'

'No, although I did do that once,' Cat said. 'All the plates came crashing down and almost took me with them. But that's not my problem today.'

He glanced up at her. 'No?'

She sighed. 'My problem today is that I think I've forgotten where my plates are. And that's just as bad as walking away from them – they come crashing down just as hard whether you meant them to or not.'

Seb smiled and gave the cocktail shaker several hard shakes. 'It sounds like you need to chill out. I bet your plates are totally under control,' he said, pouring the mixture into a glass.

'Which is what brings me here, asking for a cocktail that will help me to stop thinking,' Cat replied.

He scraped his knife across the surface of an orange, releasing a length of peel and a heady burst of citrus that made Cat's mouth water, and then picked up a lighter and ran the flame along the length of the peel. It burst into bright light for a moment, then Seb dropped the peel into the glass and pushed it towards Cat. 'Here. Try this.'

Cat held the drink up to the light, admiring the way the tawny liquid was turned amber by the orange peel garnish. Then she put the glass to her lips and downed the contents in one.

Seb studied her for a moment, then puffed out his cheeks and grinned. 'Same again?'

Elin arrived just after seven o'clock and insisted that Cat join her for something to eat. Cat wasn't sure whether Seb had summoned the chocolatier or whether, like Cat, she'd merely wanted a drink, but it didn't really matter. By mutual agreement, they ate away from Castle Court.

'So, tell me about you and Jaren,' Cat said, once steaming baskets of dim sum covered the table in front of them.

Elin paused before removing a bamboo lid and helping herself to a dumpling. 'There isn't anything to tell. We're friends, that's all.' She fixed Cat with a level stare. 'Tell me about you and Seb.'

Cat smiled. 'The same as you and Jaren. Nothing to tell.'

'Nothing to tell yet,' Elin corrected her. 'I recognise the look in Seb's eyes and believe me, if he gets his way you'll be more than just friends.'

'Oh?' Cat said, taking a sip of her jasmine tea. 'That sounds like the voice of experience.'

The blonde woman shrugged. 'It was a long time ago – I imagine there have been plenty of others after me. We went on a couple of dates, spent the night together and quickly realised we were better off as friends.'

Cat nodded; it was pretty much exactly as she'd suspected. 'And you think that's what he wants from me too.'

'It fits his pattern,' Elin said, her tone cautious. 'But I could be wrong. He might want much more for all I know. I'm an expert in chocolate, not Seb de Jager.'

'Luckily for Seb, I am very much in the market for a distraction,' Cat told the other woman.

Elin smiled and raised her bottle of beer to tap against Cat's. 'Then it sounds like you might both get what you want. Cheers!'

The bar was much busier when they returned. Powder-fine snow had begun to drift down from the blackened sky and it seemed that plenty of Saturday night revellers had decided to take refuge from the wintry chill in Seb's. Cat hovered beside Elin in the doorway, surveying the crowd and wondering whether she should head for home, but Seb spotted them and pointed at a table in the corner marked 'Reserved', close enough to the bar for him to be able to chat when he had a spare few minutes. Remembering her hangover of the week before, Cat switched to water after the first cocktail; however the rest of the night panned out, she wanted to remember it.

Elin's natural reserve loosened after a few more drinks and Cat was surprised to discover she had a wickedly sharp sense of humour hidden beneath her Scandinavian coolness. She made Cat laugh with her descriptions of Greg's pomposity and Cherie's mean-spirited miserliness. 'Honestly, if ever two crotchety souls deserved each other, it's them.'

Cat conjured up an image of Cherie's haughty demean-our and Greg's balding, rotund head. 'I must admit, I wouldn't have put them together. How long have they been a couple?'

'About a year,' Elin said. She gave Cat a shrewd smile. 'And I know what you mean – they are an odd couple. But Castle Court has a way of bringing people together.'

By the time Seb was ushering out the last reluctant leavers, Cat had developed a genuine warmth for Elin and felt better than she had for days.

'Another drink?' Seb offered, once he had turned the Open sign to Closed and locked the door.

'Not for me,' Elin said, getting to her feet. 'Two's com-pany, after all, and my bed is calling me.'

Cat smiled as the other woman winked at her and made her way to the door, pausing only to whisper something to Seb. 'Goodnight, Cat,' she called as she left. 'Have fun.'

Seb shut the door after her and turned to gaze at Cat. 'And then there were two.'

Cat watched Elin make her way along the covered pas-sageway. 'Has the snow settled?'

He ducked his head to peer out of the window. 'It's turned to sleet. We're in no danger of being snowed in tonight.'

Cat couldn't decide whether he sounded relieved or

disappointed. 'Shouldn't we call Elin a cab?' she said, as the other woman turned right and vanished into the stairwell. 'It's after eleven.'

He shook his head. 'Elin's another garret rat – she lives two doors down from me, almost directly over our heads. I think she'll be safe enough.'

'Right,' Cat said, feeling a sudden quiver of nervousness. Now that she was alone with Seb, she wasn't sure exactly what she wanted to happen next. 'Did you mention another drink?'

'I did,' Seb replied. 'Although I need to know how fast you're going to drink it. Because if you're going to down it in one like the last two I made you, I'll just pour a shot straight from the bottle.'

Cat laughed. 'That sounds perfect.'

He went behind the bar and picked up two glasses and the bottle of Jack Daniel's, then came and sat beside her. 'So,' he said, pouring a measure of whiskey into each glass. 'How are those plates doing?'

'Much better,' she said, taking a sip of the drink he handed her. 'I think they're all under control right now, even the ones I've forgotten about.'

Seb downed the shot and poured himself another. 'I'm very glad to hear that. I wouldn't want them to come crashing down in here – I have much more interesting things in mind for us to do than clearing up broken crockery.'

'Oh?' Cat said, gazing at him. 'Like what exactly?'

He studied her for a moment, as though gauging her

mood, then leaned towards her. 'Like this,' he whispered, brushing her lips with his.

She felt her mouth burn where he'd touched her and she wasn't uncertain any more; she wanted Seb. Reaching one hand behind his head, she pulled him towards her and closed her eyes, giving herself up to the moment.

When the kiss ended, they were both out of breath. Seb's sea-green eyes were cloudy. 'Want to get out of here?' he asked, and Cat nodded.

Pausing only to switch off the lights, Seb led Cat through the back of the narrow kitchen behind the bar and up a short staircase to the attic rooms above Castle Court. Another time, Cat might have spent a few minutes gazing around the low-beamed apartment, appreciating its quirky charm, but Seb was demanding all her attention. Her fingers wrapped themselves in his hair as they kissed and tumbled their way into the bed-room. And then she was fumbling with shirt buttons, jeans, punctuating each item of clothing with small, urgent kisses.

'Okay?' Seb asked, in between caresses.

Cat gazed up at him, aware that he was giving her the chance to change her mind, to back out before the ground underneath them shifted for good. For half a second, she was tempted. Then she realised it had been months – more than a year – since she'd felt this alive. She nodded and reached out to tenderly touch his cheek. 'Okay.'

Sadie knew something was different the moment she saw Cat on Monday morning. She was humming, for a start, bent over the work surface in the basement kitchen of the shop, a biscuit cutter in her hand.

'Morning,' Cat said, mouth curving into a soft smile. 'Good weekend?'

Sadie tried hard not to frown. 'Not as good as yours, from the look on your face. Is there something I should know, or are you just happy in your work?'

Cat cleared her throat. 'Uh, maybe a bit of both?'

'Tell me everything,' Sadie demanded. 'No, wait – I need coffee first. Then I want to hear all the details.'

Typically, it took her several impatient minutes to find the coffee pods, during which time Sadie ran through the possible options. There had to be a man involved – the softness of Cat's smile spoke of intimacy and connection, the kind of things you didn't get from even the most perfectly baked biscuit – the question was, which one: Jaren or Seb? There was an outside chance that it could be a stranger, Sadie mused, as she waited for the coffee machine to stop hissing, but one-night stands weren't really Cat's style. Sadie was willing to concede there was a first time for everything, however.

Placing a cup in front of an empty stool, she sat down at the table block and cradled her own drink. 'So. Tell me.'

'I was in a really weird mood on Saturday,' Cat began, not quite meeting Sadie's eyes. 'Everything felt too much, like something was going to go catastrophically wrong and it would be all my fault.'

Sadie shifted on her seat. It was understandable that Cat would feel that way, given the way her career had gone in

Paris, but this was the first time she had ever openly acknow-ledged it. 'Okay.'

'I needed to be somewhere that would take my mind off all the thoughts buzzing around it, so I went to Seb's.'

Sadie did her best to keep her face neutral, although her heart sank at the mention of Seb's name. She really had been hoping for Jaren.

'It was busy and Elin turned up, so we went for a meal. And then we went back to the bar.' Cat fixed Sadie with a crooked half-smile. 'You'll be amazed to know that I was Captain Sensible and switched to drinking water.'

'I am amazed,' Sadie said, unable to prevent a smile from creeping across her face. 'Maybe even impressed.'

Cat grinned. 'I think you can probably guess what happened next. Elin left, the bar closed and it was just me and Seb.'

'And?' Sadie asked, even though she knew exactly what was coming.

'And we didn't get much sleep, had a late lunch at a pub just outside the city walls and I slept for eleven and a half hours last night. At home, in my own bed. Alone.'

Sadie swallowed a sigh. She wanted to warn Cat, because Seb might be fun but he didn't seem to her to be boyfriend material; his track record suggested he was strictly short-term. But Cat looked so content, so happy, that Sadie didn't have the heart to burst her bubble. Besides, who was she to lecture anyone about relationships? Her own marriage had ended in infidelity and betrayal.

'How do you feel today?' she asked Cat, even though her own eyes told her everything she needed to know.

'Better,' Cat said simply. 'Like everything isn't falling apart and we can actually do this.'

Sadie tipped her head. 'And you got all of that from one night with Seb? He must be good.'

Cat laughed. 'He is. But I think it was a combination of things – getting a fresh perspective on life was one. Acting on an uncomplicated mutual attraction was another. But—' She held up a hand as Sadie opened her mouth to interject. 'I'm not stupid. I know Seb isn't going to be a long-term solution. But as temporary fixes go, he's pretty good.'

There were a million warnings Sadie wanted to give. She swallowed them all. 'So you're happy?'

'I'm happy,' Cat replied, her tone warm and gentle.

'Then that's all I care about,' Sadie said, getting up to give her friend a hug.

Chapter Seven

Sadie was surprised and delighted to see Adam tapping at the door of Smart Cookies on Wednesday morning, although she did her best to hide both. She hurried over to let him in.

'Hi,' she said, hoping she didn't sound as breathless as she felt. 'What brings you here?'

He held up a paper bag. It chinked. 'Honey,' he explained. 'Cat said she wanted to buy some for your biscuits. So here it is.'

Sadie took the bag and peered inside at the jars of crystal-clear amber. 'Great – thanks so much for dropping it in. How much do we owe you?'

Adam grimaced. 'Forty-five pounds, please. I know it sounds like a lot but it's premium, organic honey and a little goes a long way. It costs a lot more in the shops, believe me.'

'I'm sure it does,' Sadie said, charmed by his very British embarrassment at wanting to be paid for providing something of value. 'My bag is in the kitchen – hang on.'

She was halfway to the stairs when a daring thought

occurred to her. She knew very little about Adam, other than that he lived on a farm where he grew vegetables and kept bees, and she was curious. He hadn't mentioned a girlfriend, and Cat said Seb seemed to think he was single, but Sadie couldn't be sure without asking him. Maybe it was time to take a leaf out of Cat's book and go after what she wanted . . .

Taking a deep breath, she stopped and turned around. 'Actually, the kettle's not long boiled. Have you got time for a cup of tea?'

'Of course. I'd love one,' he said, smiling. 'Although it smells so good in here that you might never get rid of me.'

Sadie laughed. 'I know what you mean. Come on, I'll give you the grand tour.'

In the end, they had three cups of tea and talked almost non-stop. Adam explained how he'd fallen in love with bee-keeping after inheriting his first hive from the previous tenant of the cottage he rented on the edge of Waverton village.

'You're serious?' Sadie had said, staring at him in incredulous disbelief. 'You live at Waverton farm? That's less than a mile from my house!'

He'd let out a bark of laughter. 'You're kidding me. Where do you live – in Waverton?'

'No, in Rowton. On Rowton Lane, in fact. We're practically neighbours.'

From there, Sadie had discovered he was thirty-four and definitely single. The last time they'd talked she hadn't revealed much about her home life, other than to mention that she had a young daughter, but now she saw no reason to be coy; she told Adam honestly about Daniel's affair and the new life she was building with Lissy.

'And now you're starting a business with Cat,' he said, throwing her an admiring glance. 'It sounds as though you're going from strength to strength.'

'I hope so,' Sadie replied. 'Although opening Smart Cookies isn't the least stressful thing I've ever done. I had no idea how much time it would take to get everything in place – we're having to take on staff already and we're not even open yet.'

'I saw,' Adam said, and hesitated. 'Actually, I was going to ask you about that.'

'Oh?' Sadie said, noticing the tips of his ears had turned pink as he blushed.

'Gardening is mostly seasonal work and winter is a quiet time of year for growing – I've pretty much only got sprouts and cabbages on the go at the moment. Beekeeping is the same – the hives need all the honey reserves they have to get them through the colder months.' He paused and his cheeks grew even rosier. 'So I'm sort of between jobs right now and I wondered whether you might . . .'

'Whether we might take you on?' Sadie finished as he trailed off. She bit her lip. 'I don't know – I think we were looking for someone with actual retail experience.'

Adam nodded. 'I understand.'

Sadie eyed him thoughtfully, picturing him behind the counter upstairs. He'd certainly be popular with the hordes of female shoppers who were bound to be scouring Chester's streets in search of the perfect Christmas gifts for their loved ones. And it would give Sadie an opportunity to get to know him better . . .

She made up her mind. 'You know, I've often thought that enthusiasm is sometimes as good as experience. I'll need to speak to Cat first but, just hypothetically, when might you be able to start?'

Adam smiled, bathing Sadie in a warm glow. 'Does tomorrow sound too keen?'

Cat spent most of Wednesday evening propping up the bar at Seb's, although she stuck to virgin cocktails. At the end of the night, he'd made them both a nightcap and they'd moved to one of the leather sofas at the back of the bar.

'I hear you've given Adam a job,' Seb said, as Cat snuggled against him.

'Not me,' Cat said mildly. 'It was all Sadie's idea.'

'How do you feel about it?'

Cat shrugged. 'We'd already agreed we needed help so I don't mind, as long as he learns fast and pulls his weight.' She thought for a moment longer. 'And gives me discounted honey, of course.'

Seb laughed. 'Hey, don't overwork the supply – the rest of us need honey from those bees too. You won't be popular if he runs out.' He paused. 'And speaking of being popular, there's something you need to know. Greg and Cherie have been trying to stir things up amongst the other businesses around the Court.'

'In what way?' Cat asked, frowning.

He eased away from her and looked her in the eye. 'They're saying that you haven't been honest with us – that you're not who you say you are. Is that true?'

Cat almost dropped her drink. 'What?'

Now it was Seb's turn to shrug. 'It's all talk at the moment – no one is taking them seriously.'

She stared at him, outrage and confusion battling for supremacy. 'I don't understand what they even mean – of course I am who I say. Why would I lie?'

'I have no idea,' he said, spreading his hands helplessly. 'I'm only telling you what Andrew and Earl told me. Obviously, Greg and Cherie aren't stupid enough to approach me directly with any of their suspicions.'

Cat stiffened. 'Suspicions? What does that mean?'

Seb took a long sip of his drink and sighed. 'I think they're casting doubt on your professional qualifications. But I don't have any more detail than that. Maybe you should stop by the diner, speak to the guys there.'

Cat narrowed her eyes in fury. 'Or maybe I'll call into the bistro or the patisserie and get the dirt straight from the horses' mouths.' She shook her head in disbelief. 'I've barely even spoken to either of them. What exactly is their problem?'

'I don't know but whatever it is, it only seems to be with you,' Seb said. 'I haven't heard Sadie's name mentioned.'

'Great,' Cat said, slumping back against the sofa. 'Just great.'

Seb slipped an arm around her shoulders. 'Like I said, no

one is paying them much attention. I just thought you ought to know, that's all.'

She did her best to smile at him but she knew it was a poor effort. 'I know. Thank you.'

'Maybe you're right. Maybe you should confront them and find out what it's all about.'

'Believe me, I intend to,' Cat said, with a grim little smile. 'First thing tomorrow morning.'

Cherie didn't look surprised to see Cat when she walked into the patisserie shop early on Thursday morning. 'What do you want?' she asked, without so much as a ghost of a smile.

'I think you know,' Cat said, equally cold.

Cherie gave a single short nod and glanced at the young assistant behind the counter. 'Keris, go and grab yourself a coffee.'

The girl looked up, startled, but didn't argue. 'Yes, Cherie.'

The older woman waited until she had gone before glaring at Cat once more. 'Well? Say what you've come to say.'

'I heard you've been saying some pretty slanderous things about me,' Cat said, her tone blunt.

Cherie folded her arms. 'It's only slander if it isn't true.'

'Really?' Cat demanded. 'So you telling everyone that I'm not who I say I am – that's true, is it?'

Cherie said nothing.

'And you saying that I've lied about my qualifications – that's true as well?' Cat went on furiously. 'Because I can assure you, I haven't. I've got the framed certificates to prove it and I'm more than happy to let you see them.'

The other woman's gaze flickered with uncertainty. 'Don't be ridiculous,' she snapped.

'I'm not the one being ridiculous here,' Cat exploded. 'You are. What is your problem, Cherie? You wanted our premises, is that it?'

Cherie's eyes tightened. 'My problem is that people deserve to know the truth about the people who sell them food, especially when those people claim to be some hoity-toity chef from Paris. My problem is that you're not fit to call yourself a chef in the first place!'

Cat stared at her in complete bewilderment. 'I have no idea what you're talking about. Are you ill? Because I promise you, I was a hoity-toity chef in Paris, as you call it. Want to see my references?'

And now Cherie did allow herself a thin-lipped smile. 'No need. Greg's got all that in hand. Now, get out of my shop before I call the police and have you arrested for harassment.'

Sadie stared, open-mouthed, as Cat recounted the exchange.

'She said *what*?'

'I know,' Cat said, managing a shaky laugh as she leaned against the kitchen table. 'Another particular highlight was when she followed me along the Court, telling me she was going to ruin me. I honestly think she might be a bit unhinged.'

'That certainly explains the look she gave me yesterday morning,' Sadie said, thinking back to the ferocious scowl

Cherie had sent her way when she'd passed her in the Court and said good morning. 'How — it's just so weird.'

Cat ran a hand through her curls and glanced at the stairs that led to the shop, where Adam was painstakingly hanging biscuit baubles onto the Christmas tree. She lowered her voice. 'The thing is, even if Cherie thinks she knows something about what happened at La Perle, she's almost certainly got the wrong end of the stick. No one who knows why I left could be under any illusion that it was in some way my fault.'

Sadie shook her head. 'You had a breakdown brought on by overwork and stress,' she said gently. 'It definitely wasn't your fault.'

Cat hesitated. There *was* more to the story of why she'd left La Perle. But she wasn't sure she was ready to share that with Sadie — she wasn't sure she was ready to share it with anyone. 'I know,' she said, sighing. 'I suppose I'm going to have to confront Greg next.'

'Don't do it alone,' Sadie said, her eyes widening in alarm. 'Take Seb or Adam with you.'

'I don't need back-up,' Cat said dismissively. 'Greg's hardly likely to get violent.'

'Even so,' Sadie insisted. 'Promise me you won't confront him on your own. Apart from anything else, I need you in one piece to interview the woman who came in about the job.'

Cat sighed. 'Fine. I promise. I'll see if Seb can take a break and come with me this afternoon.'

*

They waited until the lunchtime rush was well and truly over to visit Greg's bistro. La Clé d'Argent still had plenty of customers lingering over chocolates and coffee after their meals. Greg was standing by a desk near the door, consulting a diary, when Cat and Seb walked in.

'Good afternoon, Greg,' Cat said as he looked up, her tone cool but designed to carry across the half-empty restaurant. 'I imagine you've been expecting me.'

His plump jowls quivered with disdain as he glared at her. 'Not out here, please,' he snapped. 'Or do you lack even the most basic business sense? But what am I saying – you were strictly a behind-the-scenes employee at La Perle, weren't you?'

It was such a flatly ironic statement that Cat wanted to laugh. Beside her, Seb bristled. 'Watch it, Greg. There's no need to be rude.'

'I think you'll find there's every need,' Greg responded. He snapped his fingers at them. 'Come this way.'

Cat exchanged a hard look with Seb as they followed the bistro owner to an office. Once inside, he turned to scowl at them. 'Well?'

'Have I done something to offend you?' Cat asked Greg, nonplussed. He hadn't acted this way the first time they'd met, at the after-hours drinks party.

Greg smirked. 'What makes you say that?'

'Stop playing games,' Seb said, not bothering to disguise the irritation in his voice. 'I've lost count of the number of people who've mentioned your little smear campaign about Cat. What's going on, Greg?'

'She's really sucked you in, hasn't she?' the other man sneered, tipping his head to one side. 'That's what she does – take it from one who knows.'

Cat let out an incredulous laugh. 'Knows what? I honestly have no idea what you're talking about. Until a few weeks ago we'd never even met.'

'Word gets around in this industry,' Greg replied. 'We don't need to have met for me to know all about you.'

'You're talking in riddles,' Cat said, exasperated. 'Cherie said she didn't believe I had the right to call myself a chef – that I'd somehow faked my qualifications. Is that what you're getting at?'

Greg gave her an oily smile. 'I've no doubt you've faked many things in recent years, although I am willing to concede you completed your course at catering school. But your claim that you were good enough to run the kitchens at La Perle – that is more . . . controversial, shall we say?'

'Spit it out,' Seb growled.

'He can't,' Cat said in disgust. 'Because it isn't true. I worked my arse off to make it to the top of the catering industry and you don't get to be head chef at a Michelin-starred restaurant unless you are the best. There isn't a single thing you can say that will change that.'

Greg's eyes gleamed. 'Interesting choice of phrase,' he said. 'I have no doubt you did "work your arse off". In fact, I know many people who would totally agree.'

Cat stared at him for a moment, then shrugged. 'I don't have time for this. Are you going to stop bad-mouthing me to the rest of the Castle Court shopkeepers?'

'No,' Greg said, his voice suddenly cracking like a whip. 'I don't like liars and I especially don't like those whose lies damage my friends. So you may rest assured, Cat Garcia, that I will not rest until I have exposed your deceit. Goodbye.'

White-lipped and furious, Cat turned on her heel and stalked out of the office. She waited until they were clear of the bistro and among the crowds in Castle Court before she spoke. 'What did he mean, damage his friends?' she asked Seb in bewilderment. 'Does he think I've done something to hurt Cherie?'

Seb raised his shoulders helplessly. 'Don't ask me. It's no secret she wanted your shop but that doesn't explain this level of vitriol. I've got no idea what's going on.'

'Me either,' Cat said. She pinched the bridge of her nose, feeling the start of a headache looming. 'None of this makes any sense.'

'I suppose we'll just have to hope they get bored of being so unpleasant,' Seb replied. 'And if they don't—'

He stopped and gave her a meaningful look.

'And if they don't, what?' Cat asked.

He pulled her close and dropped a kiss on her forehead. 'If they don't, they'll have me to deal with, and a few of the other business owners around here. Elin in particular is a force of nature when she's angry.'

Cat tried to picture the chocolate-shop owner in a rage about anything and failed. She sighed. 'Let's hope it doesn't come to that, eh?'

*

Thursday rolled into Friday. Cat and Sadie became wrapped up in making sure everything was ready for the shop to open on Saturday. Seb consulted the other shopkeepers and reported that Cherie and Greg appeared to have calmed down, and once Cat had filled Sadie in on the showdown with Greg, the two friends agreed to let the bizarre behaviour slip to the back of their minds. They had more important things to worry about.

'Left a bit,' Cat instructed, late on Friday afternoon, as Adam balanced on a stepladder to pin bunting on the ceiling. 'No, that's too far. Right a bit. There – perfect!'

Adam pressed the drawing pin into the plaster and climbed down to admire the effect. 'Nice,' he said, glancing around the fully stocked shop. 'It looks great, actually.'

Sadie smiled. 'It does, doesn't it? And I don't think we'd have managed it without your help, Adam.'

He blushed, causing Cat to glance at Sadie with undisguised amusement. 'Rubbish,' he said. 'All I've done is stack things on shelves.'

'Which has freed me up to finish icing the final batches of biscuits ready for the morning,' Sadie pointed out.

'And allowed me to start processing the website orders,' Cat added. 'So thank you from both of us. I think we might just about be ready.'

Sadie checked her watch, grateful that Daniel had been able to step in and collect Lissy from school. He'd been keen to help out for weeks, wearing down her instinctive refusal until she'd finally given in. But she didn't want to rely on him too much; she had no idea when, or if, the old Daniel would reappear and she didn't want Lissy to grow too used to spending time with her father if he was only going to let her down again.

'I should get going,' she told Cat reluctantly. 'Is there anything else you need me to do?'

'No,' Cat said. 'Go home and get an early night. You too, Adam. With a bit of luck, tomorrow is going to be busy.'

Sadie glanced across at Adam. 'How are you getting home?' she asked, aware that he usually relied on the infrequent bus in and out of the city. 'Do you need a lift?'

Instantly, he shook his head. 'No, don't worry. It's out of your way.'

She smiled. 'Yes, it will probably add a whole five minutes onto my journey. Don't be silly – let me drop you off at the farm.'

He hesitated, causing Cat to roll her eyes. 'Just accept, Adam, and make everyone happy.'

With one last glance at Sadie, he nodded. 'Okay. Thank you.'

Sadie felt a sudden squirm of pleasure at the thought of a whole thirty minutes alone in the car with him. 'Great,' she said, hoping her eagerness didn't show on her face. 'I'm parked at Cat's, underneath Victory Street. Grab your coat and let's go.'

When they were both ready, Sadie let Adam wander out into the fairy-lit glow of Castle Court and took a moment to stand beside Cat, gazing around at the shop.

'Well, we did it,' she said, with a little laugh of disbelief.

'We did,' Cat replied. 'And now the hard work really begins.'

Sadie puffed out a long breath. 'I suppose so. What time is the new assistant arriving tomorrow?'

'Eight-thirty,' Cat said. 'There should be just enough time to show her the ropes and then it will be showtime.'

'I hope people come,' Sadie said, gnawing at her lip.

'So do I,' Cat answered, giving her shoulders an affectionate squeeze. 'Otherwise we're going to be eating these biscuits for the rest of our lives.'

Chapter Eight

The car journey whizzed by faster than Sadie could have thought possible. Typically, there was no traffic to slow them down, no rain that meant she could rationalise driving below the speed limit; all too soon, they were pulling up outside Adam's cottage in Waverton.

'Thanks for the lift,' he said, as Sadie pulled on the handbrake. 'You've saved me around an hour and a half of standing at a freezing cold bus stop.'

She smiled. 'Don't mention it. And you should drop me a message if you're ever heading into town first thing in the morning – it's no trouble to pop down and pick you up.'

Adam nodded. 'Thanks, I might just take you up on that.' He paused and threw her an embarrassed look. 'I'd invite you in but I wasn't really expecting company when I left this morning and it's not really what you'd call guest-fresh in there.'

Sadie laughed. 'Don't worry, I have to go and collect Lissy

now anyway.' Her stomach fluttered as she glanced over at him. 'Another time, maybe?'

His hazel eyes crinkled as he smiled. 'I'd like that.'

Reaching for the door handle, he climbed out of the car, then bent to peer inside again. 'See you in the morning, then.'

Sadie nodded. 'See you then.'

He closed the car door and she watched him walk up the path to the darkened cottage. Then, worried her behaviour might seem borderline stalkerish, she put the car into gear and set off towards Christleton.

'You're later than I expected,' Daniel said when he opened the door. 'Everything okay?'

Sadie gave him a sideways glance but there was no accusation or blame on his face, just curiosity and concern.

'No, just traffic,' she fibbed. 'You know how it is. How's Lissy?'

'She's fine,' Daniel said. 'Her teacher said she had a fall in the playground at lunchtime but we patched it up with a dino-plaster and everything is right with the world again.'

He smiled and Sadie couldn't help smiling back, marvelling a little at the fact that he'd had plasters in the house, let alone dinosaur-themed ones. 'Okay,' she said. 'Well, thanks for picking her up.'

'No problem. I've given her some tea – fish fingers and rice. Is that all right?'

'Fine,' Sadie said, even more astonished. 'Thanks.'

He glanced across at her. 'You don't have to keep thanking me, Sadie. Lissy is my child too – I'm not doing anything a million other dads don't do every day.'

Sadie chose her words with care. 'Yes, but you haven't ever done it before, Daniel,' she said gently. 'That's why I'm a bit taken aback.'

He glanced towards the kitchen, where Sadie could just see Lissy's back as she sat at the table. 'Have you got a minute?' he asked, turning back to Sadie. 'There's something I've been meaning to say for a while.'

Sadie's heart lurched into her mouth. The last time Daniel had done this, it had been to confess to having an affair. What was it going to be this time – he wanted an easy divorce so that he could marry the woman?

'If you're quick,' she said, hearing the tightness in her own voice.

He led her along the hallway and into the living room. 'Have a seat. This won't take long.'

Sadie did as he asked, trying to ignore the thudding of her heart. Whatever Daniel had to say, it couldn't be more shattering, more world-destroying than last time, she reminded herself. He couldn't hurt her like that ever again.

'I've been doing a lot of thinking over the past month or so,' he began, perching nervously on the sofa beside her. 'Spending more time with Lissy has made me realise what I've been missing since the two of you moved out. I want to be part of her life, Sadie.'

'Daniel—' Sadie said but he held up both hands.

'Just hear me out. I haven't told you this because I wasn't sure how you'd take it, but I finished things with Emma. It was never serious, anyway, more of a cry for help and it soon fizzled out.' He took a deep breath. 'And I know it's crazy to even think this but there's a part of me that hopes there might still be a chance for us, Sadie. You know, in time.'

Sadie felt as though someone had tipped a bucket of ice over her. This was the last thing she'd expected to hear.

'Don't say anything now,' he urged. 'I know I've totally blindsided you. But just give it some thought. And if you decide that there's no way back then I'll accept it. But I still want to play a bigger role in Lissy's life – I want to be there for her, even if I can't be there for you.'

'Daniel,' Sadie groaned, fighting the temptation to bury her face in her hands. 'This isn't fair. What the hell has got into you?'

He hung his head. 'I'm sorry. But I can't help how I feel. It's like I'm waking up from some kind of weird out-of-body experience and only just seeing what an idiot I've been.'

She stared at him in bewilderment.

'Just say you'll think it over,' he said again. 'That's all I ask.'

There was nothing to think about, Sadie thought. He was the one who'd been unfaithful. He'd been the one who had broken their marriage. But he'd also opened her eyes to what her life could be, who she was without him; would going back rob her of the independence she'd come to value so much? There was Lissy to consider too; she'd adjusted to their new life without much difficulty. Would more upheaval simply confuse her?

Sadie sighed, sagging under the sudden weight Daniel had saddled her with. What else could she do but agree to consider what he'd said? 'Okay. I'll think about it.'

His breath whooshed out in a grateful sigh. 'Thank you.' He got to his feet, his face shining with hope. 'Now, let's go and see the walking wounded.'

When Sadie got back into her car, she saw that she had a message from Adam.

> Thanks again for the lift. Wouldn't mind
> catching a ride in the morning, if that's OK?

She sighed and glanced in the rear-view mirror at Lissy. It would mean dropping her off with Daniel first, then doubling back to collect Adam. But it would undoubtedly save him a lot of time and she'd be lying if the idea of spending more time with him didn't give her a quiet thrill. She wrestled with herself for a few more seconds, then gave in and tapped out her reply:

> Sure. See you at eight!

If Cat noticed that Sadie and Adam arrived at exactly the same time on Saturday morning, she didn't mention it.

'There's tea in the pot,' she said, as they stowed their coats away. 'If you want coffee you'll have to make it yourself.'

Just before eight-thirty, the shop door rattled and the new assistant, Clare, arrived. Sadie showed her around, explaining how the stock system worked and introducing her to the computer that powered the till system. 'And lastly, don't forget to give away the samples,' she said, pointing to the bite-sized biscuits in cellophane packets that were piled up on the counter. 'With a bit of luck once they taste them, they won't be able to resist buying some.'

Just before ten o'clock, the Lord Mayor arrived to formally declare Smart Cookies open. A small crowd had gathered to watch as, with a flourish of silver scissors, she sliced through the blue and gold ribbon. Sadie grinned as the crowd cheered – she spotted Andrew and Earl applauding near the back, and Elin and Jaren right at the front with Seb. Cherie and Greg were nowhere to be seen but Sadie found she could bear their absence very easily. The Lord Mayor posed for photos with Sadie and Cat, and seemed delighted when they presented her with her very own Smart Cookies goody bag. And throughout the day, it seemed to Sadie that the till didn't stop beeping as customer after customer fell under the spell of Sadie and Cat's efforts.

The sky was beginning to darken and the crowds were starting to thin when Sadie saw Greg and Cherie marching purposefully across the Court towards the shop. 'Adam,' she called, trying to keep her tone even and calm, 'could you do me a favour and pop across to Let's Go Dutch and The Bus Stop, please? Ask Jaren, Andrew and Earl to come here right away.' She lowered her voice and fixed him with an urgent look. 'It's an emergency.'

He didn't need to be told twice. Once he'd vanished into the crowds, Sadie hurried downstairs to where Cat was chatting to some customers about the way Smart Cookies had come about.

'I'm afraid we're going to have to cut this short,' Sadie said, interrupting with an apologetic but firm smile. 'If you stop by the till upstairs, Clare will let you have some free samples to take home and try.'

Cat gave her a puzzled look but didn't argue.

'We've got trouble,' Sadie said in an undertone. 'Greg and Cherie are coming this way and they look like they've got something on their minds.'

Cat groaned. 'Perfect. Just perfect.' She squared her shoulders. 'Okay, let's get it over with. There's no such thing as bad publicity, right?'

'Right,' Sadie said, with a confidence she didn't feel.

Then Clare's worried face appeared halfway down the stairs. 'Er . . . there's a man and a woman asking for you, Cat. They don't look happy.'

'Thanks, Clare,' Cat called and glanced across at Sadie. 'Showtime.'

Greg and Cherie were waiting outside, where Sadie assumed they'd decided they would have the biggest audience for whatever it was they wanted to say. Arms folded, they stared at Sadie and Cat with undisguised contempt.

'There she is, the fraud,' Greg called, pointing at Cat as passing shoppers slowed to a halt and exchanged puzzled looks. 'Cat Garcia, ladies and gentlemen, the worst head chef La Perle restaurant has ever had.'

Cat grimaced. 'Oh, please. Not this again.'

'Don't shop at so-called Smart Cookies,' Cherie said, loud enough to cause more passers-by to turn their heads. 'Who knows what you might catch!'

Sadie's stomach tightened in outrage. 'There's nothing wrong with our premises,' she countered, making eye contact with as many people as she could. 'You're very welcome to come inside and have a look.'

'If you're such a world-class chef, how come you're working in a poky little biscuit shop in Chester instead of running another Michelin-starred restaurant?' Greg said, his jeering tone carrying over the now-quiet court.

'Sadie and I have dreamed about running our own business since we were kids,' Cat answered in a level voice. 'I'd had enough of working eighteen-hour days so the timing was right for both of us to open Smart Cookies. I handed in my notice and came back to Chester – not that I should have to explain any of this to you.'

A murmur of agreement rippled through the crowd and Sadie saw Adam pushing his way through, with Jaren, Andrew and Earl behind him. Obviously sensing he was losing sympathy, Greg upped his game. 'There's a reason you started your own business instead of trying to get a job at another restaurant, isn't there?' he sneered. 'Something you don't want anyone to know.'

Cat stared at him. 'I don't know what you're talking—'

Greg didn't allow her to finish. He cut across her with white-hot scorn. 'You didn't leave La Perle of your own free will. You were fired, weren't you?'

Cat scowled in fury. 'That's not true,' she snapped. 'I resigned because of work-induced stress – I wasn't fired.'

Greg gave a derisory snort. 'You left before you were pushed, then. Either way, no one who worked there was sorry to see you go.'

Sadie felt Cat tense beside her. 'Go home, Greg,' she called, edging closer to Cat in support. 'You don't know what you're talking about.'

'Don't I?' Greg said, his lip curling in disgust. 'I know a lot more than you think – you convinced almost everyone with this superchef act. But not me – I saw right through you. You're a fraud who crumbled under pressure, because the truth is you slept your way to the top!'

The crowd gasped. Whispers filled the air as Cat's cheeks turned red. 'I don't know who you've been talking to, Greg, but I can assure you they are wrong.'

'It's true,' Greg crowed, turning around. 'I know people who work there – she was having an affair with the owner and that's why he gave her the job. Look at her, guilt is written all over her face.'

Sadie glanced across at Cat and saw from her expression that there was something in Greg's accusation. 'Cat?'

'It's not true,' she whispered back. Her mouth twisted with regret. 'Not all of it anyway. I'm sorry – I didn't want you to find out like this.'

Pulling herself up to her full height, Cat shook her hair down her back and gazed at Greg with contempt. 'Okay, you want to know what happened? Here it is. The truth is,

I didn't leave La Perle willingly but it wasn't because I was having an affair with anyone.' Her eyes ranged across the crowd. 'I had to leave because I *wouldn't* have an affair, and the person trying to coerce me into one refused to take no for an answer.'

Angry mumbles broke out as the crowd took in what Cat was saying. Greg looked suddenly deflated, as though someone had pricked his balloon. He leaned down to whisper furiously to a pale-faced Cherie.

'And before you demand that I tell you who it was, let me save you the trouble – I signed a non-disclosure agreement as part of my very generous settlement package when I left,' Cat went on. She fixed Greg with a final glower of disdain. 'So it seems your "source" had no idea what they were talking about. And neither do you.'

Seb pushed his way to the front and pulled Cat into a tight embrace. 'Show's over, everyone,' he called. 'And if you have any sympathy at all for what Cat has been forced to very publicly reveal, I suggest you make your way over to Smart Cookies and buy every single biscuit you can find.'

He waited until the crowd started to disperse and then made his way over to where Greg and Cherie still stood. 'As for you two, don't ever try to set foot over the doorstep of Seb's again. You're barred.'

'That goes for The Bus Stop too,' Earl called, his expression disgusted.

'And Let's Go Dutch,' Jaren added.

Elin shook her head in pity as she glared at Greg. 'Don't

expect me to supply your after-dinner chocolates any more either. Our deal is now terminated.'

'Come on,' Seb said, wrapping a protective arm around Cat's shoulders. 'Let's get you away from all these prying eyes. I don't know about you, but I could really do with a drink.'

Chapter Nine

It took several days for the trauma of having to publicly reveal her secret to leave Cat, and almost a week for her to stop feeling as though everyone was staring at her.

Sadie was horrified that she'd never guessed the truth. 'I knew there was more to it than you let on but I thought you were embarrassed about losing control. Why didn't you tell me?'

Cat sighed. 'I didn't tell anyone. I signed a non-disclosure agreement, remember?'

'But still,' Sadie said. 'I hate the thought of you coping with all this on your own.'

'I wasn't entirely alone. I had a very good, very expensive French lawyer that François de Beauvoir ended up having to pay for,' Cat said dryly.

Sadie studied her. 'Is that who it was? The owner's son?'

Cat nodded. 'As you can imagine, he denied everything

at first. But luckily for me, one of my sous-chefs had seen him trying to force me to kiss him and she wasn't afraid to speak up when he finally realised I wasn't going to give him what he wanted.' She paused and shook her head in disgust. 'It turned out I wasn't the first member of staff François had put pressure on, but hopefully I will be the last. I cost him an awful lot of money.'

'It's all behind you now,' Sadie said, squeezing her hand.

'I thought it was,' Cat said quietly. 'But it turns out François had one last parting shot to send my way. I wouldn't be surprised if he and Greg are friends, actually. That would explain Greg's venom, and all those comments about damaging his friends. I assumed he meant Cherie but perhaps he was talking about François.'

'That would make sense,' Sadie replied. 'Although he didn't have a clue what had really gone on. I don't think we'll have any more trouble with him, anyway – Jaren says he's been keeping a very low profile around the Court. But don't hold your breath waiting for an apology – from what I hear, he's too busy trying to patch things up with Cherie. She's furious he fed her a load of wrong information.'

Cat folded her arms. 'Huh – she's only furious their ridiculous plan failed. But I don't care about an apology. As long as they both stay out of my way, I'll be happy.'

News of Smart Cookies had spread like wildfire and both Cat and Sadie had to work long and hard to keep up with demand as the weeks flew by and Christmas loomed on the horizon. Their edible tree decorations were featured in *Stylist* magazine and *The One Show* sent a camera crew to film in the shop, taking particular interest in Sadie's biscuit Nativity display. Sadie found herself relying on Daniel more and more for help with Lissy; he'd even started saving her a cooked meal at the end of the day and refused to let her leave without it. And Cat had been forced to put things with Seb on hold, warning him she barely had time to brush her teeth before tumbling exhausted into bed, let alone do anything else. He hadn't seemed to mind – Christmas was a crazy time for all the Castle Court businesses.

'It's great that Daniel is helping out so much with Lissy,' Cat observed to Sadie early one morning, as they worked side by side in the basement kitchen. 'Are you sure he hasn't been captured by aliens and replaced by a newer, kinder version?'

Sadie hesitated. She'd never told Cat about her conversation with Daniel, mostly because the events of the Smart Cookies opening day had pretty much eclipsed everything but also because she knew exactly how her best friend would react. But it was festering away inside her, keeping her awake even when she was worn out from long days in the shop, and she was starting to worry that if she didn't tell someone, the whole thing would burst and poison her from the inside out.

'He wants us to get back together,' she told Cat bluntly.

But instead of looking shocked, Cat simply nodded. 'I did wonder. He's had such a personality make-over that it wasn't hard to guess what was in his head.' She gave Sadie a long, thoughtful look. 'How do you feel about the idea?'

Sadie sighed. 'There are times when I think it would be so much easier,' she admitted. 'But I haven't really had time to think about it properly, to be honest. Things have been so manic here – it's easier just to push it out of my head. You know how it is.'

Cat grimaced. 'Oh yes. I know how it is. But I also remember how being with Daniel made you feel, and what he did to you. Don't rush into anything, that's my advice. And if you do decide it's what you want, Daniel has a lot of making up to do. Let him work for it.' She paused and glanced meaningfully at the stairs. 'Or not, as the case may be. You do have other options, you know.'

She meant Adam, Sadie thought, dipping her head to hide the blush that was creeping up her cheeks. He'd been a rock since the shop had opened, cheerfully doing everything asked of him and more besides – Sadie had caught herself admiring his skill with their customers more than once as the days passed by and she could tell from the flirtatious smiles they sent back that plenty of other women appreciated his unselfconscious charm too. But it was more than just a physical attraction, she decided; she liked everything about him, from his passion for nature to his gentle, self-deprecating humour. In fact, the twenty minutes they spent together in the car travelling to and from the city was fast becoming one of the bright spots of Sadie's day. She found him incredibly easy to talk to and they had so much in common – she'd lost count of the number of times they'd spent the entire journey laughing. But as lovely as it was to get to know Adam better, Daniel still loomed large in her life and his assertion that he saw a future for him and Sadie simply muddied the emotional waters. The only way to deal with her conflicting feelings was to push them to the back of her mind and focus on her work. After Christmas, she told herself. I'll think about it all then.

Somehow, Sadie juggled Lissy's end-of-term commitments without feeling as though she had totally failed as a parent but it came as a relief when school broke up two days before Christmas Eve. She'd reluctantly agreed months earlier to Daniel's demands that he had Lissy on their first Christmas Day apart, anticipating that he might change his mind and jet off somewhere exotic and non-child-friendly with his new girlfriend instead. But Daniel had surprised her; now that he was embracing his role as a father in a way he never had before, Sadie was faced with the prospect of spending Christmas Day on her own. Unwilling to give Daniel even more time with Lissy, on the first day of the holidays Sadie packed a bag of games and toys and told Lissy she was going to visit Mummy's work. Adam took the extra passenger in his stride, spending the drive into Chester playing *I Spy* instead of chatting with Sadie. She didn't mind giving up his attention in favour of Lissy; it made her heart melt to see them getting along so well.

At the shop, everyone made a big fuss of Lissy.

'Wow,' Elin said, when she popped in with a chocolate snowman lolly for the little girl. 'She is such a mini you.'

Sadie laughed. 'She might look like me but when it comes down to getting her own way, she's definitely her father's daughter.'

Cat looked up and gave Sadie an enigmatic look, before busying herself with her work again. Lissy sat downstairs at one of the long trestle tables, colouring or playing with Sadie's discarded icing bags, enjoying the attention she was getting from the Smart Cookies staff. The system was working well, until a large last-minute order came in from a luxury hotel in the centre of Chester.

'They want how many festive gingerbread men?' Sadie squeaked, when Clare passed on the message.

'Four hundred and fifty,' Clare repeated. 'By tomorrow.'

Cat rolled up her sleeves and fired Sadie a determined look. 'Right. We can do this. You can ice the stock we have already and I'll bake some more.'

Sadie was so engrossed in her work that it took her a little while to notice Lissy was no longer perched at the long table. 'Lissy?' she called, frowning. 'Where are you?'

Cat looked up. 'Is she in the toilets?'

Lowering her icing bag, Sadie went to check. There was no sign of her daughter. Feeling uneasiness wash over her, she hurried upstairs.

'Have you seen Lissy?' she murmured to Adam, once he'd finished serving his customer.

He shook his head. 'She's not downstairs?'

'No.' Sadie looked around with a rising sense of panic. 'Did she come up here? Has she gone outside?'

Cat was upstairs too, her face tense. 'She's not under the tables. Let's spread out and check the Court. If she did wander out, she can't have gone far.'

Trying hard to control her breathing, Sadie scanned the bustling courtyard. But with only two days until Christmas, the public was out in force buying last-minute presents; it was hard to find anyone in the crowd, let alone a five-year-old.

'Please let her be okay,' she mumbled to herself, pushing her way through the shoppers as tears pricked her eyes. 'Please let one of us find her.'

But it was hopeless, she realised, as terror took over her heart. Once or twice, she caught a glimpse of auburn hair and forced her way towards it but it turned out to be someone else's child. Breaking into wild sobs, Sadie climbed up onto an empty chair and opened her mouth. 'Lissy! Lissy, where are you?'

People stared up at her as though she was mad. 'Please,' she cried. 'I've lost my daughter. She's wearing a blue dress and has red hair like mine. Please help me find her.'

Word started to make its way through the shoppers and they began to look around. Then, just as Sadie thought she would lose what little self-control she had left, a shout rang out. 'Here! She's over here!'

Sadie pushed her way forwards, not caring who she elbowed in her efforts to reach Lissy. When at last she arrived at the spot, she almost hardly dared to look. What if it wasn't her, she thought wildly. But it was – she stood holding Adam's hand under the branches of the fairy-lit oak tree. Tear-stained and terrified, Lissy's small face dissolved into tears the moment she saw Sadie. 'Mummy!' she cried. 'Mummy, I was so scared.'

Sadie gathered her daughter into her arms and held her as tightly as she dared, raining kisses onto the top of her curly head. 'You're safe now,' she said, through her own tears. 'That's all that matters. You're safe.'

She glanced up at Adam, almost too grateful to speak. 'Thank you,' she mouthed.

'No problem,' he said with a gentle smile. 'No problem at all.'

'Are you sure you don't want to go home?' Cat asked Sadie, for the fifth time. 'You've both had a terrible shock.'

They were sitting at the long table in the basement, Lissy clinging onto Sadie and only letting go to take a bite of a chocolate pancake from Jaren that was bigger than her head.

'No,' Sadie said, stroking her daughter's hair. 'We've got so many gingerbread men to decorate – I can't go.'

'So take some with you,' Cat said. 'Work on them once Lissy is asleep later and bring them back tomorrow. We've got time – we can spare you for a few hours.'

Sadie shook her head stubbornly. 'We'll never get them all done. I need to stay here.' She tried to get up but Lissy moaned, tightening her grip.

'Face it, Sadie,' Cat said in a kind voice. 'You're not getting anything else done this afternoon.'

Clare poked her head around the top of the stairs. 'I've

got an A-level in Art. If someone shows me what to do with a piping bag, I could probably copy Sadie's designs.' She hesitated and looked embarrassed. 'I'm not saying they'll be anywhere near as perfect but they'll do the job.'

'See?' Cat said, making a shooing motion. 'You're not indispensable after all.'

Sadie glanced up the stairs, where Adam was serving behind the counter. 'I need to give Adam a lift—'

Cat let out an exasperated growl. 'He's a big boy – he can get the bus. Now go – none of us is getting anything done while you're in the way.' She smiled, to let Sadie see that she was only joking. 'We'll see you in the morning.'

Defeated, Sadie managed a weary nod. 'Okay. I'm gone.'

It wasn't until later that evening, when she was tucking an exhausted Lissy under the covers, that the full emotional fall-out hit Sadie. She knelt at her daughter's bedside, stroking her sleeping head and letting enormous silent tears drop unchecked onto her lap. And afterwards, when she'd had no more tears left, she'd sat at her kitchen table, surrounded by gingerbread men and icing sugar, staring at nothing, reliving the moment when she first realised there was no way she could find Lissy in the crowd. Eventually, she gave up any pretence at work and sent a text to Daniel:

> Could you have Lissy tomorrow? I need to go
> into the shop.

His reply was almost instant.

Of course. Your place or mine?

Sadie sighed; if this evening had been anything to go by, Lissy would want the comfort of familiar things around her:

Here. Can you arrive by eight o'clock?

See you then, was his response.

And then Sadie went to bed. She lay awake for what felt like hours, then eventually fell into a dreamless sleep that was broken only by Lissy crawling into bed and nestling against her.

Getting ready to leave Lissy on Christmas Eve was even harder than Sadie expected. Daniel arrived just before eight and frowned when he saw her subdued expression. 'Cheer up,' he told her when she opened the cottage door to let him in. 'It's nearly Christmas.'

Sadie tried her best to dredge up a smile. She'd already decided not to tell him about the events of the day before; not until she had time to explain properly. 'Take it easy with her today,' she told Daniel, nodding to where Lissy was curled up on the sofa, watching a dinosaur cartoon. 'She was up in the night.'

'Sure,' he nodded. 'Everything okay?'

'Fine,' she said quickly. 'Nothing to worry about.'

The weight of Sadie's mood lifted slightly when she picked Adam up. He did almost all of the talking, describing two customers who had almost come to blows over the last angel biscuit in the shop and taking deliberate care not to ask her how she was feeling. At the shop, Cat gave her a long, warm hug and then pushed her towards row after row of gingerbread men. 'Ice,' was all she said.

Sadie didn't leave the basement kitchen all day, although she checked in with Daniel often. Visitors came and went; Elin stopped by with a cuddly woolly mammoth for Lissy, Andrew and Earl had found what seemed to be the world's largest toy school bus and had wrapped it in dinosaur paper. Jaren brought over some Stroop waffles – sweet waffles that needed to sit on top of a hot drink to melt the toffee inside – and a pair of exquisite wooden clogs. Seb had nothing for Lissy but presented Sadie with a bottle of ready-mixed cosmopolitan with a label that read: *God knows you've earned it.* And Sadie said thank you over and over, and hid her face more often than she cared to admit because their kindness was overwhelming.

When the enormous gingerbread man order had been delivered, the last frantic customer had been served, and the doors of Smart Cookies had finally closed, Sadie, Cat, Adam and Clare stood in the middle of the decimated shelves and gazed at each other.

'Well, that happened,' Cat said, shrugging in wide-eyed amazement. 'I can't quite believe we made it through but somehow, we did.'

'Thank you,' Sadie said, looking at Adam and Clare.

'It doesn't seem like enough just to say it so there's a little present to show you how grateful we are behind the counter, and you'll find a little extra bonus in your pay packets this month. We really couldn't have managed without either of you.'

'Don't forget, we open again at nine-thirty on 27 December,' Cat said, raising her eyebrows. 'The public are going to need New Year's biscuits and we're going to be the only place in Chester they can get them.'

Both Adam and Clare nodded.

'And I hope you've got the New Year's Eve party at Seb's in your diaries?' Cat went on. 'Friends and family are welcome too and Seb promises me it will be a night to remember.'

Adam glanced enquiringly at Sadie, who laughed. 'Don't tell me – you're going to need a lift.'

Cat raised her eyebrows. 'There'll probably be a couple of spare beds at my flat, if you're interested,' she said, her tone dripping with innocence. 'That way, no one has to worry about driving.'

Sadie was too embarrassed to look at Adam, especially when she saw Clare hide a quick smile behind her hand. Not for the first time, Sadie found herself wishing Cat could be less obvious – surely Adam had picked up the implication behind her offer? But when Sadie finally plucked up the courage to glance across, he looked exactly the same as always.

Cat took her arm as she was leaving. 'See you tomorrow, right? Twelve-thirty at Seb's.'

Sadie started to shake her head. 'I'll just be in the way. Why don't I stay at home?'

'Not a chance,' Cat replied. 'There's no way I'm letting you spend the day on your own.'

'Okay,' Sadie said, giving in. 'Twelve-thirty at Seb's.'

The drive home was slow but Sadie barely minded the delay. Every radio station was in relentless Christmas mode; she and Adam sang along to the well-worn tunes and chatted for the entire journey. Snow began to fall as they reached Rowton, tiny flakes that danced onto the windscreen and melted into speckles of rain. When they pulled up outside Adam's cottage, he gave Sadie a long thoughtful look. 'I've tidied up. Want to come in for a coffee?'

Sadie watched the snowflakes whirl this way and that outside the window and thought she knew how they felt; the temptation to say yes to Adam was almost more than she could resist but at the same time, her mind was full of Lissy and getting home.

She cast an anguished look at the clock on the dashboard and sighed. 'I can't today. Sorry.'

He nodded, a smile of understanding pulling at his lips. 'Another time, then.'

An awkward silence began to form. Sadie reached into the back seat of the car and retrieved a gift-wrapped box exactly the same size and shape as a Smart Cookies gift box. 'Merry Christmas. I think you can probably guess what it is – even my parents got them this year.'

Adam smiled. 'Believe it or not, I've never actually

eaten one of your biscuits. So thank you – I'll enjoy every bite.' He pulled out a badly wrapped present that looked a lot like a glass jar from his bag. 'Merry Christmas to you too.'

She shook her head in delight as she took it. 'You shouldn't have.'

He shrugged. 'Don't get excited. I'm afraid this won't be much of a surprise, either.'

Sadie tipped her head. 'It's the thought that counts,' she said, and twisted around to plant a kiss on his cheek.

For a heartbeat, neither of them moved. Then Adam slowly turned his head until he was facing her and gazed into her eyes. Sadie felt her pulse start to quicken as she psyched herself up to close the distance between them. And then, with a muffled sound that was almost a gasp, she leaned forwards and kissed him.

It only lasted a few seconds but it was enough. 'Are you sure you can't come in?' Adam murmured, when she opened her eyes. 'Not even for a minute?'

Sadie sighed again. 'I'm sure. But there's always Wednesday. We could leave work early,' she said with a wink. 'I know the boss.'

He laughed as he got out of the car. 'I might hold you to that.'

'Merry Christmas,' Sadie called, as he walked up the path. 'See you next week!'

Turning the radio up and giving in to the DJ's relentless festive cheer, she sang all the way home.

Her good mood vanished the moment she opened the front door and saw the expression on Daniel's face.

'I think we need to talk,' he said grimly, casting a meaningful look at Lissy. 'Don't you?'

Chapter Ten

Christmas Day arrived silently in Sadie's cottage. There was no excited squeal as Lissy woke up ridiculously early and discovered the overflowing stocking at the bottom of her bed; no *thud thud thud* of little feet as she made her way to Sadie's room, determined to share the unwrapping of all the presents her mother had spent the preceding few days so carefully packaging up. There was no noise at all.

Sadie lay there for a few minutes, listening to the unaccustomed hush. It was still dark; the day stretched ahead of her, long and empty in spite of her invitation to lunch with Cat and Seb. Another morning she would have revelled in the luxury of having nothing to do, no one else to cook for and run around after, but the memory of having lost Lissy in Castle Court was too fresh. Besides, this was Christmas Day and all she felt was her daughter's absence. Lissy had cried the night before, when she'd realised that Sadie wasn't coming with her to Daniel's house, and no amount of reassurance that

Sadie would see her on Boxing Day could placate her. Daniel had messaged late in the evening to say she'd worn herself out and was now sleeping and the thought had tormented Sadie. This was how it would be from now on, she thought, as the silence weighed down upon her; every other year, Christmas Day would be spent alone, while Lissy missed her and made the best of things with Daniel. Every other year, it would be something to dread rather than celebrate.

But it doesn't have to be that way, a voice whispered. Daniel was offering her another option; a way to ensure Lissy didn't have to split herself between her parents. If she accepted his offer, put everything into repairing the colossal damage their marriage had suffered, then she would never need to spend another Christmas Eve listening to Lissy sob again, or another Christmas Day aching with her absence.

Sadie and Daniel had talked for hours the night before, their voices hushed so as not to alert their daughter. Daniel had been furious; angry and scared that Lissy had been in danger but more upset that he'd had to hear it from her instead of Sadie. And as the conversation had worn on, it had inevitably swung back to their marriage. Daniel's words still echoed in Sadie's head the following morning: *You're not coping, Sadie. I'm not coping. And more importantly, Lissy is suffering because of us. We used to be happy once – can't we find a way to be happy again? For her sake as well as our own.*

She climbed out of bed and went downstairs, trying to ignore the small pile of unopened presents beneath the Christmas tree that was much more modest than the one

Lissy had been delighted to help decorate in Daniel's living room. 'Daddy had to lift me up to put the star on the top,' she'd told Sadie breathlessly when she'd arrived to pick her up the week before Christmas. 'Isn't it pretty?'

And Sadie had been forced to agree that it was; Daniel had surprised her once again.

The presents underneath Sadie's own tree were mostly for Lissy: a couple from Cat, and some from Sadie that she'd kept back so that she and Lissy could open them together on Boxing Day. The largest one had Sadie's own name on it – she had no idea what was inside; Cat had refused to give her any hints at all. And there was the small one that Adam had handed to her last night. The sight of it pierced her heart; if she went back to Daniel now, there could be no more tentative kisses with Adam. Their relationship would have to become strictly businesslike if she was to survive the journey to and from work each day and resist the temptation to accept his invitation to venture inside the cottage for coffee.

Outside, she saw in the half-light that the garden was covered in a light dusting of snow. She stood at the kitchen window, staring out at the blanket of white. Lissy would be delighted when she woke up – it gave everything a shimmering, magical air; a freshness that hinted at new beginnings and fresh starts. But above all Sadie noticed the absolute stillness, here as in the rest of the house. Would it be so very bad to wake up with Daniel again, if it also meant waking up with her daughter on Christmas Day?

Of course it wouldn't. *But Adam*, her heart agonised, *what about Adam? And what about you?*

Ultimately, there was no choice at all, Sadie realised, pulling her dressing gown tighter with a little shiver. Adam would understand that she had to put Lissy first; Cat would too, although she wouldn't approve. And Daniel had shown another side to himself these past few weeks – he had made an effort and proved he cared. They hadn't always been unhappy; perhaps, given time, they could find their way back to love. In the meantime, there was Lissy to hold them together.

In Castle Court, Cat woke up to the smell of bacon.

She stretched, gazing up at the beamed ceiling of Seb's garret, and considered getting up. But if she did that then they might not come back to bed to snuggle beneath the covers and that was something she wanted very much. So she lay still instead and waited for Seb to reappear with breakfast, wondering whether Sadie was also awake. How would she be coping on her first Christmas alone? Cat reached for her phone, intending to send her a message, and she saw that Sadie had beaten her to it. Smiling, she clicked it open.

> Spending the day at Daniel's. Don't be angry
> with me – I couldn't bear to be without Lissy.
> Will explain everything when I see you. Merry
> Christmas xx

Cat dropped her phone onto the duvet with a groan of pure frustration. She'd known this was going to happen, right from the moment that Sadie had told her that weasel Daniel had suddenly started being Father of the bloody Year. Why hadn't Sadie divorced him straight away? She'd certainly had good reason.

The bedroom door swung open just a few seconds later and Seb appeared, a tray laden with plates and steaming mugs of tea. 'Merry Christmas,' he said, sliding the tray onto the bedside table. 'You'll be delighted to hear there's at least two centimetres of snow out there. We might even manage a snowball fight later . . .'

'No thanks,' Cat drawled, then squeaked as he climbed back into bed. 'Your feet are freezing.'

He bent his head to kiss her. 'But my lips are warm.'

Cat did her best to surrender but the thought of Sadie niggled at her. After a few moments, Seb drew back and studied her. 'I'm sensing your heart isn't in this. What's the matter?'

Wordlessly, Cat showed him Sadie's message.

'Ah,' he said, slumping back against the pillow. 'Well, I can't say I am completely surprised.'

'Me neither,' Cat replied. 'And that's the most infuriating thing – I'm ninety-eight per cent sure she's in love with Adam but Daniel has somehow managed to convince her to give him a chance.'

'You can't tell her how to live her life,' Seb pointed out. 'No matter how much you want to protect her. Just like you can't make her face up to her feelings for Adam.'

123

'I know,' Cat said, sighing. 'But I wish she could see Daniel the way I do. I thought she did see him that way, to be honest.'

Seb snaked an arm around her waist and pulled her close. 'Give her time. Christmas does strange things to people – maybe she'll feel differently in the New Year.'

Cat gave her phone another troubled glance; she knew Sadie well enough to read between the lines. 'Maybe,' she said. 'There's always your party, I suppose – Daniel won't be around for that. Who knows what might happen as the clock strikes midnight?'

He nuzzled her neck. 'Exactly. And in the meantime, Christmas is doing something strange to me. I think I might need your help to take care of it.'

Reluctantly, Cat pushed the thought of Sadie out of her head; there wasn't much she could do about the situation now, anyway. It would keep until Boxing Day at least, she decided.

She gazed deep into Seb's eyes. 'You're right, there is something I need to take care of,' she told him, her lips curving into a smile of anticipation. 'I've got a bacon sandwich to eat.'

The drive to Daniel's took less than ten minutes, in spite of the snow. Sadie parked in the driveway and pulled out the front door key she'd kept in a drawer at home for emergencies. It was always possible Daniel had changed the locks but she didn't think it would have occurred to him, and her suspicion was borne out when her key turned and the door opened. She kicked off her boots, leaving them beside the front door, and padded towards the kitchen.

'Sadie?' Daniel appeared at the top of the stairs, wrapped in a dressing gown, his sleep-creased face wary and amazed. 'What are you doing here?'

Sadie took a deep breath. 'I thought about what you said. And I realised you're right – Lissy has to come first. So, if you want to try again—' She paused and sucked in another gulp of air. 'If you want to try again, then I'm up for it.'

Daniel's face lit up. He hurried down the stairs but stopped when Sadie held up a hand. 'I'm not rushing into anything, we'll take things slowly. Lissy and I will continue to stay at the cottage but – if things go well – maybe you can come over to stay occasionally, or I can sleep here.'

'Whatever you want,' Daniel said, his voice shaking a little. 'However you want it to be – I just want for us to be a family again. You, me and Lissy.'

Sadie swallowed hard. 'That's – that's what I want too.'

He stepped forwards again and she knew this time there would be no stopping him; he was going to pull her into his arms. But then a door opened somewhere upstairs and the thud of little feet she'd missed so much that morning saved her.

'Mummy!' Lissy cried as she hurtled down the stairs and the delight in her voice swept away any last doubts Sadie had about whether she was doing the right thing. 'I didn't know you were going to be here. Daddy said—'

Sadie wrapped her daughter in a warm hug and closed her eyes as she breathed in the warm, sleepy scent of her. 'I know but I bumped into Father Christmas in the snow and he offered to give me a lift so I decided to come and surprise you.'

Lissy stared at her, eyes wide. 'You got a lift on his sleigh? In the snow?'

Sadie nodded, crossing her fingers behind Lissy's back. 'I did. Are you surprised?'

'Yes,' Lissy said. 'Did he remember to leave some presents too?'

Sadie laughed. 'I'm sure he did. Shall we go and look under the tree?'

'Can we?' Lissy cried, before darting off down the hallway towards the living room. Sadie followed but Daniel caught her arm as she walked past and swung her towards him, pressing his lips to hers in a brief, fierce kiss. 'I love you. I always have. You know that, don't you?'

Sadie hesitated, then nodded. As long as he didn't expect her to feel the same way, they might just be okay. 'Yes.'

He let go and sent a swift glance towards the front door. 'I suppose I'd better go and put your car in the garage, before Lissy sees it and realises you weren't entirely telling the truth.'

A delighted squeal rang out in the living room, followed by a feverish rustling that suggested Lissy had dived head first into the presents under the tree.

'I didn't think of that,' Sadie said to Daniel. 'Would you?'

'Of course,' he said. 'Anything.'

'Oh my goodness, there are so many presents!' Lissy bellowed. 'This is the best Christmas ever!'

'You'll get no argument from me,' Daniel said. 'There's a little something for you too, under the tree. I got it in case – well, you know why.'

Sadie opened her mouth to object but Daniel hurried on. 'Don't worry that you haven't got anything for me. Now you're here I've got everything I need.'

She stared at him in silence, taken aback to see his eyes were moist with tears. 'I—'

He shook his head, as though he couldn't believe his luck, and smiled. 'Merry Christmas, Sadie.'

Time seemed to stand still as Sadie stood in the hallway. Then a particularly excitable squeal from Lissy broke the spell. Sadie took a deep breath and dug deep for a smile of her own. 'Merry Christmas, Daniel.'

Frosty Mornings at Castle Court

Chapter Eleven

Love was definitely in the air at Castle Court.

Sadie Smart made her way past the enormous oak tree that stood in the heart of the Court, presiding over the surrounding shops and restaurants like a king surveying his wintry domain. The early February sun was just peeping over the third-floor rooftops – most of the Court was still cloaked in shadow – but Sadie didn't need its rays to admire the softly lit window displays around her. Elin's had gone all out for romance, with glistening heart-shaped chocolates of all sizes nestled against rich purple satin. Patisserie Cherie had exquisitely formed swirling hearts painted onto the window, framing a mouth-watering display of sweet treats. Let's Go Dutch had posters advertising their special Loved-Up pancake, featuring white chocolate and fresh raspberry coulis. Even the big yellow school bus that formed the front of the Bus Stop diner had turned into Love Central; their menu had been given a make-over and Andrew and Earl had draped kitsch red and pink fairy lights along the length of the bus, to complement the ones wrapped around the trunk and branches of the oak tree.

St Valentine would be delighted, Sadie reflected, as she side-stepped a frost-patterned flagstone. And who knew, maybe the atmosphere could work its magic over her own tangled love life.

She felt a frown crease her forehead but, as always, the sight of the Smart Cookies Biscuit Emporium window lifted her spirits. In keeping with the rest of Castle Court, her own display was wall-to-wall romance; the city of love itself in biscuit form. A gold-flecked gingerbread Eiffel Tower glowed at one end of the window, the Arc de Triomphe presided over a glittering Champs-Elysées in the centre and Notre Dame loomed on the right. Pastel-shaded poodles frolicked with arched black cats by the Seine, beneath delicately curved lamp posts and leafy green trees. Behind the window, the shelves were stocked with souvenir tins of the City of Love collection Sadie had designed; it had given Cat more than one sleepless night as she worked out how to shape the biscuits for Sadie to ice into Parisian perfection. But the hard work had paid off: with less than a week to go until Valentine's Day, sales were picking up fast.

Sadie stood for a moment, bathed in the glow of her own handiwork, then slipped her key into the lock and went inside. As usual, the air was warm with the scent of vanilla and sugar. Cat was downstairs in the kitchen, baking up biscuits for the online orders that flooded in every day.

'Morning,' Sadie called, stopping to straighten one of the table displays before making for the stairs that led to the basement. 'Everything under control?'

Cat looked up. Her long dark curls were swept back into a severe ponytail, making her look younger than her thirty-two years, and there was a touch of what looked like flour on her nose. 'Hey. All okay here.' She paused and shook her head. 'Unless you count an especially tasteless order for a personalised Valentine's Day cookie with the words "Lick this like you lick my—"'

'*Another* one?' Sadie cut in hurriedly. 'Honestly, what is wrong with people?'

'Takes all sorts,' Cat replied, shrugging. 'But don't worry, I sent a message saying we weren't able to help on this occasion, so you'll be spared any blushes.' She sank her cookie cutter into the buttery pale dough on the worktop, leaving Sadie to wonder whether she was imagining the hint of unspoken criticism behind her best friend's words. Cat had always been less prudish than her but surely she wasn't implying they should fulfil orders for borderline obscene messages?

'It's not just to spare my blushes, though—'

'Of course not,' Cat said, without looking up. 'That kind of thing doesn't fit with the Smart Cookies brand, for a start. It doesn't exactly scream classiness, does it?'

Sadie smiled in relief. 'No, it doesn't.' She consulted the chalkboard on the wall. 'Did you order the Prosecco for tonight's icing party?'

Their first Christmas at Castle Court had been a

wonderful but crazy whirl, made all the trickier by the fact that they were still settling into their new business venture. But January had been quieter, giving Sadie the opportunity to kick-start her plan of offering icing workshops and birthday parties. Take-up had been slow at first, but they were now starting to see the bookings roll in; today's party was a hen do, due to start at six-thirty.

'I did,' Cat replied. 'How did Daniel take the news that you'd be working late?'

Sadie hesitated. She and Daniel still lived apart – Sadie in a small, two-bedroomed cottage and Daniel in the family home they'd once shared – and split the childcare between them. On the surface, Daniel had seemed fine with the idea of collecting Lissy from her after-school club and looking after her for the evening. But Sadie hated to rely on him; she couldn't shake the worry that he would go back to how he used to be, liking the idea of parenthood but wanting little to do with the realities, and suddenly decide he had somewhere better to be. It hadn't happened yet, she reminded herself; if anything, Daniel seemed to be enjoying his extra time with Lissy.

I'm probably overthinking things again, Sadie decided. 'He was fine,' she told Cat now. 'I think he's pleased at how well the business is doing.'

Cat glanced up, her expression unreadable. 'Good. I've packed all the biscuits you'll need into a basket – it's in the cupboard. Twelve guests, right?'

'That's right,' Sadie said. 'The bride, her mother and

mother-in-law-to-be, the bridesmaids – or the grown-up ones, at least – and a few friends. It should be fun.'

'It should,' Cat agreed. 'You can tell me all about it tomorrow.'

Sadie stared at her. 'Tomorrow? Aren't you going to be here?'

Cat shook her head. 'Change of plan – I'm going out for dinner with Seb. Don't worry, you won't be on your own. Adam has agreed to cover for me.'

'Oh!' Sadie exclaimed, before she could stop herself. 'But—' she trailed off, feeling her cheeks grow warm.

Her relationship with Adam had been teetering on the brink of romance before Christmas but had stayed strictly professional since she'd decided to try again with Daniel. Cat had made no secret that she'd been in Adam's corner, however, and Sadie wouldn't be at all surprised to discover Cat was looking for ways to push the two of them together.

'But what?' Cat said, raising her eyebrows. 'You can't manage the party on your own and I think he's going to prove very popular with our hens.'

And that was another problem, Sadie thought, although she'd never admit it to Cat. What if one of the guests took a tipsy shine to Adam? What if the attraction was mutual? Sadie would have to stand by and watch it happen, knowing there was nothing she could say.

'I'm sure you're right,' she said, her tone carefully neutral. 'I just wish you'd spoken to me first before making these arrangements. Clare might have been a better choice – she's getting better and better at icing.'

Clare had proved she had a natural talent for the precise decoration that had become their hallmark and Sadie was more than happy to accept her help to keep on top of the shop's orders. But Adam had a natural charm with their customers and Sadie knew his ready smile and dimples went a long way with the female visitors to Castle Court.

'It's Clare's day off,' Cat pointed out. 'You'll be taking care of all the icing, anyway. Adam will only be here as back-up.'

Sadie sighed. There wasn't much she could do about it now.

'Maybe you could take the long way home,' Cat added in an innocent tone. 'Avoid the traffic.'

Sadie gave her friend a hard look. If she'd needed further proof that Cat was meddling, here it was. 'It will be nine o'clock – there won't be any traffic.'

Cat shook her head. 'The trouble with you is that you have no imagination. How many times did Daniel lie to you when he was having his affair?'

'Two things,' Sadie said tightly. 'One, I'm not having an affair, and two, I hate lying. And . . . and three . . .' She swallowed hard against the indignant lump that had formed in her throat. 'I have plenty of imagination, actually.'

Cat was unrepentant. 'You work too hard, Sadie. When was the last time you took some time for yourself, let your hair down a bit?' She held up a hand to stop Sadie from interrupting. 'Listen, you like Adam. He likes you. You are friends. So, there's no reason you can't stop by a cosy little pub on your way home to unwind after a busy day. As *friends*.'

The trouble was that one stop might lead to another, or at least to Sadie wanting there to be another, and before she knew it, things would get complicated. Maybe it wouldn't be such a bad thing if one of the hen-party guests and Adam hit it off – at least then Cat would give up trying to tempt her into something that could only end in disaster.

'I'm perfectly capable of deciding who my friends are, thanks very much,' she said, turning to the cupboard where she kept her icing supplies.

There was a small silence. 'You're allowed to be happy,' Cat said. 'If giving things another go with Daniel makes you miserable, then maybe it's not the right thing to do.'

'I'm not miserable,' Sadie snapped. 'And even if I was, Lissy's happiness matters more than mine.'

'If *you're* happy, Lissy is happy,' Cat said firmly. 'Don't use her as an excuse because you're afraid you'll get your heart broken again.'

Sadie spun round. 'If you like Adam so much, why don't you go out with him? But for God's sake, stop trying to live my life for me, okay?'

She regretted the words as soon as they were out but it was too late: Cat's expression hardened. 'Fine. Message received, loud and clear.'

'Cat—'

'No, you're right,' Cat said, pressing the cookie cutter into the dough with more pressure than it needed. 'It's none of my business, anyway.'

She lapsed into frosty silence. Sadie stared at her for a few seconds, then got on with mixing up her first batch of icing. Cat had overstepped the mark, she thought, as she beat the smooth white mixture harder than she normally did. It really was none of her business. But she did have a point; it had been a long time since Sadie had done anything that wasn't related to the shop, Lissy or Daniel. And while going for a drink with Adam was clearly inappropriate, maybe it was time for Sadie to do something for herself. Because Cat had been spot on about something else too: deep down, Sadie knew she wasn't happy.

Adam arrived while Cat was running some lunchtime errands, meaning Sadie was spared the embarrassment of a pointed look from her best friend. A flurry of customers meant that she and Adam barely had time for more than a hurried greeting before he pulled on an apron and slid behind the upstairs counter to man the till. And when Cat did return, she nodded hello to Adam and headed back downstairs without a word to Sadie.

By mid-afternoon, Adam's curiosity was obvious.

'Have you and Cat had an argument?' he asked Sadie in a low voice.

She paused, then continued filling the gaps on the shelves left by the lunchtime shoppers. 'No. Why?'

He shrugged. 'It's just I've never known you to go more than an hour or so without speaking and you haven't exchanged a single word all afternoon.'

Sadie tried not to look guilty. 'Oh. Well, we're just busy.'

'Really?' Adam frowned. 'But she hasn't come up here, you haven't gone down to the basement and you haven't stopped frowning. It's like the stairs are some kind of no-man's-land between two unfriendly camps.'

She should have known he'd pick up on the chilly atmosphere, Sadie realised as she cringed a little inside. Now what was she supposed to do? She could hardly admit what the argument had been about – not when Adam had played such a prominent part in it. Now she'd have to do one of the things she'd objected to that morning – tell a lie. 'Just a slight business disagreement,' she said, making a special effort to relax her frown muscles. 'We'll get over it.'

'I see,' he said, nodding thoughtfully as he tapped at the screen of the till. A few minutes later, he cleared his throat. 'I'm dying of thirst – fancy a cup of tea?'

Sadie smiled. 'I'd love one.'

Adam threw her a regretful look. 'The thing is, the till software has just crashed and I need to reboot it. So, would you mind making it?'

She couldn't help laughing. The kettle was in the basement kitchen, which meant she'd have to talk to Cat. 'Been a United Nations peace envoy for long?' she called to Adam in a dry voice as she headed for the stairs.

'For about ninety seconds,' he replied, flashing her a grin. 'Don't hurry back.'

Cat was wiping down the work surfaces when Sadie reached the bottom step. She took a deep breath. 'I'm making tea if you want a cup.'

For a moment, she thought Cat would refuse. But then she looked up and nodded. 'Okay.'

Sadie set about making the tea, wondering how to break the awkward silence that had re-formed after Cat's single-word answer. But as she reached for the fridge door, Cat placed a hand on her arm.

'I'm sorry.'

All the tension Sadie hadn't even realised she'd been carrying whooshed out of her as she turned around. 'And I'm sorry too. I know you're only trying to help.'

'I'm just not very good at it,' Cat said, with a wry smile. She spread her arms wide. 'Shall we hug it out then?'

After a few moments, they separated. Anxious to avoid the subject that had caused them to fall out in the first place, Sadie racked her brain for a neutral topic of conversation. 'So, where are you and Seb going tonight?'

'A new restaurant down by the canal,' Cat replied. 'Seb's heard good things about their cocktails and he wants to check it out.'

Sadie nodded, unsurprised. She knew Seb liked to keep a sharp eye on the competition around Chester. Not that he really had anything to worry about; Castle Court was one of the most coveted foodie locations in the city and Seb's was always busy. But Sadie knew that he'd been a sought-after mixologist before settling in Chester and he hadn't got to the top of his game by sitting back and relaxing.

'How about you?' she asked Cat, raising her eyebrows. 'Are you going to have your professional chef's hat on?'

Cat laughed. 'Nope. I'm there strictly for the cocktails. Besides, Seb says the restaurant owner is mates with our friend Greg and, if that's true, I wouldn't be surprised if my food got a little extra something added to it on its way out of the kitchen.'

'You might be pleasantly surprised,' Sadie said. 'He might not be in Greg's camp.'

Cat tipped her head. 'Of course. But I think I'll test the waters first, where I can see exactly what's going into my drinks, and save the food for another time.'

Adam kept his face entirely straight when Sadie re-emerged from the stairs, ten minutes later. 'Thanks,' he said as she handed him a steaming mug of tea. His hazel eyes crinkled at the edges. 'Has goodwill been restored?'

'It has,' Sadie admitted with a grudging smile. 'Thank you.'

He sipped at his drink. 'Don't thank me. Thank tea.'

She smiled. 'But it was your idea.'

'You'd have got there eventually,' Adam said. 'I just hurried the process along, for the good of the whole hive.'

Sadie stared at him. 'Sorry?'

'In a beehive, every bee works for the good of their community,' Adam explained. 'It's in their interests to keep things running smoothly. The worker bees actually work themselves to death for the benefit of the many.'

Sadie felt the penny drop. She'd almost forgotten Adam was a keen beekeeper. Being winter, it had been ages since he'd had any honey to sell to the businesses of Castle Court, which was probably why Sadie had taken a few seconds to understand his reference.

'No need for the workers to go that far here,' she said cheerfully. 'Although I am grateful you're staying on to help with the hen party tonight.'

Adam waved her gratitude away. 'No problem. I couldn't leave you on your own.' He flexed his fingers. 'Besides, I've been itching to have a go at this icing business. I could be an undiscovered genius.'

'You could be,' Sadie said, with an amused look. 'I'll teach you everything I know.'

His eyes were steady as he gazed at her. 'I think I'd like that.'

And the image of a warm country pub popped unbidden into Sadie's head.

Chapter Twelve

It was clear from the moment they walked through the door that the hen party was going to be a handful. Sadie had assumed that Smart Cookies would be the starting point of their evening, but judging from the gentle swaying of at least one of them, they'd spent some time celebrating already. There was a definite aroma of juniper berry on the breath of the thirty-something, expensively dressed blonde who seemed to be in charge.

'Sorry we're a bit late,' she said to Sadie, the words very slightly slurred. 'We got held up in the last pub. People kept buying us drinks.'

Sadie glanced around at the hens, making sure none of them seemed too much the worse for wear. The bride was easily identifiable – she wore a white sash with 'Bride To Be' emblazoned across it in hot-pink letters. There were two older women, who Sadie assumed to be the bride's mother and future mother-in-law; one was looking around the shop with open interest and the other had her gaze firmly fixed upon Adam. But she had definite competition from some of the younger hens, who had also noticed him. Sadie swallowed a sigh and summoned up a professional smile. It was going to be a long two hours.

'Not to worry,' she told the woman before her. 'If you give Adam your coats, I'll take you downstairs and we'll get you all settled in.'

'I'd like to give him more than just my coat,' a dark-haired woman said, peeling off her plum-coloured jacket with a flirtatious smile. 'How about it, Adam?'

He coughed and glanced across at Sadie, his face flaming and apprehension in his eyes. 'I – er—'

'I'm afraid Adam's off the menu, ladies,' Sadie called. 'But don't worry, we've got plenty of other fun in store for you.'

The dark-haired woman winked. 'We'll just see about that.'

Adam managed an awkward grin as the rest of the hens handed over their coats and made increasingly lewd comments. When they were all ready, Sadie headed for the stairs.

Adam gripped her arm as she passed. 'Don't leave me alone with them, okay?'

Sadie looked up at him. His cheeks were still glowing with embarrassment and she knew he was only half joking. A shriek of laughter went up from the group and Sadie turned around to see the bride-to-be was grappling with an inflatable man. The nearest table display wobbled alarmingly. 'Believe me, I won't,' she told Adam grimly.

Once they were all downstairs and seated around the tables, Sadie handed out crisp white aprons and stickers for their names. She discovered the bride was called Elle, her mother was Lois and the dark-haired woman who'd taken a shine to Adam was called Melinda. Mr Inflatable was given a sticker that declared his name to be Roger and Sadie had a sinking suspicion he was going to end the event covered in sticky icing.

She summoned up a brisk smile. 'Now, before we get started, would anyone like a hot drink? We can offer you tea, coffee or hot chocolate."

The chief bridesmaid, whose name was Kate, frowned. 'I thought there was going to be fizz. I'm sure it said Prosecco on the website.'

So much for sobering them up, Sadie thought. 'Of course,' she said. 'I'm just giving you all the options. Adam, would you mind?'

He vanished into the kitchen and Sadie heard the clink of glasses. A moment later there was the unmistakable sound of a cork popping from a bottle.

'Sounds like someone's getting excited,' Melinda said, craning her neck to see into the kitchen. 'Do let me know if you need a hand, Adam.'

Sadie cleared her throat and took a seat at the head of the table. 'As you'll see, there are a lot of different colours of icing for us to use today. Each biscuit will need two different types – one to create the shape of the design and the other to fill it in.' She reached into the box on the table in front of her and handed round the first biscuit. It was a simple square. 'This one is going to be an L-plate for our bride-to-be.' She picked up a bag of white line icing and laid a square around the outside, with an exaggerated L in the centre, explaining the best technique as she went. 'Now it's your turn,' she said.

The noise level dropped as each hen copied what Sadie had done. She breathed a silent sigh of relief; maybe it wasn't going to be as raucous as it had first seemed.

'Now we'll leave that to dry for a minute or two and move onto our next biscuit – a celebration of the bride- and groom-to-be.'

This time, she laid out a circle and iced lacy swirls around the outside.

'If that's as easy as you make it look, then I could make you some of these as wedding favours,' Lois told her daughter.

'You'll soon get the hang of it,' Sadie said encouragingly, as Adam placed a glass of Prosecco in front of each guest.

Once the lacy circles had their outlines in place, Sadie showed the hens how to fill in their L-plate design with fuchsia flood icing. Only Melinda seemed uninterested; more than once, Sadie saw her glance across at Adam. Her glass was soon empty and she lifted it up and waggled it to catch his attention. 'How about a top-up?'

Adam's gaze flickered towards Sadie, who gave a tiny nod. The last thing she needed was for Melinda to cause a scene and spoil things for everyone else.

After the circles had been filled, Sadie lifted up a bag of red icing with the tiniest of holes snipped in the end. 'Now we'll add the initials of the bride and groom. The alphabet can be a bit tricky so you might like to practise on the greaseproof paper in front of you.'

She was not surprised to see Melinda writing her own name next to Adam's. 'See?' the dark-haired woman said. 'We make a cute couple.'

He managed an awkward, non-committal smile. This would be the last time he ever volunteered to work late, Sadie thought wryly, and who could blame him? There might not be any malice in Melinda's unsubtle attempts at flirting, but it was clearly making Adam uncomfortable.

Sadie was relieved to arrive at the last biscuit – a gingerbread self-portrait of each hen in her wedding finery.

Melinda turned her attention to Roger. 'You know, it strikes me that you're a bit lacking in the trouser department,' she said, reaching for a bag of pale pink line icing. 'Why don't I see if I can help you with that?'

'I really wouldn't if I were you,' Sadie said. 'The icing on our biscuits is going to be baked in the oven to dry it out. We can't do that for Roger – he'd melt.'

Melinda looked up, the tip of the bag hovering over the doll's plastic skin. 'Haven't you got a hairdryer?'

'I'm afraid not,' Sadie replied. 'We've never actually needed one before.'

'Then we'll leave it wet,' Melinda said, her eyes narrowing.

Sadie shrugged. 'It's up to you. He'll be a bit sticky by the end of the night.'

'Nothing wrong with that,' Melinda said. She glanced at

her fellow hens. 'What do you think – shall I give Roger a great big—'

'It's a stupid idea, Melinda,' Elle cut in. 'No one wants to get covered in icing.'

'We could always make you lick it off,' Melinda replied, clearly unwilling to give up on her idea. 'What's a hen do without a bit of fun?'

Lois tutted. 'Honestly, you're sex mad. No one is licking anything off anyone. Put Roger down and finish icing your biscuit.'

Once the last gingerbread hen was ready, Sadie and Adam loaded all the biscuits onto baking trays and put them into the oven to dry. Adam topped up the Prosecco and brought out the canapés Cat had made before she left, while Sadie offered to take some photos of the hen party. Melinda tried to drag Adam into one of the shots, but he excused himself to check on the biscuits.

'She's certainly determined,' Sadie murmured as Adam hurried past her for the safety of the kitchen.

He flashed her a pained look. 'That's one way of describing her.'

At last it was time for the hens to leave. Sadie packed their biscuits carefully into their souvenir tins, silently wondering how many would survive the evening ahead, and gave Elle a personalised memento bearing her name and the name of her husband-to-be.

Melinda kept darting little looks at Adam and made one last attempt to flirt, inviting him to join them on the next leg of their adventures.

'You could be an honorary hen,' she said, threading her arm through his. 'Or better still, you could be our magnificent co—'

Adam shook himself free and stepped back, his expression alarmed. 'No, thanks.'

'I'm afraid Adam and I still have work to do,' Sadie said, keeping her tone light to disguise her mounting irritation.

Melinda's eyes widened as she gazed back and forth between Adam and Sadie. 'Oh, you're a couple? I didn't realise.'

'No, that's not—' Adam began, but Sadie saw the chance to shut Melinda down and cut him off.

'Well, we don't like to advertise it,' she said, patting Adam's hand. 'And we never mix business with pleasure.'

Melinda leaned in closer and Sadie caught the stale whiff of alcohol on her breath. 'I would,' she said in a low voice. 'I'd mix them all the time if it was with him.'

There was absolutely nothing Sadie could say that wouldn't cause her and Adam to burn with embarrassment, so she summoned up what she hoped was a conspiratorial smile. 'Have a good evening, Melinda.'

It wasn't until the sign was turned to Closed and the door was firmly locked that Sadie allowed herself a long, heartfelt sigh of relief.

'Well,' she said, leaning against the glass door and staring at Adam. 'That happened.'

Adam ran a hand over his face and gave a shaky laugh. 'Did you have any idea they'd be so ...'

'Rude?' Sadie said.

'I was going to say drunk, but rude works too.'

Sadie shook her head. 'No. I assumed that the kind of women who booked an icing class for a hen do might be a tiny bit classier.' She paused. 'And, to be fair, most of them were. Thankfully.'

He gave her a cautious look. 'Do you think you'll be doing more parties like that?'

'Don't worry, I won't ask you to work if we do,' Sadie said, pulling a sympathetic face. 'Come on, let's get the cleaning done and get out of here.'

They worked side by side, washing up the glasses and discarding the leftover icing. Sadie wiped down the tables as Adam gathered up the empty bottles.

He held one up. 'Can you believe they got through eight of these?'

Sadie laughed. 'They drank us dry. Another lesson learned for next time – stock up on Prosecco.'

'It's a shame there's nothing left,' Adam said over his shoulder as he stacked the empties for recycling. 'I could do with a drink.'

Cat's suggestion echoed in Sadie's head. She pushed it away; the last thing Adam needed was to feel obliged to hang out with his boss after work. 'Sorry. I wish we did have some Prosecco, or anything alcoholic. I probably owe you at least one drink.'

'Don't be daft, you did nothing wrong,' he said. 'You were great, in fact – really patient. They seemed to have a good time, apart from Melinda, and I really think she was at the wrong hen party. She expected a naked butler or Magic Mike to materialise from the kitchen.'

And that presented Sadie with a mental image that was much harder to push away: the thought of a partially clad Adam glistening with baby oil. She blinked hard and hoped she didn't look as flustered as she felt. 'As long as she doesn't leave a bad review online . . .'

It was just after nine o'clock by the time they'd finished clearing up and the long day suddenly caught up with Sadie. She yawned. A second later Adam was yawning too.

'Definitely time to call it a day,' she said as they grinned at each other.

As Sadie had predicted, the traffic out of the city was quiet. She and Adam chatted in the same way as they always did, but Sadie found her gaze was drawn to the welcoming glow of the Cheshire Cat pub at the side of the road. If only she could turn into the car park and go inside; there would be a roaring fire on a cold February night like this and, if she was lucky, there might even be a pair of battered leather armchairs free beside it.

She must have slowed the car without realising because Adam stopped talking and gave her a questioning look. 'I'm up for it if you are.'

Sadie glanced at the dashboard clock: 9.17. Lissy would have been asleep for a couple of hours and Daniel would most likely be snoring in front of the TV. There was nothing to hurry home for – she could easily steal half an hour to spend with Adam. It was so tempting . . .

Reluctantly, she shook her head and put gentle pressure onto the accelerator pedal. 'I can't. Sorry.'

Adam's smile was crooked. 'I understand.'

It felt as though the air hummed with things left unsaid. She still remembered the way he'd looked when she'd first told him, stumbling over words that felt stiff and all wrong, that she and Daniel were going to give things another go; he had been quiet then too, but his eyes had been filled with hurt and frustration. This silence was busier, almost super-charged, and Sadie was both relieved and disappointed to pull up outside Adam's cottage on the edge of Waverton Farm.

'Night, then,' Adam said as he got out of the car. 'See you tomorrow.'

'Goodnight,' Sadie said. 'Thanks again.'

He made his way up the path. Fighting a sudden urge to call after him, Sadie didn't wait until he'd gone in before she turned the car towards home. Asleep or not, Daniel would be waiting for her. Daniel and Lissy. Her family.

Chapter Thirteen

Cat couldn't sleep. She lay awake for a few minutes, listening to Seb's slow, deep breathing and trying not to move; there was no need for both of them to be up at 3.16 a.m., after all. Not without a good reason. And Cat had no reason to be awake – her early morning baking routine at Smart Cookies meant that she was often yawning by ten p.m. and she'd been tired enough when she and Seb had made their way back from the restaurant by the canal just before eleven.

The restaurant itself wasn't the problem; in spite of her misgivings, it had turned out to be a pleasant but uneventful visit. She was growing used to the fact that Seb was something of a local celebrity – they seemed to run into fans everywhere they went and these fans were often female. Cat didn't mind the fluttering eyelashes and obvious flirtation while Seb was behind the bar – it was all part of his role – but she did find it grating when they were on a date and his admirers acted as though she wasn't there. Tonight had been a perfect example and although Seb's manner had been friendly but discouraging, one or two women had continued to glance over and whisper to each other, causing Cat to wryly ask Seb whether he thought he'd be safe while she popped to the ladies'.

None of that was the reason for her insomnia, Cat decided, as she stared up at Seb's shadowy bedroom ceiling. Swallowing a restless sigh, she slid her feet out of bed. Maybe a mug of warm milk would help.

The kitchen of Seb's garret flat, tucked away in the roof of Castle Court, was tiny. Cat had no idea how he managed to cook in it.

'It's got everything I need,' he'd insisted, the first time Cat had expressed her doubts about his ability to produce anything more challenging than toast. 'Small but mighty.'

She warmed some milk and carried it into the cramped living room, where a small leaded window with an abundance of cushions on the built-in seat gave her a bird's-eye view of the Court.

Up above, the sky looked ink-black, but after a few minutes of gazing at it she saw there was actually a beautiful deep indigo-blue hiding behind the darkness. It was dotted with stars and she could imagine the icy coldness outside – it would be another sub-zero morning, Cat decided as she pulled Seb's fleecy dressing gown closer against her neck, and she'd be up while the frost was still thick, to make sure there were plenty of biscuits for the day's orders.

Briefly, it occurred to her to wonder how the hen party

had been. She was certain that Sadie would have taken good care of them, no matter how raucous they might have become once the Prosecco began to flow. And maybe spending more time with Adam would encourage her to see that rekindling her relationship with Daniel wasn't the right thing for either of them, no matter how much she thought it was what Lissy needed. Cat had watched her best friend bloom as they'd worked to get Smart Cookies off the ground; she didn't want that new-found confidence to ebb away. And unless Daniel had completely changed his spots, there was a very real chance that he would want Sadie to go back to who she'd been when they were together: a quieter, less self-assured version of herself. A wife who put the needs and wishes of her family well above her own.

Cat drew her knees towards her chin and burrowed her toes beneath the cushions, sipping at her milk thoughtfully. It wasn't that Sadie had shown any signs of being less committed at work, more that there was already pressure on her from Daniel to make room for him. Which meant that Sadie had less time to ice the biscuits they needed for stock, and she was relying more and more on Clare to help. That wasn't a problem at the moment, but it would be if either of them fell ill or – disaster – Clare decided to leave. If there was one thing Cat had learned from working sixteen-hour days as a chef, it was never to rely too heavily on her staff. She always had a back-up plan. Maybe it was time to look at expanding the Smart Cookies staff further. And maybe that meant finding someone to help with the baking too – she couldn't afford to burn out here the way she had in Paris. Then she'd been able to hand in her notice and regroup, but running a business with Sadie was different. They'd both invested a lot of money to get Smart Cookies off the ground – there was a lot at stake. Additional staff meant more outlay but would hopefully pay dividends as the business grew.

Cat rubbed her forehead wearily. In some ways it had been easier running a kitchen, even one that was chasing its third Michelin star, although she hadn't been her own boss. Now the weight of her responsibilities felt much more personal; there was more to lose than professional pride. Accepting that she and Sadie couldn't do it all themselves was a step towards ensuring their dreams succeeded.

The gentle shuffle of footsteps made Cat tear her gaze away from the starry sky, just as the bedroom door swung back and Seb appeared. He looked adorably sleep-rumpled as he stared at her.

'What's going on?'

'Sorry – did I wake you up? I tried to be quiet, but I couldn't sleep, so I decided to try some warm milk.'

He rubbed his stubble-covered chin. 'Is it working?'

Cat pulled a face. 'Not exactly.'

'Then come back to bed,' he said. 'I know a much better way to make you sleepy.'

She couldn't help smiling at his rakish eyebrow waggle. 'Oh? And what's that?'

Seb shook his head. 'I can only show you once we're in bed.'

Setting her half-drunk mug of milk aside, Cat padded over

to him and planted a soft kiss on his lips. 'I can't imagine what you've got in mind.'

'Like I said, I can only prove my point in bed.' He waved towards the crumpled sheets. 'After you.'

Feeling more awake than ever, Cat went back into the bedroom and slid beneath the still-warm covers.

'Lie on your back,' he instructed her once he had joined her. 'And close your eyes.'

She did as she was told, savouring the small thrill of antici-pation that shot through her. Any minor niggles she had with Seb's behaviour in public always melted away once they were in bed. She heard him shift on the mattress and tensed, wait-ing for his touch. But it wasn't a kiss or an intimate caress; with a gentle stroke so light that it felt like a feather, he ran his finger down the length of her nose.

Cat opened her eyes to give him a questioning look.

'Keep them closed,' he said, his voice low but firm. 'Just go with it.'

It took her a few seconds to adjust, but once she had, the sensation was strangely soothing. With each slow, silent sweep, more and more tension slipped away until her limbs grew simultaneously heavy and weightless. She stirred a little as Seb nestled against her side, but he didn't stop stroking and she gave a small, contented sigh as sleep came. And then she knew nothing at all.

'I've had an idea,' Cat announced when Sadie arrived at Smart Cookies the following morning.

'Oh?' her friend said, giving her a wary look. 'Am I going to like it?'

'Maybe not right away,' Cat admitted. 'But that doesn't mean it's not good.'

Sadie sat down at the central worktop in the kitchen. 'Go on, then. Let's hear it.'

Cat explained her thoughts from the previous night.

'It is a good idea,' Sadie said, once she'd finished. 'And we could certainly use the help. But can we afford it?'

'I've done a few sums and if the business continues to grow then I think we can afford to take on one new full-timer.'

Her best friend grimaced. 'But what if it doesn't? I don't know, Cat, it's a bit of a risk. Can't we leave things as they are for a while longer? Clare and Adam are both hard-working and enthusiastic – can't we get by with just them for now?'

'We could,' Cat said. 'But I think we need to plan for the future. What happens if more orders start coming in? Have we got the capacity to increase production – without killing ourselves, I mean?'

'No.'

'Or what happens if one of us falls ill?' Cat went on. 'Even a bad cold could cause problems with our levels of production – we might not be able to meet demand. It's a disaster waiting to happen, and we need to make sure we're ready.'

Sadie stared at her with an expression of amusement mingled with doubt. 'I thought I was supposed to be the arty, overdramatic one?'

'I'm a chef,' Cat replied with a shrug. 'I can be highly

strung too. Seriously, though – we need to think about this now. Not when it's too late.'

'Okay,' Sadie conceded. 'What did you have in mind?'

Cat hesitated, marshalling her thoughts. She had to approach this in the right way. 'Well, I wondered if maybe Adam might be interested in expanding his skills.'

Sadie let out a wry laugh. 'He got a similar offer last night.'

Cat raised her eyebrows. 'Really? Only one?'

Sadie explained how the hen party had been, complete with a full rundown of Adam's embarrassment at Melinda's blatant ogling. 'So, I don't imagine he'll be up for helping out at any more evening classes,' she finished.

'No, I can imagine,' Cat said. 'But actually, what I was wondering is whether he'd be interested in learning the production side of things – baking the biscuits and icing them.'

'Oh!' Sadie looked astonished, then doubtful. 'Are you sure you'd trust him to follow the recipe? You're notoriously bad at delegating anything to do with cooking.'

'Not true,' Cat said, picturing Seb's galley kitchen. 'Chefs delegate all the time. And obviously I wouldn't just hand Adam the recipe and tell him to get on with it, any more than you'd give him a bag of icing and expect him to produce Instagram-worthy results. He'd need some training first, in the same way that we trained Clare.'

Sadie's eyes became thoughtful, then narrowed slightly. 'Is this another way for you to try and push me and Adam together? Because if it is—'

Underneath the table, Cat crossed her fingers. 'No, of

course not. I just thought a bit of on-the-job training might be useful. And that would mean we could recruit another sales assistant to take his place on the shop floor. What do you think?'

'He did say he was itching to have a go at icing. But he might have been joking – we'd have to check.'

Cat studied her. 'But in theory, you're happy?'

There was a brief silence, then Sadie tipped her head. 'Yes. In theory.'

'Great,' Cat said, mentally patting herself on the back for handling a tricky negotiation well. 'Do you want to ask him, or shall I?'

'I will,' Sadie said. 'After the relentless Melinda, he'll probably jump at the chance to hide out in the basement for a while.'

'Well, then,' Cat replied, observing the hint of a blush as Sadie spoke, 'everyone will be happy.'

Cat insisted that Sadie take Adam out for a coffee away from Castle Court to discuss his suggested change in role.

'Neutral ground is better all round,' she said firmly, when Sadie tried to argue. 'There's nowhere to chat in private here, anyway – not when the shop is open. Go and try that new café up by the cathedral.'

She waved her friend off and settled into making a new chocolate dough for a batch of Notre Dame biscuits. She had to hand it to Sadie – when it came to biscuit design, she had a talent for knowing what the biscuit-buying public wanted.

The City of Love collection was selling like proverbial hot cakes and there were still five days to go until Valentine's Day, when they could expect a flurry of last-minute sales from desperate husbands and boyfriends. And Cat had every reason to expect the Parisian-themed collection to keep on selling throughout the spring and summer – it might be *La Ville d'Amour*, but its appeal was timeless, after all.

She barely registered the arrival of the postman upstairs. His deep, cheery voice bounced down towards the basement as he exchanged a few words with Clare, but Cat was concentrating on ensuring the chocolate biscuits didn't burn in the oven; their rich brown colour made it much harder to see when they were ready and even a minute too long might ruin the whole batch. It wasn't until Sadie and Adam returned, both with pink cheeks that Cat suspected had little to do with the cold air outside, that she thought to collect the envelopes from underneath the till upstairs.

'So?' she asked Sadie in a low voice once they were downstairs. 'What did Adam say?'

'He said he'd be delighted,' Sadie said. 'But he also reminded me that this was only meant to be a temporary job – when the weather gets warmer, he'll need to spend more time gardening.'

'But by the winter, when his gardening work has dried up, he'll be ready to come back here again – just when we're building up to the Christmas rush,' Cat replied. 'So, I think it's worth finding out whether or not he's got the talent now, don't you?'

'Of course he's got the talent,' Sadie said, a faint hint of indignation in her voice.

Cat hid a smile. 'Let's see how we get on,' she said, flicking through the envelopes the postman had left. They were mostly bills or junk mail, but a French postmark on one caught her eye. It was addressed to her.

'What is it?' Sadie asked, noticing her puzzled expression.

'No idea,' Cat said, turning the letter over and ripping it open.

A flood of disbelief washed over her when she saw the letterhead: *Martin et Moreau*. The lawyers of her old employer, François de Beauvoir. She scanned the contents and let out a shaky snort.

'You have got to be kidding me.'

'What?' Sadie said in alarm.

Cat read the letter once more, trying to ignore a sense of mounting apprehension and anger. 'It's a letter of intent from François de Beauvoir. He says he's suing me for breaching the non-disclosure agreement I signed when I left La Perle.'

Chapter Fourteen

Sadie turned pale. 'Suing you? But you haven't breached the agreement. Have you?'

Cat lifted up the letter. 'No, but according to this, I described the details behind the curtailment of my employment on 2 December in a public place to a crowd of over a hundred people.'

'December?' Sadie repeated. 'But that was when you had that showdown with Greg outside the shop. How could François know about that?'

Cat stared at Sadie and a sick, acidic feeling rose up in her stomach. 'Greg told him,' she said. 'They're great friends, remember? That's the whole reason Greg had it in for me.'

'But you didn't describe the details,' Sadie said, shaking her head. 'In fact, you conspicuously avoided mentioning any names or what actually happened. François doesn't have a leg to stand on.'

'I don't suppose François is especially concerned with the

facts of the case,' Cat said, rubbing her forehead. 'He'll be going on what Greg has told him, and who knows how much that poisonous toad has twisted the truth? I've got a good mind to march over there and ask him what the bloody hell he thinks he's playing at.'

'Don't,' Sadie said. 'Let's sit down and think this through. Why don't I make us some tea?'

'It's going to take more than tea to sort this out,' Cat grumbled.

'Of course it is,' Sadie replied soothingly. 'But one step at a time, right?'

Cat read through the letter again. It demanded her attendance at a contract breach hearing on 13 February at the lawyers' offices in Paris, where she would be able to put forward any counter-evidence she might have.

What kind of evidence could she give? Cat wondered; it was going to be her word against Greg's. Unless—

'Don't worry about tea,' she told Sadie, reaching for her coat. 'I'll have some when I get back.'

Sadie stopped, kettle in hand. 'Where are you going?'

'Evidence gathering,' Cat said with a small, grim smile.

Outside, Castle Court was quiet. The temperature had barely risen above zero and Cat gave a tiny shiver as she paused beneath the blue and gold Smart Cookies awning, considering which shopkeeper to visit first. They'd all been there for her run-in with Greg, had all witnessed his aggressive, malicious treatment and taken her side. Or at least most of them had – Cherie had disliked Sadie and Cat from the moment they'd arrived at Castle Court and it had come as no surprise that she'd backed Greg up. Afterwards, when her fellow business owners had made their disgust known, Cherie had seemed to regret her actions, but she'd made no apology and Cat hadn't sought one. She tried to avoid any contact with the older woman, which was a shame, because her cakes were really rather good.

Cat's gaze came to rest on the orange and green sign above Let's Go Dutch. The pancake house didn't appear to be too busy – the lunchtime rush hadn't started to build yet. Would Jaren have time to talk to her now? Or should she try Andrew and Earl at the Bus Stop diner? She hoped they'd want to help too. She glanced around at the shops, frowning thoughtfully. No, she'd start with Elin the chocolatier; if nothing else, the heavenly scent of the shop would lift her mood.

She was a little surprised to find Seb there, leaning against one of the glass-fronted counters and chatting to Elin. Both looked up as she walked in.

'Hey,' Seb said, crossing the floor to kiss her. 'This is an unexpected treat.'

'It is,' Cat agreed, 'although it's actually Elin I've come to see. But it's good that you're here – I'm going to need your help too.'

Elin raised a cool, blonde eyebrow. 'Help? What with?'

Cat pulled the letter from her coat pocket. 'This.'

Seb and Elin huddled together to read it at the same time. Once they'd finished, Seb looked ready to punch something.

'That *doos*,' he spat, his South African accent growing suddenly more pronounced. 'Why can't he leave you alone?'

Elin gave Cat a sympathetic look. 'Because she stood up to him. I've never met François but I recognise the type – they think being rich and important gives them the right to do anything. And they hate not getting what they want.'

'She's right,' Cat said. 'With the added complication that I embarrassed him. His father, Robert, is the real power behind La Perle – he must have known how François was behaving.'

'Maybe he's the same,' Elin suggested. 'The apple sometimes doesn't fall far from the tree.'

Cat thought about that. There'd been rumours about François that she'd heard long before she'd started working for him – the catering industry was relatively small and gossip spread fast, especially about those at the top. But there had never been an outright accusation until hers. Now, of course, she knew why; the women he'd harassed had all been paid off and silenced, the same way she had. In some cases, it had probably cost them their careers. Elin was right – it wasn't much of a stretch to imagine Robert de Beauvoir was a sexual predator, just like his son.

'Maybe,' Cat said out loud. 'I only met him once or twice.'

'So, what are you going to do?' Seb asked. 'Apart from giving François the slap he deserves?'

Cat took a deep breath. 'That's why I'm here. As you'll have seen, I need to go to the meeting next week and submit my counter-evidence. And since all François has is Greg's version of events, I thought that perhaps if you all gave your version, I might be able to use that to disprove the case.'

'Of course,' Elin said immediately. 'Whatever I can do to help.'

Seb slipped an arm around Cat's shoulders. 'We'll get through this. Don't worry.'

She smiled. 'Thank you.'

Elin was studying the letter again. 'I hope you've got a good lawyer of your own, Cat. I have a feeling you're going to need one.'

'I'll use the same firm who negotiated the original settlement,' Cat replied. 'At least they'll be familiar with the case.'

'Just tell us what you need us to do,' Seb said. 'And if you need someone to do the slapping for you, I'll be happy to oblige.'

Cat shook her head. 'Tempting, but if anyone is going to hit François, it'll be me. Right after I've cut him down to size legally.'

Seb grinned. 'Attagirl. I'll hold your coat.'

Cat resisted the temptation to glare through the window of Patisserie Cherie and kept her gaze fixed resolutely ahead of her as she crossed the Court. She had no idea whether Cherie would be aware that Greg had tossed another grenade into her life, but she had no interest in finding out.

Jaren was behind the bar of Let's Go Dutch. He smiled and waved a hand when he saw her in the doorway, and Cat was struck once again by how good-looking he was; his dark hair was tumbling across his forehead in unruly curls and she could almost imagine him scowling from the pages of a glossy magazine in some perfume advert. Except that she wasn't sure she'd ever seen him scowl – he was more likely to offer up a wide, laid-back smile, no matter what the situation.

'Hey,' he said as Cat wove her way between the tables. 'Have you come for an early lunch?'

'I wish,' Cat said regretfully, glancing at the Specials menu behind the bar. 'No, it's you I've come to see. Is now a good time?'

Jaren glanced at his watch and pulled a face. 'Not really – I'm a staff member down today and the lunchtime rush is about to start. But I should be free later if that's any good?'

'Great,' Cat said. 'I don't need long.'

He spread his hands. 'I've got the evening off. As long as no one else calls in sick.'

'Shall I drop by once the shop closes? Around 6 p.m.?'

'Perfect,' he said, flashing her a lightning smile. 'Maybe we can grab a coffee or something.'

Cat returned the smile. 'I'd like that. See you later.'

Her final call was to the Bus Stop diner. She stepped through the double doors just to the right of the bright yellow bonnet and asked for Andrew or Earl.

'Hi Cat,' Earl said, beaming at her as he came nearer. 'Andrew's out saving a galaxy far, far away, but I'm here. What can I do for ya?'

Cat couldn't help grinning. Earl and Andrew were New Yorkers with exactly the same sense of humour; they were so funny that she and Sadie often remarked that they should have their own sitcom. But her smile faded away when she remembered why she was there. 'I need your help,' she said.

Earl fired an appraising look her way and gestured behind him. 'Sure – we can go and talk in the office. Can I get you a drink – tea, coffee, Banana Boozle milkshake?'

Cat shook her head. 'No, I'm fine, thanks. Although I might take you up on that milkshake another time.'

She waited until they were seated in the office before explaining her situation to Earl. When she'd finished talking, he sat back, a thunderous expression on his face.

'Of course we'll support you. We'll even have a quiet word or two with that weasel Greg, if you want us to.'

'Thanks, but the less he knows about what's going on, the better,' Cat said. 'I don't want to give him any more ammunition to pass on to François.'

Earl grunted. 'I suppose you're right. I can't believe how unlucky you've been, running into someone who'd go bleating back to the guy who harassed you.' He gave her a crooked smile. 'Of all the food courts in all the world, you had to open a shop in this one.'

'Tell me about it,' Cat sighed. 'Then again, François knows a lot of people. It was inevitable that I'd run into one of his cronies sooner or later.'

'Greg is an ass,' Earl said, dismissively. 'He and this François dude are welcome to each other. Just let us know what you need us to do – we'll happily tell this bozo what really happened in December.'

'Thanks,' Cat said, patting his arm. 'I really appreciate that.'

*

Sadie looked as though she might explode with impatience when Cat arrived back at Smart Cookies twenty minutes later.

'I was starting to get worried,' she said, giving her an exasperated look. 'Is everything okay?'

'Fine,' Cat said. 'I went to see whether I could count on Elin, Jaren and the Bus Stop boys to support me against François.'

'And?'

'Elin and Earl are on board. I'm catching up with Jaren later.'

Sadie smiled. 'Of course they want to help. No one likes a bully.'

'It does still mean at least one trip to Paris,' Cat said, frowning. 'I expect I can get away with instructing my lawyer over the phone – any witness statements I get can be emailed across to her. But I'll have to go to the meeting.'

'I'll come with you,' Sadie said instantly.

'You can't,' Cat objected. 'I need you to keep things running here. And I doubt Seb will be able to get away – the meeting is the day before Valentine's Day. The bar will be packed.'

Her best friend's shoulders sagged. 'But you can't go on your own.'

'I'll have to,' Cat said. 'Don't worry, I'll make sure we've got more than enough stock before I go. In fact, now might be the perfect time to teach Adam the recipes, just in case I get held up on my way back.'

Sadie nodded. 'That reminds me – we've just had a last-minute order for wedding favours. The bride's supplier has let her down and she needs two hundred personalised heart-shaped biscuits by – you guessed it – Valentine's Day.'

Cat let out a frustrated groan. 'Of course she does. Have you said yes?'

Sadie pulled a face. 'I haven't said no, although it's going to be a tall order to get them finished in four days, especially since you'll be away. The trouble is, she's no ordinary bride – it's Charlotte Dennis.'

The name tugged at Cat's memory. 'The one who's marrying the footballer?'

'That's the one – the wedding is going to be featured in *Hello!* and everything. And I thought it might be good PR, but we don't have to do it.'

'Are you crazy?' Cat said, widening her eyes. 'Of course we do. It's a great opportunity. We'll cope somehow.'

'I thought you'd say that,' Sadie said, with a wry twist of her lips. 'I'll get back to Charlotte now.' She started to get up and then paused to place a hand on Cat's arm. 'Are you sure you're okay, though? This François thing must be dredging up all kinds of unwanted memories.'

Cat tilted her head. 'I'm okay. I can't say I'm looking forward to seeing François again, but I'll be well armed.' She managed a half-smile. 'I'll channel my inner Amazon warrior.'

'He won't know what's hit him,' Sadie said. 'But you're not planning on confronting Greg in the meantime, are you?'

There was more than a hint of anxiety in Sadie's eyes and Cat had to fight to control her rising anger. How dare Greg and François do this? 'Don't worry,' she reassured her friend. 'I'm keeping well away from him until this is over. But afterwards? From what Seb and Earl had to say, I think we'll have to form an orderly queue.'

Sadie pressed her lips together. 'I might even join you.' She glanced at the stairs. 'Do you want me to go and tell Adam it's time for his education to begin?'

Cat gave herself a brisk mental shake and squared her shoulders. 'Send him down. Besides, there's nothing quite like dough for pounding out your frustrations – it's cheaper than therapy. And we've got a lot of biscuits to bake.'

Chapter Fifteen

'Bloody hell, Sadie, it's like an explosion in a McVitie's factory.'

Daniel stood in the doorway of Sadie's kitchen early on Friday evening, surveying the sea of iced hearts with an incredulous gaze. 'Has anyone ever explained the concept of work–life balance to you?'

'It's a rush job for the wedding of Manchester City's star striker,' she explained, concentrating on placing a series of delicate dots around the outside of the white icing heart.

'The big time, then,' Daniel observed, sounding almost impressed.

Sadie finished icing and looked up. 'Something like that. Thanks for agreeing to have Lissy tonight.'

Daniel's blue eyes were steady. 'That's okay – you know I'm happy to step in.' He hesitated. 'You know, the kitchen at my place is a lot bigger than this.'

Sadie raised her eyebrows. 'I do know – I used to live there, remember?'

'What I mean is that if you wanted more space, you could always pack this lot up and work at my house. We could get a takeaway.'

She frowned. 'The whole point of you having Lissy is that I can get on with my work uninterrupted,' she said. 'I don't have time for a takeaway.'

'But you do have to eat,' he persisted. 'And I promise not to bother you. Come on – what do you say?'

Sadie shifted uncomfortably. It wasn't a bad idea and she might be half tempted if it wasn't for one tiny problem; she'd invited Adam round for an icing lesson. Somehow, she couldn't see Daniel being quite so keen on sharing a takeaway for three . . .

She took a deep breath. 'The thing is, one of our assistants is coming round to help out. So it wouldn't just be me and—'

'Tell her to come to the house, then,' Daniel said. 'Like I said, I'll make myself scarce.'

'That's the thing,' Sadie said, wondering if the situation could possibly get any more awkward. 'It's not a—'

The doorbell rang, cutting Sadie off mid-sentence. A hot wave of panic flooded through her; it couldn't be Adam, surely? He wasn't due for another hour.

Daniel was already moving towards the hallway. 'Don't stop. I'll get it.'

'No, it's fine . . .' she started to gabble, dropping her bag of icing and jumping to her feet. But it was too late; Daniel had reached the front door.

She heard the rumble of male voices and hoped with all

her heart that it was a delivery for one of the neighbours. But she knew from Daniel's expression when he came back into the kitchen that she was out of luck. And sure enough, behind him trailed an embarrassed-looking Adam, his beanie hat twisting in his hands.

'I'm guessing you didn't get my message,' he said, red-cheeked and mortified.

Sadie lifted her sticky hands in a helpless shrug. 'I've been busy.'

Adam glanced sideways at Daniel. 'Sorry, I should have known you'd be up to your elbows in icing. Basically, I suggested that the sooner we got started the better.'

'And here you are,' Daniel said, his tone dry. 'Keen as mustard.'

Sadie flashed him a look. The words were innocent enough and maybe he meant nothing by them. But the Daniel who'd betrayed her would never have been able to resist a snide insinuation and she wasn't convinced he'd entirely changed. 'This is Adam – the assistant I was just telling you about,' she said, keeping her voice as even as she could. 'And Adam, this is my husband, Daniel.'

She watched them shake hands, guilt nipping at her nerves. It wouldn't be so bad if she could convince herself once and for all that Adam was just an employee. But the attraction she'd felt for him before Christmas was still there; the only way she could get rid of it would be to stop seeing Adam entirely and that was impossible.

'I suppose I'd better get out of your way, then,' Daniel said.

'I wouldn't want to be responsible for ruining the wedding of the year.'

Sadie managed a weak smile. 'Thanks. Are you okay to take Lissy swimming in the morning or shall I pick her up first thing?'

Daniel's gaze flickered towards Adam. 'Could you pick her up? I need to be in the office early tomorrow.'

'Of course,' Sadie said. She waited for Daniel to head into the living room to collect Lissy from where she sat colouring, but he showed no sign of moving. 'I'll just go and get Lissy's overnight bag.'

She left the two men standing in mute awkwardness while she went to gather up Lissy and her things. It took longer than she expected, mostly because Lissy insisted on taking Travis the triceratops but had no idea where she had left him. Sadie finally found the plush cuddly toy at the very bottom of her daughter's bed and, by that time, more than five minutes had ticked by.

Grabbing Lissy's coat, she hurried into the kitchen. The little girl followed and her eyes lit up when she saw Adam.

'Hello. How are your bees?'

He smiled. 'They're fine. Still shivering, I expect.'

Lissy frowned. 'Why? Are they cold?'

'Hopefully not,' Adam said. 'The bees have one job to do in winter and that's to keep the queen safe. So, they snuggle around her and flutter their wings, which makes them shiver, and the movement keeps her warm. They all move around the hive too, so no one gets too cold, and they eat some of the honey they made when the sun was shining.'

Daniel stared at him. 'Are you a beekeeper as well as a shop assistant?'

Sadie cringed. Lissy would probably miss the emphasis on the last two words but Adam wouldn't. If he was insulted, he took it all in his stride.

'Actually, I'm a gardener who fell into beekeeping when I moved into my cottage. I'm only working at Smart Cookies while things are dormant over the winter.'

'He's been a great help,' Sadie said, feeling as though she needed to stick up for him. 'We couldn't have coped over Christmas without Adam and Clare.'

'And sometimes, Mummy and Adam take me to school in the mornings,' Lissy said, beaming up at Adam.

The silence was so sharp it could have cut glass.

'Adam lives just down the road,' Sadie said hurriedly. 'At Waverton Farm. He doesn't drive and the buses are so irregular that it makes sense to car-share sometimes.'

Daniel glanced back and forth between Adam and Sadie. 'I see.'

She didn't know what to say; if she tried to explain any further, then it might seem as though she was protesting too much. But if she said nothing, then she could force Daniel into voicing the suspicions he was almost certainly considering and that would open up an entire conversation she had no intention of having – not in front of Adam and Lissy, at least. She had no doubt that Daniel would demand to know what was going on the moment they were alone.

'And, of course, it's cost-effective,' Sadie went on, clutching at straws. 'Adam contributes petrol-wise too.'

It wasn't strictly a lie; Adam had offered to pay, but Sadie hadn't ever got round to telling him how much.

'Right,' Daniel said. 'Yeah, I can see how that might be helpful.'

Adam opened his mouth to say something, but Sadie cut him off.

'Anyway, we really ought to get to work on those biscuits. They're not going to ice themselves.'

It was a clumsy attempt to change the subject and Sadie wanted to wince from the moment the words left her mouth. But Daniel took the hint.

'We'll get out of your way. Come on, Lissy, let's go and see if Travis can triumph in his battle over Ted the T-Rex.'

Lissy nodded enthusiastically: she was dinosaur mad and didn't need much encouragement to play with her many toys. 'Of course he can, Daddy. Travis can do anything.'

He reached out to ruffle her auburn hair. 'He sounds like my kind of dinosaur. Give Mummy a kiss goodbye.'

Lissy did as she was told.

Daniel shook hands with Adam again and glanced at Sadie. 'Good luck with the order. See you in the morning.'

'Thanks,' Sadie said. 'I'll come and wave you off.'

At the door, Daniel lowered his voice as Lissy danced along the path with Travis, making growling noises as she passed the darkened bushes that lined the gravel. 'You could have told me you were expecting company.'

'Honestly, I thought you'd be long gone by the time he arrived,' Sadie replied, uncomfortably aware that was only part of the reason she hadn't said anything. 'Sorry.'

Daniel grunted. 'And you could have mentioned this whole car-sharing business too. I'm entitled to know who our daughter is spending time with.'

Annoyingly, he had a point, Sadie decided. 'Yes. I'm sorry.'

'Okay,' Daniel said. He glanced at Lissy, who was now attacking the barren branches with her dinosaur. 'Apology accepted. And I really did mean it when I wished you luck tonight.'

'Thanks,' Sadie said with a rueful sigh. 'I think we're going to need it.'

He paused for a moment, studying her carefully. 'Listen, I wanted to ask you about Valentine's Day. Do you want to do something? We could get a babysitter and go out for dinner.'

Sadie blinked. He'd never made a big deal out of Valentine's Day before – the best she'd been able to hope for was a bunch of last-on-the-shelf flowers and even those had disappeared when he'd been having his affair with Emma. This was uncharted territory and definitely a milestone in their journey back to being a couple. 'Um ... okay.'

'Great,' he said, and his relieved smile reminded Sadie of the first time he'd asked her out, all those years ago. 'I looked up a couple of nanny agencies in Chester. Why don't I see if they've got anyone who can help?'

He'd given it some thought, Sadie realised. 'Okay,' she said with more conviction. 'Although we might have left it too late.'

'Then I'll cook,' he said simply. 'I promise you won't have to lift a finger.'

And that was something else that had changed, Sadie thought. A year ago she would have insisted that Daniel didn't even know where the saucepans were kept. Living on his own had encouraged him to learn how to cook and he often made her dinner now.

Even the tips of Adam's ears were red when she came back into the kitchen. 'I dropped you in it. Sorry.'

'Of course you didn't,' Sadie said, with as much firmness as she could muster. 'Everything is fine.'

He looked unconvinced. 'But—'

Sadie took a deep calming breath. 'Adam. I said it's fine and it is. Now, can I get you a drink? I don't know about you but I could use a cup of tea.'

She could actually use something stronger, Sadie thought wistfully, but she didn't say so. She needed to remember that this evening was 100 per cent work and alcohol would only make that harder.

'Okay,' she said, once she and Adam were seated side by side at the kitchen table, two steaming mugs of tea placed a safe distance from the precious batches of biscuits. 'You must have seen me do this hundreds of times already, so I don't need to explain the principle.'

He nodded. 'So, what's the best way to do this? Given that the last time I did any art was probably at primary school.'

Sadie smiled. 'As long as you've got a steady hand, you'll be fine. But how about I do the delicate outlines and you flood the middle? Then I can pipe the names of the happy couple on top.'

'Deal,' Adam said.

They worked well together, as Sadie had known they would. Adam gave the job his full attention, his movements slow and deliberate, the way she imagined he was when he handled his bees. Once they'd filled a baking tray with delicate white hearts, Sadie got up to put them in the oven.

'That wasn't so bad,' Adam said, stretching. 'How many more have we got to go?'

'A hundred and eighty-four,' Sadie replied cheerfully. 'You're going to be sick of seeing the names Charlotte and Sonny by the time we're finished.'

'I already feel a bit like that,' he confessed. 'Isn't it weird how words start to look wrong when you see them over and over?'

Sadie laughed. 'Absolutely. I live in terror of making a mistake.' She reached for the line icing. 'Ready for round two?'

Adam took a long sip of tea and smacked his lips. 'Bring it on.'

By nine-thirty, they had seventy-five perfectly iced biscuits and three that Adam had enthusiastically over-flooded so that the icing spilled over the sides of the heart. Sadie sat back and stretched, wincing as her spine cracked. 'Ow. I think it's time to call it a night.'

He nodded. 'I never thought I'd be sick of the smell of sugar. I think I've got it up my nose.'

Sadie laughed. 'And in your beard.'

He touched his face, transferring more stickiness to the sandy blond hair that half covered his cheeks and chin. 'This stuff is worse than honey.'

'Here,' she said, dampening a sheet of kitchen roll. 'Let me.'

He stood perfectly still as she reached up and wiped the sugar from his beard and cheeks. She concentrated on the task, not daring to look up at him, hoping he couldn't hear her heart thudding.

'Thank you,' he said gravely, once she'd finished.

'My pleasure,' she murmured, wondering whether he knew how true her words were. This was why she had to keep a professional distance between them, she thought, stepping back hurriedly; the attraction she'd felt for Adam back in December was always there, simmering below the surface.

Sadie reached for a box and started to pack the finished biscuits between layers of corrugated card. 'I'm working from home tomorrow, but there'll be no time for anyone to work on these at the shop,' she said, thinking of how bustling Castle Court became on an average weekend, let alone the one before Valentine's Day. 'I think you're going to be run off your feet coping with Chester's lovers, looking for the perfect gift.'

He tilted his head. 'You're right. But I'm not doing anything tomorrow night – I don't mind coming over again if it helps.'

Sadie hesitated, wondering what Daniel would think, and whether she could trust herself to behave like an employer. Then she shook the doubts away; there was a lot riding on these wedding favours and she didn't want to disappoint the bride. One way or another, the order had to be ready. 'I'll need to put Lissy to bed first – if she knows you're here then she'll never go. And maybe you could try your hand at the more detailed stuff?'

Adam started to shake his head. 'I don't think—'

'After a quick lesson and some time to practise,' Sadie pressed on. 'You've got to learn some time.'

'Maybe,' Adam said. 'You might change your mind when you see how terrible I am at drawing. I don't have an artistic bone in my body.'

'You'd be surprised how many people think that,' Sadie replied. 'And most of them are wrong. All you need is a bit of confidence.'

Adam smiled. 'Yes, miss.'

Sadie grabbed the nearest tea towel and swatted him on the arm with it. 'Careful or I'll make you do lines – ice out one hundred times, *I must not cheek the teacher.*'

'No, miss,' he said, his hazel eyes sparkling. 'Sorry, miss.'

That made Sadie giggle too and they laughed together for several long seconds.

'This was fun,' Adam said, once their amusement had died down. 'Thank you.'

She nodded her head once. 'All part of your professional development. Thanks for your help.'

'I enjoyed it,' Adam replied, meeting her gaze. A small silence stretched between them as they watched each other, then he seemed to give himself a shake. 'I'd better get going. Thanks again for the lesson.'

'You're welcome,' she said warmly. 'See you tomorrow.'

Chapter Sixteen

Castle Court was starting to fill up with the post-work Friday night crowds as Cat locked the door of Smart Cookies. The temperature had plummeted and the wind was far too bitter for anyone to dine outside, but there was a queue beside the pop-up crepe cart and a few hardened smokers were shivering beneath the oak tree. Cat checked the time and fixed her gaze on the steamed-up windows of Let's Go Dutch; with a bit of luck, Jaren would be finished work by now and they could find somewhere quiet to talk. And then she could hurry home and try to get ahead with more stock for the shop ...

She was halfway across the Court when she heard her name being called. Glancing around, her heart sank when she saw Cherie hurrying towards her. But there was a purposeful look on the older woman's face and Cat knew there was no escape.

'Hello, Cherie,' she said stonily. 'Did you want something?'

'I won't take up much of your time,' Cherie said bluntly. 'It's about Greg and this business at La Perle.'

Cat let out an impatient sigh. 'I don't have anything to say about that.'

Cherie waved her comment away. 'Look, I just want you to know that I had no idea Greg had gone telling tales to François. And for what it's worth —' she paused and threw a glance towards the glowing windows of La Clé d'Argent bistro, 'well, I'm happy to state on the record that you didn't say anything defamatory in December.'

Cat couldn't help gaping; whatever she'd been expecting, it wasn't support. 'You've changed your tune.'

The other woman raised her chin. 'I was ... mistaken about you,' she said, her tone stiff. 'When I am wrong, I admit it.'

They stared at each other for a few seconds, then Cat gave a single incredulous nod. 'Thank you. I appreciate that.'

'You'll let me know if there is anything I can do?' Cherie said. 'I'm not so well-connected as Greg, but I do have one or two friends in high places, thanks to my late husband.'

Cat was almost tempted to ask her who she meant, but time was ticking by and she didn't want Jaren to think she had forgotten him. 'I'll let you know,' she promised. 'And ... thanks again.'

Cherie's usually haughty expression softened a little. 'It's the least I can do. Goodnight, Cat.'

She turned on her heel. Cat watched her walk away, wondering whether she'd somehow dreamed the whole exchange. Of course, there was always the possibility that Cherie was playing a double agent, hoping to win Cat's confidence so she could feed back anything she learned to Greg, but Cat didn't think so. Cherie might be hard-faced, but there had been genuine consternation behind her words.

Wait until Sadie hears about this, Cat thought, setting off for the pancake house once more. *She's not going to believe her ears.*

'Wow,' Jaren said, as they dodged the crowds on Eastgate Street and headed for a quiet bar tucked away just inside the old city walls. 'That's unexpected. It's like one of those films where the old warrior suddenly comes to their senses and starts fighting for the young pretender.'

Cat grinned. 'Let's not go that far. I think she's probably just realised that it's pretty lonely on Greg's team, that's all.'

Jaren glanced sideways. 'Maybe ... I don't think anyone invited her to the last shopkeepers' drinks.'

'I rest my case,' Cat said. 'But I don't mind what her reasons are, as long as she stops trying to cause trouble for Sadie and me.'

The pub was a tiny bit dingy, but warm and welcoming and, just as Jaren had predicted, not too busy. 'It's a hidden gem,' he said, with a cheery wave at the barman. 'Not trendy enough for the hipsters and far enough from the city centre to avoid the Friday night revellers. It's a well-kept secret among the regulars.'

'So, how do you know about it?' she asked.

He smiled. 'I live around the corner. This is actually my local.'

The news surprised Cat. She didn't know much about Jaren, other than that he came from the Netherlands and had a passion for food that almost rivalled her own, and she'd never thought to wonder where he lived. Seb and Elin had garret rooms above Castle Court, Sadie and Adam were in the villages to the east of the city, and she knew Andrew and Earl shared a brand new flat in one of the converted buildings that lined the canal, much like her own home. But Jaren was more of a mystery; it was time to find out more, she decided.

They ordered their coffee and found a seat by the window. 'So,' Jaren said, leaning forwards with a curious gleam in his eye. 'What's all this about?'

Cat told him about the letter, and her visits to the other shopkeepers. When she'd finished, Jaren snapped his fingers.

'That's why Cherie has switched sides. She's finally realised what a low-life Greg is.'

'I hope so,' Cat said. 'So, what about you – will you write something to say what happened at the end of last year?'

'Of course,' Jaren said, spreading his hands. 'I'm amazed you even have to ask.'

'Thank you,' Cat said. 'Everyone has been so kind.'

He shrugged. 'Like I said when we first met, Castle Court is like a family. We look out for each other.' He paused and sipped his coffee. 'Except for Greg, obviously. He's that nasty cousin nobody likes.'

Cat smiled. 'It's certainly the perfect home for Smart Cookies.'

Jaren sat back in his seat, his dark eyes fixed on Cat. 'And you? Is it also your perfect home?'

'Yes, I think it might be,' she said honestly. 'But enough about me. How long have you been at Castle Court?'

'Three years,' he said. 'Before that, I worked in the Dutch pancake house in London. And before that, I ate a lot of pancakes at my grandmother's house. So, I guess you could say I'm a pancake expert.'

'Wow,' Cat said, straight-faced. 'That sounds like a tough job.'

Jaren shook his head sadly. 'No one appreciates how hard it's been.'

'And you don't mind the competition from the crepe cart on the Court tonight?'

He spread his hands in a gesture of openness. 'They're French – we're Dutch. There's room for both in Castle Court.'

He turned the conversation back to Cat, teasing out the details of her friendship with Sadie.

'And you've been best friends since school?'

'Yeah,' Cat said. 'Although it's hard to stay close when your lives go in such different directions; I went off travelling and Sadie married Daniel. When Lissy came along, I was working my way around Thailand, learning how to make pad thai and red curry, and then I spent most of the last three and a half years in Paris, at La Perle.'

'I think true friends can always pick up as though they

have never been apart,' he commented with a smile. 'And how are things working out with Seb? Does he make you happy?'

'Of course,' Cat said. 'I know some people might think it's a bad idea to date someone you practically work with, but we're both so busy that we haven't really had time to get bored of each other's company.'

Jaren nodded. 'He's been different since you came. More settled.'

She gave him a knowing look. 'Less of a player, you mean.'

'That too,' he agreed. 'Although why would he play elsewhere when he has you?'

Cat felt herself blush. 'What about you?' she asked, turning the tables. 'Have you got your eye on someone or are you still playing the field?'

He was quiet for a moment. 'I have my eye on someone,' he said eventually.

'I knew it!' she burst out, leaning forwards. 'It's Elin, isn't it?'

Jaren took a long swig of his drink. 'She's a very attractive woman. I'm not sure I'm her type, though.'

'Are you crazy?' Cat said incredulously. 'She's definitely interested.'

'Oh?' he said, raising one eyebrow. 'How do you know?'

'She told me. So, if you're waiting for some kind of green light, this is it. And what better time of year to make your move? Send her a Valentine – I'll even bake one for you, if you like.'

He looked thoughtful. 'That would be very kind. I don't have much room to cook in my kitchen at home.'

Cat grinned. 'It can't be much smaller than Seb's – those attic rooms are tiny. His is like a galley.'

'Ah,' Jaren said, his lips quirking into a smile, 'whereas mine actually *is* a galley. I live on a houseboat, moored on the canal.'

'No way!' Cat gasped, her jaw dropping. 'That sounds amazing!'

'It has its moments,' he said. 'The summer is obviously more enjoyable than the winter, but she's a sturdy boat and cosy enough once the wood burner is lit.'

Cat pictured Jaren sitting on the deck of a brightly painted barge at sunset, a bottle of lager in one hand. 'Wow. I'm seriously impressed.'

'You can come and see it for yourself, if you like?'

'Can I?' Cat said eagerly. 'When?'

Jaren shrugged. 'What are you doing right now?'

The canal was a five-minute walk from the pub. Jaren led Cat along the towpath that ran alongside, pointing out the boats belonging to his neighbours.

'That one is just passing through,' he said, pointing to a large black and white barge. 'We get a lot of holidaymakers on boating trips stopping here.'

Cat looked up and down the canal, taking in the warm yellow glow in some of the windows and the air of peacefulness. 'I can understand why.'

He stopped beside a beautiful green and orange boat tightly moored to a black metal post. A lantern hung at one end, sending flickering shafts of light and shadows spilling over the black roof. 'And this is mine. Cat, meet Anika.'

Cat reached a hand to touch the smooth paintwork. 'Pleased to meet you, Anika,' she said gravely. 'What a beautiful name.'

Jaren cleared his throat. 'Named after my mother. She died when I was ten.'

'I'm sorry to hear that,' Cat said softly. 'That must have been hard.'

'It was,' Jaren said. 'But life goes on. My grandmother moved in, with her amazing pancake recipes, and the rest, as they say, is history.' He held out a hand. 'Want to come aboard?'

'Absolutely,' Cat said, placing her fingers in his.

Jaren led the way, climbing down a steep, narrow staircase to a door. He unlocked it and pushed it back, flicking a switch as he did so. Inside, the boat was even more charming. Two table lamps lit up a tiny living room with old, mismatched furniture and a wood burner against one wall.

Cat gazed around in wonder. 'I love it,' she breathed. 'I really, *really* love it.'

'I doubt you'll love the kitchen,' he said dryly and led her to another door at the far end.

He wasn't wrong, Cat thought, staring at the minuscule oven and a sink that was barely wide enough to fit a frying pan.

'Don't you bang your head?' she asked, glancing up at the low ceiling; Jaren had to be six feet tall, at least.

'I used to,' he admitted. 'But now I am used to it.'

Cat's gaze travelled to a final door at the end of the boat.

'The bathroom,' he explained. 'Complete with shower.'

'But where do you sleep?' Cat said, frowning.

Jaren laughed. 'You've just been standing in my bedroom. The sofa folds out to make a bed.'

'Oh!' Cat said, feeling stupid. 'Of course it does.' She looked around again. 'No TV?'

'No TV,' he said. 'I have a tablet for watching Netflix, but most of the time, I read.' He waved a hand and now she saw the low bookcase stacked with paperbacks.

'You know this is a lot of people's idea of a dream home, right?'

Jaren beamed with pleasure. 'I'm glad you like it.'

She smiled back and they stood there for a moment. Then Cat's phone vibrated in her pocket. Pulling it out, she peered at the screen: Seb's name flashed at her.

'Sorry,' she said to Jaren and turned away to take the call. 'Hi, Seb, everything okay?'

'Are you at home?'

Cat glanced over at Jaren. 'Just on my way. Why?'

Seb's tone was grim. 'Turn around and get back over to the shop. Someone's thrown paint all over your window.'

'What a mess,' Cat said, staring in dismay at the thick black paint splattered all over the front of Smart Cookies. 'How could this happen?'

Seb shook his head. 'Obviously not by accident. And we don't have to look too far to work out who might have done it.'

'How am I going to get it off?' Cat wondered.

'Depends if it is gloss or emulsion,' Jaren said. 'Water-based paint will wash off. Gloss is trickier.'

'Only one way to find out,' Seb said. 'I'll go and get a bucket of water and a cloth.'

Cat eyed him. 'The bar must be busy tonight. Why don't I come and get the bucket? That way you can get back to your customers.'

She knew from the flash of relief that crossed his face that she was right.

'I hate to leave you to deal with this on your own.'

'She's not alone,' Jaren said, stepping forwards. 'I'll help. And there's no need to go all the way up to the third floor for water – I can get some from my place.'

Seb looked as though he was going to argue.

Cat touched his arm. 'Go on. I'll be fine.'

With a reluctant nod, Seb gave in. 'But both of you come and see me when you're done, okay? You'll be in need of a drink by then.'

Ten minutes later, Cat and Jaren stood in front of the blackened window, buckets of water and sponges in their hands.

'Let's start with a small corner,' Jaren suggested. 'If it doesn't come off, we'll need to think again.'

'If it doesn't come off, I'll have to call Sadie,' Cat said. 'She'll know what we need.'

She stepped forwards and dipped her sponge into the cold water. Raising it to the sticky glass, she held her breath and dabbed at the paint. To her immense relief, the paint began to dissolve and run in dirty charcoal-coloured rivulets down to the pale-blue window frame.

'It's emulsion,' Jaren said, coming to join her. 'Come on, we'll soon have this done.'

It took thirty minutes of hard scrubbing to clear the glass completely. Passers-by stopped to watch them from time to time and Andrew came out of the Bus Stop with a pair of stepladders to help them reach the top corners, shaking his head in disgusted sympathy. It wasn't until Cat and Jaren were standing back to admire the results of their hard work, breath puffing into steamy clouds, that they heard a familiar sneering voice.

'Oh dear, have you had an accident? Or does someone hate you almost as much as I do?'

Cat whirled around to glare into Greg's amused eyes. 'Like you don't know.'

His chubby features split into an innocent smile. 'How could I know? I've been at a meeting on the other side of the city with several important councillors.'

'Liar,' Cat snarled, her eyes narrowing.

'I can assure you I am not lying,' Greg countered. 'The meeting started at five-thirty and ended some fifteen minutes ago. So I'd be very careful who I accused, if I were you, Cat.'

'Then you paid someone else to do it,' she said flatly. 'Either way, it amounts to the same thing – a cowardly move.'

Greg laughed. 'Sticks and stones. You'll have a hard time proving this has anything to do with me and I'm sure you have better things to do with your time. Haven't you got a court hearing to prepare for?'

Cat clenched her fists and counted to ten. 'No, I have a meeting to attend. There's no way this is going back to court – it's your word against mine.'

'Or your word against a recording,' he corrected. 'It's amazing what smartphones can do these days.'

The comment gave Cat cause to pause. It was perfectly possible that Greg had recorded their run-in. But would it tell a different story to the one she and her friends remembered? They couldn't all be wrong, surely?

'You picked the wrong team, Greg,' Cat said, glowering at him. 'No matter how much you deny it, François is guilty.'

A faintly triumphant expression flashed across Greg's face. 'We'll see about that.' He glanced across at Jaren, pity in his eyes. 'Don't turn your back on this one – she might be pretty, but she'll stab you the moment you're not looking.'

Jaren scowled in dislike. 'If I want your advice, I'll ask for it. But don't hold your breath.'

Greg chuckled and shook his head. 'Don't say I didn't warn you.' He turned on his heel and walked away towards the bistro.

Jaren dropped the blackened sponge into his bucket in disgust. 'What a moron. There's no way he wasn't involved in this.'

Cat nodded, fury leaving her unable to speak. But just as

Greg had said, there was no way to prove it; Greg was too clever to have left a trail signalling his involvement.

'Come on,' Jaren said, jerking his head towards the bright windows of Let's Go Dutch. 'Why don't we get cleaned up and claim that drink from Seb? I think we've earned it, don't you?'

'We really have,' Cat replied. 'But this one is on me. I really appreciate your help, Jaren.'

He waved her thanks away. 'I keep telling you – we look after each other here. No thanks needed.'

Cat felt so grateful that she might cry. She dipped her head. 'Even so, I'm buying, okay?'

Jaren smiled. 'I think I can live with that.'

Chapter Seventeen

Sadie was filled with horror when Cat called her on Saturday morning to explain what had happened the night before.

'That's awful!' she said. 'Shall I come into the shop? Is there anything I can do?'

'No, it's mostly all cleaned up now,' Cat told her. 'At least the glass is. Our lovely blue paintwork is looking pretty grubby though.'

Sadie almost swore, then remembered Lissy was sitting at the kitchen table, drawing. 'We'll get it redone.'

'Not until after this meeting is out of the way. Seb says he'll see if anything was caught on CCTV, but I'm not hopeful.'

'And no one saw anything?'

'Not a thing,' Cat said. 'It all happened so fast – by the time Earl and Andrew came out of the diner, the culprit was long gone.'

Sadie gnawed at her lip. 'And you're sure there's nothing I can do?'

'I'm sure. Concentrate on getting those wedding favours done. I'll see you on Monday.'

Sadie was distracted for the rest of the day. She pumped Adam for information before he was even through the front door that evening, but he knew nothing more than Cat had told her earlier. The stress gave Sadie a headache and she was uncharacteristically short-tempered. After an hour of icing in virtual silence, she'd had enough.

'I'm sorry, Adam, but I think we'd better call it a night. I'm not very good company today.'

'It's understandable,' he said. He held up a finished biscuit to show her. 'Look, I'm not bad at this now. Why don't I take a box of biscuits and finish them at my place.'

Sadie hesitated. Was he good enough to work unsupervised? Then again, the order had to be completed by Tuesday and there were still over a hundred biscuits left to ice, as well as stock for the shop. She couldn't afford to say no. 'Okay,' she said. 'Just take things slow and steady.'

He nodded. 'Don't worry, I will.'

She gave him a tired smile. 'And I'm sorry for being so grumpy. This Greg business has me all on edge.'

'Get some rest,' he said sympathetically. 'I'll check in with you tomorrow.'

Sadie closed the door after him and rested her head against the cool wooden surface. She'd never expected running a business to be easy, but really, did it have to be quite so challenging?

*

By Monday morning, she was feeling more positive. The wedding favours order was complete, thanks to extra efforts from Adam and Clare. Cat reported the weekend takings were excellent, and the damage to the paintwork wasn't as bad as she'd feared. The sun was shining, bathing Castle Court in light and chasing away what was left of her despair.

Even Cat's frown when she told her about Daniel's reaction to Adam couldn't dampen Sadie's spirits.

'I'm not entirely sure it's any of Daniel's business, to be honest,' Cat said, once Sadie had finished. 'Seb doesn't know how I spend every minute of my time when I'm not with him and he certainly doesn't expect me to apologise for doing my job.'

'I think he was just surprised,' Sadie replied. 'And he's right, I should have told him.'

Cat eyed her closely. 'And how do you feel about a Valentine's Day dinner for two?'

Sadie took a deep breath. The truth was, she wasn't sure how she felt about the prospect of what would almost certainly be a romantic evening with Daniel. He'd kept his distance physically since they'd agreed to give things another go – the most they'd shared was an awkward hug. But she knew he must want more. 'He couldn't get a babysitter for tomorrow night, but there was one free tonight. So we're going tonight instead.'

'You haven't actually answered the question,' Cat pointed out dryly. 'How do you feel about it?'

Sadie hesitated, then plunged in. 'Fine. It'll be nice to have the chance to talk, away from home.'

Cat lifted her eyebrows, clearly unconvinced.

'It will,' Sadie insisted.

'If you say so,' Cat murmured.

'How about you?' Sadie asked, turning the tables. 'How are you feeling about the meeting tomorrow?'

Cat let out a long, unsteady breath. 'Okay, I think. I've sent all the witness statements over to my lawyer in Paris – he's going to meet me before we're due at Martin et Moreau to go over everything. And I've done as much as I can here, so ... I think I'm all set.'

Sadie gave her best friend a reassuring smile. 'Good. You're going to teach François a valuable lesson.'

'I hope so,' Cat said. She shifted her gaze to the boxes of wedding favours. 'Let's get these bagged up and ready to go over to the wedding venue tomorrow morning, shall we?'

They worked in silence. Sadie couldn't be sure, but she assumed Cat was thinking about the hearing. And Sadie herself was going over Cat's question in her mind: how did she feel about dinner with Daniel tonight?

'Sadie, did you check these biscuits as you were doing them?'

There was an odd tone to Cat's voice that made Sadie look up warily. 'What? Yes, of course I did. Why?'

'Because most of them have been iced as "Sonny" with an "o". And the rest say "Sunny" with a "u".'

Sadie felt the blood drain from her face. 'They can't be

wrong. I did most of them myself and the rest were done by Adam and Clare.'

And then she remembered that she hadn't checked the box Adam had taken away with him on Saturday night. Hadn't he complained that the names had started to look weird after a while? 'Let me see.'

It only took her a few seconds to see that Cat was right; a significant number of the biscuits bore the unmistakable name of Sunny.

'Can you fix it?' Cat asked.

Sadie shook her head. 'Not without making it look even worse. We'll have to do them all again.'

'We can't,' Cat said, her expression a mixture of disbelief and dawning anger. 'I'm leaving for Paris in a couple of hours – I don't have time to bake. And you've got a birthday party booked in at four o'clock – you haven't got time to ice them.'

'Haven't we got any spares?' Sadie asked, glancing at the clock. It would be tight, but she might be able to squeeze in some icing before the party, if the biscuits were already baked and cool.

'No. They're all iced, ready for the Valentine's Day rush.' Cat looked down at the biscuits in frustration. 'How could this happen?'

Sadie crossed her fingers. 'I don't know. But does it really matter? The important thing is that we find a way to fix the situation – can Adam take over the baking?'

Cat let out a short, hollow laugh. 'No. I don't think I trust anyone except me right now.'

'Okay,' Sadie said, ignoring the needle of hurt her best friend's words caused. 'Let's find out how many biscuits we need and take it from there.'

There was a tense, angry silence. Eventually, Cat nodded and reached for the nearest box. 'Fine.'

At first, Sadie was optimistic; the number of wrongly iced biscuits was low. It shouldn't take more than a few hours to bake some replacements and give them time to completely cool down. Then she could ice them and get them dry, ready to be bagged up. It was going to be fine. Then Cat unpacked the final box. Every single biscuit had the same spelling mistake.

'Sixty-one,' Cat said, once she'd counted the mistakes. 'Sixty-one Sunnys.'

Sadie groaned. 'Bloody hell. Now what?'

Cat gave a huff of irritation and reached for her phone. 'Now I see whether I can change my flight and you see whether you can cancel that icing party.'

'I can't ruin a child's birthday like that,' Sadie said, aghast. 'She'd be devastated and her mother would be furious. Can you imagine the bad publicity?'

'There's a lot more riding on the wedding favours,' Cat countered as she tapped at her screen. 'How are you going to get the new batch iced if you're tied up with the party until five-thirty?'

Now it was Sadie's turn to reach for her phone. 'I'll do them tonight. Daniel knows how important this order is — he'll understand.'

There was a long silence when she gave him the news. 'I don't suppose I've got any choice,' he said, after she'd suggested they rearrange their date.

'Does it really matter when we go out for dinner?' Sadie asked, conscious that Cat was listening.

'No, I suppose not,' Daniel said, and Sadie heard an edge of frustration in his voice. 'But it's hard not to feel like second best sometimes.'

She thought of all the times he'd called her to say he was working late – had left her alone to look after their tiny daughter – but said nothing.

He sighed, relenting. 'Do you need me to collect Lissy?'

'No. I'll pick her up from the childminder and ice the biscuits once she's gone to bed. It shouldn't take more than a couple of hours – I'll be finished by ten.'

'Okay. I'll see if I can rearrange the babysitter.'

Cat was speaking to the airline when Sadie rang off. She listened as she changed her flight to a later one and then ended the call.

'All sorted?' she asked.

Cat nodded. 'You?'

'Yeah. He's not especially happy but he's okay.'

'And you?' Cat said, giving her a searching look. 'How do you feel about having to reschedule?'

'It can't be helped,' Sadie said, hoping her shrug was nonchalant enough to stop Cat asking questions.

'No,' Cat agreed. 'But if I had to hazard a guess, I'd say you were relieved.'

Sadie focused on clearing the work surface of misspelled biscuits. 'Of course I'm not. I'm glad Daniel took the news well, that's all.'

'Hmmm,' Cat said, clearly unconvinced. She opened a drawer and pulled out an apron. 'I need to be at Manchester Airport by 5.45 p.m. We've got an hour and a half to bake seventy biscuits.'

Sadie's stomach churned with anxiety. 'Is that enough time?'

Cat lifted the stainless-steel bowl from the mixer. 'We're about to find out.'

It was almost ten o'clock when Sadie laid down her bag of white icing and stared wearily at the rows of glistening biscuits. She'd been paranoid as she'd written the names, checking and rechecking for mistakes. But this time she was certain that they were all correct.

Stretching her aching back, she glanced at her phone and saw she had a message from Daniel, sent a few minutes earlier: *How's it going?*

Done, she typed back. *They just need to dry out in the oven.*

No sooner had she placed the trays into the warm oven and set the timer for thirty minutes than the doorbell rang. Frowning, she hurried to the hallway and peered through the spyhole: Daniel was there. Her frown deepened as she opened the door.

'What – how—?' she began.

He raised his hands, in which he held a brown paper bag and a bottle of Chardonnay. 'I've got a chicken bhuna and a prawn madras. Which do you fancy?'

Sadie couldn't help smiling as she stood back to let him in. 'When have you ever known me to eat a madras?'

'There's a first time for everything,' Daniel said. He stopped by the kitchen table and shook his head. 'I'm glad you finished on time – I'd have had to eat both if you hadn't.'

Sadie laughed and took a pair of plates from the cupboard. 'Don't tell me you've been sat outside, watching the clock?'

'Of course I have,' he said. 'My car smells like the inside of a curry house and there are poppadom crumbs all over the carpet.'

The aroma of pungent spices made Sadie's stomach rumble as she lifted the lid from the foil containers. 'Thank you,' she said, filled with gratitude at his thoughtfulness.

'No problem,' he replied. 'I knew you wouldn't have eaten.'

They ate at the kitchen table, once Sadie had cleared away the bags of half-used icing and cooling racks. The curry tasted heavenly – Daniel had gone out of his way to collect it from what had always been their favourite Indian restaurant – and once again, she felt her heart soften at his kindness. He was on good form, too, making her laugh and topping up her glass the moment it was empty. But she only really relaxed once the biscuits were safely out of the oven and cooling.

'Have you heard from Cat?' Daniel asked as they carried their drinks through to the toy-strewn living room.

Sadie checked her phone. 'She says she's just cleared passport control.'

Daniel settled beside her on the sofa. 'How is she feeling?'

'Well prepared,' Sadie replied. 'Which isn't to say she's

finding it easy – I think she's hiding how much it's bothering her.'

He sipped his wine. 'Do you think this François will back down?'

Sadie sighed. 'Cat's lawyer thinks so, eventually. A lot depends on whether they accept the witness statements she's collected. I'm still a bit amazed that Cherie has swapped sides.'

'Sounds like she had an attack of conscience,' Daniel said. 'Whereas this Greg appears to be missing a conscience entirely.'

The conversation turned to other things. Slowly, the wine in the bottle grew less and less and Sadie became aware that she was laughing a lot. *I'm tipsy on a school night*, she thought as she giggled at another of Daniel's jokes. She gazed at him as he talked; was it her imagination or had his eyes grown bluer? The touch of silver at his temples was definitely new; she was surprised he hadn't had that taken care of. And then she realised he was watching her, a questioning look on his face.

'What?' she said.

'I said, it's probably time I was going.'

Sadie was surprised by her faint sense of disappointment as she checked the time. 'Oh. Yes, I suppose you're right.'

He rose, holding out a hand to help her up, and then led the way through to the kitchen to deposit the almost empty wine bottle and collect his coat.

'This was fun,' he said as they stood at the open front door. 'Not quite the romantic dinner I had planned, but nice all the same.'

Sadie's stomach fluttered at the mention of romance: so her suspicions had been correct. But he'd given it up the moment she'd asked and had gone out of his way to work around her. She was confused to realise that the butterflies his words had caused weren't unpleasant; unless she was mistaken, what she was feeling now was desire.

Almost without realising, she stepped nearer to him. 'Yes, it was fun. Thank you.'

He gave her a soft smile and dropped the briefest of kisses on her forehead. 'Any time. Sleep well, Sadie.'

The last time he'd kissed her forehead had been when he'd nursed her through a particularly bad bout of flu, long before Lissy had been born, Sadie recalled, with sudden acute recollection. He'd been kind then, too, she thought – kind and patient, exactly as he was behaving now. Giving her space but supporting her when she needed it, just like the Daniel he used to be . . .

Turning away, he stepped through the door.

Sadie caught at his sleeve. 'Daniel, wait—'

He gazed at her in surprise for a moment and then understanding dawned in his eyes. With gentle fingers, he reached out to brush her cheek. 'Yes?'

She stared at him, her heart thudding. If she did this now, there would be no turning back. Was it absolutely what she wanted?

'I . . .' she whispered uncertainly. 'Do you have to go?'

His hand moved to stroke her hair, his expression watchful. 'No, I don't have to go.'

Sadie took an unsteady breath. He was leaving it up to her, giving her every opportunity to change her mind. 'Then stay.'

His eyes darkened. 'Are you sure? I'm happy to wait – as long as it takes.'

She felt her insides constrict; she didn't want to wait. 'I'm sure.'

The hand that had been stroking her hair made its unhurried way to the small of her back. His other hand cupped her cheek. And slowly, he bent his head to kiss her.

It lasted only a few seconds. He pulled away a few centimetres, as though checking she was okay, leaving Sadie aching for more. It had been a long time since he'd kissed her like that – soft and intimate and full of tenderness. This was the man she'd loved, before everything had gone so terribly wrong. Was it possible she could love him again?

She reached up to graze his lips with her fingers. He kissed the tips, his eyes never leaving hers, silently asking her again if she was sure. And, nodding, she took his hand and led him back inside the cottage.

Chapter Eighteen

'There's something different about you today.'

Sadie kept her eyes fixed on the road on Tuesday morning, hoping Adam wouldn't notice the heat creeping up her cheeks. She and Daniel had overslept, only waking up when Lissy came in and demanded to know why Daddy was sleeping in Mummy's bed. As a result, the morning had been a flurry of disorganisation and Sadie wouldn't have been surprised to discover she'd forgotten to put on a vital piece of clothing. The passionate kiss Daniel had given her just before she left had certainly left her feeling rattled.

'Is there?' she said, self-consciously touching her hair to make sure it wasn't sticking up.

'There is,' Adam said, frowning thoughtfully. 'You look ... happier.'

'Mummy finished icing all the biscuits for the big wedding,' Lissy chimed in from the back seat. 'Maybe that's why she's happy.'

Adam stared at Sadie. 'But I thought we finished those at the weekend.'

Sadie grimaced. 'We did and we didn't. Not all of them were ... erm ... good enough to send out.'

He didn't speak for several seconds. 'You mean mine, don't you?'

'No!' Sadie insisted, unable to bear the dejection in his voice. 'No, it wasn't you ...' She took a deep breath, determined to stop him blaming himself. 'I spelled the groom's name wrong. I rushed them and didn't pay attention when it mattered. My fault, not yours.'

'You're being kind,' Adam said, looking out of the window. 'You're far too professional to make a mistake like that.'

'I'm not,' Sadie said, hoping she sounded convincing. 'Believe me, I make mistakes just like everyone else. And this one was definitely down to me. But, as Lissy says, we noticed before the order went off and I fixed it last night.'

He continued to stare out of the window. Sadie swallowed a sigh; the truth was, it had been Adam's mistake, but what did that matter now? The day had been saved, after all. But she couldn't say anything like that, so they drove for a few minutes, listening to the radio, until Sadie pulled up outside Lissy's school.

'Here we are,' she said, turning to beam at her daughter. 'Time to go and be awesome.'

'Adam is right, you're all smiley,' Lissy observed. 'Is it because you and Daddy had a special cuddle last night?'

Sadie thought she might spontaneously combust. She didn't dare look at Adam. 'Something like that. Come on, you're going to be late.'

Cheeks flaming, she fumbled with Lissy's seat belt and hurried into the playground. By the time she returned to the car, she'd stopped blushing at least, although she suspected the embarrassment would never leave her.

She started the engine. 'Right,' she said, trying not to wince at the determined brightness in her tone. She reached for the volume button on the radio. 'Ooh, I love this song.'

Adam made no response and kept his face averted. It wasn't until the song had finished and the adverts had kicked in that he spoke. 'So, you and Daniel, then.'

Sadie hesitated, searching for a way to soften the news. 'Yes,' she said finally.

He nodded and managed a smile. 'Good for you.'

She opened her mouth to say something – anything – and closed it again. What could she say, anyway? Plenty more fish in the sea?

'Lissy seems pleased,' Adam went on, staring down at his feet.

Embarrassment crawled up Sadie's spine once more. 'She wasn't this morning, when she tried to climb into bed and found someone else was already there.'

'No, I can imagine.' Now it was his turn to blush. He turned away again. 'Well, you know what I mean.'

The silence grew thick; it almost felt as though someone had built an invisible wall between them. Sadie concentrated on the traffic – a broken-down car was slowing everything to a crawl – and realised for the first time ever she couldn't wait for the journey to be over.

She glanced at Adam and the stony set of his face made her want to cry. 'I want you to know that if it wasn't for Lissy . . .' She stopped and shook her head. 'You're really great, Adam. I hope we can still be friends.'

He puffed out his cheeks in a long sigh. 'I won't lie – there was a part of me that hoped you and Daniel were just going through the motions. But I can see now that I was wrong.' He gave her a small, wistful smile. 'I'm happy that you're happy.'

'Thank you,' Sadie said.

The traffic ahead eased and they spent the rest of the journey listening to the radio. When they arrived at the underground car park beneath Cat's flat, Adam turned to Sadie.

'There's something I need to do. I'll see you at the shop, okay?'

She nodded and watched as he got out of the car and walked away. The last thing she'd wanted to do was to hurt him, but the truth was, she hadn't really known what she wanted until Daniel had kissed her last night, and then the desire to be held and loved had swept everything else aside. She'd woken in the night, his arms wrapped around her, and wondered whether she'd made a mistake, but it was too late for regrets now. Lissy's unexpected appearance had made sure of that.

*

Paris was grey and drizzly.

Cat stared out of her hotel room window at the chic, tree-lined courtyard below, and not even the bubbling fountain could lift her mood. The Hotel St Marc was a beautiful art deco hotel tucked away behind Boulevard des Italiens and she was disappointed she couldn't enjoy its charm more. But the thought of the meeting at Martin et Moreau was preying on her mind and dampening her enthusiasm for everything Paris had to offer.

Simone Collignon, Cat's lawyer, was waiting at her office. 'It's good to see you again,' she said, kissing both of Cat's cheeks. 'Although I wish it was in better circumstances.'

They went through the statements and the letter from François' lawyers. Simone was convinced they would back down as soon as they saw the evidence Cat had collected.

'But I suppose it depends what their aim is,' she said, gathering everything up into a sturdy manila folder and slipping it into her briefcase. 'François de Beauvoir likes to feel powerful – it could be he is simply trying to flex his muscles and remind you he exists.'

Cat grimaced. 'Believe me, I haven't forgotten. I'm not sure I ever will.'

Simone nodded. 'I know. But it is important we address this today and remind *him* that you will not be bullied.'

Martin et Moreau had their offices in the grand Place Vendôme. Cat tried not to feel intimidated as she sat in the ornate, high-ceilinged reception, watching the impassive face of the immaculately made-up receptionist as she tapped at her computer behind her desk.

Please let this be the last time I have to come here, Cat thought fervently.

At precisely eleven o'clock, the phone on the receptionist's desk buzzed. She listened for a moment, then gave Cat and Simone a thin-lipped smile. 'Monsieur Moreau is ready for you.' She stood and waited for them to join her. 'This way, please.'

She led them to an oak-panelled door and knocked before ushering them inside. Cat swallowed hard as she stepped into the large, red-carpeted room. An unsmiling Pierre Moreau sat behind a vast mahogany desk, white-haired and austere. Beside him was François de Beauvoir, as sharp-suited and arrogant as Cat remembered, although she was almost amused to detect the first signs of middle-aged spread behind his expensive jacket.

And just behind François, Cat saw Greg Valois. His lip curled into a sneer when he met her gaze and it was all she could do not to glare back. Instead, she dredged up a polite smile as Simone led her inside.

'Good morning, gentlemen,' Simone said, extending her hand to each of them in turn. 'I trust this meeting will not take up too much of my client's valuable time.'

Cat sat down without shaking their hands; the thought of touching François made her feel physically sick.

Pierre Moreau turned a chilly gaze towards her. 'That rather depends on Mademoiselle Garcia. Is she willing to admit that she is in breach of the agreement she signed?'

Simone smiled. 'Come now, Pierre. My client has done nothing wrong.'

'That remains to be seen,' Pierre said. 'But first, can I offer either of you some refreshment?'

Simone accepted a coffee, but Cat refused. Being in the same room as François was making her head spin, bringing back memories of the way he'd pressed himself against her in the deserted kitchen of La Perle, forcing her back against the hob, ignoring her furious demands to be let go. It was a scene she'd unwillingly replayed over and over in the days that followed and she dreaded to think what might have happened if one of the waitresses hadn't appeared. It was a memory that still gave her nightmares.

Pierre Moreau cleared his throat. 'So, as you are aware, it is alleged that on the second day of December last year, Mademoiselle Garcia broke the terms of the non-disclosure agreement she signed. Specifically, she detailed her accusations against my client in the presence of a large crowd of people, thereby defaming his character.' He paused and gazed directly at Cat. 'This is a clear breach of her contract with Monsieur de Beauvoir and we intend to pursue her for the full financial penalty detailed in the contract, which, as you'll be aware, is 750,000 euros.'

Cat felt as though the floor had fallen away from her. She didn't have anything like that amount of money.

Breathe, she told herself as Simone gave her a brief reassuring look. *Just breathe* . . .

'What is your basis for this allegation?' Simone asked, her voice cool.

Pierre waved a hand at Greg. 'Monsieur Valois here owns a

successful bistro in close proximity to Mademoiselle Garcia's business. He was present when her comments were made.'

Cat opened her mouth to speak, but Simone beat her to it. 'As I understand it, Monsieur Valois was more than present – he was the instigator. My client was forced to defend herself after he attempted to discredit her professionally.' She cast an oblique look at Greg. 'I can only assume he was jealous of her exemplary career.'

Greg let out a snort. 'I can assure you that isn't the case.'

Pierre fired a warning look at him as he steepled his hands on the desk. 'Whatever the circumstances, your client broke the terms of the contract and is therefore liable. I have a sworn witness statement from Monsieur Valois, who is a valued member of the honourable Freemen of Chester, that states the exact nature of Mademoiselle Garcia's comments – I also possess an audio recording in which she clearly identified my client as the reason she left her job at La Perle and suggested he had acted improperly.'

Cat had had enough. 'That's because he *did* act improperly,' she fired at the lawyer. 'I hardly think you'd have agreed to settle the case if there was any doubt that he was innocent.'

She glanced at François and saw that a cruel smile was playing around his lips, making her wish she'd kept quiet; he was enjoying this, as though he was a cat and she was his mouse.

'The facts of the original matter are not in dispute,' Simone said firmly. 'Let's be clear – your client sexually harassed Mademoiselle Garcia at her workplace, which caused her to leave her job. The non-disclosure agreement was agreed by both parties and my client would not breach it unless there was extreme provocation, which is what Monsieur Valois intended, given that he has boasted about being a close friend of your client.'

She reached into her briefcase and withdrew the manila folder.

'This contains seven sworn statements from other business owners who were present when you allege my client breached the agreement. They all state that she did not name your client, nor did she infer that he was the person who harassed her. Furthermore, they detail the accusations Monsieur Valois made in order to make sure my client had to defend herself.'

She placed the folder on the desk. Pierre opened it without a word and read each statement in turn, passing them onto François. He skimmed them and passed one onto Greg, eyebrows raised. Greg fired a darting look Cat's way and she thought she caught a touch of panic in his eyes. Cherie's, she decided. He wasn't expecting to see her name.

Pierre raised his head. 'I'll need to consult with my client but, to be honest, I see nothing here to change our course of action.' He fixed Cat with an aloof look. 'Be prepared to meet us in court, Mademoiselle Garcia.'

Panic swirled up inside Cat. Her head began to spin. 'But—'

Simone gripped her arm in warning. 'That is regrettable, gentlemen, but as you wish. Au revoir.' She guided Cat towards the door, her fingers still applying light pressure, reminding her to stay silent. 'It will not come to that,' she whispered. 'Don't give François the satisfaction of seeing you afraid.'

She was right, Cat decided, straightening up. But it didn't matter how much Simone insisted that she would not have to face François in court, she couldn't shake off the fear that she was about to lose everything.

Cat tried to ring Seb on her way to Charles de Gaulle airport but the call went straight to voicemail. He was the only person she could talk to, apart from Sadie, and the last thing she wanted was to worry her best friend. If François did take her to court and won, their joint business venture would almost certainly be ruined too. Thoughts of Lissy whirled around in Cat's mind as she huddled into her window seat; Sadie had worked so hard to build Smart Cookies up and she'd sacrificed so much. How would she and Lissy cope if it was all taken away?

She landed at Manchester to find a long email from Simone. Her lawyer was certain that François was trying to intimidate her. Pierre Moreau was no fool; he would know that if the case went to court, the risk of the details of the case being leaked became significantly higher. Even so, Cat still felt sick. She was sure she'd felt François watching her when Pierre had made his chilling final comment and she was willing to bet he'd enjoyed her visible shock. Simone had been right; he was trying to bully her. But that didn't mean she shouldn't be afraid.

It was rush hour by the time she'd cleared passport control and found the taxi she'd booked to collect her, and the roads out of Manchester were all snarled up. She tried Seb during the journey back to Chester, but again the call went to voicemail. Frowning, she sent him a message asking him to call her. When she was finally back within the safety of her own home, Cat double-locked the front door and showered until the water ran cold. Then she went to bed, expecting to lie awake fretting, but the stresses of the day had clearly exhausted her more than she realised. She was asleep within minutes.

Chapter Nineteen

Cat woke up early on Valentine's Day and lay for a few minutes trying to summon the courage to get out of bed. For the first time ever, she was reluctant to go to Castle Court, and even the thought of baking couldn't soothe her troubled spirits.

Glancing at her phone, she saw she had a missed call from Seb, timed at eleven-thirty the night before. Maybe she'd drop in to see him on her way to Smart Cookies; he'd know how to make her feel better.

It was still dark as she made her way along the Rows. Eastgate Street was silent; the pavement glistened with silvery frost and her breath billowed into clouds of steam as she turned down the covered alleyway that led to the Court. Instead of crossing beneath the branches of the oak tree, she took the stairs that led up to the attic rooms and knocked on Seb's door as loudly as she dared.

After the fourth knock, she started to suspect he wasn't

there. He was a heavy sleeper, especially if he'd had a couple of drinks, but there was no hint of movement inside. She was about to give up when she heard the sound of the key turning in the lock and his sleep-crumpled face peered out at her.

'Cat!' he said, his eyebrows shooting upwards. 'What are you doing here?'

'I thought I'd surprise you,' she said, smiling. 'Any chance of a cup of tea?'

He stepped back to let her in and she saw he was wearing a pair of boxers and nothing else. 'On second thoughts, I'll make the tea. You must be freezing.'

'Just a bit,' he said wryly. 'Give me a minute, okay?'

He vanished into the bedroom and Cat heard rustling as he got dressed. She busied herself with the kettle and had two steaming cups of tea waiting by the time he returned.

'You do realise it's not even six o'clock yet, right?' he said.

'Sorry,' she said. 'But I wanted to see you. Happy Valentine's Day.'

He walked across to drop a kiss on her lips. 'Of course. Sorry I missed your call yesterday – it was crazy busy in the bar. Truth be told, I've got a bit of a hangover.'

Cat hid a smile – that explained his sheepish air. 'It's fine – I came back and fell straight into bed anyway.'

He studied her for a moment. 'So, how did it go?'

She sighed, her smile ebbing away. 'It was awful.'

Seb scowled once she'd finished her description of the meeting. 'I swear I'm going to unleash hell the next time I see Greg. I'm sure he was behind the paint vandalism and now this – what's his problem?'

'I have no idea,' Cat said. 'Only that he's as thick as thieves with François.'

'But your lawyer isn't worried? She's confident it's all talk?'

'She's convinced it's all a power game for François,' Cat admitted. 'But I still don't understand what Greg is getting out of it. He must know by now that even Cherie has turned against him.'

'Want me to ask him?' Seb growled. 'I'm sure Earl and Jaren would enjoy a heart-to-heart with him too.'

Cat shook her head. 'Don't give him any more ammunition. Simone says I have to sit tight and forget about it – easier said than done.'

Seb put his arm around her shoulders and pulled her close. 'Want to stay here tonight? It's Valentine's Day, after all.'

At least that way she'd have something to look forward to, Cat decided; Seb was excellent at taking her mind off things. 'Okay – I'll head to the bar just before closing time.'

'It's a date,' he said. 'Now – hadn't you better go and get baking?'

Cat downed the last of her tea. 'No rest for the wicked.'

Seb flashed her an approving look. 'Promises, promises.'

Cat looked pale and drawn when Sadie arrived at Smart Cookies. She was filling the drawers beneath the shelves with boxes of heart-shaped Valentine's Day biscuits but glanced up as Sadie walked in.

'Morning,' she said.

Sadie dumped her bag and coat behind the counter and gazed straight into Cat's eyes. 'Right – how bad is it?'

'It depends who you ask,' Cat replied with a barely audible sigh. 'Simone isn't worried.'

'But you are?'

Cat nodded. 'François is powerful and rich and he wants to prove a point. If he can make an example out of me then it will send a message out to anyone else who might be thinking of standing up to him.'

Sadie squeezed her hand. 'All the more reason to fight him. And if Simone isn't worried . . .'

'She tells me she isn't,' Cat said, 'but I wonder if she's just trying to make me feel better.'

Sadie raised her eyebrows. 'She's not a counsellor. I'm sure she's basing her opinion on a legal point of view.'

Cat shook her head. 'You should have seen him, Sadie. He was laughing at me, like I was a fly he could squash any time he liked.'

'Then it will be even more satisfying when he loses,' Sadie said stoutly. 'Come on, this isn't like you. You're fierce.'

'I am not.'

'You are,' Sadie insisted, detecting the ghost of a smile on her best friend's face. 'Remember that time Archie Lemmon tried to steal my bag in Year Eight? You gave him a black eye.'

Cat smiled. 'I got into so much trouble for that. My mum nearly had a heart attack when the school rang her.'

'But no one ever tried to mess with me again,' Sadie said. 'You'd blazed a trail and made school a better place for me.'

'Maybe,' Cat said doubtfully.

'And you did the same thing at La Perle – you showed all the women who work there that they don't have to put up with the behaviour of men like François. I bet he thinks twice before he tries anything on with any of the female staff now.'

She sighed. 'I don't know . . . hopefully. That's what this is all about. But I'm scared the courts will take his side.'

'They won't,' Sadie said. 'And I'm going to be beside you every step of the way. So is Seb and everyone here. You're not doing this alone.'

'Thank you,' Cat said, blinking hard. 'Now, how did things go while I was away? Please tell me we met the Charlotte Dennis order.'

'We did,' Sadie said cautiously. 'Her wedding planner was over the moon – said they were exactly what Charlotte wanted and she'd make sure they featured in the magazine spread.'

'That's great,' Cat said. 'Well done. Anything else I need to know about?'

Sadie paused, wondering whether to mention her reunion with Daniel. Adam had been considerably quieter than usual and had elected to take the bus home after work last night. But she didn't need to trouble Cat with any of that now – not when she had plenty of worries of her own. It would keep, Sadie decided, and she gave her best friend a reassuring smile. 'No, nothing at all.'

*

Most of the morning whizzed by in a whirl of excited, loved-up customers. Jaren stopped by to collect his bespoke Valentine's Day order and to ask Cat how the meeting had gone. His expression was grave as she relayed the details.

'Let me know if there is anything I can do,' he said, once she'd finished. 'And thanks again for my Valentine's gift. I hope the recipient appreciates the time and effort it took.'

'Has Seb given you anything yet?' Sadie asked Cat in an undertone, after Jaren had gone.

'No, but I caught him checking out the chocolates at Elin's last week, so I know what I'm getting!' Cat replied. She glanced over at Adam, who was wrapping a heart for a hopeful-looking teenage boy. 'How about you – received any mysterious cards or gifts?'

Sadie tried not to think about the card Daniel had slipped into her handbag that morning. 'No, and I'm not expecting anything. Stop stirring.'

'Just asking,' her friend said, raising her hands.

Cat clearly hadn't noticed that Adam could hardly bring himself to look Sadie's way, she thought with an inward sigh. But between Cat and Adam, there was a subdued air in the shop and by eleven-fifteen, Sadie had decided enough was enough.

'Come on, I'm taking you out for lunch,' she said, handing Cat her coat. 'You need the kind of cheering up that only smashed avocado and chilli sauce can achieve.'

*

On the way back, they saw Elin on Watergate Street. Sadie raised her hand to wave, but the chocolatier lowered her blonde head and dodged down a side street. The two friends stared after her.

'I suppose she didn't see us,' Cat said.

Sadie pursed her lips. 'I suppose not.'

'Maybe she was out buying a Valentine's Day card for Jaren,' Cat said, winking. 'That would explain a lot and make me very happy.'

Sadie gave her a quizzical look. 'Ever thought of becoming a matchmaker, Cat? Come on, we'd better get back. It's time for Clare and Adam to take their lunch.'

Clare must have been watching out for Sadie and Cat's return because she met them at the door of Smart Cookies. 'Two things,' she said in a low voice. 'Adam's gone home sick and there's a strange man waiting to see Cat.'

'Sick?' Sadie repeated. 'Is he okay?'

'Headache, he said,' Clare replied. 'Nothing serious.'

'Good,' Cat said. 'But what do you mean by "strange"?'

Clare puffed out her cheeks. 'As in I have no idea who he is. French, I think, and looks rich.'

Cat and Sadie exchanged alarmed looks.

'I put him downstairs with a cup of coffee,' Clare said nervously. 'I hope that's okay?'

'It's fine,' Sadie said firmly. 'We'll go and see what he wants now. Together,' she added, before Cat could argue.

'Thanks,' Cat said, flashing her a wobbly smile. 'I don't think I can face him on my own.'

'I'll go first,' Sadie said, squaring her shoulders.

She led the way, plastering on a cool unfriendly smile as she made her way down the stairs. Her first thought was that François de Beauvoir was older than she'd expected; his shock of silvery white hair was swept back from his tanned, well-lined forehead in a style that reminded her of an old film star and she saw an expensive-looking walking stick leaning against the table. He glanced up as she approached and got to his feet.

'Madame Smart.'

Sadie frowned. 'Sorry, do I know you?'

Behind her, Cat stopped three-quarters of the way down the stairs. 'Monsieur de Beauvoir.'

The man looked up and his eyes widened in recognition. 'Bonjour, Mademoiselle Garcia. My apologies for intruding on you like this, Madame Smart – as your friend rightly says, I am Robert de Beauvoir. I've come to discuss my son, François.'

Sadie's gaze flew to Cat's face, which had lost all of its colour. 'If you've come here to try and bully her even more—'

Robert de Beauvoir held up his hands. 'That is not my intention at all. On the contrary, I am here to apologise to Mademoiselle Garcia. My son's behaviour has only recently been brought to my attention and it is simply unforgivable. I want you to know that I have taken steps to ensure he will not trouble you again.'

'Brought to your attention?' Cat repeated. 'You mean you didn't know?'

A flush of embarrassment coloured the old man's cheeks.

'I knew that he was a ladies' man, yes. But I had no idea that he was forcing his attentions onto the women he worked with. And I certainly did not know that the real reason you left was because you had stood up to him; I was most upset when he told me you had left La Perle, which he claimed was for personal reasons of your own.'

Cat gaped at him. 'You didn't know? But the settlement ... it was all handled by your lawyers.'

Robert shook his head. 'Jacques Martin is my lawyer. All François' affairs are handled by Pierre Moreau. I promise you I was entirely in ignorance of the settlement he made to you. And I still would be, were it not for the actions of a mutual friend of ours.'

Now it was Sadie's turn to stare. 'A mutual friend? Who on earth do you mean?'

'The widow of a dear friend of mine. She runs a patisserie here in Castle Court – her name is Cherie Louboutin.'

Cat leaned against the bannister. 'I think I need to sit down.'

'So, let me get this straight,' Sadie said, once all three of them were seated at the basement table. 'Cherie told you what François had been up to?'

Robert inclined his silver-grey head. 'She telephoned me to say he had threatened you with legal action, which led me to discover the whole sorry tale. She also admitted her own part in the matter; having known my family for many years, I think she found it hard to believe François was capable of any wrongdoing and I'm afraid she assumed you were lying, mademoiselle.'

'I suppose that explains a few things,' Sadie said weakly.

Cat nodded. 'What did you mean when you said you'd taken steps about François? Because he summoned me to Paris yesterday and both he and Pierre Moreau seemed deadly serious about taking me to court.'

Robert's expression was a mixture of sadness and disgust. 'It grieves me to learn that my son is a bully on top of his other failings. I can only apologise once again and assure you that there will be no further action. François has been removed from his role at La Perle and you will receive a letter from Martin et Moreau confirming his complaint against you has been dropped.'

Sadie could hardly believe her ears and she thought Cat might burst into tears. 'Thank you,' she said, and her voice wobbled for a moment before she pulled herself together.

'Don't thank me,' Robert said. 'Thank Cherie for making me aware of what was happening.'

'Believe me, we will,' Sadie said fervently.

He lifted his cup and drained the last of his coffee. 'I will take up no more of your time. And should you ever find yourself in Paris and in need of a job, Mademoiselle Garcia, I do hope you will remember La Perle.' He smiled. 'We would be very happy to welcome you back.'

'I'll bear that in mind,' Cat said.

At the top of the stairs, Robert paused to study the City of Love display on one of the tables. '*Très jolie*,' he said. 'I will take two boxes for my grandchildren.'

Sadie packed them into a Smart Cookies bag and waved away his payment. 'Consider them a gift.'

He shook his head firmly. 'I am afraid I must insist on paying. I remember what it is like to be just starting out, when every single sale matters to you.'

'Then thank you, again,' Sadie said, realising he would not be persuaded.

He tucked the receipt into his wallet. 'And now I must visit the excellent Patisserie Cherie – as I recall, she makes the finest macarons this side of the Channel. Au revoir, Mademoiselle Garcia, Madame Smart.' Tilting his head in farewell, he left them standing there.

'Did . . . did that really just happen?' Cat ventured after a few seconds. 'Did he really just make all my worries disappear?'

'It looks that way,' Sadie said. 'And if what he says is true, then we owe Cherie a very large drink.'

'Maybe even two,' Cat conceded. She caught sight of Clare watching them in confusion. 'We'll explain later. Why don't you take your lunch now?'

A steady stream of customers kept Cat and Sadie busy for the next hour and it wasn't until Clare came back that they had the chance to talk again.

'I wonder what's wrong with Adam,' Cat said. 'Did he seem ill this morning?'

'No,' Sadie said cautiously. 'But—'

'You don't think he knew I was going to talk to him about the wedding favours debacle, do you?' Cat interrupted.

Sadie almost groaned; the last thing Adam needed was an unnecessary lecture from Cat. 'Actually, I've realised that was me,' she said, repeating the lie she'd told Adam the day before. 'I was tired. I lost concentration. I'm sorry.'

Her friend looked askance. 'That doesn't seem like you.'

'Like I said, I was tired,' Sadie replied, trying her utmost to sound convincing. 'But there was no harm done in the end.'

'Hmm,' Cat said, with a sideways glance. 'Okay. Maybe you could send him a message to check up on him. Find out when he thinks he'll be back.'

Sadie shifted uneasily. 'All right, I'll see what I can do.'

But a moment later, Cat held up a hand. She was staring down at her phone, an expression of bewilderment on her face. 'Wait. I've got an email from Adam right here.'

'Oh?' Sadie said, swallowing hard. 'What does it say?'

'He's handed in his resignation,' Cat said. 'With immediate effect.'

Sadie felt as though she'd been dealt a physical blow. 'Does he say why?'

'No, just that he's sorry to put us in a difficult situation.' Her eyes narrowed as she studied the screen. 'Something weird is going on here. What is it?'

Sadie hesitated. Surely Adam hadn't left because of her and Daniel? But what else could it be?

'I'm calling him,' Cat announced, tapping at her screen. 'There's more to this than meets the eye.'

'No, wait,' Sadie said. Slowly, Cat lowered her phone and stared at her. 'Come downstairs and I'll explain.'

Cat listened as she poured out the whole story.

'I don't know whether to kill you or congratulate you,' Cat said, shaking her head in mock fury. 'I mean, obviously I'm disappointed that Adam has left, but you can't live your life treading on eggshells.' She gave Sadie a keen look. 'Are you happy? About Daniel?'

'I think so,' Sadie said. 'He's changed, Cat.'

Cat said nothing for a moment, then smiled. 'In that case, I'm happy for you.'

Sadie felt herself sag with relief; she hadn't realised how much she'd been dreading telling Cat the truth. 'Thank you.'

'And don't worry about Adam – he'll get over it.'

He would, Sadie knew. His pride had been hurt and maybe even his heart, but he'd be fine. And maybe in time they might even be friends again. 'Sorry.'

Cat sighed. 'Don't be. We'll just have to recruit *two* new members of staff instead of one. And maybe this time we'll check they can spell before we let them loose with the icing.'

Chapter Twenty

'Close your eyes,' Cat instructed Cherie as she led her towards Seb's after closing time on Thursday evening. 'No peeping.'

Sadie pushed open the door. The bar was apparently empty. 'Okay,' she said. 'You can open them now.'

The older woman did as she was told, just as the shopkeepers of Castle Court burst out from their hiding places. 'Surprise!'

Andrew and Earl let off giant confetti canons and Seb unfurled a banner on the front of the bar that read THANK YOU, CHERIE! Jaren snipped the cord on a net of balloons that hung overhead, causing them to tumble down around Cherie. She stood as though rooted to the spot, shock and delight chasing each other across her face.

'Just a little thank you from us to you,' Cat said, presenting her with a biscuit version of Patisserie Cherie.

Seb placed a silver cocktail on the bar. 'There's a new permanent addition to the menu here – can I offer you the very first Cherie-tini?'

'And there's a new sundae over at the Bus Stop,' Andrew said, holding up a photo of a mountain of ice cream. 'The Cherry Cherie can't wait to meet you.'

Elin stepped forwards, a small square chocolate box in her hands. 'Here are my new Cherie chocolates – white chocolate and cherry kirsch – in your honour.'

Jaren grinned. 'And, of course, I'm not going to be outdone by these guys, so there's a Cherie Amour pancake on the menu at Let's Go Dutch.'

Cat watched Cherie's face as one fat teardrop fell, followed by a second and a third. 'Here,' Cat said softly, handing her a tissue. 'I know it's a lot to take in but, as you can see, everyone really appreciates what you did for me.'

'I only did what was right,' Cherie said, her voice muffled by the tissue. 'He was such a charming little boy when he was young, but once I knew the truth, I couldn't let him destroy you.'

'Thank you,' Cat said. She glanced over at the bar and grinned. 'Now, I think Seb will explode if I don't take you over there to try his new cocktail.'

She left Cherie at the bar and came to sit beside Sadie on one of the sofas.

'Seb's going to be finding this stuff for weeks,' Sadie observed, picking several glittery strands out of Cat's dark curls.

'Worth it for the look on Cherie's face, though,' Cat said.

Sadie glanced across the room to where Elin sat talking to Jaren. 'Speaking of looks, what's going on with Elin?'

Cat stared at her. 'What do you mean?'

'She gave us the weirdest look when we came in. Didn't you see?'

'No,' Cat said, frowning. She tapped her chin as though deep in thought. 'You did spell her name right on the Valentine's heart we made for Jaren, didn't you?'

'Ha ha,' Sadie said, thumping her playfully on the arm.

Seb appeared with a tray of cocktails. 'You can't drink a toast if you don't have a glass,' he announced.

'No sign of Greg, I see,' Cat said once Seb had moved on.

'I don't think anyone has seen him since Monday,' Sadie replied. 'No one seems to be missing him – not even his staff.'

Cat paused. 'And no Adam, either. Did he reply to your invitation?'

'No.'

'Don't beat yourself up. Like I said, he'll get over it.'

Sadie looked wistful, as though she had something on her mind, but at that moment, Seb tinkled a silver cocktail spoon against his glass. 'Ladies and gentlemen, I'd like to propose a toast to our guest of honour – the fabulous Cherie Louboutin!'

'The fabulous Cherie Louboutin!' everyone chorused.

'Speech!' Jaren called.

Cherie raised one hand. 'I don't believe in giving speeches, but I would like to thank you all for this honour. My darling husband always used to say that there was nowhere quite like this little community and I am happy to say he was right. Here's to all of you, my wonderful Castle Court family!'

They raised their glasses again and this time Cat chinked hers against Sadie's. 'And here's to us, for weathering another storm. Let's hope the next few months are calmer.'

Sadie considered the ups and downs of the last few days and smiled at her best friend. 'I'll definitely drink to that.'

Stormy Weather at Castle Court

Chapter Twenty-One

'Are you sure this is a good idea?' Cat Garcia murmured, as a cluster of determined six-year-olds careened around the shop floor of the Smart Cookies Biscuit Emporium, laughing and jostling as they wove in between customers' legs to peer beneath the round display tables piled high with fragile stock.

Sadie smiled from behind the glass-topped cabinet next to the till. 'I'm sure,' she said, tipping a discreet nod towards the two women who'd come in with the children. Each was holding an Easter Bonnet biscuit collection as they stood admiring the jewel-coloured iced egg decorations dangling from the miniature tree display. 'While the kids search out the next clue, their mothers are shopping.'

Cat was less than convinced. She knew several other Castle Court businesses were taking part in Chester's Easter Egg hunt, including the stationery shop, but their stock wasn't quite so delicate. And it was the last Saturday before Easter – the city's shoppers were out in force and Castle Court was busy, in spite of the blustery skies and torrential rain. A feature in *Good Housekeeping* magazine had meant a flurry of online orders as well as an increase in footfall. Did they really need this kind of sales boost?

She sighed. 'Any minute now, one of the displays will go toppling and we'll lose all the biscuits on display.'

Now Sadie laughed. 'Who are you – the Grinch that stole Easter? Lighten up!'

'Hmmm,' Cat said, doing her best to banish the frown that had settled between her eyebrows. She glanced at the table that held the Easter Bonnet tins; it did look as though quite a few had been bought. 'I suppose you're right.'

The sandy-haired boy leading the hunt let out a shout of triumph as he pounced on the flat cardboard egg Sadie had hung on the wall near to the front door. 'Found it!'

Craning over his shoulder, the only girl in the group made a determined swipe at the pastel-green card. 'What does it say?'

'Hey, I saw it first,' the boy said, yanking it out of reach and flipping it over. 'It says, *The King of the Court holds the next clue. You won't see it here – go up to floor two!*'

The group charged for the door, causing several customers to dodge out of their way. 'Not so fast,' one of the women called. 'We have to pay for these first.'

There was a collective groan from the children.

'Don't worry – I hear the Easter Bunny has left plenty of prizes. Just follow the trail,' Sadie said with a smile as their mothers carried their purchases to the counter.

'I wish the Easter Bunny could do something about the rain,' the other mother grumbled with a backwards glance towards the window. 'It feels like it's been wet all week.'

'It's the tail end of Storm Miranda from America,' Sadie said. 'Apparently it's going to get worse before it gets better.'

Cat watched the children, who were studying the biscuit farmyard display Sadie had created. 'We sell an Ice-Your-Own Easter Biscuit kit,' she said to the women. 'It comes with everything you need to create an edible masterpiece and they're three-for-two. They might buy you an hour of peace and quiet during a rainy afternoon.'

Both mothers looked interested. 'I'll have three,' the first one said with a grateful grimace. 'Anything to keep them from climbing the walls.'

'And three for me,' the second woman said. 'I might even have a go myself, although they won't look anything like as good as yours.'

'Sadie is our resident icing artist,' Cat said. 'She's a genius with a piping bag.'

'I don't know about that,' Sadie said, her cheeks reddening as she rang up the purchases. 'But I hope the children enjoy making their biscuits – it should definitely help to take their minds off the weather. My little girl is five and she loves creating her own designs.'

'And eating them, I expect?' the first woman said, grinning.

Cat listened as Sadie and the two mothers swapped rainy day survival tips. In the early days of Smart Cookies, Sadie had brought her daughter, Lissy, to work and the whole

Court had fallen under her spell. But there was no doubt she could be a handful; Cat still felt slightly sick when she recalled the afternoon Lissy had wandered out of the shop and gone missing among the Christmas crowds in Castle Court. Thankfully, the little girl hadn't gone far but it was a wake-up call for both Cat and Sadie. Now Sadie had a reliable childminder to help her during the school holidays and Daniel took over whenever she had to work on a Saturday; as much as Cat disliked Daniel, she had to admit he appeared to have turned over a new leaf since he and Sadie had decided to try again with their marriage last Christmas. And no matter how much Cat loved having Lissy around, the shop was no place for a five-year-old, especially in the run up to Easter weekend. Although they were nowhere near as busy as Elin's, the chocolate shop – its usually cool Swiss owner looked more and more frazzled every time Cat saw her.

'Thank you,' Sadie said, handing over elegant cardboard bags bearing the blue and gold Smart Cookies logo. 'Have fun – don't forget to tag us on social media if you upload any photos of your biscuits.'

'Happy hunting,' Cat called to the children.

No sooner had they left than another excited group squelched across the damp door mat, their dripping-wet mothers in tow. 'See?' Sadie murmured in satisfaction. 'I told you it was worth hiding a clue in the shop.'

Cat shook her head. 'I'm sure you're right. But watching the shelves wobble is giving me palpitations. Why don't I go and make us a cup of tea?'

Her best friend laughed. 'When in doubt, make tea.'

'Exactly,' Cat replied, heading for the stairs that led to the basement.

She left Sadie to supervise the new group of clue hunters, breathing a sigh of relief as she passed the trestle tables they used to host icing parties and reached the calm of the kitchen. Cat had never wanted to be anything other than a chef and there was something about being surrounded by the tools of her trade that made her feel instantly soothed. But this kitchen was special, partly because it was the heart of the Smart Cookies business Cat and Sadie had poured everything into, and partly because she'd spent so many quiet, peaceful mornings there, whipping up batch after batch of biscuits for Sadie to ice into perfection. But the kitchen wasn't empty today – Delilah was there, humming to herself as she rolled out some dough. She looked up as Cat approached.

'Fancy a cuppa?' Cat asked the grey-haired assistant.

Delilah dusted her hands on her blue and gold apron. 'Of course. But I'll make it.'

'No, you carry on,' Cat said, nodding at the golden dough on the work surface. 'It looks like you're just about ready to start cutting.'

'I am,' Delilah said. 'These are going to be frolicking lambs and chicks, then I've got another batch of chocolate eggs to cut out before lunch.'

Cat sniffed the air, savouring the hint of cinnamon sweetness in the air. 'And are those spiced biscuits I can smell in the oven?'

The older woman nodded. 'I've made a start on the jewelled crosses for the Bishop's Easter Sunday feast – his housekeeper needs the completed order by next Saturday at the very latest.'

Not for the first time, Cat thanked the benevolent stars that had made Delilah answer her advert for an assistant. The plump, twinkly-eyed retired school cook had settled in so fast that it felt to Cat as though she had always been part of the Smart Cookies team but her cheery nature hid a fearsome efficiency; exactly the kind of person Cat liked to have in her kitchen. And what she didn't know about baking wasn't worth knowing. 'I don't know how I managed without you, Delilah,' Cat told her, smiling. 'Thank you.'

'Oh, stop that,' Delilah scolded, but she looked pleased. 'If Clare and Sadie can get the whole lot iced by Thursday, I can drop them off at Bishop's House on my way home. It's no trouble.'

'Then the least I can do is make you a cup of tea,' Cat replied. She edged round Delilah and flicked the kettle switch.

She was on her way back up the stairs, bearing two steaming mugs of tea, when she spotted Clare easing her way through the shoppers, a mangled umbrella in one hand.

'It's still raining, then,' Cat said, eyeing the other woman's windswept hair and soggy shoes with sympathy.

Clare's heel skidded on the wet slippery floor and she clutched at a table to steady herself. 'Just a bit – I nearly got blown off my feet on Bridge Street. I don't know who Miranda is but she's fierce.'

Cat held out one of the cups. 'Here, take this. I'll make another one.'

By the time she had boiled the kettle again and made herself a replacement drink, the rain had grown heavier. The shop was bursting with people trying to escape the downpour – Cat didn't even try to squeeze through the crowd to join Sadie behind the counter. Instead, she stood by the steamed-up window, gazing beyond Sadie's *Watership Down* window display to the raindrops thundering into the puddles outside. There was almost a river running across the Court, gushing towards the drains where it bubbled and frothed around the metal grates. The sky was an ominous slate grey laced with sullen amber and, beneath it, the branches of the oak tree in the centre of the Court waved as though they were made of paper instead of wood. Storm Miranda was gathering pace.

Sadie joined Cat, an anxious look on her face. 'Look at those puddles,' she said, as the rain began to hammer in earnest. 'It's falling faster than it can drain.'

Cat eyed the torrents of water gushing from the awnings over the shops on the floors above, her own stomach starting to twist with unease. If the rain didn't ease off soon, there was a very real chance that the Court might flood.

'I don't suppose we've got any sandbags in the basement, have we?' she asked Sadie.

Her best friend stared at her. 'No. Do you think we're going to need them?'

'I hope not,' Cat said, swallowing a sigh. 'But maybe

247

we should think about getting everyone out of here, just in case.'

Sadie looked aghast. 'We can't send them out in this – they'll get drenched.'

'If this rain carries on they'll get wet whether they're inside or out,' Cat argued. 'Think of the panic it will cause if water starts coming through the door.'

'You don't really think—' Sadie began, glancing out of the window again.

'I don't know,' Cat said. 'But better to be safe than sorry, right?'

Sadie's expression wavered between doubt and disbelief. Then she nodded. 'You're right.' She cleared her throat. 'Ladies and gentlemen, I am sorry to have to do this to you but I'm sure you can all see the level of rainwater in the Court is rising. I'm afraid that means we need to close the shop, at least temporarily, to take precautions.'

There was a swell of muttering and grumbling among the assembled shoppers. Cat tensed, preparing herself for a battle. 'We really are very sorry,' she called. 'But if you have any purchases left to make, please make your way to the till. Thank you for your co-operation.'

Those customers holding Smart Cookies tins and boxes began to shuffle towards Clare at the back of the shop. Others started to make for the door. And then a startled cry cut through the moist air. 'Look! It's too late!'

A man in a rain-dappled overcoat was pointing at the bottom of the blue shop door. Sure enough, a steady stream of water was hissing around the wood and soaking into the already soggy welcome mat.

Cat's heart plummeted. What did they do now? If they opened the door to let everyone out, then even more rain-water would flood in. But what other course of action was there?

Sadie gripped her arm. 'We'd better prepare for the worst.'

With a disconcerting sense of unreality, Cat nodded. 'We need to move any stock that's near ground level,' she said. 'Then we can open the door and let you out.'

And the water in, she added silently. Beside her, Sadie began opening the drawers underneath the round display tables and pulled out the tins and boxes inside.

The young woman next to her held out her hands. 'Where do you want them?'

'On the counter, please,' Sadie said, sounding grateful.

The woman took the boxes and passed them to the next customer, who passed them on again, forming a chain. Other shoppers started to pull open the drawers beneath the rest of the shelves and started the same process. Seeing that everything was under control, at least for the next few minutes, Cat headed for the stairs. 'I'll see what I can do in the kitchen,' she said, trying not to wince at the thought of her precious work area deluged with rain.

Delilah looked up as Cat clattered into the basement. 'What's wrong?'

'We've got a major problem,' Cat said.

Delilah listened to her terse explanation, then pursed her

lips. 'We had something similar at the school I worked in once. The first thing you'll want to do is turn the power off at the mains – safest that way. Then you can work out what needs saving and what you'll have to leave behind.'

'I'll handle the power – you grab whatever you can and get upstairs.'

For a moment, she thought Delilah would argue. But then the grey-haired woman nodded. 'I'll take as many biscuits as I can carry.'

When Cat came back from the cupboard where the mains switch was located, Delilah had gone. Working fast in the half-light filtering through the bannister, Cat whipped the plastic tablecloths from the trestle tables and threw them over her stand mixers; they were too heavy to move upstairs, and the tablecloths might just be enough to save them from any water damage. She fumbled in the drawers and threw a handful of her most used biscuit cutters into a bag, hurrying upstairs with a whispered apology to the kitchen for abandoning it in its hour of need.

Sadie had been busy – the counter was piled high with stock. Clare was doing her best to make more room. 'I don't think we've got space for any more,' Sadie sighed, with a regretful glance around.

'We're out of time, anyway,' Cat said flatly, tipping her head towards the door and the increasing stream of rain. 'Right, everyone stand back. Things are about to get wet.'

The customers shuffled backwards, clearing a path to the shop entrance. Gritting her teeth, Cat tried to ignore the squelching sound from beneath her feet; unless she was mistaken, a wet welcome mat was going to be the least of her worries once she opened the door. Taking a deep breath, she grabbed the handle and pulled.

Even though she was ready for it, the force of the water still made Cat yelp as it spurted over her shins. Behind her, the crowd muttered and shuffled backwards as the rain spread across the shop floor. Cat waited for the flood to slow to a trickle – it didn't. The flow gushed and gurgled all the way to the stairs and beyond – down to the basement.

'Okay, everybody out!' she cried, waving her arm at the door. 'Quickly but safely, please.'

Delilah stepped in front of the stairs that led to the basement, holding firm to the bannister, and began to guide people out. In the brief second before the departing shoppers blocked her view, Cat saw that the old cook was wearing a pair of hot pink wellingtons below her blue and gold Smart Cookies apron. Where did she find those? Cat wondered but there was no time to ask.

'Please accept our apologies,' she called, as the customers splashed past her and out into the blustery Court. 'Hopefully, this is just a temporary measure and it'll be business as usual tomorrow.'

Clare materialised in front of Cat, still in her coat. 'Why don't I go and see if there are any sandbags around?' she asked. 'We can't be the only shop in Castle Court with this problem.'

A gust of wind buffeted the door as Cat glanced at the

rain-lashed shops. 'We're the only one on this side of the Court with a basement but if I was one of our neighbours, I'd be using any sandbags I had as a precaution.'

Her worried gaze came to settle on the businesses opposite Smart Cookies; the rain was pounding at their windows too but it seemed to be flowing away as it hit the ground, as though the Court had a barely noticeable slope. 'Try the Bus Stop or Let's Go Dutch first,' Cat told Clare. 'They're less likely to need any sandbags they might have.'

Once the last customer had left Smart Cookies, Cat tried to close the door again. But try as she might, the wood refused to fit back into the frame. 'It's swollen in the water,' Sadie said, coming to help. The two of them struggled for a few moments, then gave up.

'Brilliant,' Cat said, resisting the temptation to kick both the rain and the door. 'Just what we need in the middle of a flash flood – a barrier that won't close.'

Delilah peered outside. 'Don't look now but the heavens have just opened even more.'

Cat pressed her lips together. Delilah was right – the rain was cascading down from a hostile sky and the roar was ever more thunderous. 'Hurry up, Clare,' she muttered.

But when Clare dashed back across the Court, she was empty-handed. 'No sandbags at all,' she puffed. 'I even went up to the shops on the second and third floors but they all said the same thing – no one was expecting this amount of rain, so the Council didn't give any out.'

'Is anyone else flooded?' Sadie asked.

'A couple of shops on this side of the Court are struggling,' Clare said with a grimace. 'Patisserie Cherie have padded the door with towels but we definitely seem to have the worst of it.'

'I suppose we must be at the lowest point of the Court,' Sadie said, sounding frustrated.

Clare nodded. 'It looks that way. Jaren suggested using scrunched-up paper to block the gaps around the door.'

'At the moment, it's just one big gap, right in the middle,' Cat said. 'The door won't close.'

'I don't know what else to suggest,' Clare replied help-lessly. 'Sorry.'

Cat waved the apology away. 'It's not your fault. We'll just have to hope that it eases off soon.'

As one, they all gazed at the heavy skies.

'Come on,' Cat said, water splashing over her feet. 'Let's get this door shut. We don't stand a chance without it.'

Sadie sighed, her expression doubtful. 'To be honest, I don't think we stand a chance anyway.'

'We'll see,' Cat said, unwilling to let go of her optimism that this was just a temporary setback. 'Now, everyone get behind it and push!'

With their combined strength, the four women managed to wedge the door into its frame, although Cat suspected it would burst free again at any moment.

'Er – you don't think we should perhaps be on the other side?' Sadie said as water began to hiss through the gaps again.

'I don't think we're in much danger,' Cat said. 'But I am

worried about the stock – the dampness in the air will affect the biscuits. Let's take Jaren's advice and use paper to stop the water.'

'There's plenty of kitchen roll downstairs,' Delilah said. 'I'll get it.'

'No, let me,' Cat said, before the older woman could move. 'The stairs are wet, they're probably slippery.'

She navigated the treacherous staircase, gripping the bannister in case her feet flew out from beneath her. Squinting through the gloom, she was relieved to see that the floor of the basement was wet but not flooded, and there didn't seem to be any water dripping through the ceiling. Yet. She opened one of the cupboards, pulling out as many industrial-sized kitchen rolls as she could find, and was just about to start back up the stairs when she heard an almighty crash and the tinkling of broken glass. It was followed by a startled scream and the unmistakeable sound of surging water.

'Watch out, Cat!' Sadie bellowed.

Cat looked up to see a frothing, dirty river pouring down the stairs. She leapt backwards, flattening herself against the wall and thrusting the kitchen roll over her head as the flood washed over her knees. The water pressure was incredible, she thought, pressing hard against the cool plaster and fighting to keep her balance. And then she felt cold raining down on her head too; when she glanced upwards, she saw water cascading through the bannister and seeping through the light fittings across the basement ceiling. Fat drips bounced off the tables and kitchen work surfaces, splashing onto the floor to join the rest of the flood, and Cat felt her heart plummet. It would definitely take more than a few days to sort this mess out.

Shoulders sagging in defeat, she waited until the deluge from the stairs died down and then trudged upwards. 'Everyone out,' she commanded. 'There's nothing we can do here until the rain stops.'

Jaren appeared in the doorway, his dark hair plastered against his head. 'Is everyone okay?' he asked, eyeing the shattered window panel in the door. 'I saw what happened.'

'We're fine,' Cat said, her tone terse. 'Smart Cookies isn't.'

Jaren's eyes widened as he took in the water streaming down the stairs. 'No, I can see that.'

'We should go,' Sadie said, glancing at the boxes piled high on the counter. 'Why don't we take what stock we can carry? Some of it might be fine and I'm sure we can find somewhere dry to store it.'

'Bring it over to Let's Go Dutch,' Jaren said instantly. 'Hang on, I'll round up some helpers – we'll form a human chain.'

Cat ushered the others out into the deserted Court. Moments later, Jaren was back, followed by the staff from the pancake house and what looked like several customers. Some held umbrellas, others had their hoods up, making Cat wish she'd thought to grab their own coats; it couldn't be good for Delilah to get a soaking at her age. Their handbags were downstairs too, containing car keys, phones and purses. There was no doubt about it – she needed to go back in.

'Sadie, you handle the stock rescue,' Cat said, just as Andrew and Earl hurried over. 'I'm going to grab our things before the water gets any higher.'

She didn't wait for Sadie to answer. At the bottom of the stairs, she let out a horrified gasp as she peered through the murky shadows. The water level was a quarter of the way up the walls; the chairs around the trestle tables were floating, along with various biscuit cutters and piping bags. Rain was now pouring through the ceiling and the white plaster had turned an ugly grey colour. Taking a deep breath, Cat plunged into the water, gasping again as the cold bit into her thighs. She waded slowly towards the cupboard where they kept their personal belongings, thankful it was currently above the level of the flood. All four handbags were still dry; Cat slung two over each shoulder before turning towards the tall cupboard where they stored their coats. Opening it was going to be a problem, she realised immediately; the door went down to ground level. She'd have to battle against the weight of the water to get to the coats hanging within.

Bracing herself, she grabbed the handle and pulled. The door didn't move. She pulled again, determined to get it open. It gave the tiniest bit. Cat put all her strength into it and managed to wedge an arm through to touch the fabric inside. But no sooner had she wound her fingers into the material than there was a gritty tearing sound from over her head. She looked up to see the plaster above her sag into an enormous round bubble. And then it burst.

Cat threw her free arm up over her head as the ceiling came down and everything went dark.

Chapter Twenty-Two

'Cat!'

The voice seemed far away and close by at the same time. Cat shook her head groggily, and then winced at the sharp pain that shot across her skull. She was freezing cold too, lying half propped up against the cupboards and up to her chest in water. One arm was suspended above her head, still wedged in the cupboard door; that ached too. And the water around her was filled with chunks of plaster; when she looked up, she could see rays of light amongst the flood that continued to pour through the floorboards above. There was no ceiling left at all.

A figure loomed into view at the bottom of the stairs. Cat tried to get up and fell back down with a loud splash that filled her mouth with water. 'Over here,' she coughed, spitting the grit-filled liquid out with a shudder. 'I'm here!'

The figure turned and waded towards her. 'Where are you? Are you hurt?'

Cat squinted in the semi-darkness. 'I think I've hit my head. It hurts, anyway.'

Jaren's concerned face swam into focus and immediately recoiled. 'Shit!' he exclaimed, staring at her. 'You look awful.'

Cat almost laughed. She reached up a shaky hand to touch her head. Her fingers came away covered in blood. 'I don't feel great,' she admitted. 'I think I ate some plaster.'

Jaren didn't smile. 'How many fingers am I holding up?'

Cat peered at his hand. 'Three. No, four.'

He shook his head. 'We need to get you to hospital.' He gave the water cascading through the sodden floorboards a worried look. 'Can you walk? I don't trust that ceiling.'

Experimentally, Cat twitched her legs. They were cold but seemed to move. 'I think so. But my arm is trapped in the cupboard.'

'I might be able to free that,' Jaren said, studying the tall wooden door. 'But you're sitting at a really funny angle and your arm is twisted. Have you injured that too?'

She tried to wiggle her fingers. 'Maybe.' Her head swam and Jaren's face grew fuzzy. She clenched her free fist and fought to cling onto consciousness. 'I can't feel very much.'

'We can't risk staying here. Hold onto me,' Jaren instructed. 'I'm opening the door now.'

Cat felt the wood give and her arm slithered down to land in the water with a splash. She gripped onto Jaren as black dots exploded behind her eyes and greyness filled the spaces in between. 'I think I'm going to ...' she mumbled as he stood, sweeping her into his arms.

'I've got you,' he said, as she slipped into unconsciousness once more.

When Cat came to again, she was in an ambulance and wearing an oxygen mask. A kind face smiled down at her.

'There you are,' the female paramedic said. 'Don't try to move – you're safe now.'

Blinking, Cat's gaze swivelled to the side and found Sadie watching her with a pinched, worried expression. 'Oh, thank God you're awake.'

The paramedic lifted the mask so Cat could speak. 'I am,' she said slowly. 'What happened?'

Sadie looked even more concerned. 'There was a flash flood at the shop, remember? The ceiling fell in while you were in the basement.'

Cat closed her eyes, trying to piece things together. It had been dark and wet, she recalled. And there'd been blood. 'I hit my head,' she murmured.

'That's right,' the paramedic said. 'You've got a nasty cut and we think you fell, so we've put you in a neck brace as a precaution. The good news is that I haven't found any obvious broken bones but we're taking you to hospital to make sure.'

That explained the strange pressure around her throat and under her chin, Cat thought groggily.

'I'm Nina, by the way, and my colleague, Doug, is driving us. Now,' the paramedic went on, 'do you think you feel up to answering a couple of questions? Nothing too difficult, we're not talking *Mastermind*.'

'Okay,' Cat said, her gaze flickering briefly to Sadie's troubled face.

'Good. I'm just going to shine a light in your eyes, so I can check how you're doing, and then we'll get started.'

Cat tried not to squint as Nina shone a thin beam first in one eye, then the other. She snapped off the light, apparently satisfied. 'Right, can you tell me what day it is?'

'Saturday,' Cat said after a moment's hesitation. It was Saturday, wasn't it? The last one before Easter . . .

'Good,' Nina said. 'And the year?'

'2018,' Cat replied, feeling on steadier ground.

Once again, Nina looked pleased. 'And lastly, I realise these are uncertain times but who is our current Prime Minister?'

Cat managed a half smile as she gave her answer. 'But ask me again next week and you might get a different reply.'

The paramedic smiled as she checked Cat's blood pressure. 'It certainly makes our job harder – sometimes, I can't tell whether a patient is confused or just not up-to-date with the latest politics.'

'I can imagine,' Sadie said with a wry twist of her mouth.

A sudden memory surfaced in Cat's brain. She threw an anxious glance at Sadie. 'The bags—'

'They're safe,' Sadie said quickly. 'A bit wet but otherwise fine. Although I still can't believe you went back for them – what the bloody hell possessed you?' Tears filled her eyes. 'It scared the life out of me when the ceiling collapsed with you still down there.'

'Sorry,' Cat mumbled, feeling her own eyes prickle with tears. 'I just thought we might need our stuff, that's all.'

'Don't upset yourself,' Nina said in a soothing voice. 'You're doing fine now. And with a bit of luck we'll discover there's no real harm done.'

Sadie tried to smile. 'Fingers crossed.'

Cat lay quietly for a moment, as her memory started to return. She listened for the tell-tale thud of rain on the ambulance roof. 'What about the shop? Is it still raining?'

Her best friend hesitated. 'No, it's stopped.' She exchanged a look with the paramedic. 'We can talk about the shop later. When you're feeling better.'

'That sounds bad,' Cat said, her lips twisting into a grimace.

'It's not great,' Sadie admitted. 'But don't think about it now. There's nothing wrong that can't be fixed.'

'And the stock?'

'Safely under various roofs around the Court,' Sadie reassured her. A look of admiration crossed her face. 'You should have seen the way Andrew and Earl rallied the troops – those guys make a tight team. At one point, they had a three-way human chain sending boxes and tins to different locations across the Court.'

Cat smiled too. 'Amazing.'

'It was,' Sadie said. 'I've left Clare and Delilah in charge – they're going to see what they can salvage and take care of the shop.'

'They'll need the insurance documents—' Cat said, trying to sit up.

Nina laid a gentle hand on her chest, pushing her back down. 'None of that, thank you. Just relax.'

'Seb has gone to pick up the paperwork from your flat,' Sadie said. 'Although he really wanted to come with you to the hospital. His face when Jaren appeared at the top of the stairs with you slumped in his arms ...'

With a shiver that was half due to embarrassment and half to the chill in her bones, Cat groaned. 'Jaren – of course. I didn't even thank him.'

'You were just a little bit unconscious,' Sadie replied with a wry smile. 'I don't think he'll hold it against you.'

'I'm afraid that's enough talking for now,' Nina said, holding the oxygen mask over Cat's mouth and observing her closely. 'We'll be at the hospital soon – try to rest until then.'

It wasn't a difficult order to follow, Cat thought; she felt as though she'd gone ten rounds with Nicola Adams. Her arm was no longer numb, but it was aching, and her legs were still cold despite the blankets piled on top of them. Belatedly, she realised there was nothing between her skin and the cotton sheet. Glancing around, she tried to spot her jeans and jumper.

'What's wrong?' Sadie asked.

Cat reached up a leaden arm and lifted the mask from her face. 'My clothes.'

'Unfortunately, I had to cut them off,' Nina said. 'They were soaked through and your temperature was already low.'

'Am I naked?' Cat squeaked.

'You've still got your underwear, damp though it is, and I popped a gown on you to save your blushes,' Nina said, entirely matter-of-fact as she replaced the oxygen mask. 'Not the height of fashion but at least it's dry.'

'I'll bring more clothes,' Sadie added hastily. 'Or Seb can pick some up, along with anything else you need. It's not a problem.'

The ambulance slowed down. 'We're here,' a male voice rumbled from the driver's seat.

'Thanks,' Nina called back. She looked at Sadie. 'Once we've got you inside, we'll leave you in the safe hands of the A & E team. They'll want to do some tests and probably a CT scan.'

Cat tried to shake her head; she might be battered and bruised but she didn't need a CT scan, for goodness sake. A stern look from Sadie quelled her protest. 'Don't argue,' she said, in a tone that told Cat she knew exactly what she'd been thinking.

A minute later, the ambulance stopped. The doors at the back opened and the male paramedic poked his head inside. 'Hello, I'm Doug. Let's get you out of here, shall we?'

Sadie climbed out and stood to one side as Nina and Doug lifted the trolley bed out of the ambulance. Cat lost sight of her as they wheeled the trolley through the double doors and into the hospital.

'I'm here,' Sadie said, from somewhere behind Cat's head. 'Still with you.'

She came to stand next to the bed as the paramedics spoke to the admissions nurse. 'How are you feeling?'

Cat resisted the urge to touch her aching head. 'I've been

better.' She paused as the moment the ceiling had crashed down loomed large in her memory. 'I suppose you could say the same about Smart Cookies.'

Sadie gave her an exasperated look. 'Will you stop worrying about the shop? *You* are what's important now.'

Nina turned back from her conversation with the nurse. 'We'll leave you with Rishi now – she'll make sure you're looked after.'

Doug nodded at Cat. 'All the best, then.'

'Thanks,' Cat said, managing a smile. 'And thanks to you too, Nina. I'll send you both some biscuits once I'm back on my feet.'

'No need for that,' Nina said, patting her waist. 'A lifetime on the hips, sadly.'

Doug grinned. 'Send them anyway – I'll eat Nina's.'

Both paramedics gave a final wave as they headed for the door.

'Right,' the nurse said, her practised gaze roving over Cat. 'As Nina said, my name is Rishi. Just a few more details and we'll see what the damage is, okay?'

It seemed to Cat that the next few hours whirled by. There were more lights shone into her eyes and a lot more questions about the day, month and year, although the people asking the questions changed. Finally, after x-rays and scans and several frowning doctors had examined her, the medical team seemed satisfied that she had no life-threatening injuries. The wound on her head had caused a concussion and her arm was badly bruised but there was no damage to her spine or anywhere else. Once the head wound was dressed, she was wheeled into a ward for the night.

'For observation,' the doctor said with a tired smile as she scribbled on the clipboard at the bottom of Cat's bed. 'If everything goes well, you should be able to go home in the next day or so.'

Cat tried to sit up. 'Do I have to stay here?'

'Yes!' Sadie said firmly. 'You absolutely do. At least if you're in here I don't need to worry about you trying to do anything else stupid.'

Cat opened her mouth to explain that rescuing their coats and bags had seemed important at the time but she was overcome by a sudden wave of exhaustion, as though the stress and pain of the afternoon's events had suddenly caught up with her.

'Okay,' she said, hearing the weariness in her own voice. 'But keep in touch, Sadie. And don't sugar-coat it – I want to know everything.'

'I promise,' Sadie replied. 'As long as you promise to get some rest.'

Cat rested against the cool cotton pillow and allowed her heavy eyelids to drift shut. 'I think I can probably manage that.'

It was starting to get dark by the time Sadie left Cat sleeping peacefully under the watchful gaze of the nursing staff and made her way out of the hospital.

In the car park, she pulled out her phone and fired off a message to Daniel: *Everything OK?*

Moments later, her phone lit up and his name appeared on the screen.

'Hello,' Sadie said. 'I wasn't sure if you'd be reading Lissy her story.'

'Not yet,' Daniel replied. 'She wanted to wait up for you.'

Sadie almost groaned. 'But I don't know how long I'm going to be – I've only just left the hospital. It's not practical for Lissy to stay up—'

'Calm down,' Daniel cut in, his voice soothing. 'I've explained that you won't be back until late – we're just having a special hot chocolate and then Lissy has promised to go straight to sleep. Haven't you?'

'Yes, Mummy.'

Lissy's voice was high and excited – Sadie didn't envy Daniel the job of making sure she stuck to her promise, especially since his special hot chocolate recipe usually involved marshmallows and Smarties. 'Good girl,' Sadie said, doing her best to sound warm and encouraging. 'I'll see you in the morning for a long cuddle.'

'How are things going?' Daniel said carefully.

'As well as can be expected,' Sadie replied, aware that Lissy might still be listening. 'But I have no idea what the situation is at the shop. I'm heading over there now.'

'At least it's stopped raining,' Daniel said.

Sadie stared up at the heavy skies overhead. The wind had died down but she didn't like the look of the thick clouds that still skulked above her. More rain could easily be on the way.

'That's something, I suppose,' she said. 'Listen, I'm not sure how late I'm going to be so don't wait up.'

A brief silence stretched. 'No problem,' Daniel said. 'But make sure you don't stay longer than you need to – it'll all still be there in the morning. In fact, it will probably look better tomorrow.'

Sadie pictured the rainwater pouring through the floor-boards and splashing into the flooded basement. She closed her eyes for a second. 'I seriously doubt it.'

'Even so,' Daniel insisted, 'make sure you look after your-self. And get something to eat. Shall I cook you something, ready for when you get home?'

He was just trying to take care of her, she knew, but food was the last thing on Sadie's mind. She was too busy imagin-ing the devastation that awaited her at Smart Cookies. 'No, don't worry,' she said, running a hand over her face. 'I'll get something later – maybe a burger or something at the diner, if I get a chance. And I'm sorry you had to cancel your plans to look after Lissy tonight. Will you be able to re-schedule?'

'Yeah, no problem,' Daniel said easily. 'It was only a few drinks with an old friend. Nothing special.'

Gratitude pulled Sadie's mouth into a reluctant smile; knowing Lissy was in safe hands had given her one less thing to think about while she worried over Cat. 'I'll make it up to you,' she promised Daniel.

'No need,' he said, his voice warm. 'Just come home safely.'

'I will. Give Lissy a kiss goodnight from me.'

She rang off and hurriedly dialled Clare's number. The

relief in the other woman's voice was clear when Sadie told her Cat wasn't in any immediate danger. 'That's such good news – Seb will be so pleased. Jaren too – all of us, really.'

'She was sleeping when I left and the doctors seem to think she's going to be fine,' Sadie said. 'I'm on my way to the shop now – how are things going?'

'Not bad,' Clare said, sounding cautious. 'Seb found the insurance paperwork and I rang the helpline number. They sent someone out to temporarily board up the door, so that it's secure overnight. An assessor will be in touch as soon as possible to see how much damage there is.'

Sadie swallowed hard. 'And how did it look to you?'

Clare hesitated. 'It's really hard to say. The power is still off and the emergency services refused to let us go inside. I'm sorry, Sadie, I don't think we'll really know the full extent until tomorrow.'

'Right,' Sadie said slowly, letting the words sink in. She'd been so wrapped up in making sure Cat was okay that she hadn't allowed herself to think too much about the devastation at the shop; the flood felt like a half-remembered dream and she needed to see the aftermath for herself to make it feel real. 'I'm still coming over. Can you hang on until I get there?'

'Of course,' Clare said. 'Jaren has given me one of the tables in the window of Let's Go Dutch so I can keep an eye on things and Earl is keeping me company. Get here when you can – no rush.'

Sadie knew exactly which table she meant; the one with

a direct view of the Smart Cookies window. She pictured the warm restaurant, filled with the scent of delicious food and buzzing with customers – it was no small thing for Jaren to have sacrificed a prime spot on a Saturday night, or for Earl to be away from the diner to make sure Clare wasn't on her own. Sadie would have to thank them both, as well as finding a way to show her gratitude to Jaren for saving her best friend's life.

'Say hi to Earl for me,' she told Clare. 'I'll be there as soon as I can.'

It wasn't until she'd hung up and begun walking across the hospital car park that Sadie remembered her car wasn't there; she'd arrived in the ambulance with Cat. She stood for a moment, staring into space, wondering how she was going to get back to Castle Court. Then her beleaguered brain kicked in and she pulled out her phone. If she couldn't get a taxi, there was always the bus. And failing that, she'd have to walk.

Chapter Twenty-Three

Sadie supposed she should have expected the anxious welcoming committee that greeted her when she walked through the door of the pancake house. Clare and Jaren were waiting by the bar, with Seb instead of Earl for company. Jaren hurried over as soon as Sadie was over the doorstep. 'This way,' he said, ushering her to a waiting seat. 'What can I get you – a coffee? A hot chocolate?'

Seb let out a growl of disgust. 'Never mind that – what she needs is a proper drink.'

'A hot chocolate sounds like heaven, actually,' Sadie said, throwing Jaren a grateful look. 'Thank you.'

The Dutchman signalled to a waiter. 'The biggest hot chocolate you can manage. And some *speculaas*, in case she's hungry.'

'How are you feeling?' Clare asked sympathetically.

Sadie resisted the urge to glance across at the darkened window of Smart Cookies. 'I'm fine. Nothing that a good night's sleep won't fix, anyway. But the shop—'

'Will keep until the morning,' Seb said, a kind expression on his face. 'Don't even think about it until then.'

And now Sadie did look across Castle Court; Smart Cookies was a black hole among the golden light of the other shops. If their neighbours had suffered from the rushing waters, none of them had been forced to switch off the power. But they hadn't escaped entirely; the awning of Patisserie Cherie had an ugly rip in the middle and the health food shop window was cracked across one corner. 'No, I suppose not,' she said and her voice started to break.

'Here,' Jaren said, putting an enormous mug on the bar next to her, along with a plate of thin, horse-shaped biscuits. 'These will help. And don't forget we managed to rescue a lot of your stock. The shop might need a bit of TLC to get her up and running again but not everything is lost and we'll all do everything we can to help.'

His warm smile banished Sadie's tears. 'Thank you,' she said, reaching across to break off a corner of biscuit. 'I don't know what would have happened if you hadn't been there today.'

He shook his head. 'It was nothing. Any of us would have done the same.'

Sadie crunched the thin biscuit, savouring the delicious warmth of the cinnamon and ginger. 'I'm sure we would have but that isn't the point,' she said. 'Your quick thinking and bravery saved Cat's life. You're a hero, Jaren.'

'Hear hear,' Clare said, gazing at Jaren with undisguised admiration. 'The way you charged down those stairs after the floor collapsed – it was like something out of a movie.'

Jaren waved the praise away. 'It all happened so fast,' he said, with an uncomfortable glance at Seb. 'And really, all that matters is that Cat is safe and on the road to recovery.'

'Thanks to you,' Clare persisted, grinning. 'You're Castle Court's answer to Superman, Jaren. Elin's a lucky girl!'

Seb cleared his throat. 'Did they say when Cat would be able to come home?'

'Not yet,' Sadie said as she nibbled on another piece of biscuit. 'They want to keep an eye on her, make sure there's nothing hiding away behind that head wound.'

'It's probably best that she stays with me for a few days,' Seb suggested. 'She'll need a bit of looking after and I'm the best person for that job.'

Sadie's eyes widened a little. Was it her imagination or did she detect a hint of jealousy behind Seb's words. Surely he didn't feel threatened by Jaren's rescue?

'I'm sure Cat will have her own thoughts about where she'll stay once she's allowed out of hospital,' she said diplomatically. 'But it's a lovely idea, Seb.'

He nodded and Sadie was relieved to see his shoulders settle. She didn't dare look at Jaren; had he picked up on the undercurrents too?

'Cat will need some clothes, though,' Sadie said, finishing the *speculaas* and taking a long sip of hot chocolate. 'And some toiletries. Have you got the keys to her flat, Seb? I can pop over in the morning and take whatever she needs to the hospital.'

'You're going to be busy with the shop,' Seb pointed out.

'Why don't you give me a list and I can drop everything in to her? I want to see for myself that she's okay, anyway.'

Sadie was too tired to argue. 'We can sort all this out in the morning – I should have a better idea how long she's going to be in hospital by then.' She stifled a yawn. 'I'm sorry, Jaren, but as delicious as it is, I don't think I can finish this hot chocolate. I need to get home before my eyelids drop any further.'

He smiled. 'No problem. I'll make you another one tomorrow.'

Clare gave her a sideways look. 'Why don't I walk you to your car? You've had a long day too.'

'And so have you,' Sadie objected, half-laughing. 'I'll be fine – it's only a ten-minute walk and the drive will be easy at this time of night.'

'She's right,' Seb said. 'Why don't I walk you back?'

'Because you have a bar to run,' Sadie countered. 'It's Saturday night and the last thing you need is to be stuck babysitting me. The same goes for you, Jaren,' she said, before the Dutchman could argue. 'You're needed here.'

She slid off her seat and fixed them with a determined look. 'Thank you for your concern but I'll be fine. And thanks for all your help today, Clare. I'll let you know what the plan is as soon as I know it myself.' She looked at Jaren and Seb. 'Thanks to both of you, too. And if you happen to see Andrew or Earl, let them know I appreciate everything they did. You were all amazing.'

With a wave, Sadie made her way to the door. Outside,

the wind was cold; she could hear the branches of the oak tree creaking and sighing as they moved. For a moment, she was tempted to cross the Court and press her nose against the window of Smart Cookies. But the darkness discouraged her; there was nothing to see – nothing good, at any rate. She hesitated for a heartbeat, then turned away and hurried to the alleyway that led out of Castle Court. As Seb had so rightly pointed out, whatever lay in wait for her at the shop would most definitely still be there in the morning.

Sunday dawned bright and clear, without a trace of the wind and rain that had caused such turmoil the day before. Sadie lay still for a few moments, feeling the weight of Daniel's arm across her middle, enjoying the warmth of his body. She'd stood in the shower for almost thirty minutes when she'd got home the night before, waiting for the hot water to banish the cold from her limbs, but the chill was still there, in her bones. She could only imagine how Cat had felt when she'd awoken in the flooded basement, injured and trapped. Thank God Jaren had been there, Sadie thought with a shiver.

'Hello,' Daniel murmured beside her. 'What time is it?'

Sadie glanced at the clock on her bedside table. 'Just after seven.'

Daniel's arm tightened around her. 'Go back to sleep, then. Lissy won't be up for a while – it took her ages to go to sleep last night.'

That would be due to the sugar overload, Sadie thought but didn't say. 'I need to get over to the shop. It was too dark to see much last night and I want to get an idea of how much damage there is.'

He opened his eyes. 'You'll stay and have breakfast with us, though, right? I didn't want to say anything on the phone last night but Lissy missed you yesterday.'

'Of course I'll stay,' Sadie said, her heart already aching at the thought of leaving her daughter. 'But I'm going to be out for pretty much the rest of the day. It can't be helped.'

Daniel frowned. 'Obviously this is an emergency situation and the shop has to come first but Lissy needs you too.'

Sadie felt the familiar stab of guilt. 'I know. And I'll be home as soon as I can but, in the meantime, why don't you take her out for the day? I'm sure she'd love a trip to the zoo.'

'Fine,' Daniel said, sitting up abruptly. His shoulders stayed high and rigid for a few seconds, then he sighed and glanced back at Sadie. 'Look, you've got enough on your plate without me giving you a hard time. It's just—'

'It's just difficult,' Sadie said, swinging her legs out of bed. 'Believe me, I know that too.'

'I'll put some toast on for Lissy,' Daniel said as he reached for his dressing gown. 'Why don't you go in and wake her up?'

'Mummy!' Lissy murmured when she opened her eyes and peered upwards through her tangle of auburn curls. 'You're home.'

'I am,' Sadie said, gathering her sleepy daughter into her arms. 'How are you this morning?'

Lissy took a moment to think before she answered. 'Hungry.'

Sadie laughed. 'You're always hungry. Daddy's put some toast on for you – shall we go downstairs and see if it's ready?'

Kicking the covers off with sudden enthusiasm, Lissy nodded. 'Yes. Can I have jam on my toast?'

'I don't think we have any,' Sadie said. 'But we've definitely got Marmite.'

'Daddy lets me have jam,' Lissy grumbled as Sadie helped her to pull her dressing gown over her dinosaur pyjamas.

'And I don't, unless it's a special occasion,' Sadie replied cheerfully. 'Never mind, only another thirteen years until you're a grown up and can eat whatever you want.'

The idea of being given free rein over her breakfast decisions caused Lissy to fall temporarily silent. It wasn't until she and Sadie were almost at the bottom of the cottage stairs that she spoke again. 'Daddy said Auntie Cat was hurt yesterday. Is she still in hospital?'

'Yes, but she's not badly hurt,' Sadie reassured her. 'In fact, I'm going to see her today. And if the doctors say it's okay, she might even be coming home later.'

Lissy's frown grew deeper. 'And Daddy said the shop is underwater. Is that true?'

'That's true too,' Sadie said, wondering how much detail her daughter would demand. 'There was too much rain and some of it washed down the stairs and into the basement.'

They'd reached the kitchen and Sadie felt the briefest flash of annoyance when she saw Lissy's toast was already spread with a thick layer of glistening red jam.

'And was it the rain that hurt Auntie Cat?' Lissy pressed

on as she slid into her seat at the kitchen table. 'Did she drown?'

Sadie stared at her daughter. 'No, she bumped her head. But as I said, she's on the mend.' She turned to Daniel, eyebrows raised. 'There is such a thing as too much information.'

He raised his hands. 'Don't blame me. I only mentioned the flood.'

Lissy took a bite of toast. 'We watched a film about a mermaid at school,' she said indistinctly. 'The prince fell in the water and drownded and the mermaid had to rescue him.'

'Right,' Sadie said, relieved. 'Don't worry – there were no mermaids or princes involved. I'll be going to the shop today to work out how we're going to get all the rain out of the basement.'

'And I'm taking you to the zoo,' Daniel put in. 'Maybe we can meet Mummy for something to eat afterwards.'

Lissy chewed in silence for a moment, then fixed Sadie with a fierce look. 'Watch out for sea hags, Mummy. If you want, you can borrow my triceratops for protection.'

Amusement bubbled up inside Sadie but she kept it well hidden. 'I'd like that, Lissy, thank you.'

'But what about us?' Daniel asked in a worried-sounding tone. 'Who's going to protect us from the lions and tigers and bears at the zoo?'

Lissy let out a heavy sigh. 'We'll take the T-Rex. Honestly, Daddy, you're so silly sometimes.'

Sadie grinned. 'What would we do without you, Lissy?'

Her daughter waved an airy hand. 'Get eaten by tigers or sharks, I expect.'

And this time, Sadie couldn't stop herself from laughing.

Sadie's phone rang just as she was leaving the house; the insurance company wanted to know when they could send someone to examine the damaged shop. Impressed and relieved to discover Cat had paid an additional premium for an emergency response service, Sadie had told them she anticipated being on the premises all day but she was still amazed to see a man in a dark, pin-striped suit waiting outside Smart Cookies as she hurried into Castle Court.

'Mrs Smart?' he said as she approached. 'I'm George Whittaker, from Sun Hill insurance company.'

'You got here fast,' Sadie said, taking in his clipboard and air of quiet efficiency. 'Did they beam you over?'

He laughed. 'No, I live locally.'

She shook his outstretched hand. 'Well, I'm pleased to meet you. Sort of.'

George Whittaker didn't seem in the least bit offended. 'Don't worry, I get that a lot. Most people only see us once there's been some kind of emergency but I'm hoping to make this as painless as possible for all concerned.'

'That would be great,' Sadie said. She waved a hand at the forlorn-looking shop beside them and tried not to notice the bloated, broken bunnies lying face down in the window. 'I'm sorry to drag you out on a Sunday. As you can see, it's all a bit of a mess.'

'Floods don't care what day of the week it is and they cause all kinds of havoc,' George said, sounding sympathetic. 'Even after the water has receded. Is the gas and electricity off? I'm afraid we can't enter the premises unless it's safe to go in.'

Sadie nodded. 'We shut them off as soon as the water started to come in.'

George examined the sturdy wooden panels over the door. 'I've arranged for the joiner to meet us to remove these. He should be here any minute.'

As Sadie glanced around the Court, she saw Jaren watching them from inside Let's Go Dutch. He mimed drinking something.

'Would you like a cup of coffee while we wait?' Sadie asked, grateful for something to do.

The insurance assessor looked appreciative. 'I wouldn't mind one. White, no sugar, please.'

By the time Sadie had answered Jaren's questions and gathered a drink for George and herself, the joiner had arrived. Quickly and methodically, he set about removing the wood that had kept Smart Cookies secure overnight. Once he'd finished, he propped open the still swollen door of the shop and cast a doubtful look at Sadie's Converse. 'I hope you've got wellington boots. It looks wet in there.'

Sadie patted the bag over her shoulder. 'I have.' She glanced at George. 'We can get changed in the pancake house if you like. I'm sure Jaren won't mind.'

The joiner shrugged. 'Right you are. I'll start measuring up for a new door.'

Five minutes later, Sadie and George were standing just inside the doorway of Smart Cookies. The insurance assessor was taking notes, his eyes sweeping across everything, from the peeling paint of the rain-soaked floorboards to the water-spattered computer behind the counter. Sadie stared at the destruction and tried her hardest not to cry; everywhere she looked, she saw more of her and Cat's hard work ruined. The display tables were bare, apart from the bright cotton bunting that had somehow tumbled from its hooks on the wall to trail across their bloated surfaces; the fish tank that had housed an *Alice in Wonderland* biscuit display was now lying sideways on the floor, its contents smashed beyond any recognition. The musty scent of damp filled the air; the smell was already overwhelming.

'I don't want you to go too far in,' George said. 'I'm not sure I trust those floorboards, to be honest. Did you say the ceiling had come down in the basement?'

'Yes,' Sadie replied. 'It landed on my business partner.'

If the insurance assessor was surprised, he didn't show it. 'I do hope she wasn't badly hurt,' he said, with a quick glance at his clipboard. 'Would that be Miss Garcia?'

Sadie nodded. 'That's right. And she seems to be okay, thankfully. Jaren from the pancake house rescued her.'

George looked impressed in spite of his professional demeanour. 'Sounds dramatic. I'll need to take a quick look at the condition of the basement – no need for you to come.'

Carefully, he picked his way towards the stairs. They creaked as he made his way down them, causing Sadie to fervently hope another rescue mission wouldn't be needed. But a few minutes later, George returned to her.

'There's still a significant amount of flooding down there,' he said, jotting some notes. 'I'll arrange for a specialist company to come and pump it out. They'll be able to provide dehumidifiers too, to help get things dried out. Once that's done, we should be able to get a better handle on what needs to be done to get you up and running again.'

Sadie bit her lip. Pumps and dehumidifiers sounded time-consuming. 'How long do you think it's going to take?'

George shook his head. 'Hard to say at this stage. Probably around a week for everything to dry out, and maybe another two to make good the damage. You're probably looking at a month all told.'

'A month?' Sadie gasped, feeling as though she'd been kicked in the stomach. 'We can't be out of business for a month!'

'A lot depends on the weather,' George conceded. 'A few sunny days will help with the drying out process. But it needs to be done properly, especially in premises used for food preparation. Mould and mildew are health and safety issues.'

He continued to talk but Sadie found it hard to focus on what he was saying. A whole month without a shop to bake and ice the biscuits in – it would ruin them. They'd built up a healthy trade among Chester's traditional shoppers and that would dwindle away to nothing when the shop itself was closed. But worse than that was the hit their online orders would take; once word got out that they couldn't provide the biscuits people wanted, savvy internet shoppers would go elsewhere. It was a disaster – a total, unmitigated disaster.

'Mrs Smart?' George said, peering at her quizzically. 'Are you all right? You've gone very pale.'

Sadie forced her legs to work. 'Will you excuse me for a moment?' she said, her voice wooden. 'I think I need to sit down.'

Chapter Twenty-Four

'A month?' Jaren's eyes widened in dismay when Sadie gave him the news. 'That's rough.'

'It's worse than that,' Sadie said, staring gloomily into the cup of tea he'd placed on the table in front of her. 'It could well mean the end of Smart Cookies.'

'That's not going to happen,' he said firmly. 'You and Cat have worked too hard for something like this to snatch everything away. Smart Cookies is your dream!'

A dream that was rapidly turning into a nightmare, Sadie wanted to point out, but she kept the thought to herself. 'We can only sell biscuits that have been produced in properly approved and licensed premises,' she replied. 'Cat's kitchen is approved, as is mine at the cottage. I'd even got Daniel's kitchen approved in case I ever decided to move back in there. But I don't know how we'll manage with three potential satellite sites, especially when one of us will need to be on site at Smart Cookies to oversee the repairs.'

Jaren puffed his curly black hair out of his eyes. 'I see your problem.'

'I don't even know how long Cat's recovery will be,' Sadie admitted. 'Maybe we should put something on the website – warn our customers that there might be a delay.'

'You could,' Jaren said, sounding unconvinced. 'But it might be worth stopping to take stock first. We rescued quite a lot of biscuits from the flood – they're split between my stock room and the one at the Bus Stop diner.' He held up a hand as she began to interrupt. 'Just hear me out. Obviously, Cat's recovery is an unknown quantity but you and I both know it'll take something serious to keep her out of the kitchen. And in the meantime, you have Delilah to bake for you and Clare to ice the biscuits. Neither of them is as expert as you and Cat but they've been trained by the best.'

Sadie barely registered the compliments. 'But they need a kitchen to work in,' she objected. 'They can't work from home.'

'They can't work from their *own* homes,' Jaren fired back. 'But they could work from yours and Cat's. They could even work from here, if they needed to.'

Sadie almost laughed. 'I've seen how busy it gets in your kitchens – it would never work.'

'Not during the day, maybe,' Jaren said, rubbing the stubble on his chin thoughtfully. 'But an early morning shift might be worth thinking about. Cat often arrives at the crack of dawn to get the day's baking out of the way – she'd be more than welcome to use the kitchens here before my staff arrive.'

Sadie stared at him. It wasn't an ideal solution but it was something to think about. 'Clare and Delilah could work together out of my kitchen to start off with. Then, once Cat is better, they might be able to work from her flat.' A slow smile started to pull at the corners of her mouth. 'You could be onto something, Jaren.'

He grinned. 'Happy to help. Hopefully, they'll be able to keep on top of the online orders so you won't have to disappoint those customers. I don't know what you can do about the ones who prefer to shop in person, though.'

'A month is a long time,' Sadie agreed, feeling her optimism start to fade. 'It would be almost like starting from scratch. Unless . . .'

She trailed off, her gaze settling on the barren paving stones at the centre of the Court. In the summer, they would be filled with tables and chairs so that diners could eat outside if they chose to. But right now, it was empty. 'I wonder if we'd be allowed . . .'

Jaren caught her meaning in a flash. 'A pop-up shop?'

Sadie nodded. 'A cute cart or a wagon of some kind.'

'You wouldn't be the first,' Jaren said, his eyes alight with enthusiasm. 'We have a coffee cart sometimes and ice-cream sellers in the summer – why not biscuits in the spring? I'm sure the management company would go for it, given the circumstances.'

'A lot would depend on the weather,' Sadie said. 'I don't fancy standing outside while April throws everything she has at us.'

'You could take each day as it comes,' he said, spreading his hands. 'What have you got to lose?'

It was a question Sadie preferred not to answer. But she felt her spirits start to rise, in spite of her misgivings; maybe things weren't as hopeless as she'd feared. 'Thanks, Jaren. You've been brilliant.'

He tilted his head and smiled. 'I'm just doing what any of the other shopkeepers would do. We look out for each other here, remember?'

Sadie couldn't help returning his smile; it was a sentiment she'd heard him express more than once and never had it felt more true. 'Even so, thank you anyway. From Cat and from me.'

'Is there any news?' he asked, his expression shifting to concern. 'How was she overnight?'

Sadie pulled a face. 'I don't think she's been given an official all-clear but I woke up to a message grumbling that the woman opposite snored like a water buffalo so I think she's on the mend. I'm going to see her as soon as I've finished with the insurance assessor.'

'Speaking of which, isn't that him at the window?' Jaren said, pointing to a figure hovering next to the door of the pancake house.

'It is. I'd better go.' Sadie drained the last of her tea and stood up. 'Thanks again, Jaren.'

The Dutchman grinned. 'Don't mention it.'

Cat was fully dressed and sitting on the edge of her bed when Sadie arrived just after midday. Her face was still pale and there was a dressing on her head but the air of badly suppressed impatience told Sadie her best friend was feeling much better.

'I see Seb has been,' she said, once Cat had explained that she was waiting to see a senior consultant before she could go home. 'Did he pick up everything you needed?'

'Surprisingly, yes,' Cat replied. 'Toothbrush, deodorant, underwear and even matching socks – which, as you know, is no mean feat with my sock collection.'

Sadie knew exactly what she meant; Cat had always maintained a relaxed attitude to matching socks, which meant her sock drawer was filled with a bewildering hotchpotch of different patterns and styles. It must have taken Seb a while to find a pair exactly the same. 'I'm impressed – it must be love if he's prepared to go to such lengths.'

'Never mind that,' Cat said, a hint of colour returning to her cheeks. 'What's the latest at the shop?'

'It's all under control,' Sadie said, holding up her hands. 'There'll be plenty of time to talk about that once you're fully recovered.'

Cat threw her a hard look. 'The x-rays say I'm recovered enough. Come on, spill the beans. How bad is it?'

Sadie swallowed a sigh. The trouble was that Cat was very unlikely to rest whether she knew the truth or not. Clearing her throat, she filled her in.

The silence stretched for several long seconds once Sadie had finished. 'A pop-up shop?' Cat echoed eventually.

'It's just an idea,' Sadie said hastily. 'A lot depends on

whether you think the kitchen-sharing arrangements with Jaren will work.'

Cat let out a soft snort. 'They'll have to work – we'll never keep the business going while the repairs are underway otherwise. Have you sounded out Delilah and Clare yet?'

'No,' Sadie replied, with a quick shake of her head. 'I wanted to speak to you first.'

'And how have you left things at the shop?'

'We've got a temporary door,' Sadie said, 'one that actually fits into the frame. A specialist company should be arriving sometime this afternoon to start pumping the water out and install the dehumidifiers, then it's a case of waiting for everything to dry out before the repairs can start.'

Cat looked thoughtful. 'The first thing we need to do is check the condition of the rescued stock – then I'll have a better idea of how much baking we need to do to catch up—'

'Woah,' Sadie interrupted, holding her hands up. 'The first thing you need to do is get some rest. The stock situation can wait.'

'No, it can't,' Cat said, her tone insistent. 'Our biscuits are dotted all over Castle Court – I need to know what we've got and what we have to replenish.'

Sadie took a deep breath and fixed her friend with a patient look. 'May I remind you that less than twenty-four hours ago, you'd been knocked unconscious by a large chunk of ceiling? The last thing you need is to start racing around a kitchen trying to bake up a biscuit storm.'

'But—'

'No buts, Cat,' Sadie said firmly. 'Delilah and I can check the stock, and we're more than capable of working out what we need to replace – we'll ask Andrew or Earl for help if we need it. You are going home – didn't Seb offer to look after you at his place?'

Cat's expression grew evasive. 'He might have done. And I might have turned him down.'

'Cat!' Sadie said, throwing her hands up in exasperation. 'I'm pretty sure you shouldn't be on your own, at least for the first day or so. I'll send him a message to say you've changed your mind.'

'I don't need a nurse,' Cat grumbled.

'You do,' Sadie replied, tapping at her phone. 'But if you won't do it for yourself, then do it for me, okay? I have enough to worry about without adding you to the list.'

Cat let out a faintly mutinous sigh. 'I suppose so.' She checked the time and peered tetchily towards the ward door. 'That's if they ever let me out of here.'

Sadie got to her feet. 'You're not their only patient,' she pointed out wryly. 'But why don't I see what I can find out?'

Two hours later, Cat walked through the alleyway that led to Castle Court. Seb was waiting in front of Smart Cookies, along with Elin, Jaren, Andrew and Earl. Several of the other shopkeepers Cat had become friends with since opening the business were there too; they cheered at the sight of her.

'Welcome back,' Seb said with a lopsided smile, stepping forwards to sweep her into a gentle cuddle.

The words were echoed by the small crowd. Every face Cat saw wore a smile, although many were tinged with concern. 'Thank you,' she said, letting go of Seb. 'I didn't expect a welcoming committee.'

Andrew rolled his eyes in mock surprise. 'Didn't you? Wow – maybe you hit your head harder than we thought!'

Cat gave an embarrassed grimace. 'Yeah, I should have known. Sorry.'

'Damn right you should have,' Earl rumbled but he was smiling. 'But it's good to have you back in one piece.'

Cat's gaze finally came to rest on Smart Cookies. The flood had taken its toll on the paintwork; the elegant blue gloss was bubbled and peeling. The empty window looked unnaturally gloomy and unloved – a far cry from its usually golden charm. Even the awning had taken a battering – a large split ran from one side to the other, matching the rip she could see in Cherie's awning at the patisserie. None of the other shops seemed to have suffered anything like as much damage; tears sprang into Cat's eyes and she looked away, blinking hard and determined not to cry in front of everyone.

'It's okay,' Sadie said softly. 'I almost cried too.'

Jaren stepped forwards. 'I must say you look a lot healthier than you did last time I saw you, Cat.'

Cat felt a rush of warmth mingled with gratitude as her gaze met his. 'I heard you were quite the hero. Thank you for rescuing me from my own stupidity.'

'It was an accident, not stupidity,' Jaren corrected before

291

giving a modest shrug. 'And I only did what any of us would have done.'

'Speak for yourself,' Andrew said, grinning. He lifted up an immaculate Converse-clad foot. 'I wouldn't risk getting these babies wet for anyone. Not even Earl!'

Earl seemed unperturbed. 'He loves me really.'

Jaren threw them both a wry look. 'Then it's a good job I was around when it mattered.' He smiled at Cat. 'I'm just glad you're all right.'

Clearing his throat, Seb wrapped a protective arm around Cat's shoulders. 'We should get you inside,' he said, planting a kiss on her cheek. 'I'm under strict orders from Sadie to put you to bed and feed you chicken soup, whether you want it or not.'

Sadie blushed, which made Cat laugh; she'd be willing to bet those were her exact orders. Now that she was back in Castle Court, the memories were returning thick and fast; she could almost feel how cold the water had been and remember the exact moment the ceiling had come down. She recalled hearing Jaren's voice too, and the fear in his eyes when he'd found her. An icy shiver ran all the way down to the soles of her feet at the thought. Maybe chicken soup and bed wasn't such a bad idea after all.

'You'll have to stop with the kid glove treatment soon,' she said, doing her best to sound unruffled. 'I'm fine.'

Sadie and Seb exchanged a knowing look. 'Why don't we fight that battle in the morning?' Sadie suggested.

As she started for the stairs that led up to Seb's attic

apartment, Cat found her eyes seeking Jaren's once more. There was so much she wanted to say – he'd saved her life and a mere 'thank you' didn't seem to be enough. He gave her a reassuring smile. 'Catch you tomorrow.'

She nodded. 'Yeah. And thanks again – for everything.'

'No problem,' he said. 'Get some rest, Cat.'

Cat turned away, reluctantly leaning on Seb for support as she climbed the stairs. But it wasn't Jaren who filled her thoughts as she settled back against the mountain of pillows Seb had rustled up out of nowhere, it was Elin. The Swiss woman had barely spoken a word, and she'd said nothing at all to Cat, although she'd smiled and joked along with everyone else. But there'd been a moment right at the end when her smile had slipped and Cat thought she'd seen something entirely unexpected underneath. Unless she'd been mistaken, it looked a lot like Elin was jealous and Cat couldn't help wondering if it was because of Jaren's heroic rescue. He and Elin were still in the early days of their relationship – maybe still early enough for the attention he'd given Cat to rankle. Cat hoped not; as Jaren had said, anyone would have done the same in his shoes and she didn't want his heroic actions to cause tension between him and Elin.

Cat closed her eyes, suddenly exhausted by the emotional and physical effort of coming back to the Court. Perhaps she'd have a quiet word with Elin, once she was feeling better. Or perhaps it was something that would resolve itself in time.

Chapter Twenty-Five

The next few days passed in a blur of noisy workmen and even louder machines. The pumps had taken the best part of a day to remove the flood water from the basement, sending it up the stairs in long rubber pipes and into the Court's drains. The front of Smart Cookies was fenced off for the procedure, something that provoked plenty of curiosity among the passing shoppers; Sadie had been able to fix a notice in the window explaining what had happened but hardly anyone could get close enough to read it.

Once the water had been pumped out, the dehumidifiers were brought in. At the same time, the ground floor was stripped of its damaged fittings and the joiner returned to inspect the floorboards and stairs. Cat had given in to demands that she spend Monday resting and kept away from the shop but Tuesday was a different story. She hovered impatiently for an hour or so in the morning, watching the various workmen go about their business, and then conceded there was nothing much for her to do, especially since Sadie seemed to have everything in hand. She took herself off to check the condition of the rescued stock and declared around fifty per cent to be undamaged.

'Which means I need to get baking, fast,' she told Sadie. 'If you need me for anything, I'll be in my kitchen.'

'Don't overdo it,' Sadie warned.

'Don't worry, I've got a plan,' Cat said, with good-natured exasperation. 'Delilah is coming over – she's going to make the dough and I'm going to cut the biscuits out. The heaviest thing I'll be lifting is a cookie cutter, okay?'

Sadie smiled. 'Okay. I'll drop in later and see what you've got that needs icing.'

The weather forecast made good on its promise of sunshine. As Tuesday turned into Wednesday, and the Easter weekend edged closer, the days grew warmer and more spring-like. After a flurry of emails, Sadie received permission from Castle Court's management company to set up her pop-up biscuit shop; they'd even arranged space in the ground-floor cleaners' cupboard so that she'd be able to store it out of harm's way overnight. Andrew and Earl had managed to source a cart – Sadie wasn't entirely sure from where – and she spent the best part of Tuesday morning painting it blue and gold to match the Smart Cookies colour scheme. The awning was white but she and Clare disguised it by pinning swathes of blue material across the top. Early on Wednesday morning, they attached bunches of blue and gold balloons to the sides and stepped back to admire their handiwork.

'Not bad,' Sadie said, her gaze roving critically over the cart.

'I think it's fabulous,' Clare said. 'And I think our customers will love it too.'

Sadie glanced up at the clear skies and crossed her fingers. 'If the weather stays like this, we might just get by. Come on, let's load her up with stock.'

The cart had a small amount of storage at the back – they left samples of their spring collections on the counter and packed as many tins as they could into the space. It wasn't ideal, Sadie thought, but it was infinitely better than nothing.

'We're going to spend a lot of time running back and forth to the pancake house and the diner for stock,' she said, biting her lip.

Clare tapped the watch on her wrist. 'I'm going to blitz my 10,000 steps, then. No gym for me this Easter!'

'And how are we going to manage the personalised icing?' Sadie fretted. Now that they were almost ready to open, all she could see were problems.

'We'll take the details and suggest they take a look around the Court while one of us ices the biscuits in Jaren's kitchen,' Clare reminded her. 'And if the customer is in a hurry, we can do it while they wait. Relax, Sadie, it's going to be fine.'

'It needs to be,' Sadie said, uncomfortably aware that she ought to be the one offering positivity and reassurance. 'We can't afford to lose any more business while the shop is being repaired.'

'Why don't I snap a few photos for social media?' Clare suggested. 'The local paper might run a piece too.'

It was something Sadie should have thought of herself, she realised; maybe she would have, if she hadn't been so busy catastrophising. 'Good idea,' she told Clare. 'Hang on, let me grab Cat.'

At least the plan to use some of Jaren's kitchen space to bake seemed to be working well, in spite of one or two territorial stand-offs between Delilah and Jaren's head chef, Meik, initially. But once things had bedded down, as long as the bakers were clear of the kitchen by eight-thirty then there didn't seem to be a problem. Sadie wasn't at all sure how things would go once Clare started to pop in and out to keep up with the personalised biscuit orders but they'd have to cross that particular bridge when they came to it.

She waved to Jaren as she made her way to the kitchen. 'Just grabbing Cat.'

'Follow your nose,' he said with a grin. 'You know, you should find a way to pipe the smell of baking biscuits into the Court – sales would go through the roof!'

Cat had just pulled a tray of chocolate biscuits from the oven when Sadie walked in. 'Have you got a minute? We've finished setting up the cart and Clare wants to snap a photo to put online.'

Cat lowered the biscuits to the worktop and undid her apron. 'Great idea,' she said, stepping back and tugging on the hairband that kept her dark curls off her face. 'Delilah, could you move these over to the baking trays to cool, please?'

The older woman looked up from the dough she was rolling out. 'Of course – leave it with me.'

Cat followed Sadie out of the kitchen. 'How's it looking?' she asked. 'Have you got everything you need?'

Sadie pulled a face. 'Not really but we'll cope. How about you? Are Jaren's ovens behaving?'

'They're wonderful,' Cat said, her face suddenly alight with enthusiasm. 'I'd forgotten what it was like to work in a big kitchen – there's so much space. It's making me hanker after La Perle a bit.'

'You know, this might be a good time to re-design things—' Sadie began.

'You can't re-design a postage stamp,' Cat said, giving her an amused look. 'But don't worry, the kitchen at the shop might be small but it's also perfectly formed – I designed it that way, remember?'

Sadie nodded. 'I know but—'

'But nothing,' Cat said firmly. 'I'll be perfectly happy to go back to Smart Cookies once the repairs are finished. I just need to make sure I don't get used to spreading out in the meantime.'

She stopped dead when she saw the cart, its balloons bumping gently against one another in the breeze. 'Oh, Sadie, it's gorgeous. Well done!'

Sadie's cheeks flushed with pleasure. 'Thank you. Clare and I did the best we could.'

'Seriously, it's so cute,' Cat said, clapping her hands in delight. 'People are going to love it.'

'All the more reason to upload some pictures,' Clare said, ushering Sadie and Cat into position. 'Say biscuits, ladies!'

Once Clare was satisfied with the photos, Cat checked her watch. 'Eight o'clock – I'd better go and make sure Delilah is out of firing range before Jaren's kitchen staff arrive.' She paused and eyed Sadie with concern. 'You look tired. Are you going to be okay to ice the last of the Bishop's jewelled cross order tonight?'

Sadie resisted the temptation to rub her eyes. She'd been up late working on replacements for the water-damaged stock but thought she'd applied plenty of concealer to mask her sallow skin and dark circles; clearly more was needed. 'I'll be fine.'

Cat looked unconvinced. 'How is Daniel behaving? Is he making sure you eat?'

'I am capable of feeding myself,' Sadie said, trying to ignore a prickle of irritation. 'And looking after Lissy.'

'Woah,' Cat said, stepping back slightly and staring at her in alarm. 'I didn't say anything about Lissy. Of course you're looking after her – I just meant that I know you sometimes get a bit engrossed and forget to eat, that's all.'

Sadie took a long deep breath and let it out again. Of course Cat hadn't meant to suggest she wasn't taking care of Lissy. But it didn't take a genius to work out why Sadie had overreacted: Daniel. He hadn't said anything but she'd seen the accusation in his eyes when she'd left the cottage at six-thirty that morning. And it was true that she was working too hard but what choice did she have? They were swimming against the tide; if she stopped for a moment, everything might go under the waves.

'Sorry,' Sadie said to Cat, summoning up a smile. 'Maybe I am tired.'

Clare stepped forwards. 'I'm more than happy to take over the Bishop's order if you want to take the night off.'

Sadie shook her head. 'Thanks but I'd feel weird watching you working in my kitchen while I lazed around in front of the TV. Let's stick to the plan – you do the Easter Bonnet tins and I'll finish the crosses.'

Cat studied her for a moment. 'If you're sure?'

'I'm sure,' Sadie said. 'Now, shouldn't you be getting back to Jaren's? We don't want a turf war between Delilah and Meik.'

'God forbid,' Cat said with a shudder. 'I'll see you in a while.'

The first shoppers started to arrive in Castle Court just after nine o'clock. A few glanced curiously at the cart; some obviously recognised the distinctive Smart Cookies branding because they came over to chat to Sadie and Clare. And to Sadie's delight, most seemed happy to support them in whatever way they could. The other shopkeepers were doing their bit too; Andrew and Earl seemed to be telling all their customers to stop by for a look and by lunchtime, Sadie's anxiety over whether the cart would be a success had all but evaporated. Cat had been right; people *loved* it.

'You should keep this going once the shop reopens,' one regular said as she cooed in delight over the painted swirls and loops Sadie had added to the cart. 'Maybe even take it out into the Rows.'

Chester's famous shopping streets dated back to medieval times and were mostly made up of covered walkways and charming gabled buildings steeped in history; there was nothing quite like them anywhere else and Sadie could easily imagine the Smart Cookies cart nestled against the city's quaint black-and-white backdrop. 'Maybe we will,' she said, sliding an extra biscuit into the bag that held the woman's purchases. 'Thanks for the suggestion.'

Trade built steadily throughout the day. Sadie and Clare just about managed to keep on top of the personalised biscuit orders, although they were both run off their feet by the time the customers thinned around five-thirty.

'Imagine what it's going to be like on Easter Saturday,' Clare said, looking worried for the first time. 'There will be crowds to contend with too.'

'We'll just have to do our best,' Sadie told her as she started to pack the cart away. 'That's all any of us can do.'

Sadie's feelings were mixed as she parked outside her childminder's house. On one hand she was happy to be collecting Lissy but it also meant she'd soon have to face Daniel. Her gaze slid uneasily to the boxes lining the passenger seat and footwell; he wouldn't be happy that Sadie had brought more work home with her. But she did her best to push her gloomy thoughts to one side as she trudged up the path to the childminder's front door. Lissy would chase her apprehensions away – she always did.

'Mummy!' the little girl cried when Sadie stepped into the living room. Rushing forwards, she flung her arms around her mother's neck.

'Hello,' Sadie said, burying her nose in Lissy's soft curls. 'Had a good day?'

'Yes,' Lissy said, beaming. 'Guess who we saw on the way home from school?'

Sadie frowned. 'Hmm, let me think. Was it the Easter Bunny?'

Lissy shook her head excitedly. 'No. Guess again.'

'The Easter Bunny's assistant?'

'No!' Lissy hopped from one foot to the other. 'You'll never guess so I'll tell you. It was Adam!'

'Oh!' Sadie said, her throat suddenly dry. Lissy was right, she would never have guessed. 'Did he see you?'

Lissy smiled. 'Yes. He stopped and talked to us. I asked him how his bees were and he said very well. And then he asked how you were and I told him all about the flood and he said that sounded very scary.'

'It was,' Sadie said absently. She felt the weight of her childminder's curious gaze; she was clearly wondering who Adam was. 'He used to work at the shop but left a little while ago.'

'And he said that if you wanted any honey, you only have to ask,' Lissy went on. 'He said the bees have finished their winter rest now and are buzzing around like anything.'

Sadie couldn't help smiling; Lissy's all-encompassing fascination with bees had been one of the best things to come out of her friendship with Adam. 'That's good to hear. I'll be sure to tell Cat — she uses the honey in her biscuit recipes.'

They said goodnight to the childminder and headed back to the car. Lissy continued to chatter and her constant questions almost prevented Sadie's anxiety from building as they finished the short journey to their cottage. Maybe Daniel wouldn't be there, Sadie thought hopefully, turning her key in the lock. Maybe he'd decided to stay at his own house this evening.

The quiet murmur of the television told her she was wrong. And sure enough, no sooner had she closed the front door behind herself and Lissy than Daniel appeared in the doorway of the living room.

'Hi,' he said, bending down to gather Lissy into a hug. 'How are my favourite girls?'

'Not bad,' Sadie answered, turning towards the kitchen to deposit the boxes of biscuits she carried. 'How was your day?'

'Boring,' he replied, following her with Lissy in his arms. 'But getting better now.'

His gaze was warm, without a trace of the accusation she'd thought she'd seen there that morning. 'Oh. Good.' She placed the boxes on the kitchen table, almost daring him to comment. 'Shall we get a takeaway tonight? I've got an order to finish for the shop and I'm not sure I have the energy to cook.'

Daniel's smile was rueful but not angry. 'I thought

you might say that so I stopped off at the supermarket for some ingredients on my way home. How does chilli con carne sound?'

Sadie eyed him warily, searching for signs of frustration. 'It sounds great.'

'Good,' Daniel said. He gave Lissy a squeeze and she giggled. 'I'll get this one bathed and into bed, then I'll make a start.'

'Not until you've read my story,' Lissy reminded him with a frown. 'Teggs Stegosaur is just about to defeat the robot T-Rex, remember?'

'So he is,' Daniel said with a laugh. He lowered the little girl to the ground. 'Why don't you go and find the right page so that we're all set for bedtime?'

In a flash, Lissy was thundering towards the narrow stairs that led upstairs.

'I can do bath time if you like,' Sadie said.

Daniel pointed at the boxes. 'You've got work to do. I don't suppose that's all you've brought back, is it?'

'No,' Sadie admitted. 'I've got four more in the car.'

He gave her a gentle nod. 'So it makes sense for me to bath Lissy and put her to bed. It's no trouble – to be honest, I really want to find out what happens to Teggs and his crew.'

Sadie felt her tension melt away. When Daniel was kind like this, he made everything better. 'Thanks.'

He shrugged. 'Don't mention it. Want me to fetch the rest of the boxes?'

'I'll get them—'

'Relax, Sadie, I'll do it.' He gave her a trademark Daniel grin. 'And if you happened to be boiling the kettle, I wouldn't say no to a cuppa. Rasping like a robot T-Rex is very thirsty work.'

He left her to get on with her work, taking Lissy upstairs for her bath and bringing her back down, warm and glowing, to say goodnight. Sadie tried to quell the little voice that told her she should be the one reading Lissy her *Astrosaurs* adventure; Daniel was her father and it did them both good to spend more time together, especially now that he seemed more invested in being part of their lives. And it was only one bedtime; as soon as the bump in the road caused by the flood was out of the way, things would get back to normal.

She concentrated on her work, creating rows of perfect jewelled crosses to grace the Bishop's table on Easter Sunday. Daniel kept out of her way as he cooked; Sadie was only really aware of his presence when she smelled the rich scent of the chilli starting to take shape and blinked in surprise as her mouth began to water. For most of their married life, she would have sworn Daniel didn't know one end of a saucepan from the other; he'd changed a lot in the year they'd spent apart.

'Dinner is served,' he announced a few minutes later, holding out a tray. 'I thought we'd eat on the sofa, since the table is out of commission.'

It took Sadie a moment to realise it wasn't a dig at her; more often than not, her kitchen table was covered in biscuits that had either been iced or that were waiting to be decorated. In fact, she couldn't remember the last time she'd eaten at the table. 'Thanks,' she said, getting to her feet and taking the tray.

'This is delicious,' Sadie commented, once they'd settled on the sofa and she'd taken a mouthful of the steaming food. 'Maybe Cat had a point after all.'

'Sorry?' Daniel said, looking puzzled. 'I don't follow.'

Sadie waved her hand. 'She asked if you were looking after me, making sure I ate. And I told her I was quite capable of cooking for myself.'

'You are,' Daniel said. 'You used to cook for me all the time. And now it seems like the least I can do is return the favour.'

'Thank you,' Sadie replied and she meant it. 'I really appreciate all the help you've given me lately. I know it isn't easy and it seems like I lurch from one disaster to another but it won't always be like this.'

'I know,' he said. A wry smile tugged at his lips. 'And for the record, you lurch beautifully.'

Sadie laughed. 'Thanks. I think.'

They ate in silence for a few minutes, then Daniel fixed Sadie with a speculative look. 'I've got something I wanted to ask you.'

'Oh?'

He cleared his throat. 'I've been invited to a christening at the end of May – one of the partners in the business is having a ceremony at the cathedral. And I wondered whether – you don't have to, of course – well, whether you and Lissy might like to come with me.'

Methodically, Sadie finished chewing the food in her mouth, although it had suddenly ceased to taste of anything. The last time she'd gone to one of Daniel's work functions, it had been as his wife. And although she was still his wife now, everyone knew they'd been separated. Everyone knew he'd had an affair. Was she really ready to face them all again?

'I don't know,' she said slowly. 'What date is it?'

'I'd have to double-check,' he said, watching her. 'It's the last Sunday of the month, if that helps? Are you doing anything?'

Sadie shook her head, trying to squash the sudden squall of anxiety his invitation had caused. With all the upheaval at Smart Cookies, she had no idea what was in her diary past next week, let alone the following month. 'I don't know. Will – will Emma be there?'

His gaze was steady. 'No. She's changed jobs – works in Manchester now, I think.'

Relief seeped into Sadie's heart. That made things a little easier; knowing she wouldn't have to face up to the woman Daniel had been cheating on her with was something, at least. That just left everyone else.

'Can I think about it?' she said. 'Let you know tomorrow, maybe?'

'Of course,' he said. 'Take as long as you need. I expect it will be a lovely ceremony and we needn't stay long – I just thought it might be nice to do something together. In public, as it were.'

She nodded, concentrating on loading her fork with chilli and rice. 'It is a nice idea.' She paused. 'Thanks for asking.'

His eyes crinkled round the edges as they met hers. 'Thanks for saying maybe.'

Chapter Twenty-Six

It was just before midnight when Cat's phone vibrated with an incoming message. She glanced across at the faint glow on the bedside table then turned her gaze back to the darkened ceiling, resisting the temptation to pick the phone up. Weren't screens supposed to disrupt the brain's ability to rest and make it harder to sleep? She certainly didn't need that; her own brain had been racing from the moment she'd turned off the light and tried to go to sleep – it didn't need more stimulation. On the other hand, who was she trying to kid? Seb would be coming up from the bar any minute and his arrival would put paid to sleep far more effectively than a quick glance at her phone. Besides, it might be something important . . .

She smiled with relief when she saw it was from Sadie: *Crosses are good to go! X*

Excellent, she tapped back. *Now sleep! X*

Cat replaced the phone and listened for sounds that Seb was on his way. She was surprised when her phone buzzed again.

PS Lissy saw Adam – he says he's got honey. Tell Seb to get his order in quick if he wants some. X

Seb would definitely want some, Cat thought as she typed her thanks. Several of his most popular cocktails used honey and Adam's bees produced a top-quality, organic product; Seb had been complaining for months that his stocks had run out.

She heard the scrape of his key in the lock just as she pressed send, and leaned over to flick the bedside lamp on. She might as well give him the good news now, before the chaos of preparing for a busy Easter weekend using someone else's kitchen drove it from her mind.

She knew the moment he walked into the bedroom that he wasn't in a good mood. His shoulders were hunched and his face had a closed expression.

'Tough night?' she asked softly as he tossed his shoes into a corner.

He grunted. 'Something like that.'

Cat wrapped her arms around her knees. 'Want to talk about it?'

'No.'

He turned away and began to undress. Cat frowned; it wasn't unknown for Seb to be grumpy after a busy night but he was usually keen to tell her about it. 'Is there anything I can do to help?'

'No.'

Her unease deepened. Like all of Castle Court's food businesses, Seb had his share of difficult customers and staffing problems but he was usually able to laugh about them and he rarely brought them upstairs once the bar was closed. Whatever had soured his mood tonight must have been bad.

She waited, watching for signs that his temper was improving. But he kept his back to her, stripping off with silent fury.

'I've got some news that might cheer you up,' she ventured, after a few more seconds had passed. 'Sadie says Adam has got honey for sale if you're interested.'

Was it her imagination or did his shoulders stiffen? 'I've got a new supplier now.'

'I know you have,' Cat said patiently. 'But the quality isn't as good, is it? I'm sure if you message Adam, he'll drop some—'

Seb gave a short laugh and turned to look at her. 'This isn't La Perle, Cat. I don't think anyone is going to complain that the drizzle of honey in their Gold Rush isn't organic, do you?'

She sat back, stung. Seb was often evangelical about getting the freshest, best ingredients for the bar – his perfectionism was one of the things that had attracted him to her. 'No, but—'

'Besides, Adam has made it clear he's not my biggest fan,' Seb went on. 'So I don't imagine he'll be going out of his way to supply me with honey.'

'That doesn't sound like him,' Cat said, blinking in confusion. As far as she knew, Seb and Adam had always been firm friends. 'Have you had an argument?'

Seb shook his head. 'Just forget it.'

Cat folded her arms. 'No. Not until you tell me what's going on.'

'There's nothing to tell,' he said, his voice flat.

She stared at him wordlessly. Why hadn't he mentioned this before? 'Is this something to do with Sadie and me? Because if it is—'

'It's not.' He climbed into bed beside her and lay down with his back towards her. 'So turn off the light and let it go.'

Frustrated, Cat glared at his still hunched shoulders for a moment. Then she snapped off the lamp and flounced huffily against the pillow. She lay there staring at the ceiling once again, until gentle snoring rose from Seb's side of the bed. Cat's glower increased; how was it that he could fall asleep so easily, even in the grip of a seriously foul mood, while she tried every trick in the book and still found it hard to doze off? It wasn't fair. And now she'd have to listen to him snore, which was just adding insult to injury.

Sighing, she turned onto her side and squeezed her eyes shut, summoning up her mother's recipe for paella and working through the ingredients and method in her head. At the very least, it should stop the argument with Seb from replaying on a loop in her head. And the memory of cooking with her mother might be exactly what she needed to soothe her troubled thoughts, although she made sure she avoided thinking about the way her mother would have sniffed at Seb's behaviour. Something was clearly bothering him and Cat didn't need her mother's fiery advice to muddy the waters. Whatever it was, Seb would tell her in his own time.

'He said *what*?'

It was Thursday morning and Sadie had stopped filling up the cart with stock for the day to stare at Cat in total confusion.

'I know,' Cat said, shrugging. 'I've got no idea either.'

'But Adam really admires Seb,' Sadie said. 'He told me so himself, when we were driving back from one of Seb's after-hours drink-ups.' Her forehead crinkled in dismay. 'This doesn't have anything to do with me getting back together with Daniel, does it?'

'No,' Cat replied, determined to prevent Sadie from feeling any more pointless guilt about the way things had worked out with Adam. 'I asked Seb if it was because of us and he said no. But I haven't got the foggiest what they could have fallen out over.'

Sadie picked up a pile of biscuit boxes and started to load them slowly into the cart. 'I suppose I could always ask Adam,' she said slowly. 'I could pop down to his cottage and pick up some honey at the same time.'

Cat did her best to keep her face neutral. She hadn't given up hope that Sadie might eventually realise she was wasting her time with Daniel and rekindle her fledgling relationship with Adam; it was definitely a good idea to keep the two of them talking where possible. But Cat also knew better than to push Sadie towards Adam; she had to come to the realisation in her own time.

'That's an idea,' Cat said. 'I really could use some of that delicious honey for the premium biscuit recipe I'm tinkering with.'

'Really?' Sadie replied, looking up. 'I didn't know you were working on a new recipe.'

'It's early days,' Cat went on quickly. 'I'm always looking for ways to improve the product, you know that.'

Sadie nodded. 'So the sooner I get the honey, the better?'

'Yes,' Cat said, crossing her fingers behind her back. 'In fact, why don't you leave a bit early today and see if you can catch him before you pick up Lissy?'

'Oh, but Lissy will be disappointed.' Sadie smiled. 'I think she's hoping to catch sight of the bees putting the honey into the jars.'

'Take her another time,' Cat suggested. 'Besides, you don't really want to ask Adam about his argument with Seb in front of Lissy, do you? There might be some dark and twisted back story we know nothing about.'

Her best friend laughed. 'I can't imagine anyone less likely to have a dark and twisted back story than Adam. But I suppose that makes sense – he might not want to talk in front of Lissy.'

'It makes perfect sense,' Cat said. A little bubble of glee rose up inside her and she clenched her hands into fists to stop it bursting into a laugh. 'You can have a nice leisurely catch-up and bring the honey in tomorrow.'

'Okay,' Sadie said. 'I'll let you know what I find out.'

Cat's happiness faded as she pictured Seb's sullen body language the night before. 'Please do.'

'Sadie!' Adam's face lit up when he opened the door of his cottage and saw who was standing there. 'What a lovely surprise.'

His light brown hair was sticking up and she could see the start of a tan building on his face but otherwise, he looked exactly as Sadie remembered. She swallowed the sudden nervous lump that had lodged itself in her throat and summoned up a smile. 'Hello, Adam. I hope you don't mind me stopping by – Lissy said she'd seen you and I wondered if I might be able to buy some honey.'

His hazel eyes widened. 'Of course!' He glanced over his shoulder and then back at her. 'Do you – er – want to wait here or have you got time to come in?'

It wasn't the first time he'd invited her inside his home and from the resigned expression on his face, he expected her to say no, the same way she had in the past. Taking a deep breath, Sadie smiled and tried to ignore the sudden thudding in her chest. 'I've got time.'

'Right,' he said, stepping back. 'Come in. And excuse the mess – I wasn't expecting a visitor.'

Sadie almost laughed; it had become a standing joke between them that Adam's home was rarely what he called guest-fresh. 'Don't worry, I'm sure I've seen worse.'

From the outside, the house looked like a typical farm

cottage; the walls were whitewashed, with small windows and a grey slate roof. Wisteria climbed around the door in thick green boughs; Sadie made a mental note to bring her sketchpad in May so she could capture it in bloom. Inside the cottage, the rooms were as small and low-ceilinged as she'd anticipated. Adam led her into a living room and Sadie was surprised by how uncluttered it was. The wooden floor was clean and polished, the bookshelves well organised and the mantelpiece over the fireplace was conspicuously clear of the letters and takeaway leaflets that covered Sadie's own. From Adam's embarrassment, she'd expected almost student levels of untidiness.

'It's lovely,' she said, gazing around in open astonishment. 'But if this is your idea of untidy, I'd hate to imagine what you think clean means.'

'In here isn't so bad. Wait until you see the bedroom.'

A look of horror crossed his face the moment he'd finished speaking and he blushed a deep rosy red that travelled all the way to the tips of his ears. 'I didn't mean that I expect you to go in there,' he said, almost tripping over the words in his hurry to correct himself. 'No reason you would, obviously.'

Sadie took pity on him. 'Did you mention a cup of tea?'

'I didn't,' he said. 'But it sounds like a really good idea.'

He vanished through a doorway that Sadie supposed led to the kitchen. Moments later, she heard the faint hum of a kettle and the rattle of spoons in a drawer. She edged closer to the bookshelves, wondering what he liked to read; there were several non-fiction titles about bees and bee-keeping, which didn't surprise her, and quite a lot of novels, ranging through everything from Iain M Banks to Terry Pratchett and Ursula Le Guin.

He found her there several minutes later, prowling the spines with her fingers.

'I don't think I realised you were a reader,' she said, as he handed her a mug of tea.

'Why would you?' he said, with a shrug. 'It's the kind of thing you only really find out about when you visit someone's home, isn't it?'

'True,' she said, thinking of her own living room with its heavily-laden bookshelf. Between her and Lissy, they had quite a collection. 'I'm glad you like reading.'

'I'm glad you're glad,' he said. 'I thought you would be.'

They stood for a moment, smiling beside the books. Then Adam cleared his throat. 'So, how much honey do you want?'

'A few jars, at least,' Sadie replied. 'Cat is experimenting with a new recipe.'

He nodded. 'The bees have been busy so my spring harvests are pretty good so far,' he said. 'It helps that the farm produces a large crop of borage – they sell it on to make Evening Primrose Oil and the bees love it.'

Sadie pictured the fields she drove past almost every day. 'The blue flowered crop?'

'That's right. You can taste it in the honey, too, if you know what you're looking for.'

Sadie couldn't help glancing towards the back of the cottage. 'And your hives are out in the garden, are they?'

Again, Adam nodded. 'That's right. I'd let you take a look but it's a warm day and there'll be a lot of traffic around the hives.'

Sadie frowned. 'Traffic?'

'Bee traffic,' he clarified. 'It helps if you think of the area at the front of a hive as the main road – all the bees travel along it as they enter and leave. If something gets in their way then word gets around and the hive might decide it's under attack. You don't want that, believe me.'

'No, I can imagine,' Sadie said, wondering whether she should start to discourage Lissy's interest in bees. 'Do you get stung much?'

'I did at first,' he said wryly. 'Back when I didn't have enough respect for them. But now I make sure I'm fully suited and approach the hives in a way that's designed to cause the least upset.' He paused. 'I've got plenty of spare kit if you'd like to have a proper look inside a hive sometime.'

It was a generous offer; Sadie knew he took his work seriously and didn't let just anyone near his bees. 'I'd like that,' she said. 'And I think it would probably blow Lissy's mind.'

Adam grinned. 'Probably. The key to bee-keeping is to stay calm. I'm pretty sure they can sense panic but if you're slow and methodical with your movements, you shouldn't have a problem. Bee-keeping is actually a pretty zen thing to do.'

His enthusiasm was very appealing, Sadie thought, taking refuge in her cup of tea; she thought she could listen to him talk about the habits of bees all afternoon. But the honey was only part of the reason she was there; she had something else to tackle too.

'Have you seen much of Seb lately?' she asked, keeping her tone as light as she could manage.

Instantly, Adam's eyes darkened. 'No.'

Sadie took in his tight-lipped expression warily. Hadn't Cat described a similar reaction in Seb? What exactly had happened between them? 'That's a shame,' she said. 'I do hope it wasn't because of your decision to leave Smart Cookies.'

His mouth dropped slightly before he got a grip. 'No! Why would you think that?'

Now it was Sadie's turn to shrug. 'What else am I supposed to think? You left so quickly after Daniel and I decided to give things another go, and Cat is practically my sister. It isn't a huge leap to assume that you and Seb disagreed over something to do with the way things worked out.'

Adam's jaw clamped suddenly shut and it was a moment before he spoke. 'No, Sadie, it wasn't anything to do with you. If you must know, Seb and I fell out over—'

He stopped and turned away, fixing his attention on the bookshelves once more.

'Over what?' Sadie pressed, dying to know the truth.

'It doesn't matter,' he said over one shoulder. 'Forget I said anything.'

'Obviously it does matter,' Sadie said, taking a step towards him. 'It matters enough for you and Seb to argue.'

'It's none of my business,' Adam said, his tone sounding strangled.

'What isn't?' Sadie asked, touching his arm.

There was a long silence that only ended when Adam let out a rough-sounding growl. 'You have to promise me you won't tell Cat.'

Sadie felt the ground lurch under her feet. It was the last thing she'd expected to hear. 'What?'

He shook his head. 'The reason Seb and I fell out concerns her.'

'Concerns her how?' Sadie said, foreboding gnawing at her insides. 'Adam, what does this have to do with Cat?'

His shoulders sagged in defeat. 'I should have told you this ages ago. But I didn't know how.'

'Told me what?' Sadie asked, taking a deep calming breath.

Adam sighed. 'Look, I think you'd better sit down.'

Hardly daring to breathe, she did as he suggested, watching with apprehension as he took a seat on the battered old armchair opposite. 'Go on.'

'There's no easy way to say this,' Adam began, 'so I'm just going to come right out with it. Seb cheated on Cat. With Elin.'

Sadie let out a horrified gasp. 'No!'

'It happened while she was in Paris, sorting out the situation with her old boss and the lawyers. Seb and Elin got drunk, one thing led to another and it all got very out of hand. I encouraged Seb to tell Cat what had happened – he disagreed. It meant nothing, he said, and Elin felt the same. But I still thought Cat had a right to know. Which is why Seb and I fell out.'

Sadie stared at him in shock. Whatever she'd expected, it hadn't been this. But suddenly the pieces started to tumble into place. Cat had been convinced there had been something wrong with Elin – she'd been unusually cool and there'd even been one or two occasions when Cat had thought she'd been avoiding them. But Seb had been the same as ever. Almost.

'I don't believe it,' she said, shaking her suspicions away. 'He wouldn't. Elin wouldn't. How do you know – did you catch them?'

'I saw Elin sneaking out of Seb's early on Valentine's Day. Let's just say she didn't look like she'd popped in to borrow a cup of sugar.'

Sadie's eyes narrowed as she racked her memory. 'That's the day you went home sick. And then you handed in your notice.'

Adam didn't meet her eyes. 'It was obvious Cat was worried by what had happened in Paris and the last thing I wanted to do was give her more bad news.' He hesitated, shame-faced. 'And you'd just got back together with Daniel, so I wasn't in the best place, mentally. It just seemed easier to run away.'

'You didn't run away,' Sadie protested, feeling a sudden jumble of unexpected emotion at his words. Pity mingled with protectiveness and a hint of something else she couldn't quite identify.

'You're very kind, Sadie, but I'm afraid that's exactly what I did,' Adam said. 'And then I didn't know how to put things right – I knew you and Cat would be furious with me for leaving at such short notice. So I told Seb exactly what I thought of him and did my best to forget all about you and Castle Court.'

He looked so vulnerable that Sadie wanted to hug him. None of this was his fault – he'd been caught in the romantic crossfire from all sides and she could hardly blame him for washing his hands of it.

Another thought occurred to her as she watched regret play across his face. 'That's around the time that Elin got together with Jaren. Does he know about Seb?'

'I don't think so,' Adam replied. 'Jaren is a very straightforward guy – he'd want everything out in the open, especially given how well he and Cat get on. No, I think I'm the only person who knows, apart from Seb and Elin.' He sat back and puffed out a long breath. 'So there you have it.'

'I wish you'd told me sooner,' Sadie said, hating the hint of rebuke behind the words. 'I know Seb is your friend but I thought I was too.'

Adam looked away. 'I'm sorry. I wanted to.'

The contrition in his voice made her feel even worse. 'No, I'm sorry. This isn't your fault.' She sighed and stared up at the ceiling. 'What a mess. You do know I have to tell Cat everything, don't you?'

'I know. How do you think she'll take it?'

Sadie managed a short laugh. 'I think she'll want to kill him, at least at first. But she isn't as tough as she seems – this is going to hurt her, at a time when she's already struggling.

So, I don't know how she'll react but I wouldn't want to be in Seb's shoes.' She thought for a second. 'Or Elin's, for that matter.'

Adam studied his mug of tea for a moment, as though it held all the answers to the situation. 'I'll get you that honey,' he said finally, placing the cup on the table to one side of his chair.

Sadie watched him go, her heart heavy. Why was nothing ever straightforward where she and Adam were concerned? It was almost as though they were cursed – something always seemed to get in the way of their friendship.

In typical Adam style, he refused to accept the money Sadie tried to give him at the front door. 'I couldn't. Not like this.'

'Take it,' she insisted. 'And give me a receipt – it's a business expense.'

'Consider it a gift,' he insisted. 'An apology for dumping a load of bad news on you.'

Sadie stared at the carrier bag she now held, laden with four jars of clear amber honey. 'I think it's going to take more than honey to make this right,' she said. 'But none of it is your fault – you're just the messenger.'

'I wish I didn't have to be.'

'No, I can understand that.' She glanced up into his wretched expression and shook her head. 'Thanks for telling me.'

He nodded. 'Yeah. Take care, Sadie.'

It took a lot of willpower for Sadie to turn away from

Adam; seeing him had reminded her how much she missed his company. But he'd obviously been more hurt than she'd realised by her reconciliation with Daniel, made all the worse by Seb's behaviour, and he'd hidden himself away to lick his wounds and recover. And it might be that he needed more time before they could begin to pick up the pieces of their friendship. Or it might be that they never would. The thought of it caused tiny needles of distress to prick at her heart.

She got halfway down the path before she plucked up enough courage to throw caution to the wind. 'Look,' she said, stopping and turning around with a quick, nervous huff, 'you might not fancy it but we're going to have a little re-opening celebration as soon as the shop repairs are finished. You'd be very welcome to join us, both as a past employee and as a friend.'

His expression was unreadable as he watched her. 'Will Seb be there?'

'I think it's highly likely Cat will bash his brains in with his own cocktail shaker, so no,' Sadie said with a slight twist of her mouth. 'I'll let you know the date, shall I?'

He managed a small wavering smile that planted hope in Sadie's soul. 'Please do.'

Chapter Twenty-Seven

'I don't believe it.'

Cat stared at Sadie, who shifted on the edge of the sofa that lined one wall of Cat's living room. Her voice sounded shrill and accusatory even to her own ears as she went on, 'Seb wouldn't do that.'

Sadie glanced across to where Lissy sat on the carpet with her dinosaurs. 'It's hard to believe, isn't it?' she said, her voice low. 'But too many details add up. Besides, why would Adam lie? He's got nothing to gain from splitting you and Seb up.'

A dull ache started behind Cat's eyes as she willed herself not to cry. 'I don't know. Maybe he's trying to get back at you.'

The look Sadie gave her was full of sympathy. 'But this isn't getting back at *me* – you're the one who's hurt. And I don't think he's the vengeful type. I'm sorry, Cat, I think he's telling the truth.'

Cat pressed her lips together hard. If she was honest with

herself, she'd known something was going on inside Seb's head for a while but she hadn't suspected this. Or at least, she hadn't suspected it would be with Elin. She was well aware that women found Seb attractive, and that he enjoyed their attention, but the fact that he'd chosen to be unfaithful with someone Cat considered a friend almost hurt more than the betrayal itself.

She put her head in her hands. 'That shit. I knew something like this would happen one day.'

Sadie cast a nervous look Lissy's way but the little girl was engrossed in her game and oblivious to the adult conversation happening on the sofa. Moving nearer to Cat, Sadie put her arm around her. 'I'm sorry. For what it's worth, I thought he was one of the good guys.'

Cat managed a short laugh. 'Good guys? Is there any such thing, outside of fiction? And on Valentine's Day too, when he knew I had the stress of being dragged over to Paris by François de Beauvoir's lawyers.' She shook her head furiously. 'Do you suppose he waited until I'd left the country to go sniffing after Elin or did he plan it before I went?'

'I'm sure it wasn't like that,' Sadie murmured. 'From what Adam said, it was a drunken mistake. I don't think either of them planned it.'

The misery that had been threatening finally overcame Cat's determination not to cry. 'It doesn't matter whether they did or they didn't,' she said, sniffing as hot, stinging tears rolled down her cheeks. 'The end result is the same. Bloody, bloody hell.'

She buried her face in Sadie's shoulder, trying her hardest to muffle her sobs so that Lissy wouldn't hear. Images flashed across her brain – glances exchanged between Seb and Elin that she'd assumed were innocent but that now took on much more significance; the moments when she'd wondered whether she'd done something to upset Elin; Seb's anger with her last night. It all made sense now that she knew the truth.

Gradually, the tears stopped although the dull ache behind her eyes remained. Sadie rummaged in her bag for a tissue and Cat took it with a grateful sniff. As she dabbed at her cheeks, feeling foolish and hurt, a small hand touched her arm.

'It's okay to cry, Auntie Cat,' Lissy said, her face solemn. 'Mummy says tears wash the sadness away so that happiness can grow again.'

She sounded so serious that a fresh crop of tears pricked at the back of Cat's eyes. Doing her best to smile, she squeezed the little girl's hand. 'She's right. I'm sure I'll feel better soon.'

Lissy held out her beloved triceratops toy. 'You can borrow Travis if you need to. He gives really good hugs, as long as you don't mind his spikes.'

'Thanks,' Cat said, and this time she didn't need to force a smile. 'If I need a hug, I'll know exactly where to come.'

She and Sadie talked over endless cups of tea, until way past Lissy's usual bedtime. When Cat caught Sadie checking her watch, she told her to go home.

'But I don't want to leave you on your own,' Sadie said, even as Lissy opened her mouth wide into a yawn. 'What are you going to do?'

'Make a gingerbread effigy of Seb and stick pins in it,' Cat said. She glanced towards the windows that overlooked the darkening canal. 'Maybe throw it in the water for good measure.'

'Be serious,' Sadie said, although Cat saw the worry lines on her best friend's forehead lessen slightly. 'Are you going to be all right if we go? I can ask Daniel to come over once I've put Lissy to bed – then I could drive back here and we can talk things through properly. With a bottle of wine and a whole lot of pins.'

For half a moment, Cat was tempted. But it was too much to ask; Sadie was already anxious about spending so much time away from her daughter and there was no way Cat was giving Daniel ammunition to suggest his wife cut back on the time she invested at Smart Cookies. 'I'll be fine,' she reassured Sadie. 'I was only joking about making a gingerbread effigy. Wax is much more effective.'

'Just promise me you're not going to confront him tonight,' Sadie said, getting to her feet and reaching for Lissy's hand. 'Sleep on it at least.'

'I will,' Cat said, crossing her fingers behind her back. 'See you tomorrow.'

It wasn't until Sadie and Lissy had gone that Cat felt the emptiness take hold. She stared at the black screen of the television, running everything Sadie had told her through her mind. Should she have known it had happened? Were there warning signs she should have looked out for? She had no idea. The more she thought about things, the hotter the embers of betrayal became, until finally she couldn't stand it any longer. Getting to her feet, she reached for a coat and her keys. There was only one person who could give her the answers she needed.

Cat thought about confronting Seb in the bar, considered causing a scene in front of all his customers; that would give them enough juicy gossip to last for weeks. But the trouble with that was that Castle Court was also her work-place – filled with people she had to continue to face each day – which meant that as satisfying as it would be to publicly shame Seb for cheating, it was also a really bad idea. Instead, she settled for using the key he'd given her to let herself into his garret apartment in the attics of Castle Court and waiting until he came upstairs.

The jolt he gave when he opened his front door and saw her might have been almost gratifying if it hadn't also flooded her body with adrenaline. It was a relief to see he was alone; Adam had said the thing with Elin had been a drunken one-night-stand, but Cat wasn't sure she could have maintained her dignity if Elin had followed him into the small living room.

'Cat,' Seb said, recovering from the shock of finding her there. 'I wasn't expecting to see you tonight.'

'I thought I would surprise you.'

He tilted his head and frowned at the obvious flatness in her tone. 'Is everything all right?'

Cat swallowed hard; she'd told herself she would be coolly

detached throughout the coming exchange but her body had other ideas and her voice was already thick with emotion. She shook her head, determined not to show how hurt she was. 'You can drop the concerned boyfriend act, Seb. I know about you and Elin.'

It was as though someone had flicked a switch; the colour drained from his face. 'What?'

'Don't even think about denying it,' Cat went on, fighting for just the right level of aloofness. 'Sadie spoke to Adam. He told her everything.'

His gaze skittered guiltily away. 'Cat, I—'

The shame on his face was all it took to sweep Cat's self-control away. 'How could you?' she cried, the words catching in her throat. 'And with Elin, of all people – why couldn't you have picked some anonymous party-girl that I wouldn't have to look in the eye every time we have a shopkeepers' meeting?'

Seb's shoulders sagged. 'It's not what you think. We didn't mean for it to happen – it was an accident.'

Cat jumped up, her hands balling into fists. 'Oh, it was an accident? That makes all the difference. That makes everything all right!'

The last two words came out as an undignified screech that Cat was sure half the Court must have heard. Her heart thundered as she glared at Seb. His face was filled with remorse as he tried to meet her eyes. 'Calm down, Cat. Can't we at least be adult about this?'

'Adult?' Cat echoed, feeling her fury erupt into white-hot

rage. 'No, we cannot be *adult* about this. The adult thing would have been not to get drunk and sleep with your ex, Seb. I think it's a bit late to try and claim the moral high-ground now.'

He ran a tired hand over his face and sighed. 'What do you want me to say? I drank too much and made a bad decision – we both did. Elin was mortified the next day, especially when you turned up before she could leave. She was all for—'

The room lurched sideways. 'What?' Cat whispered, a sudden roaring filling her ears. 'What did you say? She was still here when I arrived? She was here while I was spilling my guts about everything that happened in the meeting with François?'

Seb opened and closed his mouth. 'Yes. In the bedroom.'

Cat couldn't help glancing at the door that led to Seb's bedroom. She let out an incredulous laugh. 'I don't believe it. What did she do – hide in the bloody wardrobe?'

'It wasn't like that,' Seb insisted. 'You make it sound so sordid.'

Again, she felt a bubble of laughter threaten to escape. 'I hate to break this to you but you cheated on me. It *is* sordid.'

'I know,' he said, hanging his head. 'And it's been eating away at me all this time. Elin too, especially once she got together with Jaren. We agreed that it didn't mean any-thing – that it was just a mistake – and tried to forget about it. But I knew you'd react like this when you found out.' He sighed and stared at his feet. 'I knew you'd be hurt.'

'Of course I'm hurt,' she spat. 'I trusted you, Seb, and look what you did.'

He looked so dejected that Cat felt some of her anger start to ebb away. A sudden pang of unexpected sympathy took its place. She pushed it away, watching him wordlessly and trying to recapture her rage; she didn't want to feel sorry for him. He didn't deserve it. 'And did it mean anything?'

Seb raised his head. 'Of course it didn't. You were away – I was missing you and Elin was lonely too. It would never have happened if you hadn't gone to Paris.'

She stared at him as the implication of his words sank in. 'So it's partly my fault,' she said slowly. 'Is that what you're saying?'

'No!' He threw her a frustrated look. 'Of course it wasn't your fault. It wasn't anyone's fault – it just happened. I know you're hurt but surely you can see that?'

'I'll tell you what I see,' Cat said, forcing herself to take a deep calming breath. 'Someone who isn't prepared to take responsibility for their actions.' He tried to interrupt and she held up a hand to stop him. 'It's true – all you've done is try to shift the blame. I was away, Elin was lonely . . . maybe it's time you accepted that the only person who cheated on their partner that night was you, Seb.'

Hand shaking and blinking hard, she reached for her coat and placed the key to his apartment on the table beside her chair. 'I'll leave this here. I won't be needing it any more.'

'Cat – wait . . .' he said, his expression pleading. 'Don't go like this – stay and let's talk.'

'There's nothing left to say,' Cat said, her voice cracking as she passed him on her way to the door. 'It's over.'

She half-expected him to argue. Instead, he glanced away, hunching over in defeat. 'Okay. If that's what you want.'

This time, Cat couldn't stop her tears. 'Of course it isn't what I want. But you haven't left me any choice, Seb. It was over the moment you slept with someone else.'

She wrenched open the door and stumbled out onto the passageway. Wiping her eyes with the back of her hand, Cat hurried towards the staircase that led to the lower levels of the Court. As she passed the apartment that belonged to Elin, she thought she saw the blind twitch, as though someone had been watching and ducked out of sight. Cat didn't stop. Seb and Elin could do what they wanted to now. It was no business of hers.

Chapter Twenty-Eight

Cat thought about staying in bed when her alarm went off at six o'clock the next morning. Her eyes felt gritty and swollen; she was certain her face must be puffy from all the tears she'd shed once she got home and the adrenaline rush had worn off. The thought of dragging herself into Castle Court made her feel nauseous. But she was damned if she was going to let Seb or Elin keep her from her work; apart from anything else, she couldn't let Sadie down. Not on Good Friday.

She stood for a long time in the shower, letting the hot water soothe away her sickness, and then forced herself to get dressed. The streets of Chester were quiet, the way they always were early on a Bank Holiday, and Cat felt her anxiety about the day ahead start to lessen. She didn't think Seb would trouble her – other than by his proximity in the Court – and from what he'd said, she was certain Elin would be too ashamed to try and speak to her. Cat took several long, deep breaths as she walked; if she could concentrate on her baking and get through the hours until closing time, she'd count it as a win.

Castle Court was silent. Resolutely keeping her eyes at ground level, Cat let herself into Let's Go Dutch and punched in the alarm code before slipping into the kitchen. The cool, orderly space welcomed her like an old friend and soothed her jangling nerves. Delilah had the day off to spend with her grandchildren and Cat wasn't expecting Jaren to arrive for another hour. She pulled on an apron and switched on the oven before setting about assembling everything she needed. The biscuit dough recipe she'd perfected was so familiar that she was sure she could have made it with her eyes closed. But she still approached it as though it was the first time she'd ever made it; carefully, methodically and only deviating from the well-worn recipe to add a spoonful or two of Adam's honey into each batch of dough.

The kitchen was rich with the mingled smells of vanilla and chocolate by the time Jaren arrived. He stopped in the doorway, taking an exaggerated lungful of air before smiling at Cat. 'That smell never gets old, does it?'

Cat felt her stomach lurch at the sight of him. Did he know what Elin and Seb had done? Adam had told Sadie he didn't think so but there was always a possibility that Elin had confessed. Maybe they'd even laughed about it, Cat thought, torturing herself with the idea for several long seconds before remembering that this was Jaren. He wouldn't laugh about someone getting hurt.

'I don't really notice it any more,' she said, aware that her tone was uncharacteristically terse.

'Oh. No, I don't suppose you do ...' His smile faded as he regarded her in obvious puzzlement. 'Is something wrong, Cat?'

She shook her head, harder than was necessary. 'No. Everything's fine.'

He cocked his head. 'Really? You don't seem fine. Has something happened at the shop?'

'No. Like I said, everything is fine.'

To her horror, the last word came out as a croak. Tears surged into her eyes and flooded down her cheeks, splashing onto the stainless-steel worktop before she could stop them.

Jaren hurried forwards. Without a word, he gathered her into his arms and held her as she sobbed, murmuring soothing sounds into her hair. They stayed that way for what felt like an age to Cat as she struggled to get herself under control. But gradually, her tears subsided and she was able to step away from him.

'Thank you,' she said gratefully, looking up at him through her sodden eyelashes.

He raised a dark eyebrow. 'No problem. Are you going to tell me what this is all about?' He saw her hesitate and went on, 'You don't have to but I promise I'm a really good listener.'

Cat shook her head. 'It's nothing.'

His brown eyes regarded her solemnly. 'That is clearly untrue.'

The trouble was that a large part of Cat wanted to pour everything out. But how much should she keep to herself? It was bad enough that she'd been hurt by Seb's betrayal – was there any real need to jeopardise Jaren's relationship with Elin over something that had happened before the two of them had got together?

'Seb and I have split up,' she said, after a few moments wrestling with her conscience. 'As you can see, I'm not one hundred per cent okay about it.'

'I am very sorry to hear it,' Jaren said, shaking his head. 'No wonder you are crying. But you seemed so happy together – tell me to mind my own business if you want but how has this happened?'

Cat avoided his gaze. 'I was. But it turns out Seb wasn't. And he went elsewhere looking for happiness.'

This was it, she thought, watching him from the corner of her eye; if he knew the truth then his reaction would surely give the game away. But he looked genuinely disgusted. 'Then he is an idiot – a . . . a . . . *klootzak*.'

Cat had no idea what the Dutch word meant but she knew it wasn't complimentary. More importantly, she knew that Jaren had no idea exactly who Seb's partner in crime had been. And now the question was, should she be the one to tell him? To hurt him as she'd been hurt?

Reaching for some kitchen roll, she wiped away the last of her tears. 'He's very apologetic – says it didn't mean anything. But it's easy to say that after the event, isn't it?'

Jaren scowled. 'You deserve better than that. I mean,

everyone knows he has always had an eye for the ladies but I thought he'd changed when he met you. I can't believe he could be so stupid.'

'Me either,' Cat admitted with a sigh. 'But there you have it.'

'And the woman involved – it was a customer, I suppose. One of the girls who hangs around the bar trying to catch his eye.'

Cat held her breath. There were two ways she could answer; either by pretending she didn't know who the other woman had been or by admitting the truth and potentially endangering Jaren's own relationship. Given the way he'd reacted to the news of Seb's infidelity, Cat didn't imagine Jaren would be happy about Elin's involvement. But was it Cat's place to tell him?

She gnawed the inside of her lip as she wrestled with her conscience. Then, in a whoosh, she let go of the breath she'd been holding. 'Probably,' she said, looking Jaren squarely in the eye. 'I don't actually know all the details.'

Jaren sighed. 'Well, Seb is a fool. But you'll get over him and meet someone better. And he will die a lonely old man, muttering into a bottle with only his cocktail muddler for company.'

It was such a ridiculous image that Cat couldn't stop herself from smiling.

'There,' Jaren said, studying her with hopeful eyes. 'You are feeling better already.'

*

Sadie came to find Cat just after eight-thirty and discovered her sharing a table with Jaren, drinking coffee and looking much more cheerful than she'd been expecting.

'Good morning,' she said warily, wondering whether Jaren knew what had happened yet. 'How are you feeling?'

'Like I've just broken up with my rotten cheating boy-friend,' Cat said, pulling a face. 'But other than that, not too bad. Jaren has been cheering me up.'

Sadie looked back and forth between the two of them. 'Has he? That's good.'

'We have been devising ways for Cat to take her revenge,' Jaren said, grinning. 'I suggested hiding prawns throughout the bar, in places he'd never think to look for them.'

'And I think I should open a fabulous bar of my own right next door and steal all his customers,' Cat said.

'I see,' Sadie said. She cast a swift look Jaren's way. 'And how are you feeling about things?'

Cat flashed her a warning look. 'He's fine. Angry on my behalf, obviously.'

Sadie nodded. So Jaren had no idea that Elin was partially responsible for Cat's unhappiness. 'Well, I hate to break up the revenge party but the salvage company are just about to start stripping out the damaged equipment from the shop. Is there anything you want to keep?'

Cat gave a little shudder. 'No. I've made a list of all the equipment we lost – the insurance company have said they'll replace like for like.'

'In that case, can you come and set up the cart while I deal

339

with the paperwork? Clare isn't arriving for another half an hour.' Sadie gave her friend a searching look. 'If you feel up to it, that is?'

Cat stood up. 'Honestly, I'm fine. Thanks for the coffee, Jaren.'

'It was my pleasure,' Jaren said. 'And you know where I am if you want to talk. I also know a man who can supply any number of rotten prawns.'

Cat laughed. 'I'll bear it in mind.'

Sadie smiled in goodbye and waited until they were across the Court before firing a questioning look Cat's way. 'You didn't tell him?'

'I couldn't bring myself to,' Cat replied, sighing. 'I know they say misery loves company but not in my case.'

'You know he's bound to find out eventually.'

'I know,' Cat said. 'But I didn't want him to hear it from me. I – I wanted to give Elin the chance to tell him.'

Sadie shook her head, wondering whether Cat had been subconsciously worried Jaren might turn on her. But no matter what her motivation, Sadie found Cat's generosity of spirit to be amazing. 'You're a better person than me. I'd have set fire to everything and let it burn.'

Cat smiled. 'No, you wouldn't. I still remember how dignified you were over Daniel's affair. Where do you think I learned it from?'

Sadie wanted to laugh – if only Cat had seen the sobbing, shrieking mess she'd been when she'd first found out about her husband's affair. But she had tried to be fair, once the dust had settled, which was probably why they'd been able to try again after almost a year apart. In any case, she'd put it all behind her, for Lissy's sake as much as everyone else's.

'You're not going to forgive Seb, though, are you?' she asked, crossing her fingers.

'No, that ship has most definitely sailed,' Cat said. 'I told him so last night.'

So she had gone to see him, Sadie thought. She couldn't say she was surprised. 'Good. I hope you gave him hell.'

'I tried,' Cat said, reaching down to open the cupboards of the cart. 'But I'm not sure he really believes he did anything wrong. And until that sinks in, I don't think he'll be able to maintain any kind of long-term relationship. So all in all, I think I'm better off out of it.'

'Good,' Sadie said. She reached out to touch her best friend's hand. 'For what it's worth, I think you're going to be just fine. And I wouldn't mind betting that there's someone perfect for you just around the corner.'

Cat rolled her eyes good-naturedly. 'You know, that's pretty much what Jaren said.'

Sadie returned her friend's mocking look with wide-eyed innocence. 'Did he indeed? Great minds obviously think alike!'

The morning flew by in a blur of customers. Cat did her best to stay busy, splitting her time between managing the cart when Sadie needed to supervise the repairs in the shop and helping Clare to keep on top of the personalised orders. She kept her eyes resolutely away from both Seb's bar and Elin's chocolate shop, something that the steady stream of customers made easy. By the time closing time rolled around, Cat could see the same exhaustion she felt mirrored on the faces of Sadie and Clare.

'Wow,' Sadie said, staring at the few remaining tins of biscuits on the cart. 'I hope you baked a lot of biscuits this morning, Cat. If today is anything to go by, we're going to need a whole lot more tomorrow.'

Cat let out a long, weary breath. 'Not enough – not when I take the online orders into consideration. I guess I know what I'm going to be doing tonight.' Her gaze flickered upwards for the briefest of seconds. 'It's a good thing I don't have anything else planned.'

Sadie threw her a worried look. 'Well, yes. But how am I going to ice them?'

'We could come in early tomorrow and use Jaren's kitchen,' Clare suggested.

'But they need time to dry and I don't imagine Jaren will want his kitchen awash with bunny-shaped biscuits,' Sadie pointed out. Then she snapped her fingers. 'We'll have a baking party at my house. Cat, you bake as many as you can at home, then bring the biscuits over to me. Clare and I will ice them while you bake more.'

Cat opened her mouth to argue then closed it again. If she was totally honest, the thought of moping around her kitchen alone was a little daunting, even if she would be busy baking. 'Okay. What time?'

'Seven-thirty?' Sadie suggested. 'Clare, are you in?'

'Definitely,' the other woman said. 'Whatever you need. I can even pick you up if you like, Cat?'

Cat summoned up a warm smile. 'That would be great.'

She was just about to suggest a time when a shadow fell over the cart. Cat looked around to see Elin hovering a few feet away.

'Have you got a moment, please, Cat?' she asked in a calm but hesitant voice.

Beside her, Cat felt Sadie bristle. 'Not really,' she snapped before Cat could speak. 'We're a little bit busy, actually.'

Cat laid a hand on Sadie's arm. 'No, it's okay. This has to happen sooner or later – it might as well be now.'

'Are you sure?' Sadie asked, consternation in her eyes. 'It's very soon.'

It was soon; once again, Cat wished Seb had chosen someone she didn't know. But this was a conversation that had to happen eventually and the truth was that the faster she and Elin cleared the air, the faster Cat could move on. She didn't want to dread coming into work each day the way she had that morning.

She nodded at Sadie. 'I'm sure.'

Sadie flashed a disgusted look at Elin but didn't say what she was so obviously thinking. 'Fine.'

Clare looked mystified as Cat turned back to her. 'See you around seven pm – you've got my address, right?'

'Volunteer Street,' Clare said. 'Okay, I'll see you later.'

Pressing a reassuring hand onto Sadie's arm, Cat fixed Elin with a pointed look. 'Your place or mine?'

'Mine is closest,' Elin replied.

'Yours it is, then,' Cat said, unsmiling. 'Let's go.'

She was glad when Elin led her to the chocolate shop rather than her home. The delicious aroma as they stepped inside made Cat's mouth water, although she wasn't remotely interested in eating anything. In fact, she imagined the glistening chocolates surrounding them would taste like dust right now.

She waited for Elin to speak first, determined not to make it too easy for the chocolatier. The trouble was it didn't seem as though Elin *was* finding things easy; she looked tired and unhappy and her usually immaculate make-up couldn't hide the pinched expression around her eyes. Even her sleek blonde bob was rebelling; there was a touch of frizz around the ends. Cat wouldn't mind betting that she'd had a sleepless night and a worry-filled day.

Elin drew in a breath. 'I'm sorry.'

Again, Cat waited, maintaining her stony silence while the other woman pinned her gaze to the floor. 'I know Seb has told you what happened, and that we'd both been drinking, but the truth is that's no excuse. We knew it was wrong. And I'm sorry we hurt you – it was the last thing either of us wanted.'

Cat dug her fingernails into the palms of her hands. At least Elin wasn't trying to shift the blame, the way Seb had. 'You did hurt me,' she said quietly. 'The fact that it was you makes it a double betrayal.'

Elin's blue eyes flashed before she dipped her head again. 'I know. And if I could take it back, I would. You have no idea how wretched I felt, listening to you tell Seb how cruelly you'd been treated in Paris and knowing that we'd done something far worse.' Her gaze glittered with remorse. 'I wanted to tell you but Seb talked me out of it. He said you were too fragile.'

'Fragile?' Cat let out a bark of laughter. 'I'm not an ornament, Elin. And finding out from you would have hurt but not as much as hearing about it months after the event, when its been hardened by lies and deceit from people I thought I could trust.'

'I know,' Elin whispered, looking away. 'I'm sorry.'

A thick silence grew and Elin began to cry. An all-too-familiar pressure started behind Cat's own eyes and she blinked hard. 'I haven't told Jaren.'

Elin's gaze snapped back to her. 'What?'

'He knows that Seb slept with someone else but he doesn't know who. As you can imagine, he's pretty upset on my behalf and although it happened before you two got together, I don't think he'll be impressed when he finds out you're the other woman.' Cat paused and fixed Elin with a bleak stare. 'So if I were you, I'd tell him myself instead of letting him find out from some third-hand gossip. That way you might just save your relationship.'

'Thank you.' Elin shook her head. 'It's more than I deserve.'

'It is,' Cat agreed. 'But it's him I'm thinking of, not you.'

Elin nodded, tears dripping from her cheeks. 'I know. And I really am sorry.'

There was no doubt she meant it, Cat realised; regret was etched into every part of her. But there was something more, a deeper sadness that she wasn't sure she understood. 'Seb said it didn't mean anything – is that true?'

'Yes.'

The word had been firm and uttered quickly but Cat had caught the faintest hint of hesitation in Elin's voice. It told her everything she needed to know. 'You know he'll break your heart,' she sighed, with a pitying shake of her head.

Elin squared her shoulders. 'I know. But love isn't a choice, is it?'

Cat recalled Seb's dismissive words of the night before. 'If that's really how you feel then you need to tell Jaren. Now. Don't wait until the next time.'

Elin gave her an agonised look, causing Cat to remember that she'd been a good friend before this. She softened her voice. 'You know you have to.'

'Yes,' Elin said, her shoulders drooping. 'You're right. Thank you.'

'Don't thank me,' Cat replied. 'This isn't an easy way out – you're going to feel worse than ever for hurting him. But at least he won't be as hurt as he could be.' She headed for the door. 'I don't think we'll ever be friends again, Elin. But I wish you luck if you decide to get together with Seb. He's not the man I thought he was.'

Without waiting to hear Elin's reply, she slipped out into the Court and forced her feet to lead her towards the oak tree in the centre. Tears burned her eyes and tumbled down her cheeks. 'Enough crying,' she whispered as she passed beneath its leafy branches. She wiped her face with the sleeve of her jumper and shook her head fiercely. 'No more tears over Seb de Jager.'

Chapter Twenty-Nine

If anything, Easter Saturday was even more chaotic than Good Friday had been. Sadie was relieved to tap her final sale of the day into the virtual till system and pack the cart away; she and Cat had already decided they wouldn't open on Easter Monday.

'We've definitely earned a day off,' Cat said, surveying the few biscuits they had left. 'And besides, what would we sell?'

'You know, maybe we should stay closed for the rest of the week,' Sadie suggested. She eyed Cat with almost motherly concern. 'You need to get some rest – this time last week, you were in hospital with concussion and you've taken an emotional battering too. I could use some time to focus on the repairs to the shop, too. The plastering will be done on Tuesday and the new fittings will be in by the end of the week.'

Cat nodded. 'As much as I hate the idea of closing, it would give us the chance to build up our stock levels ready for reopening. Which reminds me, if we're going to celebrate that, we should probably send out some invitations.'

Instantly, Sadie's thoughts flew to Adam. She blushed guiltily. 'Good idea. Let's start with our regular customers and the local businesses who've supported us.'

Cat glanced over at the bright lights of Elin's shop. 'Maybe not all of them.'

Sadie swallowed the now-familiar surge of indignation she felt every time she thought of Seb or Elin; was this how Cat felt when she looked at Daniel, Sadie wondered? It would certainly explain the dislike she'd never quite managed to hide. Sadie had never really understood until now ...

Pushing the thought away, she gave her friend a support-ive smile. 'No.' Her gaze flicked to Let's Go Dutch, which was still crowded with customers. 'Have you heard anything from Jaren?'

'No. But I don't know when Elin was planning to speak to him – it could be she's waiting for the right moment.'

Sadie snorted. 'There's never a right moment to tell your boyfriend you're in love with another man.'

'I'll check in with Jaren tomorrow,' Cat said. 'If nothing else, we can mope together.'

Sadie eyed her best friend's downcast expression and reached out to pull her into a hug. 'You're both going to be okay. Give it time.'

'I know,' Cat replied, with a sigh. 'But I can't help wishing we could fast-forward a bit.'

*

The week whizzed past in a whirl of paint fumes and hammering. Sadie split her time between project managing the repairs and icing the fresh stock Cat and Delilah produced on a daily basis.

'I thought you were supposed to be resting,' Daniel said one morning, as Sadie balanced the phone between her ear and shoulder while mixing up another batch of icing. 'This doesn't look like my idea of time off.'

She threw him a wry look and continued to speak into the phone. 'No, George, I said white with a hint of peach, not the other way around.'

By the time Saturday morning dawned, the repairs were almost complete. The basement kitchen had gleaming new units and a freshly plastered ceiling. Upstairs, the warped floorboards had been replaced and the water-damaged display tables restored. Everything had been repainted and the air was heavy with the scent of emulsion.

'Don't worry,' Cat said, as Sadie stood wafting the shop door back and forth. 'The smell of baking beats paint every time.'

Clare and Delilah arrived early to help stock the shelves. By the time midday rolled around, Sadie was satisfied that everything was where it should be. She glanced over at Cat, who was filling plastic flutes with Prosecco. 'Ready?'

Cat looked up and smiled. 'Ready.'

Sadie crossed the shop floor and pulled the door back. 'Welcome to Smart Cookies,' she called to the crowd waiting in the Court outside. 'We're open for business again. And to celebrate, we're offering twenty per cent off everything!'

A cheer went up. Delilah bustled past, a tray of bite-sized cookies in her hands. 'I'll start handing these out.'

Cat lifted up a tray of drinks. 'And I'll be right behind you with these.'

'Biscuits and fizz – who could resist?' Sadie said, reaching for a flute from the table. 'Don't forget to grab a glass for yourselves, you two. It's been a hard slog to get to this point again.'

She sipped at her drink as she surveyed the crowd. It was a good turn-out, and more people seemed to be arriving with each passing minute. She was pleased to see Adam in the Court, chatting to the Smart Cookies regulars. He'd always been popular – sometimes a little too popular, Sadie thought – and he was certainly getting plenty of attention now. But he seemed to be holding his own.

'You've done an awesome job here, Sadie.'

She turned around to smile at Earl, who was gazing around in open admiration. 'When I think of what this place looked like after the flood hit ...'

'I know,' she said. 'The builders have really pulled it out of the bag.'

His eyes twinkled as he studied her. 'No, *you've* pulled it out of the bag – you and Cat. Andrew and I can't believe you guys kept going without a kitchen to bake in or a shop to sell from. We take our hats off to you and we're not the only people you've impressed.' He waved a hand towards the throng. 'Look at this turn-out. Castle Court loves Smart Cookies, just like we love you and Cat.'

Sadie felt her face flush with mingled pride and pleasure. 'Thank you, Earl. You have no idea how much that means.'

He shook his head in wonder. 'You've had some seriously stormy weather lately and you've sailed through it brilliantly. I hope you know that you've made a lot of friends here.'

Sadie resisted the temptation to glance up at the third floor. 'We do – thanks.'

'If there's ever anything we can help with, just let us know,' Earl said, reaching out to grab a biscuit from Delilah's tray as she passed. 'You can pay us in cookies.'

'Sounds like my kind of arrangement,' Sadie said, smiling.

Earl lowered his voice. 'In fact, I might have a very special commission for you soon. How good are you at keeping secrets?'

Intrigued, Sadie leaned towards him. 'The best. Tell me more . . .'

By the time the crowd started to thin out, Sadie's head was spinning with all the congratulations and lovely words that had been showered upon her and the Smart Cookies team. Tired but happy, she started to collect up some of the discarded Prosecco flutes. Adam was standing beneath the oak tree; her gaze met his, inviting her to come and talk, and she saw no reason to resist. 'You came,' she said when she reached him.

His eyes crinkled into a smile. 'I did.' He paused and looked around. 'No Daniel and Lissy today?'

'No,' Sadie said. 'I knew I'd be run off my feet and – well – I take enough work home for the novelty of biscuits to have worn off for both of them.'

Adam nodded. 'It's a shame they didn't come to see how hard you've worked – the place looks as good as new.'

She managed a tired smile. 'I don't mind admitting it's been a tough few weeks.' She looked over at Cat, who was chatting to Jaren. 'But we survived.'

Adam followed her gaze and his expression sobered. 'How is she?'

'She's been better,' Sadie replied. 'But I think she'll be okay. It helps that she's surrounded by friends here.'

'Castle Court is like that,' Adam said. He flashed a glance towards Seb's. 'Mostly.'

'And I think knowing she wasn't alone has helped,' Sadie went on, tilting her head at Jaren.

'Ah. I wondered whether she'd tell him.'

Sadie shrugged. 'Actually, that was Elin. But from what Cat has told me, Jaren wasn't as devastated as she expected him to be.'

'I'm not sure his heart was ever in that relationship, to be honest,' Adam said quietly. 'I think someone else got in there first.'

Sadie and Adam stood for a moment, watching Cat laugh at something Jaren had said. 'Yes,' Sadie said, as a smile tugged at her own lips. 'I think they're both going to be absolutely fine.'

'And you?' Adam said, his eyes coming to rest on her once more. 'Are you happy, Sadie?'

Her heart gave a flutter as she stared up at him. 'As happy as I can be,' she said, after a moment's thought. 'Happier now that we're friends again. We are friends again, aren't we?'

He smiled. 'Yes. I think it's safe to say we're friends.'

As the party wore on, Sadie lost count of the number of times she picked up and put down her glass without actually drinking any of the Prosecco inside it. When she finally had the time and space to come back to the last place she'd left it, just after closing time, she found Delilah had whisked it away.

'Sorry!' she said, obviously mortified as she stood at the sink in the kitchen. 'I thought it was an abandoned glass.'

'And the Prosecco has all gone,' Clare said, shaking her head. 'I can't believe you didn't even get to drink one glass.'

Cat appeared at the bottom of the stairs. 'Don't worry, I've got it covered.'

She squeezed past Delilah and opened one of the tall, floor to ceiling fridges to pull out a bottle of champagne. 'I've been saving this for now. Grab some glasses, Delilah – we've got some celebrating of our own to do.'

'To us,' Sadie said, once all four women had a glass of fizzing golden champagne in their hand. 'Team Smart Cookies!'

'To us,' they echoed and chinked the glasses together.

'Thanks for sticking by us,' Cat said sincerely, glancing at Clare and Delilah. 'We really couldn't have done this without you.'

'My pleasure,' Delilah said, grinning as Clare nodded her agreement. 'And there I was thinking retirement was going to be easy!'

Much later, Sadie and Cat stood side by side at the window of Smart Cookies, gazing out at the early evening diners making their way through the Court. 'I can't believe we did it,' Sadie said, glancing back at the newly restored shop.

'I can,' Cat said, smiling. 'We had the best project manager I've ever seen.'

Sadie waved the praise away. 'Stop it – I muddled through and you know it.'

'Maybe, but you still got the job done,' Cat insisted. 'In the face of some pretty heavy pressure. That's the mark of a true professional.'

'Oh shush,' Sadie scolded but she couldn't stop the warm glow Cat's words caused. 'How are you doing, anyway? I saw you talking to Jaren.'

'I'm fine,' Cat said. 'Well, maybe not fine but I will be. He's taking it better than me.'

'Hmmm,' Sadie said, studying Cat's expression for a sign that her friend had any idea why Jaren might have found Elin and Seb's betrayal easier than she had. 'That's good news at least.'

Cat gave her a sidelong look. 'And how about you? I see Adam made the effort to come back.'

Sadie forced herself not to blush. 'I'm glad he did. It's good to be friends with him again.'

'I bet,' Cat said, her tone dry.

'Don't start all that again,' Sadie said, giving her a sharp look. 'We're friends, that's all.'

'I know,' Cat replied. She raised her glass towards

Sadie and smiled. 'Here's to us, anyway, and whatever the future brings.'

'To us,' Sadie echoed, chinking her glass against Cat's. She looked over at the bright yellow splendour of the Bus Stop, hugging Earl's secret to herself, and then focused on the softly-lit windows of Let's Go Dutch. 'I have a really good feeling about what's coming next.'

Starry Skies at Castle Court

Chapter Thirty

He said YES!

Andrew and Earl

are delighted to invite you to
celebrate their wedding on

Saturday 30ᵗʰ June

at

Castle Court, Chester

RSVP to gettinhitched@busstopdiner.com

'Okay, I give in. What is that?'

Sadie stopped halfway across the basement of Smart Cookies and pointed at the glass-panelled black and red cube that sat on the work surface in the middle of the kitchen.

Cat waved a mysterious hand across the top. 'The answer to all your prayers. Or mine, anyway.'

'It's definitely not Aidan Turner,' Sadie said, raising her eyebrows. 'In fact, it looks like it just beamed here from NASA.'

'You're not a million miles from the truth, actually,' Cat said, grinning. 'I imagine these things are very popular with rocket scientists.'

Sadie's forehead wrinkled as she continued across the basement and into the small kitchen. 'Put me out of my misery. What is it?'

'You know it can sometimes be a struggle to find biscuit cutters that are the right shape for your designs?' Cat said, as Sadie peered through the glass panels.

'I do try not to be difficult,' Sadie replied wryly. 'But go on.'

Cat patted the top of the cube, feeling like a child on Christmas morning. 'Now you don't have to worry. This is a 3D printer – all we have to do is tell it what we want and it will make it for us!'

Sadie's mouth fell into an impressed-looking 'O'. 'Really?'

'Really,' Cat said. 'Obviously it's a bit more complicated than that and there might be a bit of trial and error until we get used to it. But it should mean we can create biscuits that are unique to Smart Cookies.'

She watched as Sadie's eyes widened with possibilities. 'How does it work?'

'It's really clever – you enter the dimensions into the software on the laptop and away it goes.' She beamed enthusiastically. 'I'll give you a demonstration if you like.'

'Maybe later,' Sadie said. 'I actually came down here to share some exciting news.'

She placed a cream-coloured envelope on the countertop next to the printer and gave Cat an expectant look.

'Is this what I think it is?' Cat asked, turning the envelope over and tearing it open.

Sadie grinned. 'It is. Andrew said yes – he and Earl are tying the knot!'

'Fabulous!' Cat said in delight, studying the heavy card invitation with its hot-pink lettering. 'I take it our edible proposal did the trick, then?'

'I'm not sure we can take all the credit,' Sadie replied, laughing. 'But Earl said Andrew almost burst into tears when he saw "Will You Marry Me" spelled out in biscuits. And they'd like us to provide the wedding favours, so we obviously did something right.'

The thought of stoic, bearded Andrew bursting into tears made Cat's heart melt. 'Great. Any idea what they've got in mind?'

Sadie's eyes twinkled. 'Oh, nothing too tricky. Just miniature versions of all the Castle Court shops.'

Cat felt her jaw drop as she thought of the myriad shapes and sizes of shops that lined the Court's three floors. 'It's a good job I bought this,' she said, glancing at the 3D printer. 'I think we're going to need it.'

'We're going to need a lot of icing sugar too. It's just as well we enjoy a challenge, isn't it?'

Cat's gaze came to rest on the wedding invitation once more. Andrew and Earl had been welcoming from the very first moment she and Sadie had opened Smart Cookies and they'd quickly become friends as well as neighbours. It would be an absolute pleasure to design and bake edible gifts for their fellow wedding guests.

'Mine is a plus one,' she said, looking at Sadie. 'Is yours?'

'Plus two,' her best friend answered. 'For Daniel and Lissy. In fact, they've asked Lissy to be flower girl, which I'm not sure she'll be thrilled about once she realises it involves wearing a dress.'

Cat smiled. Sadie's daughter preferred dinosaurs to dolls. 'I'm sure Andrew and Earl would be happy with a flower T-Rex instead.'

'If only,' Sadie sighed. She nodded at Cat's invitation. 'Who are you going to take?'

It was a question Cat had no answer for. Before Easter, she wouldn't have hesitated; she'd have gone with Seb. Even now, almost two months after she'd found out the devastating truth, she could hardly bear to look either of them in the eye whenever she ran into them around Castle Court.

'I'll go on my own,' she told Sadie, squaring her shoulders. 'It's not as if I won't know anyone, after all.'

Sadie opened her mouth, as though about to say something,

and then closed it again. Finally, she nodded. 'We'll have to make biscuit versions of Seb's bar and Elin's chocolate shop. That's not going to be a problem, is it?'

'I'm not that bitter,' Cat said, staring at her. 'Bloody hell, Sadie, credit me with some professionalism.'

'Sorry,' Sadie said, and Cat was slightly mollified by the blush that crept up her neck. 'It's just that it isn't very long ago that you and Jaren were discussing hiding rotten prawns around the bar. And revenge is a dessert best served cold.'

It was a conversation Cat remembered well; she and Jaren had spent the best part of an hour discussing the best ways for Cat to get her own back. That had been before Jaren had realised Seb's other woman was actually his own girlfriend . . .

'I think we've all moved on since then,' Cat told Sadie.

'Good,' Sadie said, turning around and heading for the stairs. 'Because the last thing we need is for you to go full *EastEnders* during the wedding.'

'No chance of that,' Cat called as Sadie disappeared up the stairs that led to the shop floor. 'Scandi noir, maybe . . .'

She picked up the invitation and studied it once more. It was a lovely thing for the Castle Court community and she couldn't be happier for Andrew and Earl. But she'd be lying if she said she was looking forward to the complications the wedding might cause. In fact, a lot of things in the Court were complicated these days, she thought, glancing restlessly around the basement; the only thing that stayed absolutely constant was her biscuit recipe. Although that was in danger of being *too* simple; once or twice in the last month, she'd caught herself longing for the challenge of managing a hectic restaurant kitchen.

'Make your mind up, Cat,' she muttered to herself, tucking the invitation into her pocket. She looked at the 3D printer and tried to summon up the enthusiasm she'd felt a few minutes earlier. 'Come on, then. Let's get to know each other.'

'How much longer, Mummy?'

Lissy squirmed on the cold wooden pew, gazing up at Sadie with an expression that bordered on actual pain. She'd been good up until now, absorbing the grandeur of Chester Cathedral with wide-eyed admiration, but Sadie sensed they were about to reach critical fidget overload.

'Shhh!' she whispered, glancing around to see who among the congregation had overheard. Beside her, Daniel frowned. The christening was for the daughter of a senior partner at the law firm where he worked and Sadie knew he wanted to make a good impression. It was part of the reason she'd agreed to come; a stable family life earned plenty of approval points with Daniel's bosses. But a badly behaved child could spoil everything.

Sadie slipped an arm around her daughter's shoulders. 'Not long now,' she murmured. 'Look, they're pouring the water over the baby's head.'

Lissy perked up, craning her neck to see. 'Why didn't she have a bath before she came?'

There was a muffled snort from behind them. Flustered, Sadie risked a look backwards and saw Daniel's secretary hiding a smile with one hand. Her eyes twinkled beneath her oversized hat as she leaned towards Lissy. 'That is a very good question. Would have saved us all from getting a numb bum from these horrible hard seats, right?'

Lissy giggled as everyone around them stood up.

'I now invite everyone here present to pray for Emily Rose,' the celebrant announced, his voice rich and warm.

The rest of the congregation began to read from the order of service but Lissy tugged Sadie's hand. 'Dippy wants to pray for Emily too.'

Swallowing a comment about the religious beliefs of dinosaurs, Sadie reached into her handbag and pulled out a long green diplodocus. Lissy took it eagerly and positioned the toy above the sheet in Sadie's other hand, as though reading.

'At least she's not moaning any more,' Daniel whispered, meeting Sadie's gaze with a wry look. 'Chin up, it's nearly time for fizz.'

Sadie was relieved when they reached the end of the service without any further outbursts. Outside, the sun was shining, bathing the cathedral's gothic spires in golden light against a backdrop of cloudless blue skies, and Sadie felt some of her anxiety melt away. All she had to do now was get through an hour or so of small talk with Daniel's colleagues and then she could escape, safe in the knowledge that she'd done all that he'd asked of her.

'That wasn't too bad,' he said, as they followed the crowd through the cathedral grounds to the canal-side restaurant that was hosting the party.

Sadie watched Lissy pause to offer Dippy some of the immaculate grass lawn that ran alongside the path. 'No, it wasn't. I think your secretary is smitten by Lissy.'

He smiled. 'Tell me about it – I've got a photo of us all on my desk and she keeps asking when she's going to meet you and Liss. I think today might be a dream come true.'

'Hardly,' Sadie replied, laughing in spite of the fluttering of nerves his words caused. This wasn't the first work function she'd attended with Daniel but it was the first since they'd split up and got back together and she wasn't looking forward to seeing some of his co-workers. Thankfully, his secretary was new and had missed the scandal that had followed his affair with fellow lawyer Emma. Maybe she'd be a good person to hang out with at the party, Sadie thought. If Daniel would let her.

The restaurant had made the most of the glorious weather. The courtyard overlooking the canal was bedecked with bunting and there was a grassy area filled with toys for the younger guests. A marquee gave some shade from the hot midday sunshine and there were several staff members offering up flutes of champagne. A string quartet played in one corner. Sadie looked around with tentative approval. If it wasn't for the other guests, she'd be quite happy to spend her Sunday afternoon here.

Lissy made straight for the toys, while Daniel swiped

two glasses of champagne. 'Here,' he said, handing one to Sadie. 'Cheers.'

'Cheers,' she echoed. She took a long swig, enjoying the burst of bubbles on her tongue and the crisp, buttery flavour that followed.

'Better?' Daniel asked, as she let out a small sigh of appreciation.

'Better,' she agreed. 'Although you make me feel a bit like an alcoholic.'

'Nonsense. I just know how much you appreciate good champagne.' He raised an eyebrow. 'And there's been no expense spared here, let me tell you. Nothing but the best for Emily Rose.'

Sadie believed it; hiring one of the best restaurants in Chester for an entire afternoon in high season must have cost a small fortune. And she didn't want to know what kind of strings had been pulled to have the christening held in the cathedral itself; a serious contribution to church funds must have taken place.

Daniel took her hand. 'Come on. Let's mingle.'

Sadie pulled back in alarm. 'But what about Lissy?'

'They've got staff to look after the kids,' Daniel pointed out. 'Look – there's a nanny over there, making bracelets. And another sitting on the grass, doing balloon animals. Lissy will be fine.'

Sadie frowned. On the one hand, the sooner she made the rounds, the sooner they could leave. But she didn't like the thought of leaving Lissy in the hands of strangers, no matter how qualified they were.

'Let me tell her where we'll be,' she said, passing him her glass. 'I won't be a moment.'

Quickly, she found Lissy and crouched beside her, trying to ignore the way her heels sank into the grass. 'Mummy and Daddy are going to be talking to some of the grown-ups, okay? Don't leave this area without telling one of the nice nannies. And make sure you don't go anywhere near the fence beside the water.'

Lissy nodded. 'But what if Dippy needs a drink?'

'Give him some orange juice,' Sadie said firmly.

She stood up and made her way over to the nanny surrounded by beads and elastic. 'That's my daughter, Lissy. If you need us, we'll just be chatting in the courtyard.'

The girl smiled. 'Don't worry, I'll keep an eye on her. Maybe she'd like to make a bracelet.'

Sadie eyed the explosion of pink and purple on the table in front of the girl. 'Maybe,' she said doubtfully. 'Have you got any dinosaur-shaped beads?'

By the time Sadie had chatted to what felt like a bewildering array of Daniel's colleagues and their partners, her head was starting to spin in a way that had nothing to do with the champagne and she longed to go back to the kids' area to thread beads onto elastic herself. But Daniel was obviously on a mission to schmooze; all Sadie could do was try and keep up. It wasn't as bad as she'd feared, however; if Daniel's co-workers were curious about Sadie's decision to take him back, they hid it well.

At last she found herself face-to-face with Daniel's secretary, Elizabeth.

'It's so lovely to meet you at last,' the other woman cried, shaking Sadie's hand with warm enthusiasm. 'Daniel has told me so much about you.'

Sadie couldn't help smiling. 'Lovely to meet you too. Did you enjoy the christening?'

'It was beautiful,' Elizabeth said, her plump cheeks dimpling. She glanced around, then fixed Sadie with a conspiratorial look. 'Although having it in the cathedral was a bit much, if you ask me, considering the baby won't even remember it.'

'I don't think Emily is the one who's meant to remember it,' Sadie said diplomatically. 'And how do you enjoy working for Daniel? Is he a good boss?'

'The best,' Elizabeth said instantly. 'Although I would say that, wouldn't I?'

Her giggle was infectious; Sadie realised she liked her a lot.

'And he obviously dotes on you and your little girl,' the other woman went on. 'He never stops talking about you. I don't know how he's going to cope with all these nights away he's got coming up.'

'Nights away?' Sadie repeated, frowning.

Elizabeth clapped one hand over her mouth. 'Hasn't he told you? Oh, bugger.'

Sadie shifted uncomfortably and took a long sip of too-warm champagne. 'He might have mentioned them,' she lied. 'When is the first one again?'

'Next month,' Elizabeth said. 'But I'm sure Daniel will give you the details himself. It's probably slipped his mind, that's all.'

The trouble was that this was how his affair with Emma had begun, Sadie thought miserably, with sudden nights away and a lack of communication about where he'd be. But Elizabeth wasn't to know that. And besides, Emma had moved away. She wasn't a threat any more.

'I'm sure you're right,' Sadie said, summoning up what she hoped was a carefree smile. 'He's got a memory like a sieve sometimes.'

Daniel found her later, sitting at one of the tables on the edge of the grass, watching Lissy play with her balloon dinosaur. He'd loosened his tie and his gaze was soft as he sat beside Sadie. 'Have you had enough?'

'Yes,' she answered truthfully.

He laughed. 'Honest, at least. I'm sorry to drag you along – has it been as bad as you expected?'

This time, Sadie shook her head. 'No. I had a lovely chat with Elizabeth – she's nice.' She paused, and then hurried on before she lost her nerve. 'I hear you're going to be working away.'

Daniel frowned. 'Am I? Oh, you mean next month? It's just the odd night, here and there. I've been roped in to advise on a merger down in London, that's all.' He studied her with concern. 'It's no big deal. I was going to tell you.'

Sadie swallowed. She was being paranoid. 'I – I need the dates to make sure I sort things out at Smart Cookies. You know how busy we are.'

He leaned over to kiss her on the cheek. 'Of course. I'll dig them out of my diary as soon as we get home.'

'Okay,' Sadie said. She gazed at Lissy for a few moments, trying to quell the lingering sense of unease in her stomach.

'Listen, I've been thinking,' Daniel said, taking her hand. 'Lissy spends a lot of time on her own and I'm not sure it's good for her.'

'No, she doesn't,' Sadie said, stung. 'One of us is always with her.'

He ran one hand through his hair. 'That's not what I mean. She doesn't have anyone else to play with. And we're back together again now – things seem to be going pretty well – so I wondered if . . . whether it was time to think about . . .'

He trailed off awkwardly, firing a hopeful look her way, and all of a sudden she knew exactly what he meant. 'A baby,' she said slowly. 'You want another baby.'

His eyes lit up. 'Wouldn't it be wonderful? A brother or sister for Lissy, although obviously she'd prefer a brontosaurus, but what do you think?' He paused to give her a tentative smile. 'Isn't it time?'

No, Sadie wanted to tell him. No, it was not time. Things might be better between them but they were a long way from perfect. And then there was the business she was building with Cat; there was no way Sadie could abandon that for a year to look after a baby, no matter how much Daniel wanted one. Her gaze lurched wildly around the party and came to rest on Lissy's auburn curls once more. But now wasn't the right time to tell Daniel that.

'I – wow. This is a bit of a shock,' she admitted, glancing at him.

'Just think about it,' he urged her, squeezing her listless fingers. 'Don't answer now.'

Sadie did her best to smile, but inside she already knew what her answer was going to be. The question was, how would Daniel take it?

Chapter Thirty-One

'Is this your work?'

A newspaper was slapped onto the glass-topped Smart Cookies counter, causing Cat to look up. Greg Valois stood glaring down at her, his bald head red and quivering with barely suppressed fury.

'Good afternoon to you too,' she said drily, straightening up. 'What can I help you with today?'

He jabbed a meaty finger at the paper. 'This hatchet job of a review of La Clé d'Argent, supposedly written by the *Observer*'s food critic. I assume I have you to thank?'

Cat blinked. It just so happened that Mariette Noble *was* a good friend of hers but she'd had no idea the restaurant critic had been in Chester. She would have arranged to meet up for cocktails if she'd known.

'How have you reached that conclusion?' she asked Greg, trying not to glance down at the review. 'And do be careful with your answer. I'd hate for you to slander anyone.'

Greg turned even redder, telling Cat her jibe had hit the mark. Greg had kept a low profile ever since accusing her of slander. Cat had assumed he'd been concentrating on running his bistro, but clearly he'd been biding his time, waiting for an opportunity to strike.

'Don't try to deny it,' he blustered. 'I know you and Mariette are thick as thieves. Tell me, did she even eat at my restaurant or did you make it all up yourself?'

Cat couldn't resist it any longer. She waved a hand at the folded newspaper. 'May I?'

She didn't wait for him to reply. Instead, she began to skim the article. Almost immediately, she could see why he was spitting feathers: the review was scathing. Mariette did not have a good word to say about anything, from the tired decor to the disengaged staff and uninspired menu options. But her worst criticism was reserved for the food. The snails, she claimed, were so springy that she feared they might leap off the table and dance a jig. The sea trout looked embarrassed to be on her plate and tasted as though it had been through the dishwasher, and the pastry chef appeared to have confused her order for a passion fruit soufflé with one for a crêpe; she'd certainly seen more air in a pancake. The wine, Mariette conceded, was tolerable but it was difficult to ruin a good Chablis. All in all, it was the kind of write-up that would have had Cat reaching for her coat or some gin, and quite possibly both.

She looked up at Greg. 'I understand why you're upset—'

'Upset?' he roared, spit flecking his lips. 'I am more than upset. I – I am *furieux*.'

'I promise you this has nothing to do with me.'

Greg's eyes narrowed. 'I don't believe you.' He reached across to prod Cat's shoulder. 'And let me make a promise of my own. This is war, Mademoiselle Garcia.'

'What's going on?'

Cat could have cried with relief to see Jaren standing in the shop doorway, his black eyebrows drawn together in a forbidding frown. She straightened up and gave Greg an imperious look. 'Nothing. Monsieur Valois was just leaving.'

The seething bistro owner snatched the review from her hands. 'You haven't heard the last of this,' he snarled. 'I'll find a way to prove you're behind it.'

He spun around and barged past the Dutchman, who watched him go with a mixture of disbelief and amusement. 'I think he's been watching too many pantomimes,' Jaren said, with a shake of his black curls. 'What was that all about?'

'He thinks I wrote a terrible review of his restaurant,' Cat said, trying her hardest to sound light-hearted. 'Or he thinks I asked a friend to do it instead. He's not sure which.'

'Ah, right,' Jaren said, heading towards her. 'Because no one could eat at his bistro and actually think it was terrible, am I right?'

Cat laughed but she knew it was a weak effort. Now that Greg was gone, her hands had begun to shake. Hiding them beneath the counter, she gazed at Jaren. 'Forget him. What can I do for you?'

He pulled out a familiar-looking envelope. 'I need

help,' he said, sliding the invitation out and placing it onto the counter. 'What do you get for the men who have everything?'

Cat puffed out her cheeks. 'I have absolutely no idea,' she confessed. 'We're providing their wedding favours so I don't think we need to buy a gift and I'm incredibly grateful for that.'

Jaren sighed. 'You're so lucky. I asked Earl what they wanted – he just smiled and said, "Your beautiful face among the crowd."'

This time, Cat's laugh wasn't forced. 'That does sound like him. Why don't we both have a think and then compare notes? I'm sure we can come up with something between us.'

'Okay,' Jaren said. His long fingers toyed with the invitation. 'Have you thought about who you might take?'

'No,' Cat replied. 'Have you?'

'No,' he said, and hesitated. 'I did think—'

'I don't know what's in this, Cat, but it weighs a ton,' Delilah said, bustling up to the counter with a large brown-paper parcel in her arms. She placed it on the glass top and pushed her grey hair back from her face. 'Hello, Jaren. What are you two plotting – his 'n' hers wedding outfits?'

Cat's cheeks exploded into heat. She patted the parcel in an effort to change the subject. 'Thanks for going to collect this,' she said. 'I'm sorry it was so heavy – I'd have gone myself if I'd realised.'

Delilah shrugged off the apology. 'The exercise did me good. What's inside?'

'New colouring gels, amongst other things,' Cat said.

'Recreating Castle Court in biscuit form is going to take a lot of trial and error.'

Jaren looked delighted. 'Is that what you're doing for the wedding favours?'

'Don't tell anyone,' Cat warned. 'It's supposed to be a surprise.'

Jaren smiled. 'I won't breathe a word. As long as you help me find a gift of my own.'

Cat nodded. 'I'll get my thinking hat on.'

'And if Greg gives you any more trouble, you send him over to me,' Jaren said, collecting his wedding invitation and making for the door. 'Maybe it's time someone told him a few home truths about his precious bistro.'

Delilah didn't try to prevent her sigh of admiration as the Dutchman left the shop. 'He's so handsome. Oh, if only I was forty years younger.'

'Mmm,' Cat said, suddenly busying herself at the till.

'It's a crime that someone so good-looking is single,' she went on, and Cat could almost feel Delilah's eyes boring into her. 'He's clever too, and successful. In fact, he's quite the catch. If I were you, I'd—'

'Haven't you got some biscuits to bake, Delilah?' Cat said, glancing at her assistant with an exasperated but not unkind expression.

The older woman was entirely unruffled as she made for the stairs that led to the basement kitchen. 'I do. But don't dither about too long. He might decide you're not interested and invite someone else to the wedding.'

Cat opened her mouth to say that it was perfectly fine if he did, but the words died in her throat. Because it wasn't. If Jaren brought someone else to the wedding, Cat would mind very much. And she didn't know quite what she was going to do about that.

*

How are your honey supplies looking?

Sadie had drafted the message to Adam three times on Wednesday morning before she hit send. There was something about the word honey that seemed to give the wrong impression.

I need your honey.

Can I come round for some honey?

Have you got some honey for me?

It wasn't that she thought Adam would get the wrong idea – after he'd spilled the beans about Seb and Elin, they'd begun to build up a tentative friendship again but they both knew that was all it could ever be. No, it was more that Sadie burned with embarrassment at the mere thought of sending Adam a suggestive message. Even if that wasn't what she meant at all.

She leaned against her kitchen counter, waiting for his reply. Cat wanted to increase production in preparation for the wedding order and the honey from Adam's bee hives was a vital ingredient. A few minutes later, Sadie's phone buzzed and lit up:

> Pretty good! Want me to drop some in
> to the shop?

> Only if you're heading into town. Or I could
> collect? When are you around?

She popped her mug into the dishwasher and wiped a few crumbs from the counter while she waited. Adam only lived a few minutes' drive away; it made sense to call in on her way into the shop if he was home.

> Now?

> Perfect! See you in five x

It wasn't until after she'd pressed the send button that she noticed the kiss.

'Sorry about the kiss,' Sadie blurted out, the moment Adam opened the door of his cottage.

His eyebrows shot up so far they almost mingled with his untidy brown fringe. 'Pardon?'

Sadie took a deep breath and started again. 'I added a kiss to the bottom of my last message. Sorry.'

A look of enlightenment crossed his freckled face. 'Ah,

did you? I can't say I noticed.' He smiled and held the door wide. 'Don't worry, I won't hold you to it.'

Of course he hadn't noticed it, Sadie told herself, burning with mortification as she followed him across the low-ceilinged living room. Adam wasn't the type to spend hours staring at his phone, especially at this time of year. He'd be too busy tending to his organic fruit and vegetable patches, or checking on his bees.

'How are things at the shop?' he asked once they'd reached the kitchen. 'How's Cat?'

'Things are pretty crazy, as usual,' she told him, glancing around as she spoke. Was it her imagination or had he tidied up? The kitchen was gleaming and she knew from many previous conversations that he wasn't normally so house-proud. 'Cat's fine – stressed, but fine.'

'That's because she thrives on stress,' Adam said, waving a teabag in Sadie's direction.

She nodded. 'I suppose so. You can't run a double-Michelin-starred restaurant without enjoying life on the edge.'

'Exactly,' Adam said. 'But I meant how's she feeling – you know, about the whole Seb and Elin thing.'

Sadie smiled. He'd been so reluctant to be the bearer of bad news when he'd told her about Seb's infidelity, and he never missed an opportunity to ask after Cat's well-being. 'Better. And I have high hopes for Andrew and Earl's wedding – there's nothing like "I do" to make people wonder what they might be missing.'

He flashed her a thoughtful look and for one awful

moment, she thought he'd misunderstood. But he went back to stirring the tea. 'You're right. Somehow it makes people see what's been right under their nose all along.'

Sadie cleared her throat. 'So, how many jars of honey can you spare?'

Adam spread his hands. 'As many as you need. The bees have been working hard and there's a great supply of borage in the fields. The honeysuckle is in bloom and it's been a good year for foxgloves – honey bees love both.'

Sadie followed his gaze out of the kitchen window, to where the enormous walled garden was basking in the morning sun, neatly set out in rows and beds. She could see what he meant – the honeysuckle was running riot over one wall, and there was a forest of tall foxgloves nodding underneath. It would make a great watercolour, she thought, and her hands twitched at the thought. Maybe she'd pop back some time, with her paints and brushes.

'Are those your hives?' she asked, nodding at a cluster of peaked boxes tucked almost out of sight towards the back of the garden.

'They are,' he said, before pausing to give her a speculative look. 'Do you fancy meeting the neighbours?'

Sadie felt a sudden surge of anticipation. She'd heard him talk so much about his bees that she practically felt as though she knew them. And Lissy would be thrilled to hear what the hives were like on the inside; she'd been fascinated by the thought of bee houses ever since Adam had first explained where honey came from.

'Can I?' Sadie asked, feeling a flutter of excitement mingled with nervousness at the thought of getting close to so many bees.

'Of course,' he said, smiling. 'Let me finish my tea and I'll take you out to say hello.'

She'd guessed there'd be some protective clothing to wear but Sadie still wasn't prepared for the outfit Adam presented her with fifteen minutes later. The jumpsuit looked like a cross between a hazmat suit and something a scenes of crime officer would wear. And the hat made her feel every inch the Edwardian lady once the wide-brimmed, heavily veiled construction was resting on her head.

'Wellies?' she said, gazing down at the scuffed khaki boots Adam was holding out. 'Is it muddy?'

'No, but the trick is to make it very hard for a bee to sting you.' He peered through her veil. 'I probably should have asked this earlier, but you're not allergic to bee venom, are you?'

Sadie shook her head carefully. 'No. Are they likely to try to sting me?'

'Hopefully not,' Adam said, gesturing at the wellingtons. 'But you never know what mood they'll be in, so it's better to be safe than sorry.'

Swallowing an apprehensive sigh, Sadie slid her feet inside the boots and allowed Adam to pull the legs of her suit over the rubber. *What must I look like?* she wondered, almost embarrassed. Then she remembered this was Adam's job; in a few minutes, he'd be wearing an outfit very much like hers.

'Have you been stung much?' she asked, once they were both ready.

He held open the kitchen door. 'A few times,' he admitted. 'But only when I haven't been giving the bees my full attention or the proper respect. And I do have a secret weapon – it's over here.'

Adam led her over to a dark–green storage cupboard and reached inside to pull out the weirdest-looking contraption Sadie had ever seen. It looked like a silver jug inside a wire cage, with a round, pointed nozzle covering the top and what looked a lot like a tiny set of bellows on the side.

'Any idea what this is?' Adam asked, holding it up.

Sadie studied it, observing the blackened tip of the nozzle. It looked as though it had been burned, but surely fire and bees were a bad combination? 'None at all,' she admitted. 'What does it do?'

He reached into the shed once more and pulled out a sheet of newspaper. 'We're technically going to be breaking and entering in a minute and the bees won't like it. Don't ask why, but smoke makes them hungry, which in turn makes them sleepy and less likely to object when we disturb their homes.'

'So you use that to create smoke,' Sadie said, watching as he flipped the nozzle off the jug to reveal a blackened empty cylinder inside. He held a lighter underneath the ball of newspaper and stuffed it inside. 'Won't paper burn too fast?'

Adam nodded and reached into the cupboard again. 'I use dried grass to create the smoke but there are loads of other things you can use. Some beekeepers swear by woodchips, others buy specialist fuel.' He pushed a handful of yellow-green grass on top of the burning paper. 'What you want is plenty of smoke without any flame.'

His fingers gave the bellows a careful squeeze and a grey cloud poured from the jug. 'The secret is to pack plenty of fuel into the smoker – that way you get embers that last a long time so that you don't have to break off to refuel.'

He added more grass, pushing it into the cylinder until he was evidently satisfied, and replaced the nozzle. 'Here,' he said, passing it to Sadie. 'Give it a squeeze.'

She did as he suggested and a puff of smoke filled the air.

'So that's our secret weapon,' he said, smiling through his veil. 'Ready to meet the bees now?'

Sadie wrinkled her nose. 'I think so.'

As they got nearer to the hives, she could see the bees buzzing up to the wooden houses and disappearing into a slender gap between the slats at the bottom. Adam held out an arm to stop her. 'This is the motorway,' he said, gesturing to the area in front of the hives. 'We'll use the back road.'

He circled around to the rear of the wooden boxes. Sadie followed. The buzzing was louder now, a constant low-pitched hum that she found oddly soothing. She felt some of the tension in her shoulders lessen and allowed herself a wry smile. No wonder Adam was one of the most chilled-out people she knew – being up close with bees was unexpectedly calming.

She felt slightly differently when Adam lifted the top off the hive, however. The tone of the buzzing changed immediately as the inhabitants realised something had changed. Several veered upwards towards Adam's head. Sadie took an involuntary step back but he seemed unconcerned by the bees flying suspiciously around his veil. 'These are called frames,' he explained, beckoning her close and pointing at the vertical slats that were sticky with a mixture of wax and golden-yellow honeycomb. 'If you hand me the smoker, I'll pull one out for a closer look.'

Directing the nozzle between the frames, he sent a lazy stream of smoke curling into the hive. The change in the bees was remarkable; instantly, they began to crawl to where the honey was. Adam gave another puff and waited, observing the tiny winged creatures. Finally, he seemed satisfied and handed the smoker to Sadie.

'Now we'll see how busy you've been,' he murmured, sliding one of the honeycomb-laden frames up in a slow, methodical manner so that she could see it.

The hexagonal cells were covered in bees. Sadie watched in fascination as they crawled around the sticky surface; she knew from listening to Adam talk about the hives before that each one had a job to do and that they all worked tirelessly for the benefit of the colony.

'Somewhere in there is the queen,' Adam said, his finger hovering over the cluster of bees. 'I like to find her every time I open the hive, if I can, just to make sure she's okay. The whole hive revolves around her.'

Sadie smiled. 'Nice work if you can get it.'

'Sort of,' Adam replied. 'She's basically an egg-laying machine who can't actually feed or clean herself. And as she gets older, the colony might decide to replace her with a younger model. There's only really room for one queen in a hive.'

Unbidden, an image of Emma flashed into Sadie's mind. She shook it away. 'Can't she fight back?'

'Not really,' Adam replied. 'If the colony loses faith in the queen, they'll drive her out to die. The only option she has is to swarm with the bees that have stayed loyal and go in search of a new home.'

Sadie felt a shiver go through her. Wasn't that exactly what she'd done with Lissy? Flown away and started up a new home while Daniel made honey with his new queen? Except that things with Emma hadn't worked out and Daniel had decided he wanted his old queen back. And now he wanted a baby too . . .

'There she is,' Adam said, pointing at a noticeably larger bee with a red spot on her back. 'See? She's bigger than the others.'

Sadie frowned. 'And she's born red?'

He laughed. 'No, that's my handiwork so I can find her easily. Beekeepers rotate the colours over a five-year cycle so that it's easy to tell how old a queen is but it's not unusual for the workers to clean the paint from her back – bees are often very hygienic.'

Sadie listened as he pointed out the eggs and larvae in

various stages of growth, marvelling at his knowledge and enthusiasm. Eventually, he slotted the frame back into place and eased the roof of the hive back on top. They walked slowly away until the bees were just dots flying in and out of the hives.

'Thanks,' Sadie said, as Adam helped her to remove the veiled hat.

'No problem,' he said. 'It's always a good idea to make sure you don't have any hitch-hikers before you get too far from the hives.'

Sadie's eyes widened as she looked down at her white overalls. Adam smiled. 'Don't worry, you're clear.'

'Thank you for introducing me to your bees,' Sadie said. 'I can see why you love them – they're fascinating.'

He glanced across the garden, his smile widening. 'Yeah, they're pretty amazing. Thanks for letting me show off a bit.' His gaze drifted upwards, to where the sun was climbing high in the sky. 'But I've kept you long enough – Cat will be thinking I've kidnapped you.'

Sadie shook her head. 'She won't mind once she knows I've been with you.'

The words replayed themselves in her head and she felt the familiar burn of embarrassment. What was wrong with her – first the kiss, and now this, making it seem as though Cat was trying to push the two of them together. Which she was, Sadie thought wretchedly, but there was no need for Adam to know that. 'What I meant was—'

His eyes creased at the edges. 'I know what you meant.'

They stood smiling at one another for a few long seconds, then Adam seemed to give himself a mental shake. 'Come on. Let's see if I can find a box for your honey. Cat will definitely have my head if you leave without that.'

Chapter Thirty-Two

'Do you ever dream about just . . . sailing away?'

Jaren took a long swig from his pint glass and leaned back against the brick wall of the pub, shading his eyes against the evening sunshine as he considered Cat's question. 'I used to,' he said, after a while. 'But not recently. Why – do you?'

Cat watched what was left of a heat haze shimmer over the canal and sighed. 'Not sailing, no – I only mentioned that because you live on a houseboat. It would be mad not to take it with you if you suddenly upped and left Chester.'

He studied her over the top of his drink. 'But you have thought about leaving?'

She hesitated. It wasn't a fully formed thought, more a reaction to the stress of the last few months; she'd been injured in a flood, had to defend herself against scurrilous lies and discovered that her boyfriend had betrayed her with a woman she'd thought of as a friend. And now Greg Valois had declared war on her over something she hadn't done. Who wouldn't dream about escaping all of that?

'Not seriously,' she said, after a thoughtful sip of her wine. 'But maybe if I lived on a canal boat, I might be more tempted.'

Jaren grinned. 'Typical landlubber – imagining it's all cocktails at sunset and pub lunches at old boating inns. Whereas the truth is nothing like that – the mooring points are few and far between, you never know if they'll be busy when you get there and don't get me started about the toilet facilities.'

Cat frowned. 'But you have a toilet on board the boat.'

'I do,' he replied, pulling a face. 'But – how can I put this delicately? It has a tank that needs to be emptied. That needs to be factored into your journey plans.'

'So what you're basically saying is that even running away generates admin. There's no such thing as living the dream, is that it?'

Jaren spread his hands. 'Broadly. Or maybe that shit happens, I'm not sure.' He regarded her with concern. 'But what's brought this on? Is it your run-in with Greg?'

'Partly,' Cat admitted with a sigh. 'But it's not just him – it's everything. I even found myself looking at a job advert for a restaurant in New York yesterday. That's how bad it's got.'

She knew without having to look at Jaren that he was shocked. Why wouldn't he be? Cat hardly knew what to make of it herself. Sipping her drink, she lapsed into silence. She was sure Jaren had his own problems to deal with; he didn't need hers dumped on top.

'I'm sorry you feel like this,' Jaren said, a few moments later. 'Have you spoken to Sadie about any of it?'

'No,' Cat replied quietly. 'I don't want to bother her.'

Jaren leaned forwards and gazed at her intently. 'It's not bothering her. You are business partners and best friends – she'd want to know. In fact, she needs to know, especially if there's a chance you might apply for another job.' He gave a little shake of the head. 'Look at it this way – if the situation was reversed and Sadie was looking at other jobs, or talking about walking away, wouldn't you want to know?'

He was right, she realised; she would want to know. The trouble was that Sadie's artistic flair meant that she was integral to Smart Cookies, whereas Cat was starting to feel that anyone could bake the biscuits, now that she'd perfected the recipe. And the wedding favours had given her a new challenge – one she was enjoying – but she still felt a little as though she was treading water. Cat was also acutely aware that Sadie never seemed to struggle this way; obviously, she'd been through some difficult times when Daniel's affair was revealed but she had faced her problems head on. And Cat might not agree that taking Daniel back was the right course of action but she couldn't deny her best friend's courage in doing what she thought was best for her family. Sadie was strong, even if she didn't always believe it; she didn't run, the way Cat wanted to.

'Cat?' Jaren said softly, taking her hand. 'If you don't want to tell Sadie how you feel then I hope you know you can always talk to me.'

His dark eyes were so sincere that a lump grew in Cat's throat. She didn't trust herself to speak and nodded instead.

'I like to think I'm a really good listener,' he went on and a wry smile tugged at his mouth. 'When I'm not talking about toilet tanks, that is.'

The words lifted Cat's spirits enough for a little laugh to escape her. 'Yeah – thanks for ruining that particular dream.'

'I prefer to think of it as keeping it real,' he said. 'Or a reminder that the water isn't always bluer on the other side.'

Cat watched a couple strolling along the canal, their arms wrapped around each other. 'No, I know. Thanks, Jaren. You are a good listener.'

He twined his fingers around hers. 'That is what friends are for, Cat Garcia.'

The opportunity to talk to Sadie failed to materialise over the next few days; business in the shop was brisk, and whenever there was a quiet moment and Cat was able to build up the courage to start the conversation, someone always seemed to appear. In the end, Cat offered to come over to cook at Sadie's cottage on Friday, once she'd established that Daniel would be out at a work function.

'I can't quite believe I have a two-Michelin-starred chef cooking in my own home,' Sadie said, leaning back in her seat at the kitchen table to watch Cat work. 'I hope you haven't gone all Blumenthal on me.'

'Not exactly,' Cat said, stirring the bubbling pan of paella.

'You're a bit lacking in basic equipment for that – no liquid nitrogen, for a start.'

Sadie grimaced. 'Please tell me that wasn't a regular feature of the menu at La Perle?'

Cat summoned up a mental image of the menu she had created for the most famous restaurant in Paris. She'd taken a pinch of classic French cookery and mixed it with the best flavours from around the world to create recipes that couldn't be found anywhere else. Food lovers and critics alike had flocked to the restaurant, earning Cat the two highly coveted Michelin stars Sadie had mentioned with such awe. And she'd never needed gimmicks or dangerous chemicals to win the praise of her customers and colleagues; it had all come from a deep understanding of food and flavour.

'No,' she said, dipping a spoon into the pan to taste the sauce. 'I failed GCSE Chemistry, remember?'

'That's right, you did,' Sadie replied, a twinkling look in her eyes. 'Didn't you almost blow up the lab once?'

'Exactly,' Cat said. 'So it's probably safest if I stick to traditional cooking. It's ready, by the way, if you want to help me plate up.'

Sadie got to her feet and reached for an oven glove. 'I feel like a proper chef. What do you need me to do?'

The conversation slid inevitably towards Smart Cookies business as they ate. Once they'd finished, Sadie got up to clear the plates and Cat touched her arm. 'Leave those a minute, will you? There's something I need to tell you.'

Concern flickered over her best friend's face. 'What's wrong?'

'Nothing's wrong,' Cat reassured her. 'Well, nothing major, anyway. It's just that I've been feeling a bit ... not overwhelmed exactly, but struggling with everything that's happened this year. And rather than stick my head in the sand and pretend everything was fine, I decided the grown-up thing to do was talk to you.'

Sadie listened as Cat spilled out everything she'd told Jaren, although she didn't mention the job in New York, telling herself it was just a symptom of the deeper problem. When she'd finished, Sadie shook her head. 'You've been under so much pressure that I can't believe I didn't see this coming. What can I do to help?'

'That's just it,' Cat said wretchedly. 'I don't know. I mean, obviously if you could arrange for Greg to vanish into a puff of smoke then that would be great but he's only part of the problem. I don't expect you to manage the same trick with Seb and Elin.'

'No,' Sadie said thoughtfully. 'They're not going any-where, I'm afraid. But what if you took a few days off?'

'You know I can't – not at the weekend. We've got way too many orders for me to skive off, plus I'm still working on the designs for the wedding favours.'

'So work from home, then,' Sadie suggested. 'You said yourself that you're enjoying designing them and it's work that can be done on a laptop – you don't need to be at the shop for that.'

Cat considered the idea; it would be good not to have to run the gauntlet of bumping into her ex, or mouth-frothing Greg, each morning. 'Are you sure?' she asked Sadie, with a frown. 'Won't you need extra cover in the shop?'

'We'll manage,' Sadie said, her tone firm. 'I'm sure Clare and Delilah will be happy to do a bit of overtime if I need them to. No, don't argue – it's happening.'

The sudden surge of relief Cat felt at knowing she didn't have to go to Smart Cookies in the morning made her slightly tearful. 'Thank you. You're the best business partner I've ever had.'

Sadie smiled. 'I'm the only business partner you've ever had.' Her smile faded into mock severity. 'Just promise me you won't bottle everything up again, okay? I can't help you if I don't know there's a problem.'

'I promise,' Cat said, sniffing. 'Now enough about me – what's new with you?'

'There's nothing new with me,' Sadie replied firmly. 'Nothing to write home about at all.'

'Really?' Cat said, glad to shift the conversation away from herself. 'Had any more romantic trips to Adam's apiary recently?'

Her friend laughed. 'None. And if you'd seen what I had to wear that morning, you'd know that it was anything but romantic.'

'Are you sure?' Cat asked, raising her eyebrows. 'I assume there were birds in the garden – couldn't you think up some subtly sexy questions to ask Adam about the relationship between them and the bees?'

'I'm not sure Adam would have got the hint,' Sadie said in amusement. 'There might have been birds and there were definitely bees but, believe me, romance was the last thing on either of our minds. We're friends, that's all.'

'For now,' Cat added.

'For ever,' Sadie insisted. 'And you need to stop trying to push Adam and me together – sooner or later he's going to notice and I'm happy with Daniel.'

Her gaze skittered away at the very last second, telling Cat more in that one action than Sadie seemed willing to admit, even to herself. With a thoughtful look at her friend, Cat rose to start the clearing up. It appeared she wasn't the only one pretending everything was perfect in her life.

When Sadie awoke early on Saturday morning, the first thing she noticed was Daniel's absence. His side of the bed was unruffled, the sheets cool, meaning he hadn't come home last night. That wasn't an issue, Sadie decided as she stared at the ceiling and yawned; he'd probably been a little the worse for wear and decided to sleep it off at his own house rather than disturb her. He'd be along soon, carrying fresh bread from the village bakery and a hangover.

Checking the time and deciding there was no point in going back to sleep, Sadie slid out of bed and padded downstairs to put the kettle on. The kitchen was immaculate; Cat had insisted on helping her to clean up, despite Sadie's insistence that she sit down and leave it all to her. Outside, the sun was already warm. Birdsong floated through the window and if she listened very carefully, she could just about hear the crow of a cockerel. Could it be the one at Waverton farm? she wondered. Was Adam listening to exactly the same sound as he stood in his own kitchen, sipping a cup of tea like her? The thought made her smile, although she drew the line at reaching for her phone to ask. It would be even harder to draft than the honey message . . .

Lissy woke up just before seven and came thundering downstairs when she discovered her mother was already up.

'Where's Daddy?' the little girl asked, upon finding Sadie alone in the kitchen.

'I don't know,' Sadie replied. 'I think he must have stayed at his house last night.'

Lissy nodded; she was used to Daniel spending some nights away from the cottage, although they had happened less and less frequently as he and Sadie rebuilt their marriage. 'He needs to come home soon – he promised to take me to Dino Golf today. And you'll be late for work.'

Sadie glanced at the clock. 'It's okay. We've got plenty of time before I need to leave.'

By eight-fifteen, she was starting to worry. Daniel hadn't read her message asking what time she could expect him, nor was he answering his home phone, and she needed to set off by half past eight to reach Smart Cookies in time to open up; there was no way she was calling Cat to do it for her, not after their conversation the night before. Lissy was fidgeting on the sofa, listening out for the crunch of Daniel's feet on the gravel path that led to the front door.

'Where's Daddy?' the little girl asked again.

'I don't know,' Sadie repeated, listening to Daniel's phone ring and ring through her mobile. Finally, she gave up and went to find her daughter's shoes. 'Sorry, Lissy, you'll have to come to work with me today.'

Lissy's expression drooped. 'But I wanted to play Dino Golf with Daddy.'

Bending down, Sadie tugged the shoes onto Lissy's feet. 'I know. Maybe he'll be able to pick you up later and take you this afternoon.'

She hoped she sounded more confident than she felt. There had to be a rational explanation – a good reason for not being where he'd promised to be – because it wasn't like Daniel to let either of them down like this; at least, it wasn't like the new and improved Daniel. The old version had never been around when Sadie had needed him but she'd finally come to believe that those days were gone. Until now.

Now it felt very much as though she and Lissy had travelled back in time.

'Can I decorate some biscuits like you do, Mummy?' Lissy asked from the back seat, as Sadie turned the car around and pointed it towards Chester.

'Of course,' Sadie said, smoothing out the frown lines and doing her best to smile at her daughter in the rear-view mirror. 'You can decorate as many as you like. Just don't leave the shop.'

Sadie was keen to avoid a repeat of Lissy's last disappearing act. Apart from anything else, it had aged her five years in fifteen minutes.

'I'm going to decorate a gingerbread man to look like Daddy,' Lissy went on. 'And then I'm going to tell him off.'

'Good plan,' Sadie murmured. There were a few choice words she'd like to say to Gingerbread Daniel herself.

Chapter Thirty-Three

'Look, I've said I'm sorry,' Daniel said, perching on the edge of Sadie's sofa and folding his arms defensively. 'I don't know what more you want from me.'

Sadie glared at him. 'How about a sense that you actually mean that apology? Or even offer some kind of explanation.' Her gaze flicked up towards the stairs. 'Lissy waited all day for you to come and get her – she was really upset when you didn't show up.'

He ran a hand though his hair. 'I told you I'm sorry. One drink led to another and before I knew it, we were going for a kebab. I didn't think you'd appreciate my chilli breath in the early hours of the morning so I went back to my place, that's all.'

There wasn't a lot Sadie could say to that; he was right, she wouldn't have appreciated it. But she didn't understand why he hadn't messaged her to explain. Her phone had been resolutely silent throughout the day, apart from the occasional message from Cat.

'And then what – you slept through my phone calls?'

Daniel winced. 'Could you not shout? I still have a hangover.'

'You should have let me know you were okay,' she insisted, not in the least bit sympathetic. 'I was worried about you.'

His expression softened a bit. 'As I said, I'm sorry. And you're right, I should have let you know.' He paused. 'But we wouldn't even be having this conversation if we all lived in one house. Isn't it time you thought about coming home?'

The words caused a scythe of anxiety to cut through Sadie. He meant *his* home – the one they'd all shared before she'd uncovered his affair. And it wasn't unheard of for Sadie and Lissy to stay at Daniel's, but he tended to spend more time at the cottage and it had been a long time since either Lissy or Sadie had thought of his big, echoing house as home. And Sadie wasn't at all sure she was ready to give up her cosy two-bedroomed cottage, with its just-exactly-right kitchen and peaceful atmosphere. This was her home now. Hers and Lissy's.

'I have thought about it,' Sadie said, fighting to keep her voice level. 'And I've told you, we're not ready for that yet.'

Daniel took her hand. 'But this place isn't big enough. Where would we put the nursery, for a start?'

The words set alarm bells ringing in Sadie's head. The last time they'd spoken about having another baby, she'd told Daniel she'd think about it. She hadn't, not really, but he obviously had. And he'd taken her reluctant maybe to mean yes.

'Daniel—'

'I know, I know, you're still thinking about it. But we have to plan for the future, Sadie. And whichever way you look at it, this house doesn't have enough room. Not for a growing family.'

She shook her head in disbelief. 'We're not growing.'

'Lissy is,' he replied, lightning fast. 'Or haven't you noticed that the trousers she had on today are too short for her?'

'They are not,' Sadie said.

'They are. And she needs some new shoes – those trainers are only held together by the laces and she didn't even have matching socks.' He took a deep breath and gave her a disappointed look. 'I've only ever been supportive about how hard you work at Smart Cookies but I can't keep quiet when I see Lissy looking like she's got dressed in the dark.'

Sadie swallowed her wounded gasp, determined not to let Daniel see how much his comments hurt. 'That's not fair,' she said quietly. 'I wasn't expecting to take Lissy with me this morning, remember? She had to get ready in a hurry, which is why her socks didn't match and I might have picked up an old pair of trousers. But that wasn't my fault – if you'd been here then I wouldn't have had to take her at all.'

'That's right, blame it all on me,' Daniel replied, folding his arms. 'The thing is, I'm not the one standing in the way of us being a proper family, Sadie. You need to think about what you want.'

'What I want is for Lissy to have a father she can rely on,' Sadie retorted, trying not to raise her voice.

Daniel's eyes narrowed. 'I'm not the one working every weekend. And I'm not the one who lost her in a busy shopping centre. Just think about that before you call me unreliable.'

This time, Sadie couldn't stop herself from gasping. 'How dare you?'

He shook his head. 'You can't cope on your own – that's one of the reasons we got back together in the first place. And isn't it better to live together in one house than waste money on two? We could rent this one out, earn a nice bit of money for a family holiday and give Lissy some quality time.'

Sadie heard the words but they whirled around her head, barely making sense. Daniel earned more than enough money to pay for a family holiday if that was what he wanted to do; why did he need her to rent out the cottage? And why was he implying she'd be a bad parent if she didn't?

'It'd be for us, Sadie,' he said, reaching for her hand again. 'You, me and our kids. What do you say – will you move back in with me?'

His blue eyes were so wide and appealing that she was almost convinced. But then she replayed the words in her head – *our kids* – and she knew it would be a mistake to agree. 'I don't think it's a good idea at the moment. Sorry, Daniel.'

His gaze hovered between shock and incredulity. It hardened as he dropped her hand and stood up. 'Then I don't think it's a good idea for me to stay here tonight.'

Heart pounding, Sadie took a deep breath and rose. 'And while we're being honest, I don't think it's the right time to consider another baby, either.'

'I don't suppose it matters what I want, does it?' he said, his lip curling. 'Only what's right for you.'

'Daniel,' she said, laying a hand on his sleeve but he shook her off.

'I thought we wanted the same thing,' he said, and she saw pain flit across his eyes. 'But if you can't even bear to live with me, what future do we have?'

He turned on his heel and walked out, leaving Sadie staring after him. Moments later, the front door slammed and she heard the roar of his car as he sped away. And then she heard the gentle thud of small feet as Lissy appeared at the top of the stairs.

'Where's Daddy gone?' she asked, her face round and pale.

'Back to his house,' Sadie said, trying to sound calm and reassuring. 'He's tired so he's going to sleep there tonight.'

Lissy yawned. 'I'm tired.'

'Then go back to bed,' Sadie said, half-exasperated.

'Dippy wants you to tuck him in,' Lissy said. 'Will you?'

And Sadie was filled with a rush of love for her daughter. 'Of course I will.' Climbing the stairs, she slipped her hand into Lissy's. 'Would you mind if I tuck you in at the same time?'

The little girl gave a sleepy smile. 'No, Mummy. I wouldn't mind that at all.'

*

404

'This is nice,' Jaren said approvingly as he glanced out of the balcony that overlooked the canal, taking in the early evening view. 'How long have you lived here?'

Cat handed him a glass of water and frowned thoughtfully. 'Almost a year. I moved in last August.'

The Dutchman nodded. 'Well, I like the view. It's not a houseboat but it's pretty close.'

Cat grinned. 'Damn right it's not a houseboat. When the toilet flushes here, that's the last I ever see of the contents.'

Jaren threw her a pained look. 'I thought we agreed never to mention that again?'

'You're right,' Cat agreed, glancing at the bulging jute carrier bag he'd brought with him. 'So, what's on the menu?'

'I am going to teach you the noble art of making *garnalencocktail*,' he said. 'It's a shrimp cocktail starter in a whisky sauce, served on a bun. And afterwards, I might share my grandmother's secret pancake recipe with you. But, of course, then I'd—'

'Have to kill me?' Cat said, her eyebrows raised.

'Be quite full, I was going to say,' Jaren went on with a teasing smile. 'Obviously, things are a lot more cut-throat in the restaurants of Paris.'

Cat laughed. 'Obviously. Your *garnalencocktail* sounds delicious.'

He tipped his head, accepting the compliment. 'And what are you going to cook for me?'

Mentally, Cat flicked through her knowledge of Dutch cuisine; it was fair to say that apart from pancakes and waffles, they weren't exactly renowned for having recipe books packed with world-beating recipes. She seemed to remember a lot of potato dishes, and a split-pea soup that was filling but not especially adventurous. But the point of this evening wasn't to cook something that Jaren would recognise from his life back in the Netherlands, it was to teach him something he didn't already know. The idea was that they would each show the other a technique or recipe that they hadn't tried before. And that gave Cat a serious advantage, even though they'd both agreed it wasn't a competition.

'How do you feel about Thai green curry?' she asked.

Jaren's brown eyes gleamed. 'I love it.'

'Then that's our main course. Ready?'

He bent to collect the jute bag. 'Ready.'

They worked well together, moving around each other in Cat's compact kitchen with such synchronicity that it almost felt as though they were dancing. Jaren told her that the tastiest shrimp of all were the grey shrimp caught in the North Sea. 'That's what we have here, although as you can see, they are so small that they have to be shelled by hand.'

Once the whisky sauce was complete, Cat showed him how to layer the flavours in the Thai green curry so that they would unfold in waves when eaten, combining to create a curry that was fresh and fiery at the same time. By the time the sauce had thickened around the morsels of chicken, both Cat and Jaren were starving. They sat down to eat, each complimenting the other on their recipes.

'We made a good team,' Jaren said, scraping the last of the

curry onto his fork and eating it. 'You can be my assistant any time.'

Cat smiled. 'Sure. And I'll consider letting you be my sous-chef next time I have a dinner party.'

Jaren raised an eyebrow. 'But you haven't tasted my pancake recipe yet. Like I said, it's my grandmother's recipe and the secret of my success.'

Cat pushed her chair back and began to clear the plates. 'Then what are we waiting for?'

She had to admit, the pancakes were good; their lighter-than-air crispiness was pure heaven on her taste buds. But she enjoyed stepping back to watch Jaren cook even more; he gave off an air of being at home in the kitchen that she found very attractive. Once or twice, he looked up and caught her staring. The first time she looked away. The next time she didn't.

'So,' Jaren said, as they sat beside each other on the sofa, full and satisfied. 'That was fun.'

'It was,' Cat agreed. 'You were right about the pancake recipe – it's amazing.'

He nodded. 'My grandmother is an amazing woman. I think you'd like her.'

Cat studied him from the corner of her eye, remembering how he'd told her that he'd been raised by his grandmother after his mother's death. 'I think I'd like her too,' she said softly. 'And not just for her pancakes.'

Jaren smiled. 'You seem happier – more settled. Did you talk to Sadie?'

'I did,' Cat said. 'She told me to take some time away from Castle Court, which is why you haven't seen me around as much.'

'The change obviously agrees with you.' He hesitated and glanced sideways at her. 'Are you still thinking about applying for other jobs?'

There was something unreadable behind his eyes. Cat hardly dared hope that it was the same spark of attraction she felt. 'Not at this moment in time,' she said truthfully.

'But later,' he persisted. 'Is there a chance you might leave Chester for good?'

It wasn't a question she could answer; who knew what the future held? But right then, all she wanted was to be close to Jaren. 'It depends.'

'On what?'

She leaned in. 'On whether there's a good enough reason to stay.'

His brown eyes were fixed on hers. 'Is this a good enough reason?' he said, closing the final few centimetres between them.

The feel of his mouth on hers was unlike anything Cat had felt before, soft and gentle but passionate at the same time. Her eyes drifted shut as she eased into him and felt one hand tenderly brush her cheek. A slow curl of interest rose inside her as his lips moved against hers, bursting into full-blooded desire when he pressed harder. Her mouth opened and the kiss deepened.

Cat had no idea how long they stayed that way, slowly

teasing and exploring each other. But when they did finally part, she felt bereft by his absence.

'That was . . .' she began, then trailed off.

He smiled gently. 'Unexpectedly good? Better than the pancakes?'

Cat couldn't help smiling back. 'Definitely better than the pancakes. With all due respect to your grandmother.'

Jaren laughed. 'She'd say that was exactly as it should be.' He paused to give Cat a searching look. 'So shall we do it again sometime?'

'I'd like that,' Cat said, feeling a sudden burst of happiness. 'I really would.'

Cat hugged the memory of her kiss with Jaren close over the next few days. He'd left just before midnight, promising to take her out on a real date soon, and the thought gave her the courage to brave Castle Court once again.

The early morning sun was cresting the rooftops when she arrived on Tuesday, bathing the oak tree at the heart of the Court in beams of brilliant gold. There was no breeze; the weather forecast promised heat all day long, but Cat fancied she could hear the dark-green leaves rustle as she paused underneath. She loved the peace and quiet of the paved courtyard at this time of day, when the shop windows glowed with temptation and there was no one else around to break the silence. No one, that was, except Greg.

He was outside La Clé d'Argent, fumbling with the keys. Cat watched him for a moment, frowning as several plastic folders slithered from his grasp. He muttered a curse in French that carried across the still air, and shifted an over-loaded rucksack further onto his shoulder as he picked the folders up from the floor. Cat's frown deepened. There was something furtive about his behaviour; was that a strong-box under his arm? And what on earth was he doing there so early? The bistro didn't open until midday and even the food deliveries didn't arrive at dawn in the summer. Besides, Greg didn't appear to be taking a delivery. It looked more as though he was leaving.

Cat made a decision. Stepping out from the shelter of the tree, she cleared her throat. 'Need any help, Greg?'

She was sure she heard him yelp as the folders tumbled to the ground again. He turned around and his expression soured immediately. 'Oh, it's you. No, I think you've done enough.'

Cat stopped in front of him, her eyes roaming curiously across the items he carried. 'What exactly is it you think I've done now?'

'Isn't it obvious?' He gestured to an A4 sheet of paper stuck in the window.

Mystified, Cat moved close enough to read the untidy handwritten scrawl. 'Closed until further notice?' she said, blinking.

'I hope you're pleased with yourself,' the Frenchman said. 'That poisonous review you set up was the last nail in the coffin.'

Cat waved an impatient hand. 'I told you that had nothing

to do with me.' Her gaze slid to the strongbox that rested on his well-padded hip. 'But that still doesn't explain what you're doing with *that*.'

Defensiveness flashed across his features. 'I'm only taking what's mine. I built this business up from scratch – I deserve to be rewarded, even if Robert de Beauvoir thinks otherwise.'

The mention of the old restaurateur created a light bulb in Cat's brain. 'You don't own La Clé d'Argent,' she breathed. 'You just ran it on Robert's behalf. Of course.'

'Not for Robert,' Greg sneered. 'For François. And don't worry, I'll be sure to make sure he knows about your part in the failure of the business.'

'I'd like to wish you good luck,' she said, stepping back from Greg without smiling. 'I think you're going to need it.'

'I'm not the one who's going to need luck,' Greg said, glowering at her bitterly. 'François is going to ruin you.'

Cat summoned up a carefree laugh. 'He tried once and it didn't end well. I don't fancy his chances a second time.'

She left him standing there, spluttering and struggling with his ill-gotten gains, and strode purposefully towards Smart Cookies. It was too early to call Paris yet but Cat intended to be on the phone to Robert the moment it was decent to ring. She had no intention of letting Greg get away with anything.

Chapter Thirty-Four

Earl's eyes twinkled as he regarded Sadie across the counter in Smart Cookies later that morning.

'Can it be true? Has Greg really pulled a Loki?'

Sadie blinked. Both the American owners of the Bus Stop diner were keen film and TV buffs and often threw fandom references into conversation. Most of them seemed to relate to *Star Wars* but this one was lost on her. 'Sorry?'

'Loki,' Earl repeated. 'Evil genius, tries to steal the secrets of Asgard to use against his enemies, often makes terrible choices?'

Sadie waited until a customer had moved away before lowering her voice. 'If you're asking whether Greg has absconded from the bistro, disabling their stock ordering system, taking their bookings diary and a large amount of cash, then yes, I suppose he has pulled a Loki,' she said, taking a deep breath. 'I don't know about the secrets of Asgard, though.'

Earl whistled, his expression sobering. 'Man, I knew

things weren't going well for him, but this? It sounds like he's really done a number on the place.'

Sadie sighed. 'Not to mention the poor staff. The maître d' has stepped up and they've reopened, despite Greg's efforts, but it's safe to say everything is a bit chaotic over there. Cat has been talking to the owner in Paris – he's sending some-one over to take charge, at least temporarily.'

'That's something, at least,' Earl said. 'Are they going to involve the police?'

'Cat says no,' Sadie replied. 'But the de Beauvoirs know a lot of people in the catering industry – I hope Greg isn't planning to get another restaurant job.'

Earl shook his head. 'What a tool.'

'Anyway, I'm sure you didn't come here just to gossip about Greg,' Sadie said. 'Is there something I can do for you?'

'You overestimate me,' Earl said, grinning. 'Gossip is exactly why I'm here. But I might as well check up on the wedding favours too, although I'm sure you and Cat have everything in hand.'

Sadie spared a guilty thought for the boxes of shop-shaped biscuits sat on her kitchen table, awaiting her attention. She'd been unsettled ever since her argument with Daniel and the strain on their relationship had made it harder for her to con-centrate at home. 'Of course,' she said, crossing her fingers beneath the counter. 'Do you want to see the designs?'

He waved the offer away. 'No, no. I want them to be a surprise.'

'I think you'll definitely be surprised,' Sadie said, picturing not only the wedding favours but the additional project she and Cat had cooked up between them to present to the grooms on the day. 'In a good way.'

'Fantastic,' Earl said warmly. 'I suppose I'd better get back before the lunchtime rush hits. May the Force be with you, Sadie.'

'Er – and you,' Sadie said as he dodged the browsing customers and made his way across the shop floor.

'Oh,' Earl said, turning as he reached the door. 'We're having a double stag party at the Bus Stop on Saturday – it's a lot like a normal stag, but hornier. Are you and Cat in?''

Sadie couldn't help grinning. 'When you put it like that, how could we say no?'

Cat was up to her elbows in dough when Clare appeared in the Smart Cookies kitchen.

'You have a visitor,' she told Cat. 'It's that French guy who turned up a few months ago, when you had all that trouble with Greg.'

She held out a business card but Cat didn't need to take it to know who was waiting upstairs: Robert de Beauvoir. Dusting off her hands, she reached for the cling film to wrap up the dough. 'Tell him I'll be straight up.'

Robert was as elegant as ever. His silver-grey hair was swept back in a way that made him seem taller than he was, in spite of the walking stick he leaned upon. He wore a dark-grey three-piece-suit that murmured expensive tailoring and a pair of black patent-leather shoes in which Cat could see herself reflected. 'Bonjour, Mademoiselle Garcia. It is a pleasure to see you again.'

Cat shook his outstretched hand. 'The pleasure is mine, monsieur.'

He glanced around the busy shop and lowered his voice discreetly. 'Is there somewhere we could go to talk?'

Cat hesitated, glancing over at Clare. Sadie had left early to make a start on Earl and Andrew's wedding favours and Delilah was delivering an order of bespoke book cover biscuits to the local bookshop for a launch party that evening. She hated leaving Clare to handle the shop alone, especially when business was brisk. But Robert wasn't someone who was used to being refused; he might not be her boss any more but that didn't mean she could simply turn down his request.

She thought quickly. 'Of course,' she told Robert. 'Just give me one second to make an enquiry.'

Hurrying across the sun-drenched Court, Cat wove in and out of the crowd, hoping Jaren would be able to spare one of his employees to help out at Smart Cookies. But her heart sank as she pushed back the door of Let's Go Dutch; almost every table was occupied.

'Hey,' Jaren called from behind the bar, his face lighting up when he saw Cat. 'How's my favourite assistant?'

'Stressed,' she said, making her way between the diners. 'I've got a problem.'

He listened as she explained, then spread his hands. 'I'm all yours.'

Cat felt warmth creep up her cheeks, even though

she knew exactly what Jaren meant. 'Really? Aren't you too busy?'

He shrugged. 'These guys have everything under control,' he said, patting the barman beside him on the shoulder. 'Really, I'm only here to make myself feel useful. I can spare some time to help you out.'

Cat's hesitation only lasted a few seconds. 'Great. Come on, I'll tell you more as we walk.'

Inside Smart Cookies, Robert was examining their Blooming Summer collection with evident enjoyment. He put the tin back on the shelf when he saw Cat and came towards her.

'Robert de Beauvoir, I'd like you to meet Jaren Smit,' she said, and the two men shook hands. 'Jaren owns the very successful Let's Go Dutch pancake house on the other side of Castle Court.'

'Delighted to meet you,' the Frenchman said. 'My grand-mother was Dutch and made the most wonderful pancakes.'

Cat and Jaren exchanged grins. 'Mine too,' Jaren observed. 'It's a pleasure to meet you, monsieur.'

Robert glanced at Cat, his expression appraising. 'Shall we?'

'Of course,' she said and turned to Jaren. 'Speak to Clare, she'll tell you what to do. I'll be as quick as I can.'

With a final smile of appreciation, she led Robert out of the shop and through the alleyway that led to the Rows. Mindful of his slower pace, she chose a café tucked away under the shadow of the cathedral, where she knew they might find somewhere to sit and talk without being overheard.

'I recommend the lemon and poppy seed muffins,' she said, as Robert studied the menu.

'Then that's what I'll have,' Robert said to the waitress. 'And a black coffee, *s'il vous plaît*.'

He waited until they were alone again to fix Cat with a serious look. 'I'm sure you know why I am here,' he said in French.

Cat inclined her head, hoping her grasp of the language was up to the demands of the conversation. It had been more than a year since she'd needed to say much more than please and thank you. 'I do. Although when you said you would send a representative, I didn't expect for one moment to see you.'

Robert shrugged. 'If you want a job done properly, you do it yourself. And so here I am.'

'Here you are,' Cat agreed. 'I assume you've visited La Clé d'Argent?'

'I have. The situation is grave, even worse than I suspected. Monsieur Valois has been mismanaging things there for far too long – it will take a steady hand and talented management to turn things around.'

He paused while the waitress arranged their coffee and cakes on the table, then gazed at Cat with undisguised candour. 'In short, Cat, I think it will take *you*.'

'Me?' Cat squeaked in English. 'Surely you don't mean that.'

'But I do,' Robert said, switching languages as smoothly

as Cat. 'Your reputation precedes you – even if I hadn't seen and tasted your work first hand at La Perle, I know enough about you to be certain you are the right person for the job.'

Cat gaped at him in shocked amazement. 'But you need a proper manager – someone with experience of running a whole restaurant, not a chef like me.'

'A head chef,' Robert reminded her. 'And on the contrary, you are exactly who I need. I want someone with the vision to turn La Clé d'Argent around – to make it the best restaurant in Chester. That someone is you and I am prepared to pay you handsomely to do it.'

'It's not about money,' Cat said, shaking her head to clear the buzz of confusion his offer had created. 'I don't have the experience to run a whole restaurant.'

'And yet you run Smart Cookies.'

'That's different,' she pointed out quickly. 'I'm not on my own there – Sadie is there too. We're a team.'

Robert took a long draught of his coffee. 'So recruit some help. What about that Dutchman who looked at you as though he would jump through rings of fire to please you? Didn't you say he runs his own restaurant in Castle Court?'

She had, Cat realised, and wondered for one incredulous second whether Robert had planned things this way. But he couldn't have anticipated she would bring Jaren over to meet him, even if he had known about Let's Go Dutch beforehand. 'We're both busy,' she said flatly. 'Running our own businesses. What makes you think we'd have time to run yours too?'

Robert smiled. 'I know you, Cat. You enjoy a challenge. And while Smart Cookies appears to be doing very well indeed, I wonder whether it really stretches you.' He leaned forwards, steepling his hands. 'Wouldn't you like the opportunity to make La Clé d'Argent rise like a phoenix from the ashes of disaster? I can assure you that you'd have free rein to remodel the restaurant as you wish. Money is no object.'

Cat imagined the bistro lighting up Castle Court with warm yellow lighting and chic Art Deco interior design, a throwback to the elegant dining experiences of the 1920s, with food that was unparalleled in quality and flavour. The staff would need training, she thought, mentally spooling through the employees she remembered seeing there under Greg's management. And she'd have to recruit an entirely new kitchen team; Mariette's stinging review suggested none of the chefs currently employed were up to the job. And then she adjusted her assessment, reminding herself that they'd probably been held back by Greg; perhaps some of them might make the grade, with the right head chef. The image faded. Robert was right: it would be a challenge. And there was something else too.

'Greg will be furious if I take the job,' Cat said, pulling a face. 'He warned me François was.'

Robert shook his head. 'You don't need to worry about François – he is in no position to ruin anyone. And you may forget about Greg Valois too. His days in the restaurant business are over and he knows that if he so much as sets foot in Castle Court again, I will prosecute him for theft.'

His expression was so momentarily stern that Cat found herself almost feeling sorry for both men.

'*Alors*, you don't have to give me your answer now,' Robert said, his gaze watchful but encouraging once more. 'Take some time, think it over. You know how to contact me when you have made your decision.'

'And if I say no?'

He raised his shoulders in a quintessentially French gesture. 'Then I will find someone else for the job and perhaps it will become the second- or third-best restaurant in the city. Life will go on.'

Cat almost laughed, her respect for Robert increasing. Underneath his Parisian charm and gentlemanly demeanour lay an arch-manipulator, someone who knew exactly which buttons to press to pique Cat's interest. But she didn't resent him for it; the challenge he'd laid out was an attractive one. Her most pressing question was, could she do it? And the question right behind that was, did she want to?

Cat didn't mention Robert's offer to Jaren. She wanted to keep it to herself, turn it over in her mind before she shared it with anyone else. And, when she was ready, the first person she spoke to would be Sadie.

It took her a few days to work her way through the implications. Being a head chef was a high-pressure role and she'd almost burned out before she'd left La Perle. If François hadn't made her life so miserable and left her with no choice but to quit, perhaps she would have worked herself into a breakdown, like so many of her friends and colleagues. Did she really want to get back into that life? Things at Smart Cookies were steady and left her time for a social life; she'd be a fool to trade that for the undoubted stress, long hours and headaches managing La Clé d'Argent would bring.

And yet she couldn't quite dismiss the idea. At the back of her mind, she could hear Robert's persuasive voice reminding her that she didn't have to do it all by herself, that money was no object. She'd be able to bring talent in, chefs who could absorb the day-to-day stresses while ultimately following her vision. If things had been different, she might even have considered investing in the businesses around Castle Court; buying chocolates from Elin's and asking Seb to design a cocktail menu, but she couldn't bear the thought of working with either of them now.

Her nerves had almost got the better of her by the time she sat down in the basement kitchen with Sadie on Friday morning to fill her in. Sadie listened in silence, her expression growing more and more pensive as Cat went on.

'So what do you think?' Cat said eventually. 'And be honest – I want your opinions.'

Sadie puffed out her cheeks. 'I don't actually know what I think. It's a great opportunity for you but where would it leave me?' she asked. 'I'm not sure I can commit to spending any more time at Smart Cookies. Things at home are ...'

She trailed off, her expression pinched and anxious. Cat frowned. 'What is it? Has something happened?'

Sadie shook her head. 'It's nothing. Just Daniel playing silly buggers, that's all.'

'In what way?' Cat demanded. 'Tell me.'

'He's been a bit weird,' her best friend admitted. 'You know he's been pushing me to move back in with him? Well, now he's decided that he wants—' Sadie stopped and took a deep breath. 'He wants another baby.'

Cat's mouth dropped in sudden understanding. Of course Sadie would be worried about Cat vanishing off on another project, or even to another job, if she was thinking about the consequences of falling pregnant. Although having a baby with Daniel was the last thing Sadie should do, as far as Cat was concerned. 'Right. And how do you feel about that?' she asked carefully.

Sadie let out a shaky sigh. 'I think it's the worst idea I've ever heard.'

Cat resisted the temptation to whoop with relief. 'Oh, thank god. For one horrible moment, I thought you were actually considering it.'

'No,' Sadie said. 'But we had a huge argument about it and ever since then, he's been off with me. Nothing major, just little digs here and there about how much time I spend here, the way I look after Lissy, that kind of thing.'

Cat let out a growl of irritation. 'So he's reverted to type, has he? Want me to come round and talk to him?'

'You can't,' Sadie said, with a half-smile. 'He's working in London today – won't be back until tomorrow. It's a bit of a relief not having him around, if I'm honest.'

Cat studied her friend's downcast expression and considered her next words carefully. 'You know it isn't meant to be like this, don't you? He's meant to make you happy, not miserable.'

'I know.'

Cat squared her shoulders. 'And you know that you don't have to put up with it if you don't want to.'

'I know that too,' Sadie said with an anguished sigh. 'But there's Lissy to think about.'

'Lissy will be just fine,' Cat said firmly. 'She was before and she will be again. What won't be good for her is growing up with a mother trapped in a loveless marriage with a tosspot husband.'

'Cat!' Sadie said, almost laughing. 'He's not a tosspot.'

Cat folded her arms. 'You're right, he isn't. He's a borderline sociopath with narcissistic tendencies. And you don't need him.'

Sadie was quiet for a moment, then gave herself a shake. 'Maybe. Anyway, enough about me. What are you going to do about Robert's offer? Have you considered asking Jaren to join forces with you?'

A mental image of Jaren, close enough to kiss, flashed into Cat's mind. She pushed it away. 'Sort of. But it's never a good idea to mix business with pleasure, is it?'

Her best friend sat up straight and stared at her. 'Pleasure? Cat Garcia, is there something you need to tell me?'

Cat's cheeks began to burn. 'Possibly. It's nothing major, Jaren and I just had a little *moment* last week, when he came over to cook dinner.'

Sadie's eyes widened with indignation. 'And you didn't think to tell me? Bloody hell, Cat, this is front-page news! What kind of a moment?'

'A very nice one,' Cat admitted, her face flaming even more. 'But it was just a kiss, before you go ordering a wedding hat.'

Delight spread across Sadie's features. 'This is excellent news.'

'It was,' Cat said with a wry twist of her lips. 'But then Robert suggested we work together and now I don't know what I want. I don't think I can have both.'

'Of course you can,' Sadie said, frowning. 'Plenty of people do.'

'But rebuilding the restaurant would be really intense,' Cat argued. 'We'd spend a lot of time together and there are bound to be times when we don't agree. I'm worried that it would be too much, I don't want it to be paring knives at dawn before we've even got over the honeymoon period.'

Sadie looked thoughtful. 'So what are you going to do?'

'What can I do except think about it some more?' Cat said helplessly. 'But I wanted to talk to you first. If you think it's a bad idea then there'll be nothing to discuss with Jaren. I'll tell Robert I can't help and that will be that.'

'You could always outsource the project management side of things,' Sadie said slowly.

'I'd have to,' Cat said, with a snort. 'Give me a seven-course meal to plan and I'm fine. Anything else is beyond me.'

'That's not actually true,' Sadie pointed out, waving a

hand at the kitchen around them. 'You did manage to pull together all of this before we opened the shop.'

Cat cocked her head. 'And you did exactly the same after the flood. We make a pretty good team, don't we?'

'We do,' Sadie replied, squeezing her arm. 'But that doesn't mean you can't move on. We can take on more staff here if we need to – I could even promote Clare. You do what's right for you.'

Cat placed her hand on top of Sadie's and squeezed back. 'Thanks.'

'But you will have to decide what to do about Jaren.'

'I know,' Cat said, feeling the little buzz of happiness that came from bonding with Sadie start to ebb away. 'I know.'

Chapter Thirty-Five

The music was so loud that Sadie could barely hear what Cat was saying.

'What?' she shouted above Britney's 'Toxic', sliding along one of the leatherette seats towards her friend. 'I didn't catch a word of that.'

It was Saturday night and the Bus Stop was closed to the public in honour of Andrew and Earl's joint stag party. The party was in full swing – everyone from the Court was there, along with plenty of the couple's other friends, jammed into the diner's booths and perched on tables. Part of the room had been turned into an impromptu dance floor, where Earl was demonstrating the caterpillar while Andrew cheered him on. Everywhere Sadie looked, she saw photos of the two grooms, often in costume and having the time of their lives. They'd been together a long time and it warmed her heart to see that their relationship seemed stronger than ever.

'I said, it's too hot in here,' Cat bellowed, once Sadie was within shouting distance. 'Want to go and get some fresh air?'

Nodding, Sadie slid out of the booth and made for the door. They weren't the first guests to think of it; quite a few people had spilled out into the starlit court, which was marginally cooler than inside the diner. They were sitting on the metal chairs outside the Bus Stop's yellow exterior, drinking and laughing.

'That's better,' Sadie said, relieved to be able to hear herself think once more. 'I love a bit of Britney as much as the next woman but not when it feels as though she's stomping around inside my head.'

Cat stretched, tilting her head back to look at the stars, twinkling against the inky black sky. 'If you could make a wish right now, what would it be?'

'I don't know,' Sadie said, pulling a face as she sipped her virgin piña colada. 'Probably for some more ice in my drink.'

'I'm being serious,' Cat said, only slurring the words a little. 'What do you want more than anything?'

There was no point in wishing for that, Sadie thought, glancing across to where Adam sat chatting to Cherie. 'For Daniel to stop being an idiot.'

'Sorry, I'm afraid I'll have to take your first answer,' Cat said, following her gaze with a tipsy wink.

'How about you?' Sadie asked, relieved that her cheeks were already pink from the heat. 'What do you want?'

Cat waved her glass, splashing some of her pink cocktail onto the paving stones at her feet. 'I want a fairy godmother to tell me what to do about that place.' She pointed to La Clé d'Argent, which was shrouded in darkness. 'Because I can't make up my mind. Sometimes, I think it's the perfect challenge and at other times, it looks like a mountain of hard work I don't need.'

Sadie cast a sideways look at her friend. 'Have you discussed it with Jaren yet?'

The expression in Cat's eyes became hunted. 'No. I keep thinking of all the ways it could go wrong and before I know it, another day has gone by and I'm no nearer to working out what to do.' She sent a reproachful look skywards. 'Which is why I need that fairy godmother.'

She was right to be worried, Sadie thought. Relationships were hard enough without the added stress of a refurbishment project, although it was quite hard to imagine laid-back Jaren losing the plot about anything 'And have you and Jaren had any more moments?'

'No.' Cat's gaze didn't quite meet Sadie's. 'I've – erm – been avoiding him a bit – it seems easier that way.'

Sadie shook her head. 'You can't keep avoiding the poor guy – I bet he's wondering what he's done wrong. He's looked over here at least twelve times already.' Cat examined her drink silently for a moment, then took a long swig and sighed. 'You're right. I need to grow up, don't I?'

'At the very least go and say hi,' Sadie said.

'I'll go on one condition,' Cat replied, raising her chin. 'That you go and talk to Adam at the same time.'

Sadie looked over to where Adam sat. Cherie had

vanished and he was now deep in conversation with an attractive brunette. Her heart sank; he was obviously chatting her up and the last thing he needed was for Sadie to blunder in and ruin his chances. 'Okay, but not now. I'll do it later.'

'Now,' Cat said firmly, draining her glass. 'Before you conveniently forget, or he goes home early or something.'

'But he's talking to someone,' Sadie objected. 'A woman.'

Cat glanced at Adam. 'All the more reason to interrupt,' she said meaningfully. 'Go on. Go now.'

Inwardly cringing, Sadie squared her shoulders and crossed the Court to where Adam stood chatting to the brunette. He broke off when he saw Sadie. 'Hello.'

'Hi,' Sadie said. She smiled at the other woman. 'I'm Sadie.'

'And I'm Kirsty. Pleased to meet you.'

'Kirsty was just telling me where she met Andrew and Earl,' Adam said.

The dark-haired woman grinned. 'Oh, we go way back. They used to be a right pair of party animals back in the day, although they've calmed down now.'

'It sounds like you might have some stories to share,' Sadie said, intrigued in spite of the unpleasant coil of jealousy squeezing at her stomach.

Kirsty held up a half-drunk cocktail. 'I do. Ask me again after a few more of these and I might even tell you.'

Adam smiled. 'I wouldn't expect anything less from the best woman. Although you might want to save your most embarrassing ones for your speech.'

'Oh, don't worry,' Kirsty said, a wicked gleam in her eye. 'Between Lara and me, we have an almost inexhaustible supply.'

'Lara?' Sadie repeated, wondering whether Andrew or Earl had a sister who might have a tale or two to tell.

'My girlfriend,' Kirsty said, glancing over at a blonde woman by the entrance to the diner. 'She's their bridesmaid.'

Sadie wasn't proud of the flood of relief she felt upon hearing that Kirsty wasn't single. 'Oh! Then you're going to meet Lissy, my daughter. She's the flower girl.'

'Although she might be greener than the average flower girl, if she gets her way,' Adam said, with an affectionate grin.

'She's determined to come dressed as a triceratops,' Sadie explained. 'She doesn't believe that it's not a traditional flower girl outfit.'

Kirsty laughed. 'She sounds great. You don't see enough dinosaurs at weddings.'

The conversation went on for several more minutes, then Kirsty excused herself. 'I can't leave Lara unattended around the cocktails for long,' she confided, with a mischievous grin. 'No one wants a repeat of the Screaming Orgasm incident.'

Sadie watched the other woman pick her way across the Court to Lara. 'She seems nice.'

'She does,' Adam replied. 'But you're nicer.'

The compliment caused a pleasurable blush to warm Sadie's cheeks. 'Thank you.'

'It's true,' he said, and Sadie noticed the tips of his ears had turned pink, the way they always did when he was embarrassed. 'How have you been, anyway?'

'Fine,' she replied briskly. 'Busy, you know how it is.'

He nodded. 'I do. And how's Lissy?'

'She's fine too,' Sadie said, and this time her response was less brisk. 'She was fascinated by my description of the hives. Now she wants to be a bee-keeping diplodocus when she grows up.'

Adam laughed. 'I can't see a problem with that.' He paused and gave her a searching look. 'Everything okay with you? Apart from being busy, I mean.'

Sadie meant to give a glib answer, one that glossed over the turmoil she felt about the situation with Daniel, but Adam's hazel eyes were so warm and inviting that somehow, she found herself pouring out the details of her argument with Daniel. Adam listened without interrupting, his expression hardening when she reached the part about her care of Lissy. When she'd finished, he looked angrier than she'd ever seen him.

'I can't believe the way he's treating you,' he said, his voice tight. 'What kind of a man tries to undermine his wife like that? I think you're an amazing mum – Lissy is happy and confident and a total joy, most of which is down to you.'

Sadie shook her head. 'Thank you. It's a shame Daniel doesn't see it like that.'

Adam looked even more incensed. 'Seriously, what is going on with him? You're brilliant, Sadie – a successful businesswoman, a dedicated mother and you're really kind and generous. Daniel should be thanking his lucky stars he has you at all, not criticising you or making you feel bad about yourself.'

Tears gathered in Sadie's eyes. She tried to blink them away. 'You sound like Cat. She's not his biggest fan either.'

Adam's forehead creased in concern. 'You deserve so much better. Honestly, I'd never presume to tell anyone how to live their life, but I care too much about you and Lissy to stand by while Daniel treats you like this.' He paused and reached for her hand. 'I can't stand to see you unhappy.'

It was too much for Sadie; big fat teardrops spilled down her face. 'I don't know what to do. Lissy loves having him in her life.'

Fumbling in his pocket, Adam pulled out a tissue and handed it to her. 'But that doesn't mean you have to stay together,' he said gently. 'My parents split up when I was young and it was hard for a while but I eventually came to understand that they were much happier apart. Lissy's a smart kid – she'll see that too.'

It wasn't just Lissy, Sadie thought, dabbing at the tears that refused to stop falling. It was the horrible sense that she was giving up, that she'd failed at being married. The last time she and Daniel had split up, there'd been a reason. This time, there was no catalyst driving her towards the end of her marriage, only the increasing sense that she was making a mistake. And she wasn't sure it was enough to put her daughter through the upheaval of another acrimonious break-up.

'What a mess,' she mumbled.

Adam was silent for a moment, studying Sadie with such compassion that she felt she might start crying all over again. 'I suppose what it comes down to is this – do you love Daniel?'

It was a question Sadie hadn't dared to ask herself. She had, once upon a time, and she'd thought she might love him again. But it had proved harder than she'd expected to get back to where she'd once been. 'I – I don't know.'

'That's what you need to work out,' he said with a pensive smile. 'Once you know the answer to that, you'll know what to do about everything else.'

He was right, Sadie realised. She glanced up at him gratefully. 'Thanks for listening, Adam. Sorry to blub all over you.'

He pressed his fingers against hers. 'Any time.'

Cat watched Adam and Sadie chatting, her eyes narrowing as she observed the obvious chemistry between them. Adam said something that made Sadie blush; she responded in a way that made him turn red. They were so perfect for each other, Cat decided with some satisfaction – if only Sadie would let go of her stubborn insistence that staying with Daniel was the right thing. Then again, who was she to be giving relationship advice, Cat thought wryly. She'd spent the best part of the last few days avoiding Jaren so that she wouldn't have to make any difficult decisions. But not any more; Sadie had kept her side of the deal, now it was time for Cat to step up to hers.

She spied his dark curly head among a cluster of others at the rear of the yellow bus and was halfway across the Court when Seb appeared out of nowhere to intercept her.

'Hello, Cat,' he said, his green eyes wary. 'Long time no speak.'

She stared at him, taking in his mussed-up brown hair and golden stubble trimmed to just the right thickness to frame his tanned jaw. He was as charming and handsome as ever, but then good looks had never been the problem with Seb. It was the way he treated women that was the issue.

'Hi,' she said stiffly. 'How are you?'

'I've been better,' he admitted. 'Look, I know this probably isn't a great time but have you got a minute to talk?'

Cat eyed him doubtfully. 'I don't think there's anything left to say, is there?'

'Come on, Cat, don't be like that,' Seb said, and Cat thought she detected a familiar hint of impatience behind the words. 'I just want to talk, that's all. You know, like adults?'

She was tempted to toss the remains of her cocktail in his face; it would be immensely satisfying to watch the sticky pink liquid dripping from his chin. But the comment about being an adult touched a nerve and she took a steadying breath instead.

'Okay. You've got exactly one minute.'

'Not here,' he said, scouting around for somewhere more private. 'How about under the tree?'

Cat glanced over at the shadowy branches of the oak tree.

There was no one else near the vast trunk but it was still within easy sight of the other party-goers. 'Fine.'

'You're looking good,' he said, once they were standing under the leafy canopy.

Cat threw him an impatient glare. 'One minute, Seb. Please don't tell me you brought me over here to hit on me.'

His expression sobered. 'Of course I didn't. But you do look good. And I don't think I appreciated that enough while we were together, so I'm saying it now. Okay?'

'Not really,' Cat said, wondering what on earth he was playing at. Where was Elin? Did she have any idea Seb was trying to charm his way back into Cat's good books? 'Get to the point, please.'

Seb's jaw tightened, which gave Cat a small flicker of satisfaction. 'Fine, if that's how you want to be. It's about Jaren.'

'What about him?' Cat said, frowning.

'I've been watching you around him—'

Her eyebrows shot up. 'Really?'

Seb sighed. 'Not in a creepy way. In an – I don't know – let's call it a friendly way. As in, a looking-out-for-you kind of way.'

Maintaining her expression of disbelief, Cat tilted her head. 'O-kay.'

'And I can see there's something between you.' He shrugged. 'Maybe you always liked him, I don't know. But I see it now and I wanted to warn you not to get too involved. Not yet, anyway.'

Cat's jaw dropped. 'What?'

He raised his hands. 'Just hear me out. I'm worried that it's too soon after his split with Elin – I think he's on the rebound. And I'd hate to see you get hurt.'

'I think that's a bit rich coming from you,' Cat said, letting out a small huff of incredulity. 'Jaren has never shown any sign of wanting to hurt me – in fact, he's been there for me ever since I met him. Whereas you—'

'I know, I know,' Seb cut in, his expression a mixture of resignation and regret. 'I'm a dick. But there are things Elin told me – stuff I can't repeat, but trust me, you'd see Jaren differently if you knew. So I'm warning you now, before you get in too deep. He's still in love with Elin.'

The words cut at Cat's heart. Could it be true? Could Jaren still be holding a torch for beautiful, blonde, Swiss Elin? It hadn't felt as though he was when he'd kissed Cat after they'd cooked together but then Seb hadn't shown any sign of his duplicity in the weeks after sleeping with Elin; in fact, he'd been as attentive to Cat as ever, although she knew the signs were there, in hindsight. Could she have missed something similar in Jaren?

'You're lying,' she said.

'Am I?' Seb said softly. 'You know how hard he chased her – he even got you to make his Valentine's Day gift to her. Did you get any kind of sense that he wasn't really into her then?'

'No,' Cat said reluctantly, thinking of all the times she and Jaren had talked about how much he liked Elin. 'But that was before she cheated on him with you.'

Seb shook his head. 'She didn't cheat, though – they weren't a couple then. What if Jaren didn't really want to break up with Elin but did it out of loyalty to you?'

It did sound like the kind of thing he might do, Cat realised with a sinking heart. He'd been furious with Seb, too; what if that fury had actually been fuelled by jealousy?

Maybe Seb was right. Maybe Jaren *was* still in love with his ex-girlfriend.

Her shoulders slumped. 'I don't know what to say.'

Seb gave her a half-smile. 'You'll thank me one day. Regardless of how you feel about me, I still care about you. And I hope – sometime in the future – we can be friends again. I miss you, Cat.'

She shook her head distractedly. 'Sure, maybe.'

'I'm sorry to be the bearer of bad news,' Seb went on. 'But better to hear it now than a few months down the line, right?'

'Right,' she echoed. 'Look, will you excuse me? I think I need a drink.'

Seb stepped back, his gaze concerned. 'Are you going to be okay? Do you want me to take you home?'

With a huge effort, Cat pulled her scattered thoughts together. 'I'll be fine. Like I said, I need a drink.'

She walked away, replaying Seb's revelation in her head, struggling to process how it made her feel. On the one hand, she was hurt and upset to think she'd failed to suspect how Jaren really felt; she had begun to hope that their friendship was about to bloom into more and the idea that he was still in love with Elin hurt more than she was prepared to admit.

But on the other hand, Seb's assertions might make her decision about La Clé d'Argent much simpler. If she couldn't have Jaren as a boyfriend, then at least she could have him as a business partner.

Maybe this is all for the best, a little voice whispered at the back of her mind. But if that was the case, Cat thought as she headed for the bar, why did she feel so desolate?

Chapter Thirty-Six

'What happened to you on Saturday?' Sadie demanded, the moment she walked into Smart Cookies on Monday morning. 'One minute you were there, insisting I talk to Adam, and the next you'd vanished.'

Cat didn't look up from the gingerbread dough she was rolling out. 'I did message you. I had a headache and decided to call it a night.'

Sadie pushed her bag into a cupboard and grabbed a Smart Cookies apron. 'I know you messaged me,' she said, giving her best friend an impatient look. 'But you didn't have a headache when I spoke to you. Did something happen? Did Jaren upset you?'

'No one upset me,' Cat said. 'I got a migraine and went home, end of story.'

'A migraine?' Sadie repeated, frowning. 'How long have you been getting those?'

'A while,' Cat said evasively. 'But I'm fine now. How was your chat with Adam?'

Sadie cleared her throat. 'Good,' she said slowly. 'Unexpectedly emotional, actually. I ended up telling him all about Daniel.'

Now Cat did look up, her face a picture of sympathy. 'Oh, Sadie. What did he say? Anything useful?'

A shiver of embarrassment crawled over Sadie as she remembered the way she had sobbed in front of him. 'He said some really nice things – told me he thought I was a good mum and reassured me that Lissy seems happy.' She paused. 'And he asked me whether I still love Daniel.'

Cat lowered the rolling pin to study Sadie. 'And?'

'And I told him I don't know. Which is the truth.'

'Is it?' Cat said, giving her a penetrating stare. 'Because I've got to be honest, Sadie – I see the way you look at Adam, and I see the way you look at Daniel, and I know who my money is on.'

'Cat!' Sadie ground out, glancing towards the stairs that led to the shop to see if Clare or Delilah might overhear. 'I told you to stop trying to force me and Adam together.'

'Sorry,' Cat said, looking entirely unrepentant. 'I'm just telling you how I see it. However you feel about Adam, you definitely don't love Daniel.'

Sadie busied herself at the sink, scrubbing her hands longer than she needed to so that she wouldn't have to meet Cat's knowing gaze. Deep down, Sadie knew her friend was right. But it wasn't as simple as just knowing.

She turned back. 'What about Jaren? When are you going to speak to him?'

Instantly, Cat's eyes dropped to the gingerbread dough she was shaping. 'I don't know. Later, maybe.'

'But you've decided what you're going to do?'

Cat nodded. 'Yes, I think I have.'

Now it was Sadie's turn to stare. 'And?'

'I'll tell you once I've spoken to Jaren,' Cat said, with an air of finality that told Sadie the subject was very firmly closed. 'Now, it's less than a week to Andrew and Earl's wedding and we've still got fifty shops to finish. Do you think it might be time for less talking and more icing?'

Sadie blinked and pulled off a mock salute. 'Yes, chef.'

It was late afternoon by the time Cat walked through the door of Let's Go Dutch. Jaren was nowhere to be seen, however, and she was just about to leave when Meik, the restaurant's head chef, appeared, clearly having finished his shift.

'Looking for the boss?' he asked when he spotted her. 'He's out the back. You can go through if you want.'

'Thanks,' Cat called and headed for the door that led to the kitchen. She knew the way well, having spent weeks baking there in the early mornings after Smart Cookies had been decimated by a flash flood. The kitchen wasn't empty now, however; it was dotted with white-clad chefs, clearing up after the lunch service and completing the last few orders. Cat hovered in the doorway for a moment, then stepped inside.

Jaren was peering into the walk-in fridge, a clipboard and pen in his hand.

'This is a lovely surprise,' he said, beaming at her. 'Just give me a second to finish this stock check and I'm all yours.'

Cat glanced around for a spot that was out of the way of the other kitchen staff, ignoring the sudden rush of butterflies the sight of him had caused, and managed to summon up the ghost of a smile. 'No rush.'

'And that's twenty-four avocados, right?' he called into the fridge.

Listening to the muffled response, he scribbled something on his clipboard. Cat used the time to gaze around her, making professional mental notes as she did so. It was sparkling clean, she observed; each staff member seemed to be meticulous about cleaning up as they worked. And the communication was good – calm and clear. Everyone knew what they were doing and got on with it. She watched as a burst of flame erupted from an expertly wielded frying pan and took a deep breath of the rich, sizzling air that resulted. It was a well-run kitchen but then she hadn't really expected anything else.

'Done,' Jaren announced in satisfaction. 'Now, what can I do for you? Is this business or pleasure?'

His eyes twinkled as he spoke and Cat had to forcibly remind herself why she was there. 'Strictly business, I'm afraid.'

'Ah,' Jaren said, flashing her a quizzical look. 'In that case, shall we head to the office?'

He led her out of the kitchen and along the cool corridor. Once they were seated in the office, he studied her curiously. 'So, business then. What's up?'

Cat hesitated, marshalling her thoughts. They'd been so clear when she was in the basement at Smart Cookies: lay out Robert's proposal, establish whether Jaren was interested in working together professionally and leave. But now that she was next to Jaren, all her preparation had flown out of her head. 'I've – erm – got a proposition for you.'

Jaren raised his eyebrows. 'I like it already.'

Cat shook her head, flustered. 'A business proposition. As you know, I had a visit from Robert de Beauvoir last week. He's looking to relaunch La Clé d'Argent as Chester's top restaurant and he's asked me to oversee the project.'

Jaren's face lit up. 'But that's amazing. I think you'd be brilliant at it.'

'I don't,' Cat said bluntly. 'I'm not experienced enough, for one thing. But Robert said I could work with someone else, put together a team of experienced professionals. He suggested I ask you to be my partner.'

He stroked his chin, pretending to think. 'Let's see – I get to spend time with one of my favourite people, designing a dream restaurant, and – I assume – get paid handsomely for doing it?'

Cat nodded uncomfortably. 'Yes, but—'

'I'm in,' Jaren went on, grinning. 'We already know what a great team we make. Hey, we can have cookery evenings – try out new recipes on each other. It'll be fun!'

443

He looked so enthusiastic that Cat had to steel herself to say the words she knew needed to be said. 'There's just one thing,' she said, and swallowed hard. 'I think we'd have to keep things professional between us.'

'What do you mean?' he said, his enthusiasm dimming a little.

'Between us,' she went on, remembering Seb's certainty when he'd told her Jaren still loved Elin. 'It's going to be a difficult enough task to pull off as it is, without complicating things with ... personal relationships.'

The light in his eyes faded. 'Oh.'

'So no cooking evenings,' she ploughed on, forcing herself to ignore the dawning hurt on his face. 'Nothing that might compromise our working relationship. Strictly business.'

Jaren gazed at her without speaking for a moment. 'I see,' he said softly. 'Well, if that's what you want, Cat.'

She felt her heart crack a little as she returned his gaze. 'It's how it has to be.'

Again, he was silent. 'And if I turn the opportunity down, can we be more than friends?' he asked eventually.

A picture of Elin seared itself across Cat's brain. 'I don't think so, no. I'm going to be so busy that it wouldn't be fair on you – on either of us. I'm sorry.'

'So it's work together or nothing,' he murmured, almost to himself.

'Obviously, we can still be friends,' Cat said, clamping her lips shut on the sudden wild temptation to declare she didn't mean it.

Jaren shook his head and held out a hand. 'Business partners it is, then.'

Cat took it, hoping she didn't look as forlorn as she felt. 'Here's to working together.'

'Absolutely,' he said, his expression unreadable. 'Here's to us.'

The following few days were even more of a blur than usual for Sadie. Her kitchen was a sea of miniature shops as she worked on the last of the wedding favours, and when she wasn't icing biscuits, she was working on the secret wedding gift she and Cat had devised, which was being stored in Cat's spare room. In between work and ferrying Lissy around, she hadn't seen much of Daniel; he was still spending the nights at his own house and had been sporadic with messages and phone calls. It was a situation she was going to have to deal with sooner or later, she knew, especially since Lissy was questioning her father's absence more and more, but it would have to keep at least until her evenings were not consumed by fifty shades of icing.

By Wednesday, she was beginning to feel as though she could breathe. The miniature Castle Court shops were individually wrapped in their cellophane bags and the secret project was almost complete, although she had no idea how they were going to transport it to the wedding in one piece and without anyone seeing it. Everything seemed to be coming together. So when Sadie's phone rang and the number of Daniel's office flashed up, she took a deep breath and answered.

'Hello, Daniel,' she said coolly, giving Clare an apologetic look as she stepped outside into the Court. 'Good to hear from you.'

There was a brief pause and then a female voice tumbled out of the handset. 'It's not Daniel. It's Elizabeth.'

'Oh,' Sadie said, frowning. 'Hi Elizabeth, is everything okay?'

'Not really, no.'

Sadie felt her forehead crease even further. The other woman sounded upset. 'What's wrong?'

Elizabeth let out a deep sigh. 'I don't know if I should be telling you this,' she said, her voice fluttering with anxiety. 'But you seemed so nice when I met you and there's that lovely little girl of yours to consider and – well – I don't think I could live with myself if I kept quiet.'

An ominous sense of foreboding settled over Sadie. 'Kept quiet about what?'

Silence. 'It's Daniel, Sadie. He's having an affair.'

The pit of Sadie's stomach plummeted. She clutched at the doorpost for support. 'What?'

'I know, it's hard to believe – he seems so devoted to you. But there was some discrepancy over the hotel bill for his business trip last week so I called the hotel to ask for a copy.' Elizabeth sounded wretched. 'And there was two of everything – two meals at dinner, two bottles of champagne, two breakfasts in bed. Even then, I thought there'd been some mistake so I rang them. And they confirmed that there were two guests in that room – a man and a woman. Mr and Mrs Smart. They said they were regulars.'

Sadie felt the world around her spin as the words sank in. All this time Daniel had been pressuring her to move in – his suggestion that they try for another baby – and he'd been having an affair. Another affair.

'I'm really sorry, Sadie,' Elizabeth said, and she sounded it. 'I wish I'd been able to tell you face-to-face but I thought you needed to know sooner rather than later. I'd want to, if it was me.'

'Thank you,' Sadie heard herself say. 'I appreciate that. Thanks for letting me know.'

'I've requested a transfer,' Elizabeth went on. 'I've told the senior partners that I won't work for anyone I can't respect, so I probably won't see you again. But I wanted to wish you good luck, anyway. And give Lissy a high-five from me.'

She rang off, leaving Sadie staring into Castle Court.

'Sadie?' Clare's voice floated out of the Smart Cookies door. 'Is everything all right?'

'No,' Sadie said, feeling her face start to crumple. 'No, it isn't.'

Sadie sat on the sofa in Daniel's living room, waiting to hear his key turn in the lock. She'd collected Lissy from the childminder as normal and driven her back into Chester for a cooking lesson with Auntie Cat.

Cat had hugged her fiercely as she left. 'Good luck. And if you need help to bury the body, give me a call.'

Sadie had gone through every piece of paperwork in Daniel's study; every receipt, invoice and delivery note until finally she found a thin cardboard wallet tucked inside a box file labelled 'Work Expenses'. And inside the wallet was a trail of hotel bills going back six months, beside florists and jewellery receipts and a handwritten thank you that was signed Emma.

It was funny, Sadie thought as she stared at the name, she'd expected anger but instead she felt numb. Numb, with a curious sense of relief that the niggling doubts she'd put down to paranoia were now vindicated. She'd been right to suspect Daniel. She'd been right to hold back.

She saw from his face when he walked into the room that he knew. He lowered his briefcase to the floor with a heavy thud. 'Sadie, I can explain.'

'I'm sure you can,' she said, surprised by the evenness of her tone. 'I expect you've got a long, complicated story of how you didn't want to have an affair, I drove you to it. It probably all comes down to how busy I've been – I neglected you, much the same way that you accused me of neglecting our daughter. Is that it, Daniel? Is it because you couldn't stand the fact that I didn't put you first this time round?'

His shoulders slumped. 'Partly. But you've got to believe me, I didn't mean for this to happen. Emma wouldn't leave me alone, she made my life hell until I gave her what she wanted.' He threw Sadie a pleading look. 'It's been eating me up inside. I'm almost glad you know so that we can talk and sort this whole mess out.'

Sadie couldn't help it; she gaped at him. 'You think we can sort this out?'

Daniel hurried across the room to kneel at her feet. 'Of course we can. Look, I know you think you hate me right now but we need each other. You can't cope without me and I – I don't want to be a Sunday father.'

Sadie felt the slow burn of anger at last. 'I can't cope without you? That's a joke. I can't cope *with* you, Daniel – you make everything ten times harder. And the only way you'll be a Sunday father is if you choose to be. I won't stop you from seeing Lissy.'

His expression set as he looked at her, as though the realisation that he wasn't going to be able to talk her round was dawning at last. 'That's assuming you have custody of her. I'm not convinced you're a fit and proper parent, Sadie. Imagine if I went to court and told them how you lost her, or how you send her to school in ill-fitting clothes and spend all your time working. Imagine how a judge might view that.'

And now Sadie's anger burst into incandescence. 'You're not going to fight me for custody, Daniel,' she said, each word ringing with ice-cold fury. 'Because if you do, I'll tell the senior partners at your work just how long you've been fiddling your expenses and charging your sordid little nights away to the law firm. I imagine they'll take a pretty dim view of that, don't you?'

The last vestiges of colour drained from his face. 'You wouldn't.'

She held up the cardboard folder. 'I would. And please don't think I need you financially. Smart Cookies is doing well enough that I can support Lissy all on my own now.'

Getting to her feet, she stared down at him. 'I feel sorry for you, Daniel. You had everything you claimed you wanted and it still wasn't enough.'

'Sadie, wait—'

She ignored him and strode to the door. 'I'll let you know when you can see Lissy. Until then, don't contact me.'

The sense of fevered euphoria lasted all the way back to Chester. It carried her from the underground car park beneath Cat's apartment building and up the stairs to her penthouse flat. And it lasted until she saw Lissy curled up asleep on the sofa. Only then did Sadie's strength fail her.

'Oh Cat,' she wailed, turning into her best friend's waiting arms. 'What am I going to do?'

Chapter Thirty-Seven

The day of the wedding dawned clear and bright.

Castle Court was closed. The alleyway that led into the courtyard was decked with ribbons and bunting and neon-pink hearts, and posters on elegant silver stands stood on either side, proclaiming what was happening within.

In the middle of the Court itself, a pergola had been built around the oak tree. Its beams criss-crossed in a lattice, around which thousands of fairy lights had been twisted. And inside that was a small raised dais, where Andrew and Earl would exchange their vows. The effect would be magical when darkness fell, Cat thought as she stood in the doorway of Smart Cookies at ten o'clock and surveyed the rows and rows of ribbon-trimmed seats, just waiting to be filled with the grooms' family and friends. It looked pretty amazing now.

Delilah appeared at her elbow, carrying a steaming cup of tea. 'You look like you need this.'

'Thanks,' Cat said, taking it gratefully. 'I hope it's strong – I need the caffeine.'

Delilah smiled. 'Rough night, was it?'

Cat grimaced; rough didn't begin to describe it. Sadie and Lissy had stayed with her, to avoid any potential traffic disasters in the morning. At least, that's what Sadie said but Cat secretly suspected she was finding Daniel's permanent absence from the cottage harder to bear than she'd expected. On Thursday morning, a locksmith had been summoned to change the locks and while he worked, Cat and Sadie had removed every trace of Daniel from the house. They'd deposited the bulging black binliners in Daniel's hallway, after which Cat had taken a quiet satisfaction in watching Sadie post his house keys back through the letterbox.

'Done?' she'd asked her friend, squeezing her arm in a mixture of sympathy and solidarity.

Sadie had swallowed hard and managed a brave smile. 'Done.'

Her bravery was wavering by Friday and Cat wasn't entirely surprised when Sadie asked if she would mind two house guests on Friday night. It wasn't that Cat minded their company; they'd ordered pizza and played silly games until Lissy began to yawn. Then Sadie and Cat had stayed up late, talking and reminiscing, and that was fine too. What Cat had found hard to cope with was the Lissy invasion at the crack of dawn, roaring like a T. Rex and demanding a fight to the death.

'There was a lot more dinosaur talk than I'm used to,' Cat told Delilah wearily. 'Especially at 4.48 in the morning.'

'Bless her little heart,' Delilah said indulgently. 'She's had a rough time herself.'

Cat couldn't argue, although she'd been amazed at the way Lissy had coped with the news that Daddy was moving out. She'd been quiet initially, Sadie said, but then had accepted the news and asked for a bowl of ice cream. Cat supposed it helped that Andrew and Earl had been only too delighted to have a dinosaur flower girl and Lissy was now the proud owner of a size five to six years triceratops suit.

Cat stretched and sighed. 'I suppose we'd better get a move on. Our gift is going to take a bit of reassembling. I only hope I remember which piece goes where – Sadie will kill me if I get it wrong.'

'We'll manage,' Delilah reassured her. 'And there's always the internet if we get stuck.'

By eleven o'clock, things were starting to happen in the Court. The caterers had set up in the kitchen of Let's Go Dutch and Cat had given permission for the wine waiters to use La Clé d'Argent as their base. The celebrant had arrived too and had been greeted by the brunette woman Cat had seen talking to Adam at the stag party. And Cat and Delilah had laid wedding favours on every seat, along with the order of service, and put the finishing touches to their surprise gift to the grooms.

Cat checked the time and let out a yelp. 'Time for me to get ready. Let me know when Sadie and Lissy arrive, please, Delilah?' She paused on her way to the stairs that led to the basement and glanced at the satin-covered mountain that sat on top of the Smart Cookies counter. 'And guard that with your life.'

She'd just applied her lipstick when she heard Delilah calling her. 'Yoo hoo – are you decent?'

Cat grinned. 'As decent as I'll ever be. Send them down.'

But it wasn't Sadie and Lissy who made their way to the basement. It was Elin.

Cat watched the elegant blonde woman walk down the last few steps. 'Hello. This is a surprise.'

Elin didn't smile. 'How are you, Cat?'

Better than you, by the looks of things, Cat thought but she didn't say it. Elin had the world-weary look of a woman who'd been disappointed too many times. 'I'm fine. Looking forward to celebrating with Andrew and Earl. How are you?'

Elin gave her a bleak smile. 'Oh, you know. Up and down. But I didn't come here to exchange pleasantries. I understand you had a conversation with Seb last week.'

'That's right,' Cat said, suddenly wary.

'What did he tell you?'

Cat frowned. Had Elin seen her skulking underneath the tree with Seb and put two and two together to make six? Was that what this was? 'About Jaren, mostly. Why?'

The Swiss woman did not seem surprised. 'Let me guess – he was warning you off.'

Now Cat's eyebrows shot up in astonishment. 'That's right – how did you know?'

'Because he's jealous,' Elin said bluntly. 'Of Jaren and Adam and anyone else he thinks might be a rival. If Andrew

454

and Earl weren't getting married today, I'm sure he'd develop an unreasonable dislike of them too, despite the fact that they've been together for seventeen years.'

'But why would Seb be jealous?' Cat said, with a sceptical shrug. 'He cheated on me with you. There's no way he can pretend to still be interested in me.'

Elin let out a hollow laugh. 'You'd think so, wouldn't you? But Seb's one of those men who always wants what he can't have. When he had you, he wanted me. And now that he's got me . . .'

Understanding washed over Cat. 'He wants me.'

Elin nodded in mute resignation.

'But—' Cat paused, going back over her conversation with Seb the week before. 'He told me you'd said Jaren wasn't really interested in me. He said Jaren was still in love with you.'

'I thought it might be something like that,' Elin said, with a soft sigh. 'He lied, I'm afraid. Jaren was never in love with me. As a matter of fact, I think he's always been in love with you.'

The words jolted through Cat like electricity. 'You're wrong.'

'I assure you I am not,' Elin said, the ghost of a smile flickering across her face. 'Believe me, I've seen the way he looks at you, the way he has always looked at you. And you should have seen the way he raced into the flood waters to rescue you – if that isn't love, I don't know what is.'

Jaren loves me, Cat thought, testing the idea out. Could it be true? And then something else occurred to her; how dispirited must Elin be feeling, when it turned out both the men in her life were carrying a torch for the same woman? 'Oh, Elin, I'm sorry. You must hate me.'

'Of course I don't,' Elin replied, although she looked a long way from happy. 'But I do want something good to come out of this mess. Jaren is a good man and he deserves to be happy. I hope you might be the person to do that.'

Cat could have wept; if only Elin had spoken to her earlier, before she'd told Jaren they could only ever be business partners. Now it was too late. 'I don't know – it's complicated.'

'Then uncomplicate it,' the Swiss woman urged. 'Don't wait for the problems to unknot themselves. Be happy now, Cat.'

Could it work? Cat asked herself. More importantly, could she take a risk that it might all go wrong and cause ripples in her professional life? 'I'll think about it,' she said slowly, then her eyes met Elin's. 'But what about you? What are you going to do?'

Elin sighed. 'Join a convent? I'm sure they'd welcome a chocolatier.'

Cat smiled. 'I'm sure they would.'

'But maybe I'll just try celibacy for a while,' Elin went on. 'There's no need to go overboard, after all.'

'Thank you,' Cat said, closing the gap between them to take Elin's hand. 'I know this can't have been easy for you.'

'No,' Elin said, her mouth twisting into a sad smile. 'But it's been harder on you. I'm glad I can unpick some of the damage I caused, at least.'

A roar floated down the stairs, causing both women to look up.

'I think that means Lissy's here,' Cat said, her lips quirking into a half-smile. 'And if Lissy is here then the grooms can't be far away. We'd better go and find a seat.'

'Try to sit next to Jaren,' Elin whispered as they reached the top of the stairs. 'A wedding is a good time to show someone you love them, right?'

With one final look, she was gone, leaving Cat to stare after her.

'Everything okay?' Sadie asked, frowning. 'What did Elin want?'

'Oh, nothing,' Cat said hastily. 'Something to do with the bistro, that's all.' She turned her attention to Lissy, who was clutching a small, hand-tied bouquet to her bright-green triceratops outfit, and patted her cream-coloured horns. 'Look at you and your lovely lilac flowers. I hope you're not going to eat them on the way down the aisle.'

Sadie let out a strangled groan. 'Please don't give her ideas. If we end up in A&E later, I'm blaming you.'

Lissy did not eat the flowers. Instead, she followed sedately behind Andrew and Earl, roaring quietly at the assembled guests as a harp played. And behind Lissy came Kirsty and Lara, each in fitted lilac dresses that matched the colour of Lissy's flowers perfectly. Their bouquets were twin tumbles of greenery to mirror Lissy's triceratops scales. Sadie held her breath as they passed and let out a heartfelt sigh of relief when the procession reached the front without mishap. Now she could relax into enjoying the ceremony, she thought, until she caught sight of Lissy's horns bobbing up and down in the front row. Mostly relax, she corrected herself silently.

'Look at those suits,' Cat whispered as they settled into their seats again.

Sadie nodded. Earl, always the more flamboyant of the two, wore a white morning suit with a slate-grey cravat. And Andrew was his mirror, in a grey morning suit with cream accessories. They both removed their top hats, handing them to Kirsty and Lara before turning to face the celebrant.

She spread her hands and smiled. 'Friends, we have gathered here today to witness the marriage of Andrew and Earl and celebrate the love they share. My name is Juliet and I have the great pleasure of performing the ceremony today.'

Everyone's attention was fixed on Andrew and Earl. Sadie took the opportunity to study Adam's profile. He'd sat in the row in front of her, a few seats along, so she could appreciate how good he looked in his suit without making it obvious what she was doing. Nothing escaped Cat's notice, however. She leaned towards Sadie. 'Scrubs up well, doesn't he?'

Sadie gave a slight shake of her head, hoping she wasn't as red as she felt, and saw Cat grin as she sat back. As the ceremony went on, Sadie found her gaze drawn back to Adam more and more often, until she began to worry he must be able to feel her staring. Fixing her eyes on the grooms, she concentrated on the vows.

Earl cleared his throat. 'Andrew, from the first moment

we met, you have brought me joy. I promise to do everything in my power to return that joy to you. In this world, I believe everyone is capable of choosing love and that when we open our hearts, amazing things happen. I will always be grateful that you chose to love me and I promise to always love you.'

Sadie felt her eyes swim with tears. 'How beautiful,' she murmured to Cat, who took her hand and gripped it hard.

Then it was Andrew's turn. 'Earl, you are Leia to my Han, Snape to my Dumbledore, Picard to my Riker. I promise to always return your "I love you", to keep our unbreakable vow and to make it so whenever I can. Together, we'll boldly go where no one has gone before.'

Spontaneous cheering broke out here and there. Sadie glanced at Cat and saw that her friend's eyes were now suspiciously damp too.

Juliet smiled. 'Lovely. And now the rings.'

Lara and Kirsty stepped forwards, each carrying a cushion that matched the grooms' suits.

Juliet turned to Earl. 'Do you, Earl Eric Jones, take this man, Andrew Godric Samuels, to be your husband?'

Earl gazed at Andrew with such tenderness that Sadie allowed a small sob to escape her.

'I do,' he said, sliding a golden band onto his finger.

'And do you, Andrew Godric Samuels, take Earl Eric Jones to be your husband?'

Andrew took Earl's hand and beamed at him as he put the ring on. 'I do.'

Sadie sniffed. The other guests smiled and Adam twisted in his seat to hand her a fresh tissue. Beside her, Cat winked.

'I now pronounce you partners for life,' Juliet said. 'You may kiss the groom.'

As they leaned towards each other, the congregation got to their feet and burst into applause. Sadie dabbed at her eyes with Adam's tissue and cheered as loudly as she could.

Holding hands, Andrew and Earl made their way down the aisle, grinning as though their faces would split, although their progress was slowed by the number of guests trying to shake their hands. Lissy hopped along behind, waving her bouquet like a floral lightsaber. Sadie blew her daughter a kiss as she passed by and was rewarded with a beatific smile. And at the rear came Kirsty and Lara, arm in arm.

'If that doesn't restore your faith in love then nothing will,' Cat said, with evident satisfaction.

Adam turned around. 'Amazing ceremony.' He grinned at Sadie. 'I think everyone will be having dino-maids next year.'

The pop of champagne corks announced that drinks were being served and the guests started to drift away.

'Warm, isn't it?' Cat said, fanning herself with the order of service. 'Why don't I go and grab us some drinks?'

She gave Sadie a meaningful stare before making her way towards the bistro. Adam watched her stop to tickle Lissy, then turned back to Sadie. 'Lissy did so well. You must be very proud of her.'

'I am,' Sadie said, smiling. 'I brought a change of

clothes – it's too hot for her to stay in that triceratops suit all day but I don't suppose I'll be able to get her out of it. Today was basically a dream come true for her.'

'I can imagine,' Adam said, laughing. He glanced around. 'No Daniel today?'

Sadie felt her good mood slip. 'No. Not today. Or any day for that matter.' She took a deep breath and looked him squarely in the eye. 'We've split up, for good this time.'

Adam's face fell. 'Bloody hell, I'm sorry. I shouldn't have mentioned him.'

'It's okay,' Sadie reassured him. 'I'm fine, really. It was a bit of a shock and I'm still adjusting but – well, as you know, I've had my doubts for a while now and let's just say he confirmed them in spectacular fashion.'

'Not—' Adam said, breaking off with a hesitant look.

Sadie nodded. 'Yes, he was having an affair, with the same woman as before.' She drew in a long, ragged breath. 'It's been going on for months. In fact, I'm not sure he ever really stopped seeing her.'

'Fuck,' Adam swore, then blushed a deep crimson. 'Sorry. But I can't get my head around it. Why would he even so much as look at another woman when he had you?'

The compliment caused all the air to whoosh from Sadie's lungs. She gazed up at him, feeling slightly dazed and not sure how to respond without seeming to agree with him. Adam noticed her discomfort and blushed even harder. 'Sorry,' he said again. 'I'm sure the last thing you need is idiots like me saying stuff like that. But the real moron here is Daniel.'

'Hear, hear,' Cat said, materialising at Adam's elbow and handing him a flute of champagne. 'I will most definitely drink to that.'

She passed the second glass to Sadie and raised her own into the air. 'To Daniel, for finally showing his true colours and setting Sadie free at last.'

Now it was Sadie's turn to flush scarlet but she lifted her glass all the same. 'To the future.'

'To the future,' Adam and Cat both echoed.

'Mummy, Mummy, did you hear me roar?' Lissy came barrelling towards them, her face alight with happiness. 'Andrew says I was the best triceratops flower girl he's ever had and he's going to throw a dinosaur party in the diner to say thank you and I can invite all my friends!'

Sadie laughed as the little girl wrapped her arms around her legs in a sweaty hug. 'That's amazing, and of course I heard you roar. Adam says he thinks everyone is going to want a dinosaur for a bridesmaid now.'

Lissy shot Adam a worried look. 'But I don't know if I can go to all of their weddings. What if they live a long way away?'

'Don't worry, I expect there are plenty of other children who would love to wear a dinosaur suit to a wedding,' Sadie said, smoothing Lissy's damp hair from her forehead. 'Speaking of which – do you think it might be time to get changed? You look awfully hot in there.'

'No,' Lissy said instantly, shaking her head. 'I'm not hot.'

Sadie studied her daughter's red cheeks and feverish eyes.

'I disagree. Come on, let's go and find you something cooler to wear. You can still be a triceratops on the inside.'

'That's true,' Adam confirmed. 'I'm actually a diplodocus.'

Lissy eyed him suspiciously. 'If that's true then what do you eat?'

'Leaves, mostly,' Adam said, not missing a beat. 'Ice cream, if I can get it. Look, there's a stand over there. Maybe we can go and get some once you've got changed.'

The little girl nodded, evidently satisfied he'd passed the test. 'Okay. As long as I don't have to wear a dress.'

Sadie smiled. 'No, Lissy. I wouldn't dream of it.' She handed her champagne to Cat. 'Sorry. Mummy duty calls.'

'See you soon,' Cat called.

By the time Sadie came back, with a noticeably cooler Lissy dressed in shorts and a dinosaur T-shirt, Adam was nowhere to be seen.

'You didn't say anything to him, did you?' Sadie asked Cat, grabbing her champagne flute and taking a long sip.

'Of course not,' Cat said innocently. 'We both stood here entirely mute for several minutes and then he went off to find the toilets.'

'Cat,' Sadie warned.

Her friend rolled her eyes. 'All right, if you must know, he asked me how you were coping and I said not brilliantly but you were getting there.'

'Cat!'

'What? It's the truth,' Cat said. She glanced at Lissy, whose attention had been caught by another child wearing a similar T-shirt on the other side of the Court, and lowered her voice. 'I didn't suggest he gave you a practical lesson on the birds and the bees at the first opportunity. But I did tell him that I knew you valued his friendship and friends were something you really needed right now.'

Sadie opened and closed her mouth. 'Thank you,' she said after a few seconds had passed. She caught sight of Elin and remembered the evasive look she'd seen in Cat's eyes earlier. 'So, are you going to tell me what Elin wanted or do I have to go and ask her myself? And don't say it was something to do with the bistro. I've known you for over twenty-five years, Cat Garcia – I know when you're lying.'

Her friend hesitated, then sighed. 'Okay, I'll tell you. But you have to promise not to lecture me or tell me how stupid I've been.'

Sadie was intrigued. 'I promise.'

She listened as Cat explained first about her conversation with Seb, then the discussion she'd had with Jaren and finally what Elin had revealed that morning.

'Oh my god, what an arsehole!' Sadie blurted out, before remembering that Lissy was standing right beside her and clamping a hand over her mouth.

'Yeah,' Cat agreed. 'And now I don't know what to do. I mean, I made it very clear to Jaren that we could only be business partners – it's too late to go back on that now.'

Sadie gave her a sideways look. 'Is it? Are you sure?'

Cat sighed. 'Pretty sure.'

'What if you explained? Jaren is the most reasonable person I know – he'll understand.'

'There's still the bistro?'

'So?' Sadie asked, exasperated. 'I know it's important, Cat, but it's not the be-all and end-all. Work won't snuggle up to you after a long day, and it won't bring you a cup of tea in bed on a Sunday morning.'

'You might be right,' Cat mumbled but she looked unconvinced.

Remembering her promise not to lecture, Sadie tried another tack. 'What did you say earlier, as Andrew and Earl were coming back down the aisle?'

A hunted expression crossed Cat's face. 'I don't remember.'

'Yes, you do. You said, "If that doesn't restore your faith in love, I don't know what will."'

'Okay,' Cat said, folding her arms. 'I might have said that. What's your point?'

Lissy's hand started to twist in Sadie's, a sure sign she was getting bored. 'Don't you want that?' she asked Cat. 'Don't you want someone to look at you the way Earl looked at Andrew during that ceremony? Don't you want to be Leia to someone's Han?'

A look of yearning flitted across Cat's face and was quickly hidden. Her gaze flicked towards Smart Cookies. 'Speaking of which, don't you think we'd better—'

'Don't change the subject,' Sadie warned, as Lissy began to hop from one foot to the other. 'Tell Jaren what happened. If you don't, I will.'

465

'You wouldn't dare,' Cat said, raising her chin in challenge.

Sadie smiled. 'Watch me.'

Cat opened her mouth to speak, just as Adam appeared with the most enormous ice-cream cornet Sadie had ever seen. 'Special dino delivery for Lissy Smart,' he said, bending down to hand her the ice cream. 'One Strawberry Sensation, all the way from Cornwall, just for you!'

Cat tilted her head to one side and smiled at Sadie. 'What was that you were saying about Leia and Han?'

Chapter Thirty-Eight

It was much later. The wedding breakfast had been served and speeches had been made. Andrew's father, a hale and hearty logger from Oregon, had made everyone cry by describing the moment he first realised his son was gay and how happy he was to be gaining another son. Kirsty's best woman speech had made everyone cry again, but this time with laughter. And both Andrew and Earl had gone into raptures over Sadie and Cat's special gift to them – a Millennium Falcon made entirely from gingerbread.

Eventually the shadows had grown longer and day had become night. As Cat had predicted, the fairy lights sprinkled magic over the Court and crowd-pleasing music from the band encouraged people to dance beneath them. Cat was delighted to see Cherie from the patisserie dancing with an older gentleman and gazing shyly into his eyes; could it be she was finally ready to let go of the ghost of her beloved husband? Cat hoped so; if anyone deserved a second chance at love it was Cherie, who'd been widowed far too young.

She sat for a moment, allowing her heart to warm at the sight of so many people having fun, then shuffled back in her seat and tilted her face towards the sky. The first few stars were twinkling into view, making Cat recall her wish from a week earlier. It still held, she decided, staring up at the stars. She still needed a fairy godmother to sort everything out.

'A euro for your thoughts.'

She blinked and looked around to see Jaren standing beside her, a golden flute of champagne in each hand. She smiled, remembering another time he'd used exactly the same phrase. 'They're definitely not worth that much,' she replied.

'I'm sure that's not true.' He held out a glass. 'Do you mind if I join you?'

Cat's smile vanished as her heart began to thud. 'Pull up a chair.'

He settled beside her. 'Do you remember the first time we met?'

She nodded, wondering if he had any idea how many times she'd thought of that moment since. 'You came into the shop, just before we were due to open.'

'I did,' he agreed. 'But that wasn't the first time I'd seen you. I'd been watching you coming and going for weeks – always in a hurry, always with your head down. And then one time, you walked into the Court and stopped to admire the oak tree, as though you were noticing it for the first time.'

'Did I?' Cat gave a self-conscious laugh and took a gulp of her drink. 'I don't remember.'

Jaren's dark eyes fixed hers. 'I do,' he said quietly. 'It was the first time I'd seen your face. And I remember thinking you were the most beautiful woman I'd ever seen.'

The breath caught in Cat's throat. She couldn't speak.

He smiled. 'I think that was the moment I fell in love with you, although I didn't realise it for some time. And by then you were mixed up with Seb and there was nothing I could do. So I resigned myself to being your friend and tried to move on. But that was easier said than done.'

Warmth stole over Cat like a cashmere blanket as she gazed at him. She didn't dare interrupt in case she broke the spell.

'Eventually, Seb ruined things, as I suspected he would, although I was sorry to see you get hurt. I was sorry for Elin too, because she didn't deserve what happened and I think she always knew she was second choice to you for both of us.' He looked away. 'I'm not especially proud of that. But I still thought I could get over you then.'

Cat found her voice. 'Jaren—'

He held up a hand. 'No, I have to say it all now. If I stop then my courage will fail.' He took a long sip from his glass and carried on. 'Then we cooked together and I finally summoned up the courage to kiss you. It was the best moment of my life – anything seemed possible – but afterwards, you started to avoid me and I thought you had decided our kiss had been a mistake. When you told me we should be business partners and nothing more, I became even more convinced that you regretted what had happened between us.' His gaze met hers once more. 'But now I know differently.'

In a flash, Cat knew what had happened. 'Sadie.'

Jaren tipped his head. 'No, not Sadie. It was Elin. She told me that Seb had lied to you, made it seem as though it was her I wanted and not you. And it gave me hope that maybe – maybe all was not lost.'

Cat sat very still, her heart racing as she tried to process everything Jaren had told her. He loved her, just as Elin had said – had always loved her, even before she'd known he was there. And the kiss they'd shared had been the best moment of his life, until she'd ruined it. Yet he still had hope, in spite of everything she'd said about remaining colleagues.

'But the bistro . . .' she said weakly, trailing off.

'I resign,' he said promptly. 'If I have to make a choice then there is no contest. I choose you, if you'll have me. Will you, Cat?'

He looked so vulnerable at that moment that Cat wanted to pull him into her arms there and then. But she didn't. Instead, she stayed still, watching the other guests swaying to the music and allowing the tumultuous thoughts in her head to settle. 'Do you want to dance?'

He raised his eyebrows. 'Now?'

She smiled. 'Yes, now. I want to feel your arms around me and that can't happen if we're both sat in different chairs.'

His eyes lit up from within. Taking her glass, he placed it

on a nearby table and held out a hand. 'Then I would love to dance.'

Once they were beneath the fairy lights, Jaren slid his hands carefully around Cat's waist and held her. Scarcely believing it was happening, Cat leaned into him and breathed in his scent. They swayed gently, gazing at each other in wonder. 'You smell like vanilla and sugar,' he murmured as he pulled her closer, and she felt his smile curve against her hair. 'I knew you would.'

As the song ended, Jaren drew his head back. 'I've just realised you didn't answer my question.'

'Which one?' Cat asked.

'The one where I asked whether you would have me.'

'Oh,' she said, reaching up to stroke his cheek. 'Isn't it obvious? Of course, I'll have you. I love you, Jaren.'

His eyes closed for the briefest of seconds, as though he was celebrating a prayer that had been answered. Then he bent his head to kiss her. Feeling as though her heart would burst, Cat kissed him back and all the misery and uncertainty of the last week melted away. She sank into him, feeling as though she'd been on a very long journey, one that had taken her far from home, but now, finally, she was back where she belonged. And she never wanted to leave again.

Sadie sat on the far side of the court, a sleeping Lissy in her lap, and watched Cat and Jaren kiss. A grin of total satisfaction crossed her face and she allowed herself a quiet, 'Yes!' as she cradled her daughter.

'About time,' a voice said, and she craned her neck to see Adam standing behind her.

'It certainly is,' she said. 'I was beginning to think it was never going to happen at all.'

'Good for them,' he said. 'They'll make a great couple.'

Sadie raised her eyebrows. 'They'll make a scary couple – with his business brains and her culinary expertise, I think they might just take over the world. At the very least, they're going to take over the city.'

Adam gave her a sidelong look. 'Where does that leave you?'

'Oh, I'll be fine,' Sadie said briskly. 'Cat and I talked everything through weeks ago – she'll step back from Smart Cookies for a while and I'll step up, employ more staff and promote Clare. I'm pretty sure she's ready for more responsibility and it's not as though Cat's going to be a million miles away, after all.'

He sat down beside her with an admiring glance. 'It sounds like you've got it all worked out. Unsurprisingly.'

'Do you really think so?' Sadie asked, fighting a sudden burst of hysterical laughter. 'Honestly, I'm just making it up as I go along.'

'Well, it doesn't look that way from the outside.' He paused and looked at her shyly. 'Cat said earlier that the thing you needed most was a friend. And I want you to know that I'm here for you – anything you need, no matter how small, just let me know.'

Sadie wasn't sure if it was the champagne she'd drunk or

the stars that twinkled over Castle Court like sparkling dew, but she turned her head towards Adam. 'There is something you can do,' she said.

'Anything,' Adam said.

Sadie took a deep breath and gathered up every bit of bravery she had. 'You can kiss me.'

Adam blinked and blushed to the very tips of his ears, in a way that Sadie was becoming very familiar with. He glanced down at the sleeping Lissy. 'Are you sure—'

'Please kiss me,' she said, praying he wouldn't make her ask a third time. 'Or I can kiss you. The way I did on Christmas Eve.'

For one stuttering heartbeat, she thought he might say no. But then he tilted his head to one side and leaned forwards to brush her mouth softly with his. A moment later, he pulled back to gaze uncertainly into her eyes. 'Like this?'

Sadie bit her lower lip. 'Very much like that,' she whispered. 'But longer.'

This time Adam didn't break the kiss. It went on and on, growing and deepening, until Sadie felt as though she never wanted it to end. It didn't matter that they were in the middle of the Court; it didn't matter who saw them. It didn't even matter that Lissy lay slumbering in her arms – what the little girl didn't know couldn't hurt her. But eventually, Sadie felt her daughter start to stir and she pulled gently away to gaze into Adam's wondering eyes.

He swallowed hard. 'That was . . .'

'Not a bad start?' Sadie finished his sentence with a gentle smile as Lissy raised her head and opened one eye to gaze blearily upwards.

'Mummy,' she said, her voice thick with sleep as she opened one eye. 'What's a narsehole?'

'Never you mind,' Sadie said, swallowing a wildly inappropriate snort of laughter. 'Go back to sleep. I'll tell you in the morning.'

Adam was watching her, his expression still dazed. 'Is this . . . just a one-night thing?' he whispered. 'Just because you're here and I'm here and it's a wedding?'

Sadie rocked Lissy gently as she studied him. 'Do you want it to be?'

'No! I mean, not unless that's all you want it to be.'

She gazed at him, taking in his flushed cheeks and untidy hair and uncertain hazel eyes, and explored the new thoughts and ideas that had suddenly blossomed inside her. 'No, that's not what I want, Adam. I want to wake up with you each morning and I want you to kiss me like that every day. But,' she paused to rest her cheek on Lissy's head, 'we come as a package. So if you love me, then you have to love Lissy too. Do you think you can do that?'

He sat back, staring first at Lissy, then at Sadie. Then a slow, tentative smile crept across his face. 'Are you kidding? It's all I've ever wanted.'

And Sadie found herself blinking back tears for the second time that day. But this time she didn't mind at all.

Epilogue

Halloween was in full swing at Castle Court. The doorway of Smart Cookies was draped with thick white cobwebs and a creepy, echoing laugh sounded each time anyone went in or out. The Court itself was awash with swirling fog, courtesy of a dry-ice machine tucked away beneath the oak tree, and every now and then the haunting howl of a wolf floated into the chilly autumn air.

'Neeg ang maw noogies?' Clare called up the stairs from the basement, before realising her vampire fangs were causing a communication problem. 'Sorry, Sadie. I said, do you need any more cookies?'

'Yes, please,' Sadie called back, glancing at the almost empty basket by the till. They were free to any child brave enough to enter the ghostly Court. There'd been plenty of visitors earlier but trick-or-treaters were appearing with less regularity now. Sadie checked the time: six-fifteen. The Halloween icing party Clare was hosting in the basement kitchen was due to finish in fifteen minutes, by which time Sadie hoped Adam would have returned with Lissy. She also hoped he'd heeded her warning not to let the six-year-old eat too many sweets on their travels, otherwise they would have an excitable and doubtless high-pitched journey home.

She was laying the fresh skull-shaped cookies from Clare out in the basket when the door cackled and Cat walked in. 'Hello,' she said, beaming at Sadie. 'Ooh, I'll have one of those.'

She bit into the biscuit and let out a sigh of pleasure. 'Just as good as ever.'

Sadie gave her a mildly affronted look. 'Were you expecting something different? Just because it's Delilah and not you that bakes our biscuits now doesn't mean they won't taste as good. She's still using your recipe, after all.'

'True,' Cat said, entirely unruffled. 'How are things?'

'Good,' Sadie replied. 'Clare says the new trainees seem promising and sales of the Spooky collection have been amazing. How are things over at the bistro?'

Cat pulled a face. 'Stressful.'

Sadie gave her best friend an appraising look. 'But nothing you can't handle.'

'No,' Cat agreed, 'nothing we can't handle, although I think Jaren may be about to murder one of the workmen. You know the guy who fitted our oven downstairs?'

Sadie wrinkled her forehead thoughtfully. 'The one you wanted to bury underneath the concrete floor?'

'That's the one. He's part of the team putting in the

appliances over at La Clé d'Argent and – well – let's just say his skills haven't improved much.'

'Poor Jaren,' Sadie said, trying not to laugh. 'You'll have to come round for dinner one night and tell us all about it.'

Cat smiled. 'That sounds like an offer I can't refuse. Just tell me when and we'll be there.' Reaching into her pocket, she pulled out an envelope. 'Oh, and before I forget, this is for you.'

'What is it?' Sadie asked, frowning.

'Open it and find out.'

With another curious look at her friend, Sadie did as she was instructed. 'Happy anniversary?'

Cat shook her head in mock sorrow. 'I can't believe you've forgotten our one-year anniversary.'

'Oh!' Sadie exclaimed and clapped a hand over her mouth. 'It's a year since we signed the lease and took over the shop, isn't it? How could I have forgotten?'

'Don't worry, I nearly did too. It was only the reminder for the insurance policy renewal that jogged my memory.'

Sadie reached under the counter, suddenly nervous. 'I do have something for you, as it happens. It's not quite an anniversary card, though.'

Cat's eyes gleamed. 'Is it a copy of your decree nisi? That must be due soon.'

'It's due any day now, but that's not what I have here.' Sadie swallowed hard and handed over a little gold and blue Smart Cookies box, her nerves twanging unbearably.

'I hope there's another biscuit in here,' Cat said, lifting the shiny black layer of corrugated cardboard. 'I didn't have time for lunch – I'm starving.'

Sadie held her breath, watching her best friend's expression change from puzzlement to astonishment as she lifted the delicate white pram from the box. 'A baby?' she said, staring at Sadie with questioning eyes. 'You're going to have a baby?'

'Due in March next year,' Sadie said, feeling herself blush. 'You look how I felt when I first saw the pregnancy test.'

Cat's expression transformed from amazement to pure delight. She hurried around the counter to pull Sadie into a gentle hug. 'This is wonderful news! How does Adam feel about it? And Lissy?'

Sadie leaned into her, relief coursing through her. She'd hoped Cat would be as thrilled as she was but she hadn't known for sure how her best friend would react; it would mean more upheaval for the shop and yet more changes in routine. But although the baby hadn't been planned, she and Adam couldn't be happier. 'They're both over the moon,' she told Cat, stepping back. 'Although Lissy has somehow got the idea that it's going to be a dinosaur-human hybrid, so I'm managing her expectations.'

Cat laughed. 'That sounds like Lissy. And how are you feeling?' She shook her head in wonderment. 'I can't believe you didn't tell me. I can't believe I didn't guess.'

'I'm sure you would have, if you'd still been working here every day,' Sadie admitted. 'Delilah worked it out straight away and I had to swear her to secrecy. I think she might have known even before I did.'

'Not much gets past Delilah,' Cat said. She gave Sadie a marvelling look. 'I swear you are actually glowing with happiness. You've come a long way in a year.'

'We both have,' Sadie said, smiling as she gazed at the brightly lit shop around them. 'Has it really been a year? It's flown by so fast.'

'I know,' Cat agreed. 'It doesn't seem like five minutes since Smart Cookies first opened and now look at us – we've got employees and regular customers and a really bright future.'

Sadie gripped her best friend's hand and squeezed. 'Thanks for making our dream come true, Cat. I couldn't have done this without you.'

'Stop that right now,' Cat said, squeezing back. 'I couldn't have done any of it without *you*.'

'I wonder what the next year will bring,' Sadie said, reaching into the basket and taking out a biscuit to nibble.

Cat grinned. 'Lots of broken nights and smelly nappies for you,' she teased.

'And lots of praise and rave reviews for you,' Sadie said. She pulled a wry face. 'Want to swap?'

'Not a chance,' Cat said, laughing. 'But I don't mind babysitting every once in a while.'

Sadie gave her warning look. 'Be careful, I might hold you to that.'

'Please do,' Cat said. 'In fact, if you don't I might have to insist.'

Sadie felt her expression sober. 'Thanks for being so supportive. I know maternity leave wasn't part of our plans.'

'Oh, shush,' Cat said, pulling her into another heartfelt hug. 'If you're happy, I'm happy. As long as I get to keep my position as favourite auntie?'

'Of course,' Sadie said, smiling once more. 'Even so, thank you. It means a lot.'

Cat smiled back. 'No problem. What are best friends for, after all?'

Acknowledgements

My sweetest thanks go, as ever, to Jo Williamson at Antony Harwood Ltd, without whom I'm certain I would not be able to do this. Your support means everything and I am very proud to call you my agent and my friend.

Next in line is my ever-patient editor, Emma Capron – thanks for helping me create Castle Court and the stories that happen within its spell-binding walls. If writing witty yet encouraging comments in the margins of a manuscript was a superpower, you'd rule the world.

A huge heartfelt thank you to all at Simon & Schuster UK, in particular SJ Virtue, Laura Hough and Jess Barratt: your professionalism, wisdom and excellent noses for cracking cocktail venues make being published by you a total dream.

I am very lucky to have some wonderful friends who help with everything from brainstorming plot points to finding the fuse box after midnight in Venice: Cally Taylor, Julie Cohen, Kate Harrison, Miranda Dickinson and Rowan

Coleman, I bow down before your brilliance. Please do pass the gin.

Special thanks to Michelle Whittaker and Dave Canham of South East Herts Bee Keepers Association, for letting me visit their hives and meet the bees – I learned so many fascinating bee facts, some of which found their way into this book. Any mistakes are most definitely my own.

As always, love, thanks and big squishy hugs to T and E for lighting up even the darkest days.

And last of all, thank you to everyone who reads my books. I hope you enjoyed shopping at Castle Court!

A Year at the Star and Sixpence

Holly Hepburn

When sisters Nessie and Sam inherit a little
pub in a beautiful country village, they jump at
the chance to escape their messy lives and start
afresh. But when they arrive at the Star and
Sixpence, it's not quite what they imagined . . .

Determined to make the best of this new
life, they set about making the pub the
heart of the village once again.

But when the sisters' past comes back to haunt
them, they start to think that the fresh start
they needed is very far away indeed . . .

'You'll fall in love with this fantastic novel from
a new star of women's fiction'
Miranda Dickinson

**AVAILABLE IN PAPERBACK
AND EBOOK NOW**

SIMON &
SCHUSTER

The Picture House by the Sea

Holly Hepburn

The Palace at Polwhipple is a lovely art deco cinema, nestled in front of azure Cornish seas. But it's long past its heyday now. Its only saving grace is Ferrelli's, the family run ice-cream concession in the foyer.

When Ferdie, the owner of Ferelli's, breaks his leg, his granddaughter Gina drops everything to come and help out. But when she arrives she is dismayed by the state of the cinema, which she remembers fondly from childhood holidays. Along with local renovation expert Ben, she sets about reviving the Palace to its former glory.

But the cinema needs more than a lick of paint. Its very future is under threat from a developer with greed in his eyes. Can Gina save the place before it's too late?

'Fabulously feel-good, funny and fresh, it will sweep you off your feet'
Rowan Coleman

**AVAILABLE IN PAPERBACK
AND EBOOK NOW**

**SIMON &
SCHUSTER**

COMING SOON

Last Orders at the Star and Sixpence

Roaring fires, cosy nooks and friendly locals, welcome back to the perfect village pub . . .

It is September and the new season is bringing change to the village of Little Monkham. **Nessie** has moved in with the lovely **Owen** and his son **Luke**, leaving her sister **Sam** next door in their renovated pub, the Star and Sixpence. But is all change for the good? Sam and **Joss** have gone their separate ways and he's left Little Monkham for good.

New chef **Gabriel Santiago** is causing a flutter among the women of the village but Sam is determined not to make the same mistake again and keeps things strictly business between them. But an inconvenient attraction to Gabe is the least of Sam's worries when an unexpected visitor arrives at the Star and Sixpence. Who is **Laurie Marsh** and what does he want from the sisters?

'Warm, witty and laced with intriguing secrets! I want to pull up a bar stool, order a large G&T and soak up all the gossip at the Star and Sixpence!' **Cathy Bramley**

If you loved *A Year at the Star and Sixpence*, you will adore *Last Orders at the Star and Sixpence*! It is like being reunited with old friends (in a pub!)

SIMON &
SCHUSTER